] Promised
Lands [

Brandeis Series in
American Jewish History, Culture, and Life

Jonathan D. Sarna, *Editor*
Sylvia Barack Fishman, *Associate Editor*

For a complete list of books that are available in the series,
visit www.upne.com

HBI Series on Jewish Women

Shulamit Reinharz, *General Editor*
Sylvia Barack Fishman, *Associate Editor*

The HBI Series on Jewish Women, created by the
Hadassah-Brandeis Institute, publishes a wide range of
books by and about Jewish women in diverse contexts
and time periods. Of interest to scholars and the educated
public, the HBI Series on Jewish Women fills major gaps in
Jewish Studies and in Women and Gender Studies as well
as their intersection.

The HBI Series on Jewish Women is supported by a
generous gift from Dr. Laura S. Schor.

For the complete list of books that are available in this series,
please see www.upne.com

Sonja M. Hedgepeth and Rochelle G. Saidel, editors
  Sexual Violence against Jewish Women during the Holocaust
Julia R. Lieberman, editor
  Sephardi Family Life in the Early Modern Diaspora
Derek Rubin, editor
  Promised Lands:
  New Jewish American Fiction on Longing and Belonging
Carol K. Ingall, editor
  The Women Who Reconstructed American Jewish Education:
  1910-1965
Gaby Brimmer and Elena Poniatowska
  Gaby Brimmer
Harriet Hartman and Moshe Hartman
  Gender and American Jews: Patterns in Work, Education,
  and Family in Contemporary Life
Dvora E. Weisberg
  Levirate Marriage and the Family in Ancient Judaism
Ellen M. Umansky and Dianne Ashton, editors
  Four Centuries of Jewish Women's Spirituality:
  A Sourcebook
Carole S. Kessner
  Marie Syrkin: Values Beyond the Self

]Promised Lands[

New Jewish American Fiction on Longing and Belonging

EDITED BY **DEREK RUBIN**

BRANDEIS UNIVERSITY PRESS

Waltham, Massachusetts

Published by

University Press of New England

Hanover and London

BRANDEIS UNIVERSITY PRESS

Published by

University Press of New England

www.upne.com

© 2010 Brandeis University

"Sovereignty" © 2010 Nessa Rapoport

"The Yehudah Triangle" © 2010 Thane Rosenbaum

All rights reserved

Manufactured in the United States of America

Designed by Eric M. Brooks

Typeset in Fresco and Fresco Sans

by Keystone Typesetting, Inc.

University Press of New England is a member of the
Green Press Initiative. The paper used in this book meets
their minimum requirement for recycled paper.

For permission to reproduce any of the material in this
book, contact Permissions, University Press of New England,
One Court Street, Suite 250, Lebanon NH 03766; or visit
www.upne.com

Library of Congress Cataloging-in-Publication Data
Promised lands: new Jewish American fiction on longing and
belonging / edited by Derek Rubin. — 1st ed.
    p. cm. — (Brandeis series in American Jewish history,
culture, and life)
(HBI series on Jewish women)
ISBN 978-1-58465-939-6 (cloth: alk. paper) —
ISBN 978-1-58465-920-4 (pbk.: alk. paper)
1. American fiction—Jewish authors. 2. Jews—United
States—Fiction. 3. Desire—Fiction. 4. Jewish women—
Fiction. I. Rubin, Derek.
PS648.J4P76   2010
813.008'09287'089924—dc22   2010029160

5 4 3 2 1

TO MARIJKE

Contents

Preface

Promised Lands: New Jewish American Fiction on Longing and Belonging is a collection of twenty-three short stories by leading contemporary writers. Their stories offer striking variations on the core Jewish theme of the Promised Land and how it continues to shape the collective consciousness of contemporary American Jews. Taken together, the stories provide an illuminating window onto Jewish American life and culture today. *Promised Lands* is different from most other fiction anthologies in two ways. Rather than gathering previously published stories, it looks forward, showing the state of Jewish fiction in the United States at the beginning of the twenty-first century and where it is headed. It does so by presenting new, unpublished short stories written exclusively for this collection by Jewish American writers, ranging in age from their late twenties to early sixties. And rather than comprising an eclectic collection of discrete short stories, *Promised Lands* reads like a unified book, consisting of fictions that cohere around, explore, and shed light on a single theme—the Promised Land.

Why the Promised Land as the thematic focus for this collection? Because it is both narrow enough to lend the book coherence and yet wide enough to guarantee a rich and diverse collection of stories. As a concept, it is quintessentially Jewish *and* American and therefore enabled the contributing authors to direct their gaze toward either Israel or America, or to negotiate imaginatively between the two. Furthermore, as perhaps the key metaphor of longing in Jewish experience, the Promised Land has a specific referent *and* it can be applied more generally to any place at which one directs one's hopes and longing—the New World for the immigrant and the children of immigrants, the Old World or Israel for some members of the third or fourth generations, or California or Buenos Aires, for example, for a fully Americanized Jewish American in search of himself. Finally, given its multivalence, the Promised Land can be perceived either in concrete or in abstract terms, either as a physical space or as a metaphorical space of great promise.

The essays in my earlier anthology, *Who We Are: On Being (and Not Being) a Jewish American Writer* (2005), placed contemporary Jewish

American writers in conversation with each other, highlighting the continuities and discontinuities among generations. For the first time, younger writers voiced the range of their concerns, dilemmas, and goals as Jews writing in America today. The aim of this new collection is to look ahead and explore—with the kind of depth and imagination that only fiction allows—the next stage of Jewish writing by showing that the ideal of the Promised Land, while radically transformed from the geographic, religious, and political to the metaphorical and deeply personal, continues to shape, indeed inspire, this new generation. That it exists as a vibrant idea among young Jewish Americans was borne out by the contributing authors' overwhelming enthusiasm when I proposed the theme of *Promised Lands*. Some of them had been working on or had completed stories in which they explored the idea of the Promised Land and which they immediately expressed a willingness to publish in the anthology. Those who did not have such a story in progress eagerly rose to the challenge of the assignment. Together, all of them have produced—separately yet collectively—a richly nuanced literary mural that is at once poignant, shocking, hilarious, and always deeply felt.

D.R.

Introduction

The Promised Land: Variations on a Theme

The Mosaic ideal of the Promised Land has sustained the Jews throughout their history in the Diaspora. For centuries, the Jews of Eastern Europe found sustenance and meaning in the belief that they would one day return home to the Land of Israel. With their coming to America at the end of the nineteenth and the beginning of the twentieth century, the exilic experience changed fundamentally, and with it, their ideal of the Promised Land. For most Jewish immigrants and their American-born children, the geographic, religious, and—in more recent history—political longing expressed by the phrase "Next year in Jerusalem" was replaced by a new geographic longing and by the cultural and material desire to make a home for themselves in America. Insofar as the best immigrant and post-immigrant fiction written by Jewish writers in America displayed a strong assimilationist impulse, it gave powerful imaginative expression to this new, secularized dream of the *Goldene Medineh* as Promised Land. Where the idea of Israel as the Promised Land has persisted among American Jews, it has maintained its geographic and political meaning mainly as a haven or home for Jews from countries in which they have been less welcome than in the United States. The vast majority of American Jews were never interested in making aliyah. For those who were, however, with the birth of the State of Israel and its rapid emergence as a modern, affluent Western nation just an airplane ride away from New York and Los Angeles, the longing expressed by the phrase "Next year in Jerusalem" came to an end. American Jews who wished to, could, after all, easily immigrate to Israel, or visit frequently, and in this way maintain close ties with the Jewish homeland.

With this promise fulfilled and with younger generations of American Jews now fully Americanized, has the idea of the Promised Land lost its power, or even become obsolete? Has the exilic experience, which played such a key role in Jewish history, culture, and literature, come to an end for the Jews of America? If so, how does this final arrival home affect their sense of identity? Do they still subscribe to the ideal of the Promised Land, or has this fundamental Jewish concept been transformed into something else? Does it even figure in their way of looking at the world?

The stories in *Promised Lands* confront these questions and show vividly how the theme of the Promised Land maintains an abiding allure, now largely metaphorical but no less powerful than the geographic, religious, and political ideas that inspired the preceding generation of Jewish American writers. The writers of that post-immigrant generation—such as Saul Bellow, Grace Paley, and Chaim Potok—were preoccupied with the tangled experience of being caught between past and present, between the Jewish Old World of their parents and present-day America. Their fiction was fueled by the need to find a home within the tension between these two worlds to which they felt strong ties but did not fully belong. By contrast, most of the younger writers represented in *Promised Lands* are fully at home—in *both* of these worlds. They are comfortable with being Jewish *and* American; indeed, many of them move easily between the two, whether in real life, as reflected, for example, in Jonathan Rosen's nonfiction work *Talmud and the Internet*, or in their fictions—think, for example, of Rebecca Newberger Goldstein's "Jewish" and "non-Jewish" novels *Mazel* and *The Dark Sister*. In a wonderful essay titled "Against Logic," Goldstein explores this sense of being imaginatively at home in different worlds, both Jewish and non-Jewish. She talks there about how it is out of *love* and *against all logic* that she—a secular and fully Americanized Jew with a PhD from Princeton in the philosophy of science—*chooses* to write "Jewish" fiction alongside her "non-Jewish" stories and novels.

Yet paradoxically, for the writers in *Promised Lands*, having multiple roots means a new kind of rootlessness. However much the younger generations of Jewish writers may be continuing the literary tradition begun by their immigrant and post-immigrant predecessors, they are also expressing something entirely new in *Promised Lands*: They are writing in and responding to today's fractured world in which many individuals are simultaneously at home in multiple settings and yet not completely rooted in any. In most of the stories gathered here, the Promised Land is an ever-elusive phantom, and the central, sustaining value is not necessarily the ideal that one longs to *attain* but the very *longing* itself. In terms of the Mosaic ideal of the Promised Land, these stories can be said to be driven not by a longing to *be* in Jerusalem next year, but by hopes and aspirations that spring from a variation of that longing expressed by the phrase "Next year in Jerusalem."

Longing has often shaped Jewish understanding of the ideal of the Promised Land. There have been periods in history when the Jews of the Diaspora have found themselves in such hopeless circumstances that they have felt that they would never be able to reach the Promised Land, whether real or metaphorical. One way of coping with the devastating heartache, or at best passive resignation, that such lack of hope could lead to was to turn their longing *itself* into a sustaining value. For Jews of the *shtetl*, for example, acknowledging the futility of their hope for deliverance often served as a comic defense mechanism. This Yiddish folktale, "Why the Night Watchman of Chelm Was Denied a Raise," tells it beautifully:

> It was once rumored that the Messiah was about to appear. So the Chelmites, fearing that he might bypass their town, engaged a watchman, who was to be on the lookout for the divine guest and welcome him if he should happen along.
>
> The watchman meanwhile bethought himself that his weekly salary of ten gulden was mighty little with which to support a wife and children, and so he applied to the town elders for an increase.
>
> The rabbi turned down his request. "True enough," he argued, "that ten gulden a week is an inadequate salary. But one must take into account that this is a permanent job" (Irving Howe and Eliezer Greenberg, eds., *A Treasury of Yiddish Stories.* (1953; New York: Schocken, 1973, 626)

The idea of unfulfilled longing as a self-sustaining value features not only in earlier Jewish folklore but also in the work of some of the towering figures of modern Jewish literature—for example, in Franz Kafka's "A Hunger Artist"—and in Jewish immigrant fiction in America, such as Abraham Cahan's *The Rise of David Levinsky*. In a fascinating essay on Cahan's rags-to-riches immigrant classic, Isaac Rosenfeld describes David Levinsky as the embodiment of the "Diaspora Man," the person for whom, as Rosenfeld puts it, "[t]he hunger must be preserved at all cost." Longing is the core value that drives Levinsky's ambition and nourishes him—even after he has attained the wealth and position he aspired to in America and finds himself yearning for what he lost spiritually as he made his way up in the world. However, a fundamental difference exists between the unfulfilled longing found in these early examples and the unfulfilled longing that resides at the center of the stories in *Promised Lands*. The former, whether comic or serious, was shaped by the powerlessness of the diasporic Jew and by the uncertainty and lack of hope caused by the constant threat of spiritual and physical destruction. In contrast, the new generation of writers are fully secure; they are at home in America, and are looking for an anchor in an ever more spiritually depleted yet materially over-abundant world. This search leads them back to the age-old Jewish emotion of unfulfilled longing, which serves for them as a source of moral, spiritual, and creative sustenance.

Writing from Home:
Looking Backward, Looking Forward

Back in the 1970s, some critics such as Irving Howe and Ruth Wisse wondered whether successive generations of writers would have the resources to sustain and give new direction to the great tradition of Jewish American fiction that began in the late nineteenth and early twentieth centuries with immigrant writers like Abraham Cahan and Anzia Yezierska and that was taken to new heights by postwar luminaries such as Saul Bellow, Grace Paley, and Bernard Malamud. Today, however, there is little doubt that the skeptics have been proven wrong. Writers such as Melvin Jules Bukiet, Dara Horn, Rebecca Newberger Goldstein, Binnie Kirshenbaum, Jonathan Rosen, Thane Rosenbaum, Steve Stern, and a host of others have produced numerous works of fiction that have significantly enriched and diversified the canon of Jewish American writing. Indeed, with an even-younger generation of highly talented writers appearing on the literary scene, Jewish American fiction is in a particularly creative, transitional phase as it moves beyond the literary heritage left by the post-immigrant generation and explores new themes and literary forms in response to contemporary American life.

In a 1997 symposium organized in *Tikkun* magazine by Thane Rosenbaum, Morris Dickstein discussed the nature of the creative revival among young Jewish American writers. While praising their work, he argued that it was "too early to tell whether this new wave would achieve the stature or create the body of major work of a Bellow or a Roth." He further pointed out that "[t]he ultimate test is not quantity but the challenge of taking possession of one's experience in an inimitable way that resonates beyond the writer's own life, as books like *The Magic Barrel*, *Herzog*, and *Portnoy's Complaint* definitely did." Critics have argued that the post-immigrant Jewish writers broke through as major *American* writers in the 1950s and 1960s because their particular experience as the children of Jewish immigrants placed them in the unique position to articulate the concerns of many Americans, both Jewish and non-Jewish. *Promised Lands* suggests that the fiction of the younger generation of writers has a similar broader relevance. By responding imaginatively to the age-old Jewish ideal of the Promised Land, their stories, separately and together, not only speak to the lives of American Jews today but also go to the heart of the experience of many Americans at large who are fully at home in different worlds and yet experience the same kind of rootlessness that gives rise to a sense of unfulfilled longing.

Because the authors approach this subject from a range of perspectives, their voices crisscross and echo each other in a rich and surprising conversation. Some of the writers in *Promised Lands* situate the unattainable object of their yearning for home in the imagined past of their imagined forebears. Others express this unfulfilled longing through the lingering ideal of Israel as homeland and safe haven. Then there are those who express a yearning for a more meaningful existence in present-day America. If, for all of the writers in *Promised Lands*, longing issues from a profound need to extract themselves from a sense of being adrift, between past and present, present and future, there are those who overtly explore this sense of "in-betweenness" as a consequence of the Holocaust. And finally, there are writers who emphasize the value of longing as a source of spiritual sustenance by paradoxically locating the unattainable Promised Land in the here-and-now.

[

] What follows is a discussion of the organization of *Promised Lands* that aims to illuminate connections among the stories and to suggest some of the many ways in which the multivalent idea of the Promised Land features in this book. The reader who wishes to approach the stories with a fresh gaze and without prior knowledge of their content may prefer to skip this section of the Introduction and return to it after having read them.

The Past as Impossible Promised Land

Of the writers in *Promised Lands* who direct their unfulfilled longing for home to the past, some locate the Promised Land in the vanished world of the *shtetl* or *Yiddishkeit* and some locate it in the American immigrant ghetto. In her story, "Shtetl World," Dara Horn dramatizes the question of cultural authenticity and the inaccessibility of the past to painfully hilarious effect. She does this through the story of Leah, a graduate student of Yiddish, who unwillingly winds up with a summer job running the dry-goods store in a *shtetl* theme park in Western Massachusetts and is angered by her own role in what she considers a shamefully trite reconstruction of the past. Horn's story expresses disappointment in contemporary America, where the trivialization of the Jewish past threatens to cut American Jews off from the legacy of *shtetl* culture, with which Leah so profoundly wishes to connect.

In contrast, Tova Mirvis's story "Potatoes," which is set in the immigrant past, presents a view of America as offering the hope of renewal and regeneration. To Mirvis's newly arrived young protagonist, Bella, America is the Promised Land that holds out the possibility of liberation from the psychic prison of her nightmarish past. Paradoxically, she longs to return to Eastern Europe because her suffering there has rendered her incapable of living fully in the New World. However, the love and kindness with which she is met in Memphis, Tennessee, where her family has settled, provide the promise of healing and overcoming the pain she experienced in Grodno.

Whereas Mirvis's protagonist comes to see America as a safe, nurturing home, Avigdor Bronfman, the protagonist of Steve Stern's "Avigdor of the Apes" experiences the harsh everyday life of the American immigrant ghetto as exile. To him, the unattainable Promised Land is the realm of the purely physical, where he can transcend the crush of the Lower East Side and his cramped, constricting existence as the son of a *mohel*. In his youth, the constant butt of jokes and the target of local bullies, Avigdor is inspired by the figure of Tarzan. He trains himself to soar above the jungle-like city where "his apprehension dissolved, his brain ceased its caviling, and he became a pure expression of the physical." However, Avigdor's ability to dwell in this "timeless space" proves to be only very brief and he spends the rest of his life longing for this unattainable Promised Land.

In contrast to Mirvis and Stern, who set their stories in the past, Joey Rubin and Melvin Jules Bukiet, like Horn, set theirs in the present as a means of talking about the links between contemporary American Jews and the world of the *shtetl*. Rubin's "Toward Lithuania" is a comic yet poignant tale of a young New Yorker in his twenties who is drifting, in search of himself and his patrimony as he retraces his deceased father's footsteps back to Argentina. The vehemence with which his father had turned his back on his homeland once he had settled in America prompts the unnamed protagonist to travel to Buenos Aires, where his father grew up, the son of a Jewish immigrant from Lithuania. The young man earns a living in Buenos Aires as an English tutor. One of his students is Elías, a retired Jewish doctor who has been studying English in vain for twenty-five years. Through a personal tale of exile and homeland that Elías recounts in his mangled English one evening, "Toward Lithuania" becomes a parable of the jumbled tension between Jewish exile and homeland played out through the conundrums of language and place.

While Rubin's tale probes the complexities involved in the quest for one's heritage, Bukiet's disturbing story, "The Florida Sunshine Tree," sardonically suggests that such a quest is futile. It does this by describing how Sandy Levinson, an adolescent growing up in an affluent suburb in south Florida, kills the Gentile neighbors' baby boy and drinks his blood in the belief that he is fulfilling the Chosen People's covenant with God. To Sandy, the Promised Land is the inaccessible world of his forefathers in Eastern Europe as recounted to him by his two recently deceased grandfathers, Max and Nate. He is profoundly moved by their accounts of the kidnapping of Jewish children by *khoppers* and especially by their tales of blood libel. Jewish life in Eastern Europe as Max and Nate described it to Sandy is so remote from his world that reality and imagination fuse in his mind, and he begins to think the unthinkable: "What . . . if blood was the ultimate Old World flavor that had been denied in the New World?" The story thus suggests in darkly humorous and absurdist fashion that in America, where Jewish history has been reversed and the "outsiders [are] insiders," where Jews enjoy unprecedented affluence and unparalleled security, the vanished world of their forefathers is gone forever. If it can be accessed, it is only imaginatively, via the psychotic mind of a boy like Sandy.

Israel as Elusive Promised Land

In some of the stories in *Promised Lands*, Israel is perceived as a place of healing and regeneration. Like Mirvis's young immigrant from Eastern Europe, the American protagonist of Joan Leegant's "Remittances" is seeking healing from a brutal crime committed against her. Her empathic Israeli boyfriend's hard-nosed attitude toward violence in general and her pain and suffering in particular helps to heal her psychic wounds and to ease her profound sense of guilt that she may have brought the act of violence upon herself. Ironically, however, this story suggests that "post-Zionist" Israel is not the place that Jews of the Diaspora necessarily travel to in the hope of reconnecting with their Jewish roots as a means of regeneration, but rather "the country of wishfully amnesiac Jews" that has its own guilty conscience to salve.

Whereas Leegant's story offers a troubling reassessment of the Zionist achievement, Rivka Lovett's "Leo's Squid" paints a comic, if poignant, picture of Israel as a site for spiritual renewal. The Israel that Leo, the protagonist, travels to with his twin brother is offbeat and odd. As quirky as this version of Israel may be, however, it turns out to be just the right place for Leo to find the regeneration he desperately yearns for. Nearing forty, he is single and lonely and suffers from the sense that his life lacks the fulfillment that Jerry, who is the more on track and assertive of the two, enjoys, being happily married and with two children. During their trip, Leo gets a glimpse of the Promised Land he so longs to reach when he spends the night, not with a beautiful Sabra but with a Filipino woman whom he met in "the only restaurant in Jerusalem that served seafood," and thereby in his own way asserts himself, if only momentarily, in his complicated relationship with Jerry.

Like Leegant and Lovett, Nessa Rapoport also portrays Israel as a site of regeneration. The unnamed protagonist of her story, "Sovereignty," is a forty-year-old New Yorker whose husband has given her a trip to wherever she chooses as a gift on the occasion of their twins' first birthday. She travels to Jerusalem, where she lived as a student and fell deeply in love with the city and with a young Israeli soldier. Back in the

Holy City after an absence of twenty years, her visit turns into a futile quest to recapture the pristine sensual beauty and carefree happiness of her youth that were closely bound up with the city that has now changed so much she hardly recognizes it. In this story, Rapoport employs vocabulary that links Jerusalem to the body and the body to Jerusalem, and that allows the past and present to reverberate within and between the two, while all the time maintaining a balance between the poetic and the everyday. She thereby turns this moving tale of exile and homecoming into a parable of the female Jewish body as a trope for the rich Jewish history of unfulfilled longing for the Promised Land.

If some of the stories in *Promised Lands* explore the idea of Israel as a place of healing and regeneration, in others Israel serves as the locus for the characters' futile longings and aspirations: artistic, amorous, or political. Jonathan Wilson's "The Liars" tells of a twenty-six-year-old aspiring poet from London who travels to Jerusalem in the hope of finding love with the "perfect Sabra" and the key to literary success as embodied in his ideal of the Israeli poet-hero. The story of the young man's sojourn in the home of his Israeli mentor provides a telling portrayal of the diasporic Jew's experience of contemporary Israel as unattainable Promised Land. Rachel Kadish's "Come on Zion Put Your Hands Together" lyrically recounts the painful tale of unfulfilled love between Ahmed Almasi, a Palestinian who has spent most of his life abroad, and Karen Reed, who is Jewish and, like Wilson's protagonist, from England. Almasi and Reed, who run a top international mediation consultancy firm, are in Israel to coach a team of government negotiators. It is here, ironically in the Promised Land, that Karen is confronted with both the depth and the futility of their love for each other. Kadish's story dramatizes the complex paradox of the unattainable Promised Land as played out in the tangled crisscrossing forces of love, lineage, and land that have shaped the lives of her two would-be lovers.

As in Kadish's story, in Binnie Kirshenbaum's "The Lunatic," love and politics play an important role in the protagonist's relation to Israel. This is the story of a young Jewish American "Princess" who has a crush on a high-school classmate, Stanley, a loner who, unlike her and her friends, does not intend to go to college but is set on joining the Israeli army when he graduates from high school. She is drawn to him, but his being deliberately different, belligerently self-contained, and extremist makes him inaccessible to her, especially since she subscribes fully to the shared values of her peer group. Because to her and her friends the affluent suburban existence they lead and all that it promises *is* the Promised Land, Kirshenbaum's protagonist cannot imagine forfeiting everything in order to win over Stanley. The story is framed by a brief description of Stanley and the narrator each "at home" as adults in their respective Promised Lands. The narrator in her comfortable American home recognizes Stanley on television amidst a crowd of extremists in Israel joyfully celebrating the assassination of Yitzhak Rabin. "The Lunatic" presents Israel and America as competing promised lands with different ideals, cultures, and lifestyles as embodied by these two affluent New York suburban high-school students. It does so by vividly dramatizing the way competing value systems can be tangled up with the basic feelings that one young person has for another.

Beyond the American Dream

The stories in *Promised Lands* that perceive the futile yearning for the Promised Land as a means of imaginatively going beyond or through the American dream are rich and varied. Lauren Grodstein and Elisa Albert spin fascinating tales of the affluent worlds of Manhattan and Los Angeles, in which longing takes the form of a hopeless desire for marriage and a meaningful relationship with a person one loves and with one's children. Grodstein dramatizes this theme by painfully laying bare the complexities of a romantic relationship between a Jew and a Gentile, while Albert does so in conjunction with the theme of the Internet as new, "virtual" Promised Land through which people try in vain to connect meaningfully with others. Their respective stories, "Homewrecker" and "One Good Reason Why Not," expose with wit and sensitivity the myriad factors—personal, religious, social, cultural, and generational—that complicate and frustrate the longing for the Promised Land of domestic bliss in America today.

In both of these stories, the problematic relationship between divorced parents and their children plays a role, while in his story "Midhusband" Edward Schwarzschild explores the bruising upheaval in a marriage brought on by the birth of a first child and the obstacles that his main character, Michael, and his wife, Kate, have to overcome in order to fully acknowledge their love for their child and regain their commitment to, and love for, each other. Michael and Kate are torn between their love for their six-week-old baby boy, Drew, their fear of having to raise a child, and their anger at him for the upheaval that his birth has wrought upon their lives. As a consequence, they have drifted apart. Away to attend the funeral of a high-school friend, Michael is tempted to commit adultery and is confronted with the depth of his love for Kate and Drew as he is forced to choose between taking an irrevocable step toward destroying his marriage or committing to his wife and child. The story thus describes Michael's emotional journey back to his family—his metaphorical Promised Land.

Whereas Grodstein, Albert, and Schwarzschild present the children in their stories from the perspective of the parents, Adam Wilson's story is told from the perspective of the child. "The Porchies" is a haunting story about the consequences of a young man's inability to connect with himself and with those closest to him. Ben, the narrator, describes himself as "a Jewish boy with a dead father, and a child of the spiritually devoid East Coast suburbs." Living in a post-adolescent world without substance and direction, he does everything he can to avoid the emotional pain caused by his general lack of purpose and the sense of loss brought on by his father's death. Ben is therefore drawn to the uncomplicated, carefree "Porchies," a group of friends who while away their summer evenings drinking and joking around on the porch of the house he lives in. However, trapped in his misery, as time passes and he enters adulthood, Ben is unable to attain the ease and peace of mind that in his youth he associated with California—his unreachable, mythic Promised Land—and that the Gentile Porchies seem to be able to achieve so easily.

In contrast to Ben, who doesn't fit in because he is more sensitive and reflective than the Porchies, Alan, the teenage protagonist of Aaron Hamburger's "The End of Anti-Semitism" is isolated because of his homosexuality. Being Jewish and gay in America in the 1980s, Alan longs for a Promised Land in which an end has come, not to antisemitism, as the title of the story suggests, but to homophobia. His Promised Land is one in which he can openly be gay and enjoy a romantic relationship with his first love, his classmate Mark Taborsky. As Alan negotiates worlds at home and at school in which being gay is taboo, he gradually comes to understand that what is at stake in his secret relationship with

Mark, who is the class bully and is careful to hide his feelings for Alan, is whether he will be able to remain true to who he is or will succumb to the pressure to suppress his homosexuality and live a lie.

Whereas Adam Wilson and Hamburger's stories are tales of youthful Americans longing for self-fulfillment, Lara Vapnyar's "Things That Are Not Yours" is a sardonic, latter-day immigrant story of the post-Soviet era. As such, it ironically echoes Anzia Yezierska's romantic tales of Jewish immigration from Eastern Europe and the short story by Mirvis in this volume. "Things That Are Not Yours" is written in the form of a letter addressed by a Russian immigrant living in the United States to a friend, Masha, who is about to emigrate. The letter begins humorously with the well-intentioned purpose of offering Masha advice on what she should bring with her to America, but as it unfolds it turns into a bitter lesson about America as a failed Promised Land.

In contrast to Vapnyar's story, Janice Eidus's "A *Bisel* This, a *Bisel* That," is a touchingly humorous celebration of contemporary multi-cultural America. As in Albert's "One Good Reason Why Not," here, too, the Internet is depicted as adversely affecting meaningful aspects of people's lives. *The Promised Text*, "the monthly independent Jewish newspaper 'for progressive Jews, their friends, and everyone else' " that Myron Gerstler, the protagonist of the story, has worked for as book editor for twenty-five years, is about to shut down. Like other fringe newspapers, *The Promised Text* is being squeezed out of existence by the proliferation of digital media and the popularity of the Internet. Through Myron's interaction with a motley group of colleagues lamenting the disappearance of their "medium" and the lack of an audience for their "message," the story presents us with an endearing image of present-day multicultural America as the true alternative to the digital Promised Land of the twenty-first century.

The Holocaust and Unattainable Promised Lands

In stories far less celebratory and light-hearted than Eidus's "A *Bisel* This, a *Bisel* That," Thane Rosenbaum, Lev Raphael, and Yael Goldstein Love dramatize the longing for an unattainable Promised Land against the backdrop of the Holocaust. While Rosenbaum and Rafael approach this theme from the perspective of the American-born children of survivors, Love does so by focusing on a group of Jewish émigrés from Europe living in America during the time of the Holocaust.

In the fractured world of his absurdist, semi-allegorical story, "The Yehudah Triangle," Rosenbaum addresses the psychic implications for members of the second generation of their ties to Israel and America as homes to which they simultaneously belong but to which they cannot commit fully. The son of survivors, born and raised in Florida, and currently living in New York, Jerry Bender (or Yehudah Ben-David, as he has renamed himself) is caught in the unfathomable vacuum left in the aftermath of the Holocaust. Scarred by his parents nightmarish memories of events that he himself never witnessed—what Marianne Hirsch tellingly refers to as "postmemory"—he exists in a state of in-betweenness into which, like the ships and airplanes in the mythic Bermuda Triangle, he is in continuous danger of vanishing. He has three non-Jewish ex-wives who converted to Judaism, three daughters living with their mothers in different parts of the world, and three homelands: America, where he resides as a citizen, Israel to which he belongs as a Jew, and his parents' traumatic past in which he is trapped but which he never will be able to access fully. Rosenbaum's story darkly suggests that his protagonist, as the son of Holocaust survivors, is doomed to longing for an unattainable Promised Land in which he is at home within this painfully tangled state of in-betweenness.

Like Rosenbaum's story, Lev Raphael's "Money" presents us with the vulnerability of members of the second generation, who have been exposed vicariously to the trauma of the Holocaust. This vulnerability is conveyed through the second-generation narrator and his friend Joyce, who has invited him over to her house to unburden herself because she recently discovered that her German husband, Fred, has squandered the fortune that he inherited from his father. During their conversation, Joyce unexpectedly reveals that she too is Jewish and the child of Holocaust survivors. As he is confronted with Joyce's confession, the narrator, who had always believed that he had not been damaged by his parents' traumatic past and was able to live a regular life like other Americans, gradually discovers that he has, in fact, been deeply scarred. The story dramatizes the unfulfilled longing felt by many members of the second generation to live lives free of the fears and insecurities that they have inherited from their parents. Although born and raised in

America, as members of the second generation they are doomed never to feel fully at home.

While Rosenbaum sounds the implications of the Holocaust with reference to Israel and America as promised lands, Yael Goldstein Love's "Lonely, Lonely, Lonely Is the Lord of Hosts" does so with reference to the utopian ideal of a community based on its members' supreme commitment to their "loving responsibility" for each other. The story presents such a community established by Jewish émigrés from Europe in the Berkshires in the 1930s. Set during the Second World War, "Lonely, Lonely, Lonely Is the Lord of Hosts" describes how the main character, Anna, is torn between her urgent need to use the community's funds to save her younger sister from the Nazis, and her lover Alfie's unswerving belief that fulfillment of the community's covenant as a means of making this a better world must take precedence over any exigencies of the moment. The story becomes a parable of the impossible choice between two ideals: personal love and moral commitment in the here-and-now versus "immaculate kindness" that ignores the immediate suffering of one's fellow humans. "Lonely, Lonely, Lonely Is the Lord of Hosts" takes on an inter-generational dimension that links it to Rosenbaum's and Raphael's tales of second-generation experience when at the end of the narrative we learn that it has been presented to us by Anna's granddaughter as a means of coming to grips with "the chill remove [her mother] had always felt in [Anna's] way of loving."

The Here-and-Now as Promised Land

Rebecca Newberger Goldstein's "The Afterlife of Skeptics" contains several promised lands, all of which prove to be illusory for her protagonist, Max Besserling, because they involve great personal loss. Besserling, a Jewish émigré from Cracow, is an ambitious, selfish, and spiteful skeptic. As he is about to die, he looks back and realizes that everything he had desired and attained—marriage with Nina, the love of his youth; a beautiful daughter; a life in America; and academic success built on the philosophical rigor of relentless rationalism—meant turning his back on the world. He finally understands that although his youthful friend Jakob Binder—a romantic metaphysician with whom he competed jealously for Nina and came to hold in contempt for his ideas—died in the Holocaust, he had lived to the full in the here-and-now and it was therefore Binder, rather than Besserling, who had understood what constituted the true Promised Land.

The final story in *Promised Lands*, which like "The Afterlife of Skeptics" focuses on the here-and-now as unattainable Promised Land, is paradigmatic of the theme of unfulfilled longing at the heart of this volume. "The True World," an entertaining yet enigmatic parable-like story by Jonathan Rosen, captures succinctly the idea that spiritual sustenance can be derived from the awareness that the Promised Land is unreachable. Rosen presents the ideal of unfulfilled longing as the source of artistic sustenance. He does so by linking it as a key value to the Emersonian ideal of artistic self-reliance. Believing that "literature was finished" and "the future was with the dead," the protagonist of the story—who remains unnamed, but the suggestion is that he is a fictional projection of Rosen himself—travels by boat from Ellis Island to the Beyond in order to interview the deceased Saul Bellow for a magazine. Bellow, who in real life believed firmly that death is silent and that one can be a writer only if one says "yes" to life, teaches the young man that the Promised Land must be sought in the present, in the everyday world that he inhabits. But how can one believe in an ideal that is within the realm of the real? That is, after all, the very problem Rosen's protagonist was faced with in the first place. By *acknowledging* that it is unattainable and yet still *longing* to attain it—this is the deeply Jewish answer given, not explicitly within the story, but by the story as a whole, as summed up in its epigraph, taken from Isaac Bashevis Singer's masterpiece "Gimpel the Fool":

> No doubt the world is entirely an imaginary world, but it is only once removed from the true world.

Singer's legendary schlemiel embodies the Eastern European Jew's self-sustaining spirit in the face of powerlessness. Duped and fooled all his life, the lesson Gimpel learns when he reaches old age is that one has to *choose* to believe even when there are no grounds for belief, because not to believe is to lose faith, and to lose faith is to give up on the value of life. This simple wisdom is what prompts the imaginary Jews of Chelm to appoint a watchman to look out for a messiah they know will not come. It is also expressive of the belief in the importance of longing for an unattainable Promised Land—the Jewish essence from which the stories in *Promised Lands* spring. Longing and belonging are, of course, at the heart of human experience. Given the centrality of the ideal of the Promised Land in both Jewish and American culture, it is not surprising that it should shape, indeed inspire, the literary imagination of contemporary Jewish American writers. Drawing on the crucial role that longing plays in the Mosaic ideal of the Promised Land, the writers in *Promised Lands* highlight the importance of longing even when one belongs fully, both as an American and as a Jew. In doing so, they speak to the experience of many readers, Jewish and non-Jewish alike, who are at home in multiple worlds yet share the condition of rootlessness—an enabling legacy that continues to define the manifold richness of contemporary Jewish American experience.

] Promised
Lands [

] Shtetl World

It was just a summer job, Leah kept reminding herself. Just a summer job to earn some money, because she hadn't gotten the grant she needed to spend the summer doing her graduate work on Yiddish periodicals, and because the job was at least ostensibly related to her research, and because the apartment she had shared with her boyfriend had very abruptly stopped being hers, and because her parents had decided to rent out their house and spend the year in Madagascar, and because her life as a scholar and even as a person during that summer of 2006 needed a break, and because it was better than working at Starbucks. It was only a summer job.

Her job was to run the dry-goods store. It was easy, really. Much easier than being the milkman, who actually had to learn how to milk a cow, or the melamed, who had to pretend to smack kids' hands with a ruler in his little shack of a school, or the badkhen, who had to make up corny rhymes about every visitor who passed him by, or the rebbe, who had to recite the same sermon three times every day, or the shabbes-goy, who had to lug buckets of water all over town (but at least only worked weekends), or the crippled beggar, who had to sit by the front gate of the complex all day long even in ninety-degree heat, begging for alms while winding and unwinding the bandages around his legs and occasionally, very subtly, letting on to a visitor that he was the Messiah. She might have preferred to be the bride, whose wedding they celebrated in the town square every afternoon at two o'clock, if she had been pretty enough. But Leah's job wasn't bad. All she had to do was sit behind the counter of her store and wait for someone to come in and buy a tallis. Or, theoretically, a bag of flour, though that had never happened. Her store was even air-conditioned, through a small unit hidden under a pile of chuppah poles, which made her costume's woolen ankle-length skirt, long sleeves, and enormous plastic-pearl-brocaded headscarf a little more bearable. No, the job didn't bother her much at all. What bothered her was that along with the tallises in her shop, there were also T-shirts for sale emblazoned with the words "Farshtoonkineh Zaideh"—a phrase which, in addition to being written in English characters that didn't conform to standardized translitera-tion, wasn't even grammatically correct. What bothered her was that the musical overture to *Fiddler on the Roof* was piped through her shop on a repeating loop. What bothered her was that there was an actual fiddler sitting on the roof of the house across from her shop. What bothered her was that there were rides.

Something else that bothered her was that every day at exactly 4:30 P.M., right before closing, there was a pogrom. Most of the staff loved the pogrom—particularly Mendele the book peddler, in reality a sixth-year senior at Amherst College named Jason Resnick, who at 4:20 P.M. each day would abandon his cart full of books, slip off to the backstage area behind the *World of Our Fathers* ride, change out of his black hat and knickers and into an embroidered Cossack blouse, and come charg-ing out from behind the ride to smash the windows of her shop with an axe, to the shock and delight of visitors in their Farshtoonkineh Zaideh T-shirts. After a while it began to get old.

But the main thing that bothered her about the job was Mendele himself. Lately he had started waiting for her behind her shop during her afternoon break. Except for the daily wedding—which was at least a good way to stretch her legs with a few rounds of horahs after sitting behind the counter all day long—her break was her only time out of the shop during working hours. For lunch, one of her six daughters (she tried to get their names right, not that any of the visitors noticed) would come by with a bialy or two, or, on a particularly bad day, a bowl of kasha. The portions were small, cheap. It was an attempt at authen-ticity; either that, or the bequest for the complex didn't cover food. Usually the herring at the wedding made up for it, though, so she didn't need anything to eat during her break, just a chance to get outside and look at the woods behind the building (Western Massachusetts, she noted, was almost as wooded as Poland) and daydream about being somewhere else. It was a moment to herself during the day that she had begun to treasure, so she was genuinely irritated when Mendele began showing up behind her shop with his cart full of books, pretending that he just happened to be there, always finishing a cell phone call just as she stepped outside, muttering a pro forma "Love you" into the mouthpiece. And then he would flick the phone closed, slip it back into his tallis bag, and pull out a cigarette.

"I never see you making any calls out here," he said to her one day, pushing one of his sidelocks behind his ear. "I never even see you smoke. What's the point of a break if you don't use it?"

"Phones aren't allowed," she said. She was embarrassed by how smarmy she sounded. He was attractive, she had to admit, under his beard. He was developing a beard tan, his nose and cheekbones ruddy from the distinctly un-Polish summer sun.

"You forget that I'm the book peddler," he said. "I'm the vanguard of the enlightenment." He blew smoke at the wall. "Leah, right?"

"Yes, Mendele," she said, and noticed he was hiding a smile. Had he been on the phone with a girlfriend, or his mother? "How's business?"

He let out a groan. "They never buy the books," he whined. "It's a problem for my commission. You're so damn lucky to be selling T-shirts. In air-conditioning."

"You can stop by for some buckwheat whenever you'd like," she said. The truth was that she'd have loved to be the book peddler, even if it meant being outside all day, just to have something to read, even if all there was to read were the book cart's remaindered copies of Mark Zborowski's *Life Is with People* and Irving Howe's *World of Our Fathers*. But it wasn't a job for a girl.

"I'm getting better at the pogrom," Mendele said eagerly. "The other day I figured out how to throw the axe so that it just misses the tourists. I've been practicing. Check it out when I come to the store today."

She snorted. "You're a lawsuit waiting to happen."

He pulled one of his tefillin out of his pocket and unfurled a strand of it, letting it tumble out of its coil until he snapped it back into his hand like a yo-yo, just clearing the ground. "Me and the rebbetsin are going out for a beer after the pogrom," he said, winding the leather strap. The rebbetsin was beautiful, Leah remembered, a bombshell from U-Mass who even managed to look hot in a headscarf. "They've got a happy hour at the place down the road. Super-cheap. Wanna come?"

"I wouldn't want to intrude on your date," she said.

"It's not a date," he retorted. "We're just blowing off some steam."

"I'm working evenings on my research," she heard herself say. "There's a pile of photocopies at my place, and it's going to take me all summer just to read through them."

He flipped the tefillin by its strap toward the wall, then snapped it back. "What kind of research?" he asked.

He actually seemed interested, but Leah hated talking about her work to people outside her field. "Yiddish magazines," she conceded.

He opened his eyes wide. "Oh, so you're *living* it! Day and night!" He laughed out loud, then burst into one of the songs from her shop's sound track. "Who, day and night, must scramble for a living . . ." He squatted down, doing the kazatski dance that he would perform an hour later at the wedding. It made Leah nervous to watch it; at one point, she had seen a tourist actually break his leg trying. Finally he stood up. "You're really living it!" he announced, out of breath.

She tried to decide how to respond—indignant and enraged? Or indifferent and bored? It was like dealing with a child, though Mendele couldn't have been younger than twenty-two. A century ago, he would have already been a father of four. Leah was twenty-five, and she felt like his mother.

She was about to answer when the beadle came by, rapping on the window at the front of her shop to summon people to afternoon prayers. Mendele dropped his cigarette and started wrapping the tefillin strap around his arm, dusting ashes off his beard. "I gotta go to minyan. Catch ya later," he called, and wheeled his cart around the corner.

Leah's break wasn't over yet, but the woods suddenly felt hot to her, oppressive. She went back into the air-conditioned shop, where someone was already waiting at the door, wanting to know the price of a T-shirt.

[

] Life is with people, Leah discovered: Mendele wouldn't leave her alone. She had tried to time her break to avoid him when she saw his book peddler's cart pass by her window, but he seemed to be waiting for her. She would check outside to see whether he was there and venture out when the woods seemed empty, only to see him pop out from behind a tree, clapping his cell phone shut. He was one of those parasitic types who need to be with others in order to believe in their own existence. People avoided him, Leah had noticed, particularly the women; Leah had overheard the mikvah lady complaining about him at the wedding, and the rebbetsin had blown him off. But Leah couldn't think of a way to get rid of him. He was her special curse, it seemed. Her bashert.

"So why are you studying this stuff?" he asked one day after hanging up his phone. "I mean, this is just a summer job. You really do this all year long?"

"I don't do 'this' all year long," Leah said. "I don't sell tallises. I don't eat bialys. I wear jeans. I have hair."

"But your name really is Leah," he said.

"That's not my fault."

Mendele didn't care. "You're an all-year-rounder. A shtetl townie." He grinned, and lit a cigarette. "Seriously, why?"

Leah looked at his squinting eyes, wondering if telling him anything was a waste of breath. "I needed a foreign language in college," she said. "Yiddish fit my schedule, and it was only three times a week instead of five. Stupid, right? But when I started learning it, I just felt like I discovered an entire world that no one knows about at all." Mendele looked intrigued. She was surprised by how pleased she was to see that he was interested. "It's nothing like this," she said, waving a hand at the buildings behind them. "It kind of makes me sick, being here."

Mendele nodded. "Me, too," he said, and for a moment she revised her opinion of him. Then he took off his hat and wiped his dripping forehead. "It's so damn hot all the time. Pay's good, though. Better than Starbucks."

She sighed. His tallis bag shuddered, and he fumbled to open it, grabbing his vibrating cell phone. He flipped it open and said, "Not now, I'm at work." He listened for a moment, then shouted, "Mom! Later!" and hung up. Leah tried not to laugh. He dropped the phone back in the bag, then continued smoking. "What did you say you're researching again?" he asked, looking back at her with a surprising lack of embarrassment. "Yiddish what?"

"Yiddish magazines," she said. He was cute, she thought. Did it matter that he was a moron? It was just a summer job.

Mendele laughed. "Like *Yiddish Seventeen*? 'What to Wear to Your Yeshiva Prom!' Or *Yiddish Cosmo*? 'Give the Shabbes-Goy an Orgasm He'll Never Forget!'"

"You're an ass," Leah told him.

Mendele smirked at his cigarette. "There can't seriously be such a thing as a Yiddish magazine."

"Of course there is," Leah said. "There were hundreds. Some still exist. There are even new ones, mostly for Hasidim."

But the book peddler had lost interest. "I bet you're one of those SuperJews," he said. "Like you've spent your whole life at Jewish summer camps, and your parents work for the Elders of Zion or something, and they just want you to find some nice Jewish boy." He smiled.

Leah felt her face turning red. Why was she embarrassed in front of this idiot? "I never went to a Jewish camp," she said. "And my parents are in Madagascar."

Mendele stopped smoking. "What's that?"

"It's an island off the coast of Africa." Truly, she thought, I am working in Chelm.

But now Mendele was actually interested. "What the hell are they doing there?"

The phrase "midlife crisis" sounded as spoiled and clichéd as the concept actually was, so Leah had started making things up that were even more ridiculous. "They're animal-rights activists," she lied. "They're taking animals from American zoos back home to their former environments and helping them adjust."

Mendele didn't get the joke. "Wow, cool," he said, awed. "I bet that's really tough for the animals. I mean, they're not used to having predators and stuff. You can't really go back after that kind of change."

"That's why they're actually building the animals a little artificial habitat, to acclimate them to their former world," Leah said. "It's become a tourist attraction."

"That's awesome," Mendele gaped. Just then the beadle came by and shouted the time for prayers. Grumbling, Mendele started pushing his cart back around the corner. "I wish I was in Madagascar," he muttered.

Leah laughed. "I wish I was at Starbucks."

[

] The weekend before the Fourth of July was busy at the dry-goods store, and unbearably hot, which gave Leah a chance to avoid Mendele. She barely had time to take a break at all, which was a relief, since it meant she didn't leave the air-conditioning except at the wedding—and it also meant that she didn't have to talk to Mendele, though she could hear him lurking behind her shop with his book peddler's cart, whining on his cell phone to his mother. Other than that, she had barely seen him, except during the pogrom. Lately his pogrom antics had evolved. The previous afternoon, he had attempted a "rape" while attacking her shop, which consisted of his jumping on her behind the counter. She had screamed, following protocol. But he had really touched her breast. She should have reported him, but to her astonishment she hadn't minded. In fact, she had begun to look forward to the next pogrom.

But the next time Mendele approached her was at the wedding. She was standing off to the side, escaping with a piece of herring to the ambiguous area beyond the makeshift fence dividing men and women, where no one would pull her into a horah. The bride was flying high in a chair, throwing cloth napkins at the man who was being lifted up on the chair on the opposite side of the fence. In real life, Leah had heard, the bride was a radical feminist at Smith, majoring in performance art.

Mendele had beat his way through the dancing yeshiva students to track Leah down. He waved to her so insistently that she couldn't pretend she hadn't seen him, and eventually he edged toward her and lured her farther to the side with more insistent hand-waving, since they weren't allowed to touch each other in public—except when he transformed into a Cossack, of course. Now they were standing just in front of the study-house, right above the grave of the bride and groom who, according to the gravestone's English inscription, had been murdered under their own wedding canopy during the 1648 Chmielnitski massacre—an event that used to be reenacted during the daily wedding, until a tourist was accidentally hit by an airborne chair.

"So how are the magazines coming?" Mendele asked. "Did you do a translation yet of the *Yiddish Maxim*? 'Good Times at the Mikvah'? 'Wigged Girls Gone Wild'?"

"Shut up," Leah muttered. But there was something amusing about him, something innocent in his lack of self-awareness. She smiled.

They watched from a distance as the rebbe and the melamed performed a carefully choreographed dance with wine bottles balanced on their yarmulkes. It was considerably less impressive when you knew about the Velcro. Mendele tilted his head toward Leah. "Me and the rebbe," he said, speaking under his breath and stroking his beard, "we're thinking about starting a pogrom."

"You're already in the pogrom," Leah said.

"No, I mean a real pogrom," Mendele replied. "Like burning down the *World of Our Fathers*."

Leah sucked in her breath. *World of Our Fathers* was the most popular attraction in the entire complex—partly, she liked to think, because it didn't involve any actual people, just audio-animatrons of people acting out various moments in Eastern European Jewish history, on a loop, while the visitors sat in little book-peddler carts on a slow-moving track. It also had the benefit of being a place to sit, in air-conditioning. People would wait on line for it. Mendele couldn't possibly be serious, Leah thought. She stared at the dancing rebbe and pretended she hadn't heard him.

But Mendele wasn't someone you could easily ignore. He glanced around, then furtively tugged at her sleeve. "Are you in?"

A joke, she was sure now. She forced a laugh. He looked at her and smiled. "If you're interested, let me know tomorrow during your break," he said, as the drunken fiddler threw his violin at the bride. "I'll be by the yeshiva, corrupting the youth."

The next day, she glanced across the square and saw Mendele idling at the door of the yeshiva, waiting for her. But she didn't go. No one came out of the yeshiva either; even the tourists were ignoring him. Apparently the youth had already been corrupted enough.

[

] Leah felt they should have been given the day off on the Fourth of July, but unfortunately it was one of the busiest days of the year, with record numbers of visitors. She had people coming in and out of her store all day long—delighted old people, amused middle-aged people, and children who were so angry to be there that some were already throwing bagels before noon. The day lingered on like the final prayers on Yom Kippur, long and exhausting. Fifteen minutes before the pogrom, the dry-goods store was finally empty for a moment. Leah was leaning back against the wall of T-shirts, anticipating her own collapse beneath Mendele's axe-wielding form, when a tiny elderly woman with dyed black hair walked into her shop.

"Where are the magazines?" the woman asked. Her accent was heavy. Most of the old people who came here were American-born, the farshtoonkineh zaidehs. Occasionally there would be an old survivor, but usually they were brought there by their fifty-five-year-old children or their twenty-five-year-old grandchildren, and usually they were already lost to Alzheimer's. Leah listened, trying to determine whether or not the woman was demented.

"What magazines?" Leah asked. It was hot outside, short-sleeve weather. She glanced at the numbers on the woman's bare forearm.

"Magazines," the woman repeated, with deliberate slowness, as if Leah were a child, or an idiot. "Don't you have magazines to sell?"

Demented, Leah decided. Or very sane, and severely bored. "You'll have to go and see Mendele the book peddler," she told her, using her most courteous voice. "He's around the corner, next to the mikvah."

"All he has are stupid English books," the woman huffed.

Leah looked up, startled.

"When I was a girl in Krakow we used to go to a country resort like this in Kazimierz, a little phony village for tourists, in the summer," she continued. "Nobody ever lived in a place like this for a hundred years, you know—it was just a movie set. But even there, at the fake one, they had the magazines. Don't you think these people knew how to read a magazine?"

Leah felt the chill of the air-conditioning on the back of her neck, and held her breath. Finally she decided on what to say. "Which magazines would you read?" she asked. In Yiddish.

She expected the woman to be surprised to hear her speaking Yiddish, but the woman simply answered, in Yiddish. "I would look for *In Zikh*," she said.

"*In Zikh*! You mean Yankev Glatshteyn's magazine?" Leah asked. She felt, for the first time in months, genuine joy.

"Not just Glatshteyn," the woman said. "Sutzkever wrote for it also. And Leyeles, but I never liked him."

"Avrom Sutzkever!" Leah sang. She was astonished by her own happiness.

The woman grinned, elated. "You like Sutzkever?"

"I love him," Leah murmured, swooning. "The 'Siberia' poem is the most wonderful thing I've ever read. In any language. And his 'Green Aquarium' . . ."

The woman grabbed Leah's hand, clutching it. "We moved to Vilna, and then in the Vilna ghetto, Sutzkever was living there," she said.

Her speech was level, her pronunciation careful; an educated person's voice. "His wife worked in the ghetto library. I was only fourteen maybe, but my mother had me read everything, even then. He won the Ghetto Prize for 'The Grave Child.' It's an exceptional poem. Exceptional. I haven't been able to find a copy of it since then." Leah's hand turned white under the pressure of the woman's fingers.

"I've seen it on microfilm," Leah mumbled, saying the word "microfilm" in English. But it didn't matter. She was gripping, and gripped.

"He's still alive, you know," the woman said. "He lives in Tel Aviv. Unfortunately he's very ill. Disfigured by skin cancer. He doesn't take visitors anymore."

Leah felt the store revolving around her, sliding out of her vision. If only Sutzkever took visitors, she thought. If only all of the visitors who came to her shop, every last farshtoonkineh zaideh who came here in the hope of finding something real, if only they could go to visit Sutzkever instead—if only the whole place could be dismantled and the bequest given to the visitors themselves, in the form of plane tickets to Tel Aviv, so that all of them could line up like they did for the rides and visit Sutzkever at his bedside, to gather at his feet, to drink in his words.

"But all you have here are stupid T-shirts, and no magazines," the woman said loudly, in English. She pulled her hand away, leaving the white imprint of her fingers on Leah's skin. The woman looked at the T-shirts, and then at Leah, with utter contempt. *"Dos iz take a farsh-tunkene shtetl,"* she said. *"Un ir ale—ir zayt take a farshtunkene shtetl-folk."* Leah gaped, breathless, thoughtless, heartless. For an instant the world stopped. And then she heard the explosion. She looked out the shop window, not yet broken, and saw *World of Our Fathers* burning to the ground.

[

] The fire engines arrived minutes later, but not before Mendele the book peddler burst into Leah's shop in his Cossack costume, his baggy sleeves charred. "What the hell did you do?" Leah screamed at him. The door was open now, revealing the brilliant conflagration as the giant map of the Pale of Settlement was consumed by a wave of flames. The blaze was growing quickly. The ride had closed at four as usual, Leah remembered with relief; still, through the windows of her shop across the town square, she could see the smoke billowing up and out until it completely obscured the mikvah. Next door, the yeshiva had already been evacuated. A group of Cossacks on horseback were driving a pack of screaming tourists into the woods. "What the hell did you do?" Leah shouted again, grabbing Mendele by the shoulders.

"It wasn't me!" Mendele wailed. "I swear to God it wasn't me! I was just changing my clothes! I swear!" The sirens began wailing, amplifying Mendele's whines. "I was just changing my clothes! I was taking off my tefillin, and I threw them down so I could change my shirt, and I had the new shirt over my head, and then the whole thing just—"

The old woman who had come for the magazines was still standing at the counter, the expression of disdain frozen on her face. She had turned now, and was staring at the fire through the open door. Then she turned back to see Mendele in his burned Cossack blouse, and shared with him her look of contempt.

"Antisemites," the woman muttered. And before Leah could come out from behind the counter, she walked out the door.

[

] A mechanical failure, it turned out. The ride was actually very old, a refurbished remnant of a carnival ride from eighty years earlier, but no one had realized what a poor idea it was to rely on the old equipment. The wiring had short-circuited, and, the fire department deduced, someone had been smoking a cigarette at just the wrong moment. The rebbe claimed that Mendele had been planning it all along. Mendele blamed the rebbe, but no one believed the book peddler. Later, Leah heard that Mendele was being sued. Meanwhile, other rumors abounded. The melamed was convinced that it was actually an elaborate plot by the administrators of the site, who had failed to turn a profit and were planning to collect the insurance by "lighting shabbes candles in the middle of the week." The mikvah lady said that the gas pipe used to turn on the fake wooden fires for heating the mikvah had been routed under the ride, and she was convinced there was a leak from the shoddy construction job. The badkhen blamed a ten-year-old tourist he had seen dressed in red, white and blue, claiming that he knew for a fact that the kid had a fistful of roman candles in his pocket. The rebbetsin said that a goat from the tailor's backyard had gotten loose and was wreaking all kinds of havoc, and must have chewed at the wires before the ride blew up. And the Messiah swore that he had seen a young man walking into the complex wearing a puffy winter coat on a hot summer day while he sat at the gate with his wounded feet, and he was sure that microscopic pieces of the suicide bomber's corpse were scattered across the ruins of the electronic map of the Pale of Settlement. But no one believed the Messiah.

In the very apologetic letter Leah received in the mail three weeks later, she was offered a job for the following year, when the complex was scheduled to reopen. But Leah turned it down. She had decided to spend next year in Jerusalem. Or, failing that, Starbucks.

] Potatoes

Everyone who passed, Bella had seen before. For the five months in which she'd lived in Memphis, every shopkeeper was not from here, but from Grodno. The man delivering newspapers was the butcher from back home. Every young woman she caught sight of from a distance was her next-door neighbor's daughter. And now just ahead, the eight-year-old boy on the street was her youngest brother Shale, walking hand in hand with a short, skinny woman who, Bella's eyes assured her, was her mother.

Bella followed them from a distance so that they wouldn't see her. On a Friday afternoon, Market Street bustled with words. She recognized those that were in Yiddish, but the rest were locked away, as foreign as every face would be had her mind not invented a way to lessen the shock of being in a strange city. In this neighborhood known as the Pinch, there were Irish and Italian immigrants too, and in their eyes she recognized her own fear, and wondered if despite their best efforts, they too still lived in the countries they had left behind. Did the faces, the houses, the streets live fully formed inside their heads?

Bella, her father, and two of her brothers had come to Memphis as opposed to any other city because her father had a third cousin here. In Grodno, such a tenuous connection meant little. Here it meant everything, as had the words this cousin wrote in a letter to another cousin, who had shared it with them: *you can make a living here*, slim words they'd heaped so much expectation upon it was a wonder they had not sunk; words they'd traveled upon as surely as the ocean liner that sailed from Dansk to New York. When they'd arrived, Shale's trachoma had prevented him from entering, so he and her mother had been sent back to await his recovery.

When Bella reached the corner of Market and Main, she lost sight of the boy and the mother amid the bustle of people, the rowdy group of boys talking and laughing. At the outskirts of the crowd was another young boy, this one taller, in a different cap, with a burst of freckles Shale didn't have, but it was Shale nonetheless.

Of her three brothers, Shale was the only one for whom she felt the fealty of love. Perhaps because he was the youngest, perhaps because he had always been frail, she thought of herself as his protector. At the sight of this latest Shale, she couldn't hold herself back; she ventured closer to the group of boys. One of the oldest of the boys, actually closer to a man than a boy, turned away from the group and watched her, though she didn't know why. Perhaps his mind too fell victim to this rampant misconfiguration where everyone was at the same time someone else.

Stepping closer, she realized that she knew him, not from home, but from the Neighborhood House where she had gone the first few months she was here to study English. His name was Sam Goldberger and he had been the teacher of her class, thirty young women and men crammed into a classroom better suited for children, and he, the lone male teacher, standing at the front, calling out English words for them to repeat. He was not much older than she. His eyes were pale blue, his hair that peeked out from under his cap was the color and texture of wet straw. She wanted to learn English—desperately wanted a way to free her tongue from the paralysis it suffered since they had arrived in Memphis—but she sat silently at her desk, afraid to call attention to herself, afraid she would be asked to speak aloud on her own.

One Wednesday night each month, the desks and chairs were moved aside, and a dance was held. Though she longed to go home before the music began, she forced herself to stay because she heard the voice of her mother, urging her to smile, to enjoy herself. Her mother would not recognize her now, how serious, how downtrodden she had become. At home, she had tried to help out, but had known how to slink away for a quick visit to her friend next door, then to lose track of time, and return only once the cleaning was done, dinner made.

Though she had feigned disinterest, she had listened carefully to the conversations of the other girls who made a habit of whispering and giggling about Sam and had learned that he was from Memphis, born here to parents who had been born here as well. He lived not in the

Pinch, but farther east, on Bellaire Drive. He was reputed to be serious and smart, a boy of whom great things were expected, who already was planning with his older brothers to open a printing press, who brimmed with books he had read and places he would visit. It had to be a matter of pity that Sam showed any interest in she who was besieged with a shyness so malevolent that had it been visible on her face, she too would surely have been sent back along with her mother and Shale.

"Would you like to dance?" he had asked her, in English, in front of a group of girls whom she'd stood near though didn't know by name.

Bella's face burned with embarrassment, and she pretended not to have understood. She wondered if the other girls had put him up to it, if her loneliness was so visible on her face that only the cruelest of men could ignore it.

"Dance," he articulated in slow, careful English as he did in class, as though he expected her to repeat after him.

Her own private lesson, but she was too shy and ashamed to say anything.

"Music," he said, pointing to the lone woman who played piano in the corner.

"Food," he said, pointing to the cookies laid out on tin trays on a table.

"Smile," he said, touching her lips, tracing the shape.

"One day," he promised, "you will talk to us."

She had looked away. In Grodno, she had loved to dance, but here, she could no more make her feet obey her than her tongue. She agreed because she saw no other choice but she had not looked at his face, only at his shoes, light brown leather that was well-worn, though not as worn as her own. She studied the other pairs of shoes dancing across the floor, the sturdy leathers, the upturned delicate pairs, some with buttons, some with bows, some a welcome departure from black or brown.

Across the floor, beneath a rustling skirt, danced a pair of light gray slippers, the prettiest she'd ever seen. The sight of them stirred in her a longing for the shoes she'd once had. It was silly, surely, to care about the shoes—that loss of those black leather boots, with the row of tiny buttons up each side, was the least of it—and yet she couldn't help but remember the pleasure she'd taken in setting them by her bed each night and covering them with a spare scrap of cloth. She had lost them the time she'd taken Shale to dig for potatoes in a field that lay on the outskirts of town, where it was said you were allowed to dig and take what you found. The outing had seemed like an easy way to entertain Shale and to help her mother; it was also a way to spend the spring afternoon outside. When she and Shale arrived at this field after an hour's walk, farther and more strenuous than she'd anticipated, she'd taken her shoes off so as not to get them dirty. It had never occurred to her that when she and Shale returned for them, they'd be gone.

Now, on the street, Sam was waiting for her to say something. After the dance, she had stopped going to class, even though it was the only hour all week that felt like her own. In a cave inside her heart, where she dared to admit the truth to herself, she knew that it wasn't just the lessons that made her so nervous, but the way she had been unable to remove her eyes from Sam's face. She had been afraid that he would see how she hung upon his words, not speaking them aloud, but once she was home, practicing them in front of the mirror.

"Where have you been?" Sam asked her, again assuming that she could speak English.

Bella shrugged her shoulders, looked away. But he was not going to let her evade the conversation so easily. He switched to Yiddish, which, he'd told the class, he'd learned from his grandparents who themselves had come to Memphis as teenagers.

"We've been looking for you. Five weeks and you haven't come," he said.

"My family needs me," she whispered, not sure he could hear her.

"Our class needs you as well," he said, but the look on his face made it plain that he spoke only of himself.

So she had not imagined it. His interest wasn't one more thing her mind had conjured up. Bella gave have him a shy, quick glance; she looked away, then met his eyes and smiled. If he could speak the silent language of her face, he would know that it was an invitation to pursue her. He was as surprised by the sweetness of the gesture as she. Was this a brief appearance of her former self, peeking out? If only she could free her tongue, she would be far more bold. She would grab him by the arm and ask him what he saw when he looked at her: Somewhere in the flecks of her eyes, in the now lustreless braids of her hair, did he see an inkling of who she used to be?

Another group of boys, similar in age and dress, but louder, more boisterous, approached. This time it wasn't a trick of her eyes, but she actually did recognize two people, her brothers Eli and Reuven, who were at that moment supposed to be in school. Within two weeks of their arrival, they began attending Fairview Junior High, which stood at the edge of the neighborhood. There had been no conversation about the fact that they would attend and that she, needed at home, would not. She had said nothing, but her brothers had felt her disappointment; on their first morning of school, as they brimmed with excitement and bustle, they had shocked her when, in a rare moment of seriousness and kindness, they promised to attend school on her behalf; whatever we learn, they'd said, we will teach you.

Angrily, Bella walked toward them. In the three months in which they'd attended school, they not only hadn't made good on their promise, but had managed to alienate every teacher with whom they'd had contact, managed to be called into the principal's office on an almost daily basis, where their knuckles were rapped, their bravado tested. Her father sent her to talk to the principal, though Bella's English was no better than his, and she had the additional burden of needing to explain why it was that she had come in place of a parent.

"Why are you here?" she scolded Reuven and Eli quietly.

"Who are you?" they asked.

"Never seen you before."

In the eyes of the other boys, she could have been any of their older sisters, come to call them home. They waited for her to say something, but even with her brothers, her mouth had swallowed her tongue.

"School is already over for the day," Reuven said.

"If you went to school, you would know that," Eli said and the other boys laughed as well.

If her mother were here, she would be in school too. If her mother were here, she would not have to try to summon a love for Reuven and Eli that she did not feel. Nor would she feel the impossibility of walking into one more store, to buy another day's worth of groceries, would not have to worry about preparing their food, washing their clothes, would not have to remake herself constantly into the shape others needed her to be.

"She's lost her tongue," one of the boys with them said.

"We have one brother with bad eyes, now a sister with no tongue," Reuven and Eli said to each other.

They looked at her with a hatred she couldn't understand. At home, her brothers had been required to listen to her. But here, they saw her weakness and rebelled. No longer did the fact that she was the oldest matter anymore; no longer did she have any means to stop their behavior that grew increasingly out of control. But none of this did she report to her mother in the letters she wrote each week, not wanting to worry her. Instead, Bella took pains to fill the lines with as much practical information as possible, the layout of the small apartment that their cousin had helped them find, the foods she prepared for their meals, the look of the stores, the sounds of the streets, all in the hope that if her mother could envision where they were, neither of them would feel so alone.

"What kind of brothers are you?" said Sam, who had been watching their exchange, and came over, playfully cuffing Eli on the shoulder, then doing the same to Reuven. "You don't even let her go to school one night a week?"

"She doesn't want to go. That's what she told us," said Eli, rubbing with exaggerated gestures the spot on his arm that Sam had touched.

"She does want to go. You listen to me. Even if she says she doesn't want to go, she does."

"She doesn't say anything, or haven't you noticed that yet?"

"I've noticed plenty," he said. "You take care of her, do you understand me?"

He was expecting her to thank him, but only because he didn't understand her shame. To hide, she focused her attention on her brothers, on whose faces she saw, for the first time, a flash of Shale's vulnerability. Suddenly, a rare moment of pity for them: What did they know of why their father had suddenly changed his mind about the need to leave Grodno, what hushed conversations about her had they overheard in their own beds. Even though they, as twins, were inseparable, what burdens did they now bear? It was not just she who suffered the fact that though they had left Grodno as a family, they had each arrived here alone.

Without speaking further to Sam, without looking at her brothers or buying food as she'd intended, Bella turned and ran home, where she lay on the sofa. It was cooler now in Memphis, and for the first time in months, the windows could be closed. When they first arrived, in August, she had been shocked by how hot it was; who could have imagined that the air itself had arms that could wrap around her neck? Then, and now once again, she fell prey to the thought that perhaps it had been better in Grodno. To give into this thought would open an abyss beneath her, but she could no longer prevent herself from doing so. She remembered the Grodno in which she'd known where to walk and how to talk, a city in which she and Shale had confidently set out, that time when she took him to dig for potatoes, and they'd sung as they walked, she telling him fantastical stories of the food she would make him when she returned with potatoes.

The sounds of streets and songs and people, both here and there, grew faint, and she closed her eyes, thinking with dismay of the last letter she received from her mother which said that Shale's eye infection had not yet healed. To hide herself from the interminability of the separation, she took refuge in another memory, this one of her mother on the boat, a week into the journey, pulling from her pocket an orange, slightly battered and turning brown, but an orange nonetheless, as miraculous as though she'd plucked it from a grove springing forth from the salty water. Into each of their outstretched hands, she'd placed a wedge, which they'd hungrily consumed. Then her mother had come up behind her, her body a whispering touch against her own. Her mouth close to her ear, her words were soft but unmistakable. "Forget everything that happened."

When Bella turned to face her, wondering if she was being offered either a warning or blessing, her mother's gaze had shifted outward, her face concealing her intentions as surely as the sea would close over her were she to fall overboard.

Bella awoke to Reuven and Eli bursting into the apartment. It was almost sundown, and they looked around expectantly, in search of dinner.

"We invited your friend for dinner," Reuven announced.

"Who?" she asked, as confused as if he'd spoken in English.

"Your teacher," Eli said.

Her heart fluttered with an excitement she tried to mask from her brothers, unsure whether they intended this as retribution or reconciliation. She rummaged through the cupboard, thinking she would make potato soup, but there were only a few potatoes, not enough to feed her family, let alone an unexpected guest. Alarmed, she looked around the kitchen, which despite her efforts remained gray, dirty, dingy. She'd walked instead of shopped, slept instead of cooked. If Sam were to come to an empty table and a messy home, the shame she'd felt in class would be magnified. In her own eyes too, she would cease to be someone he might seek out.

With sundown less than an hour away, Bella ran from the apartment. She turned first onto Market Street, but all the stores were closed. She checked each store, knocking impatiently in the hope that one of the shopkeepers would recognize her and let her in. The sun was setting, but she couldn't go home without food. She had no choice but to venture into unfamiliar streets that were becoming cloaked in darkness. Until now, she had been afraid to leave the neighborhood; she scarcely believed there was more to this city than these streets. Only the nearby presence of the Mississippi River assured her that the world had not closed off. Were she to find her way onto one of these boats, its captain might transport her from this river to the ocean, and by magic, into the Bovar River, because despite what forms the maps drew, all the waters of the world connected somewhere.

Bella walked past the closed stores, past Market Street Square, past any vestige of familiarity. She came to a church, a cemetery, a court house. She passed houses so large that her mouth dropped in envy. She tried to keep track of where she'd turned and in what direction she'd gone, but soon she couldn't turn back because she didn't know which way back was. She would never find her way home; she'd spend her night on these streets. She'd walk to the edge of the city, to the edge of this country and never find her way back.

The fear which she'd tried to hide from since she arrived pounced upon her. She was back, not in the Grodno which she longed for, but the real one whose borders mapped the terrain of her fear. When she'd realized that the shoes weren't there and had looked up to see them in the hands of two boys she didn't know, she was initially just angry. But as the two boys drew closer, suddenly older than she'd first realized, she became afraid. Dangling the shoes by their laces, so that they danced in the air, the boys taunted her. "Come and get your shoes," one had said. "If you steal potatoes, why can't we steal shoes?" the other yelled out. For the boys, this was a game. For her and for Shale, it was the hidden world of nighttime fears come to life, standing before them in the afternoon sun. Detecting the malice in their voices, she grabbed Shale's hand and began to run, sure that home could not be so far away. She ran to the screams of their laughter. She ran to the sound of footsteps behind her, wild like hoof-beats.

She hadn't been able to outrun those footsteps then, and now, separated by the passage of an ocean, by the passage of many months, she was still unable to outrun them. Those pounding sounds had followed her—were they the only thing that had, in actuality, come with her from there to here? She'd tried to listen to her mother's advice, but the more she tried to push Grodno from her mind, the more it insisted upon following her.

In Memphis too, the sound of footsteps followed her, in the distance but coming closer. This time it was not just the screams of laughter but her name being called, Bella, Bella, Bella, a threat, a taunt. At least in Grodno, she had known what to fear. Here, she didn't know the shape fear could take, when it ambushed her from all the places where it liked to hide.

She came to the end of a street, and there was the entrance to Confederacy Park, whose name her brothers had mentioned, having gleaned from their classmates' tales of the dangers lurking there. They recounted these stories with bravado, sure they would be able to defend themselves when necessary, because they didn't know what it was to be able to protect neither yourself nor those you loved.

The path inside the park was lined with trees, but it was so dark that she couldn't see their branches, only felt aware of their presence above her. This time she didn't run against pebble-laden roads with no shoes; her feet were not cut and bleeding; this time she didn't hear Shale's voice screaming in fear, making her stop in order to help him, not realizing until it was too late that the boys weren't interested in Shale. This time she didn't have Shale to think about, didn't have to choose between saving herself and thinking she needed to save him. This time the voice calling her name grew fainter, and there were no arms pushing her down, no need to worry that Shale was just off in the distance, witnessing her struggle to be free from the assault upon her body and the part inside herself that she used to think of as her soul. She was free too from the look in Shale's eyes—as much as she missed him, she didn't have to live with his futile attempts to ease her pain.

Faster, and stronger, Bella ran, emerging from the park with a speed and force she didn't know she still possessed. Across the street, a light was illuminated, a store still open. Inside, a shopkeeper was wiping off a counter. Panting, she banged against the glass door. She'd never seen him before, neither here nor in Grodno, but even so, he opened the door, alarmed by the wild look on her face and the disheveled state of her hair.

He brought her a glass of water and she drank. He motioned to a chair and she sat.

"How can I help you?" he asked, in English, and though she only partially understood what he had said, she was moved by the kindly way in which he spoke.

"*Kertofle?*" Bella asked, the Yiddish word for potato.

He stared uncomprehendingly at her.

"*Kertofle*, she repeated, "*kertofle, kertofle, kertofle*," her voice growing louder and more desperate with each repetition. In the air before him, she drew the shape of a potato, but he could read nothing from her wild gestures.

Still to no avail, but the patience and kindness on his face were unexpected. As she searched for what to say, someone burst through the door, as winded, as flushed as she had been moments before. His face had not been concocted in her mind. It was not one born of the past, but one that lived here: it was Sam, who was supposed to be sitting down now at her family's table. Somewhere inside the thicket in her head, where she knew more than she had allowed herself to believe, she pulled out an English word. She opened her mouth, which formed a small solid object.

"Potato?" Bella asked. Her pronunciation was mangled, her accent thick, but the word was right.

"Potato," Bella said again. "Potato."

Only once the shopkeeper went to get what she'd requested would she meet Sam's beseeching gaze. Bella turned to him and began to speak.

] Avigdor of the Apes

*What ails you now, that you have gone up entirely
to the roofs?*
ZOHAR

Avigdor Bronfman, an indifferent scholar, made his way across Orchard Street at twilight, on his way home from his Talmud Torah class.
He sidled between the vendors of nickel spectacles, celluloid collars,
and cotton waists, and avoided a shrill woman in the process of slap-
ping a peddler with his own stinking carp. He skirted a starving draft
horse with ribs like hood louvers dropping a steaming pile into the
gutter, and stepped onto the opposite curb. Mounting the stoop, he
entered a cabbage-rank tenement beneath a sign in Hebrew characters
advertising the second-floor occupant's profession of circumciser. That
was his father. The boy climbed a flight of stairs, opened the door
to a stuffy apartment wherein his bearded papa stood swaying in his
prayer shawl, his mama pumping her sewing machine, and tossed in
his books. Then he closed the door and continued his ascent up the five
remaining flights to the top of the building, where he pushed open a tin-
plated door onto the tar-papered roof. Crossing the roof, he shed his
reefer jacket and hopped onto the low parapet, stood a moment admiring the salmon-pink sunset, and plunged into the crisp autumn air.
[
] His flights had begun soon after Avigdor and his friend Shaky Gruber
went to a Shabbos matinee of *Tarzan of the Apes* at the Grand Street
flickers. The film starred Mr. Elmo Lincoln in the role of the ape man, an
actor so gross and lumbering that even when battling an authentic lion—
a mange-ridden beast whose drugged movements were even clumsier
than those of its human prey—he failed to convince. Nevertheless,

while his pal Shaky snickered irreverently, Avigdor was transfixed. Sunk in the plush seats of the dark picture palace, a sanctuary from the clamor and menace of the neighborhood streets, he experienced a kind of savage freedom. He was a scrawny kid, Avigdor, tethered to a claustrophobic household in the sump of the East Side ghetto, and the progress of an orphan raised to manhood by anthropoid apes struck a chord in his pigeon breast. It was not so much Tarzan's brute power and ferocity that thrilled him—though such attributes were nothing to sniff at—as his ability to maintain a largely aerial existence, navigating the lush canopy of the Congo high above the earth without ever having to come down.

Excited as he was by the film, though, Avigdor was not immediately moved to emulate its hero. Raised in an atmosphere where sedulous study was valued above action, he first visited the Seward Park Library, where he obtained a copy of the novel by Edgar Rice Burroughs from which the photoplay had been adapted. He read it in secret, since his pious papa regarded all secular literature as obscenity. Then he found himself doubly spellbound, the exploits of the boy adopted by a tribe of great apes further validated by their translation into print. The son of a *mohel*, a ritual clipper of infant foreskins, Avigdor had been the object of countless jokes at his own and his father's expense, as well as a frequent victim of bullies. He knew he was the unlikeliest of candidates for a transformation from *yeshivah bocher* to jungle denizen, but on the strength of his enchantment with the ape man he determined to reinvent himself.

"Grow up already," sneered his friend Shaky Gruber—himself no model of maturity—when Avigdor confided his resolution; and ambivalent until then, Avigdor was briefly inclined to agree. Then he surprised himself by dissolving his friendship with Shaky on the spot.

Soon after, on an early March evening, he climbed to the windy roof of his six-floor tenement. He'd been there before, on sweltering nights when his family joined others escaping their oven-like apartments to bed down beneath lusterless stars on the so-called tar beach. But at those times Avigdor had felt uncomfortably vulnerable, lying awake amid alien bodies emitting rude noises, some crying out from troubled dreams. Now, as he surveyed the scene, he had to admit that the rooftops of the Lower East Side had little in common with the dense arboreal expanse of equatorial Africa. Except for a few scraggly plane trees over in Seward Park, there were no boughs to perch on, no luxuriant creepers or lianas to swing from. The realization came almost as a relief, since now he could dispense with the passing compulsion and resume his ordinary life. But look again with less-civilized eyes and there were no end of purchases and footholds, of aeries and swallows' nests and lofty towers affording panoramic views. There were ledges, catwalks, drainpipes, and lampposts, an urban skyscape with any number of features that a sprightly young primate might employ in eluding jungle predators.

But how to proceed? You could beat your shallow chest with your fists gorilla-style—which Avigdor commenced to do; and the gesture did lend him a certain Dutch courage, not to mention giving a vibrato quality to his yawp. But after that it seemed incumbent on him to perform some feat of simian athleticism. Avigdor had never before demonstrated the least hint of athletic ability, nor had it ever occurred to him to try; until now his body had been a rickety construction wherein he was forced to dwell for lack of a sturdier container. Then he invoked a passage from the novel, which he recited under his breath like a portion of scripture: "He could spring twenty feet across space at the dizzy heights of the forest top . . . ," after which Avigdor made a dash for the surrounding parapet. Bounding onto it he launched himself with cycling legs over the airshaft onto the neighboring roof. The distance was not very far; other boys routinely cleared the shafts flat-footed, the taller ones able almost to step across. But something happened as soon as Avigdor felt himself airborne: his apprehension dissolved, his brain ceased its caviling, and he became a pure expression of the physical. Instinct supplanted self-consciousness and his limbs assumed an integrity of their own.

So it seemed that Avigdor had a gift, which he straightaway began to nurture, developing it along with the strength he needed to enhance his prowess. Over time, his gaunt body acquired a tough and sinewy armature of muscle, a tempered vitality he augmented with various devices either scavenged or manufactured by his own hand. From modest monkey-like efforts at swinging, leaping, and vaulting, he graduated to circus-grade acrobatic feats. For these he was not above consulting library books on gymnastics and even the physics of leverage and balance. But while the information might be useful to some, the boy found the technical language a distraction, calling his attention back to the pedestrian plane, and in the end he left the books behind in the world where they belonged.

On any given afternoon, abandoning his studies, Avigdor might step to the edge of the roof and throw himself off, perhaps catching hold of a clothesline fastened by pulleys to an adjacent tenement wall. Then he would "brachiate" arm over arm along the sagging line above a flagstone courtyard, where far below a mother patsched a whining child's tush and a vendor of sheet music intoned a music hall air. He might drop neatly onto the fire escape of an opposite building and clamber up a ladder to the roof, where he fetched from under a pile of rubble beside a spinning air vent a rope tied to an iron hook. Then he would twirl the rope lasso-fashion above his head in ever-widening circles and release the grappling hook, watching it arc over Ludlow or Essex Street to clank onto a scaffold or wrap itself serpent-like around a balcony rail. He might swing out over the jostling thoroughfare and let go before smashing into a wall, free-falling ass over elbows to land plump in the tent of a consumptive erected on the pebbly roof of a candy store. (So what if the tent collapsed, traumatizing the invalid inside? The law of the jungle made allowances for such damage.) He might land in an awning or a canvas tarp stretched over a seedframe and bounce back into the air like a shot from a sling.

In lieu of vines Avigdor scaled walls of jutting masonry—"He could gain the utmost pinnacle of the loftiest tropical giant with the ease and swiftness of a squirrel . . ." Reaching the top, he might locate a limber flagstaff hidden in a cache of scrap lumber, and making a run across the tarpaper, plant the pole and vault over an alley; or hurl himself feet-first against a bulkhead and, shooting his legs like a jack-in-the-box, catapult himself onto the pitched roof of a rowhouse several stories below. Clattering down the shingled slope, he might leap onto the top of an omnibus, dropping into a seat beside a frightened passenger. The bus would turn a corner into Orchard Street, forging like a pachyderm lumbering upstream through hordes of hawkers and market wives, passing under a hanging ladder that the apeboy would then grab hold of, hoisting himself onto another fire escape where he opened a window and tumbled inside.

As he rolled onto the creaking floorboards, his pear-shaped mama, placing a dish of stuffed derma beside his place at the table, would ask him, "Where's your jacket?"; while his papa, already seated with a napkin tucked under his chin, called him apostate and invited him to say the prayer over breaking bread.

[

] You might ask what became of his fear, for he'd always been a timid kid. But once he'd overcome his trepidation through blind faith and flung himself into the vapory air, Avigdor discovered that the ghetto's higher plateaus had been his element all along. Swarming over the rooftops, he remained in a state of pure rapture. The rest of the time— forced to sit in dusty classrooms and run the gauntlet of his discordant neighborhood—he regarded as misspent. It was true that his new physicality had toughened his frame, making him a less objectionable companion, but Avigdor shunned the society of his peers, whom he'd yet to forgive for ridiculing him as his father's son. Now he lived only for the moment when he could climb above the choking grid of the Lower East Side. Down below, amid the mercantile crush, he endured the monotonous passage of days, while above he dwelled in a timeless space where he would never grow old. He liked spying on the ethereal activities of his neighbors: the women kneeling to spread their freshly washed hair over a skylight to dry, the pigeon-fanciers wielding their hooples shaped like snowshoes to shoo the birds back into their coops. Blind children performed calisthenics on the caged roof of their academy on Pitt Street; artists erected their easels atop the Educational Alliance on East Broadway.

Ultimately, however, he felt the pull to range farther afield. There were towers that beckoned with their Babel-like altitudes, roof gardens where orchestras played for tea dances and gentlemen waltzed slinky ladies about the upper reaches of the metropolitan night. You had rooftops where grass grew and barnyard animals grazed, rooftops with whole parlors under awnings, penthouse terraces designed to resemble the decks of ships. There were kite fliers and laundry thieves whom Avigdor furtively observed, lovers entangled in trysts among flapping sheets. In Herald Square, there was a giant billboard in the shape of a windmill on whose turning arms you could ride. All this he viewed through the eyes of a curious young savage looking onto a strange civilization, its inhabitants aspiring to the heights while remaining anchored to the terrestrial world.

Sometimes the boy felt sorry for them. So freighted were they with their worries and piecework, so bound by the shackles of their phylacteries, that they could never know his high-flying freedom. While they required so much to sustain the little they had, Avigdor needed next to nothing—only an occasional taste of his mother's soup afloat with medallions of fat to keep him nourished, and his dexterous limbs to give him access to a city that had become his own personal jungle gym. Still, it was a solitary life, and there were times when he might feel sorry for himself as well, a sentiment that actually sweetened his life aloft.

Summers swelled the population of the ghetto's elevated real estate, and Avigdor occasionally confronted gangs of other boys in his wanderings. As the Jews were likelier to remain earthbound, these were typically Irish lads in their floppy caps or Italians east of the Bowery, youth auxiliaries of the older gangs that were the strong arm of Tammany Hall. When they spotted a sheeny trespassing in their territory—Avigdor's beak was a dead giveaway—they were quick to give chase across the sticky tarpaper. The boy exulted in these encounters even to the extent of seeking them out, nor was he above baiting his enemies in a Yiddish as exotic to them as the language of apes:

"*Putzim mit oyren*," he might shout, "pricks with ears," hopping up and down on a chimney pot.

Then he would turn a backwards somersault over a gap between buildings and lead them on an obstacle course across the housetops. At first they followed in a threatening mob, though their ranks would soon thin, some hanging back in the face of their quarry's more perilous leaps. The more stalwart persisted, only to be brought up short in the end, arriving on a roof in time to see Avigdor atop a facing tenement reeling in the ladder he'd just danced across; they halted at the sight of him running up a plank that was slanted against a trestle, weighted at its foot by a keg of nails. The yammering plank, which served as a springboard, would toss the nimble yid whooping onto some far-flung height, where he turned to raise his fist and voice a victory cry,

"*Kish mikh vi di yidn hobm gereet*, kiss me where the Jews reposed!"

And while he still wore his shopworn sweater, knee pants, and tramping shoes, he imagined himself prancing in a loincloth—"his brown, sweat-streaked body glistening in the moonlight, supple and graceful among the awkward, hairy brutes about him."

Occasionally it occurred to Avigdor that he might stand and fight, that with his "mighty thews" he might tear out their hearts as Tarzan did to

Sabor the lion and Horta the boar, but it was frankly more fun to lead them on a merry chase. Eventually, though, they wearied of the sport, after which he would have to egg them on, pelting them with insults and standing on ledges to pish on their games of alley craps. When the weather began to turn and the roofs became less tenanted, he sorely missed their cat-and-mouse games.

By then he'd become something of a legend in the neighborhood, the feats ascribed to him including aspects of the miraculous. (The more credulous spoke of flying carpets and wings.) Though he never made any effort to disguise himself in his flights, no one on the ground ever confused the apeboy with the son of the *mohel* who remained the butt of jokes: "Whaddaya call Reb Bronfman's toolbox? A bris kit." But the fact of his double identity only added spice to his aerial exploits.

With the return of cold weather, however, Avigdor sometimes found it a stretch to sustain his fantasy, so incompatible were the frosty altitudes with his vision of the jungle's verdant humidity. His fingers and toes stiffened, his frigid scalp chilled his brain, and occasionally as he scrambled up a stone façade or swung from a rope above an arcade, the lemony light from a window might beckon him back indoors. Sometimes, however much he might judge himself to be of another species, Avigdor missed the life of the tribe. But always his exhilaration renewed itself, and winter had its virtues: the clotheslines, for instance, bereft now of garments and coated in ice, gave the passenger—dangling from a walking stick hooked over them—a streamlined ride at breakneck speed. Though once, while he was zinging above the courtyards via this mode of travel, the brittle line snapped from his weight, and unable to arrest his forward momentum, Avigdor was thrust headlong through the flimsy frame of a tenement window.

He crashed into the railroad flat in a cataclysm of splinters and glass and went sprawling onto the floor of a kitchen, where a woman stood dusted to the elbows in flour from a kneading trough and a girl sat naked in her bath. The woman—face like a pomegranate in a lopsided wig—came at the boy with her upraised rolling pin as he attempted to get to his feet. The girl in the inclined porcelain tub covered her breasts with her arms and shrieked hysterically; but Avigdor, lacerated head to toe, was deaf to the sound, insensitive to everything but her radiance, which shone through the lather that festooned her pink flesh like surf.

"A mermaid," thought the boy, frozen in his fascination until the rolling pin descended on his skull. Lightning struck a baobab tree in his head as he crumpled onto the floorboards again.

He came to in a paddy wagon from which he was unceremoniously hauled through dank corridors and tossed into a holding cell in the Tombs. With blood crusted like war paint over one whole side of his face, he climbed the bars and rattled his cage, uttering guttural cries—until he noticed that he wasn't alone in the long cell. A number of desperate-looking parties in equally gore-stained attire sat slumped against the walls frowning at his antics. Their censure had an inhibiting effect on Avigdor's outbursts, and realizing that he ached exquisitely in every fiber and joint, he satisfied himself with gingerly thumping his chest. At length he was allowed to send a message to his family, whereupon his father, who for all his piety understood how the system worked, paid a visit to the Honorable Max Hochstim in the backroom of an Essex Market saloon. Mr. Hochstim, local ward heeler and trafficker in Jewish girls, had a son at whose bris Reb Bronfman had presided, and at the request of the distraught *mohel* he appealed to the Tammany boss Big Tim Sullivan, who saw to it that Avigdor was released from captivity.

"Now you going to be a good boy?" Reb Bronfman inquired of his son, whose head was swathed in gauze bandages; and the chastened Avigdor assured him that that was the case. But no sooner did his wounds begin to heal than the boy, heeding once more the call of the wild, took again to the roofs.

But instead of traveling by leaps and bounds to remote destinations about the city, Avigdor kept close to his own native quarter; close, to be precise, to a railroad tenement on Attorney Street, whose unmended window was covered with a dingy gray blanket whipped by the wind. Perched on a ledge supported by stone gargoyles, whose squat pose the apeboy duplicated, Avigdor maintained his vigil, waiting for a glimpse of the girl in the tub. Not that he expected to see her naked again. In fact, he was a little ashamed of having first viewed her in her natural state; for despite the tension that troubled his heart and loins, Avigdor still respected her modesty. In anticipating a second sighting, he clothed her in his mind, though not in the drab shirtwaists and buttoned boots of her peers. Rather was she wreathed in spindrift, hobbleskirted in rainbow scales, a creature of the sea as he was a creature of the air. That was the vision that had surfaced in his brain to displace the vertiginous throbbing left there by the rolling pin. It was a vision that vied with the dominion of the riotous jungle canopy that had lured him so far from the commonplace, an image he'd seen not just with his eyes but with organs of perception Avigdor could not even name—and he knew that every nerve in his body would sing out when he saw her again. So he watched from a neighboring ledge and sometimes dropped onto her fire escape to peer through windows, all to no avail. He spied the pomegranate-faced woman at her breadboard and a bald man reading a Yiddish newspaper at a table, rocking a cradle with his foot, and a daughter occasionally moving among them to perform chores; but how could she, who resembled so many others, be the same girl whose rosy essence permeated his waking dream?

From time to time, Avigdor's restlessness would get the better of him. Now that the season was milder, his body revived its involuntary agenda, and he was compelled to turn circles about a horizontal flagpole or shove off on a housepainter's ladder, riding it like a giant second hand across an alley. He might skip over an avenue on the tops of the cabs of trucks as if across the armored backs of a herd of rhinoceros. But always he returned to his perch to watch for her, aware that "in his savage, untutored breast new emotions were stirring." He wanted to rescue her from jungle cats and mamba snakes, from the shark-like youths in yellow spats who preyed on pretty Jewish daughters. "He knew that she was created to be protected, and that he was created to protect her." Scrutinizing the girls on the sidewalks or at school, he wondered if he were missing her among them, so much did he distrust his own senses at street level. On earth he was only the son of a poor father who wore a suspensory and muttered benedictions into a beard so strewn with scraps you could boil it for soup; whereas aloft . . . but aloft was not where she lived.

Then came an afternoon in late April when the wind started up, the drizzling rain gathered into a cloudburst, and a girl appeared on the tenement roof to take her turn among the women bringing in laundry from the lines. From his roost, Avigdor watched her struggling to stuff the billowing garments into her basket in the downpour: how her ginger hair was plastered to her forehead and cheeks, her white frock drenched until it clung to the contours of the sylph-like form beneath. So dizzy with desire was the boy that he nearly pitched head foremost from his perch; for this one he recognized as his *rusalka*, his sea-borne *maidel* and destined mate. The other ladies had abandoned the roof, leaving the girl still wrestling chemises and sheets, while Avigdor mounted the terrace behind him. Impervious to the driving rain, he stepped onto a cedar plank arched over the fulcrum of a railroad tie, which was wedged under a water barrel at one end, lashed with ropes at the other. He took up a fireman's axe he'd left propped there for the purpose and—bracing for the release of tension that would fling him over the chasm between buildings—severed the ropes at a stroke. But nothing happened; the wet plank retained its warp—his devices were growing outworn from neglect. So he forsook the mechanism and hurtled the abyss on his own steam, clapping hold of a ceramic drainpipe on the opposite wall; he shinnied up its slippery length and sprang onto the roof in time to place himself between the girl and the door to the stairs.

"Then Tarzan of the Apes did just what his first ancestor would have done. He took his woman in his arms and carried her into the jungle," and Avigdor, believing he'd detected a hint of compliance in her attitude, made to follow suit. He grabbed her arm with a force that caused her to drop her basket and pulled her to him, intoxicated by his own strength, trying his best to ignore her panic as he looked about for the readiest route of absconding with the girl. He saw walls whose irregular bricks he might ascend spider-like with his burden, chimneys he could bound across like stepping stones, a distant bell tower that might provide a temporary nest. There he would deposit her after she'd come "to trust this strange wild creature as she would have trusted but few of the men of her acquaintance." He would make her a bed of ferns and grasses and leave her to sleep in the leafy bower while he lay across the entrance to keep watch. In the morning he would bring her coconuts, and when he lifted her up and offered to return her to civilization, she would throw her arms about his neck and unashamedly declare her love.

But that was not how things fell out. Furiously beating her fists against his chest, she cried, "Lemme go!" in a voice whose stridency froze his bones. When he relaxed his embrace, she tore herself from his grasp spitting curses: "*Boolvan!* Idiot!" while he remained at a loss for words, having ruled out the language of the great apes as inadequate. Recovered enough to take up her basket and make for the stair-well, she hissed, "A cholera in your guts!" as she swept through the bulkhead door.

Standing there with the rain buffeting his upturned face, he declared, "I'm Avigdor, Lord of the Rooftops," then asked of the closed tin door, "What's *your* name?"

[

] It was Fanny, Fanny Podhoretz, but he wouldn't learn it for a time. For a time he continued to lurk in the vicinity of her building, squatting on elevations that afforded him an unobstructed view of her roof. But if she appeared at all (and it was seldom), it was in the company of other girls, as she was clearly not of a mind to risk solitary exposure again. Though she wore the same calicos as her companions and seemed to share in their conspiracies, Avigdor could now discern that, wet or dry, she was a rare creature composed of pure light. By summer, when he spotted her beating a rug or featherbed with her companions, or braid-ing another girl's hair, he wondered if she even remembered their en-counter. Forgetting it would be in his favor, though the thought also filled him with regret. There were occasions when he saw her eyes stray from their occupation to scan the rooftops, and although at those times he read a certain uneasiness in her expression, he also believed he saw something else—which gave him cause to hope. Nurturing that hope, he would station himself on a cornice or atop a water tower so that, when she looked up, she might observe him hunkering there. But if ever she caught sight of him, she quickly averted her glance. Of course, Avigdor continued his aerial sorties, but he no longer plummeted and soared for the sheer animal sport of it; always now he liked to imagine she was watching, that he was showing off his agility for her sake. Such self-consciousness had already in some degree compromised his free-dom, or so Avigdor supposed, even as he despaired of ever seeing her alone again. Then early one evening in June, as dusk stained the sky a plum-purple over the river, there she was by herself on the roof taking clothes from a line.

And before she could release the other corner of a hanging pillowslip, he was standing right in front of her.

The clothespin fell from between her clenched teeth as her jaw dropped open. "*Meshugah ahf toit!*" she cried, taking a step backward with a hand to her breast; but that was the extent of her retreat. Perhaps she'd had a change of heart, or was she merely too frightened to flee? In either case, Avigdor felt encouraged, but while he knew better than to try and abduct her, he was still unable to find his tongue. How after all did humans pay court? Then it seemed to him a great mercy that she was the first to speak, demanding in her unladylike voice,

"What are you, a man or a monkey?"

The question demanded an earnest answer and the boy hung his head to consider. "Both?" he replied at length.

"You can't be both," she insisted almost angrily.

He did not contradict her.

Then she cautiously submitted, "You look more like a monkey."

Again he let the statement stand.

She shrugged as if having determined his harmlessness and began hurriedly to fold a sheet that was dragging the tarpaper, then dropped it into her wicker basket. "In monkeys I ain't innerested," she snapped, but unless he was mistaken, there was a trace of coyness in her tone. Emboldened, Avigdor rallied all the courage he had at his command, which wasn't much—it was only the untried courage of a callow youth, which had little in common with the fearlessness of apes.

"In what then you innerested?" he asked.

She gave another tug at the clothesline on its pulley, causing a tendril of russet hair to come loose from its bun. It spiraled, thought Avigdor, like an auger that could drill to the core of your soul. "I tell you what I ain't innerested; I ain't innerested in talking no more to you. You're bughouse."

But she made no effort to depart, dropping another item of clothing into her basket, an intimate article at which Avigdor saw her blush. He felt again the urge to snatch her up and swing aloft with her, to feel her supple body in his arms. He wanted to battle the rogue anthropoid Terkoz over her, vanquishing him just in time to pull her out of the quicksand in which she was sinking. An apeboy had many options unavailable to the son of a *mohel*. Then she blessedly took the initiative again, uttering somewhere between an insult and advice,

"Go walk up a wall, why dontcha. What are you always spying on me?"

"Because," in his mind he let go of a vine with no notion of what he might next catch hold of, "I love you."

"Feh!" She made a disgusted face, pulling another scanty item from the line, stuffing it into the basket without folding it as she turned on her heel. "Bughouse!" But the next evening she was on the roof alone again.

[

] He offered her the celestial altitudes and she assured him that the roof of No. 76 Attorney Street was lofty enough for her, thank you very much. He told her that with him she could fly and she said there was nowhere she was going that she couldn't get to on the 3rd Avenue El. Thus disparaged, he had the presence of mind, once he got around to introducing himself as Avigdor, to insert a "formerly" before "of the Apes." She sniffed and said she was Fanny of the Lower East Side Podhoretzes, her father the proprietor of Podhoretz's Foundation Garments, one of a dozen such hole-in-the-wall establishments on Orchard Street. Then she told him in no uncertain terms that rooftop rendezvous were not her style; they were the kind of thing that could give a girl a reputation, and personally she preferred being closer to the ground. If he wanted to see her again—which wasn't to say that she wanted to see *him*—he could come calling at her family's apartment like a regular person. As she spoke, Avigdor became a student of her emerald eyes set slightly aslant in the cameo pink oval of her face, and realized he was hopelessly torn. To be with her would mean coming down from up above, a bodeful prospect for a youth who had no other prospects in the world of men; and to present himself as a candidate for Fanny's hand he must have prospects.

So, with a heavy heart, he temporarily abandoned the roofs in order to indenture himself to his mother, whose finished piecework he delivered to the rag-trade jobbers after school—school having become a place where his attendance seemed daily less imperative, while the cheder was already history. Neither of his parents were especially troubled that his tasks abetted his truancy, both already resigned to the fact that scholarship would not save their son from the life of a wage slave. At first Avigdor thought he might make short work of his deliveries by taking aerial routes to the uptown emporiums, but given the bundles he had to carry, that method of transport proved impractical. And so he became a shlepper, identifying more with the native bearers the Lord of the Jungle viewed from the treetops than the Lord of the Jungle himself. Still he was making a salary, if only a pittance, and with his inaugural pennies he purchased a bouquet of chrysanthemums, brilliantined his hair, and turned up with palpitations at the threshold of the Podhoretz flat. He was relieved when, opening the door, Fanny's mother failed to recognize the interloper who'd crash-landed on her kitchen floor, though he still had to submit to what amounted to an inquisition from her father. Once it was established, however, that the merchant Podhoretz and the ritual circumciser Bronfman both hailed from the Ukrainian town of Drogobych—once determined that, un-Jewish musculature notwithstanding, Avigdor was an ordinary kid from the neighborhood—Fanny was allowed to step out with the reformed apeboy.

They went to a candy store with a fountain on Delancey Street, where Fanny had a charlotte russe, Avigdor a phosphate, and overcoming his disappointment at finding her less siren than sensible Jewish daughter, Avigdor asked her to marry him.

"Behave yourself," simpered Fanny, licking her spoon with a tentacular tongue, but the boy had developed no talent for small talk. In fact, he had no facility for conversing with a young lady in any conventional fashion, when by all rights they ought to be frolicking among branches reached only by the most intrepid of tropical birds. But as he sat there at the marble counter looking out onto the sidewalk aswarm with toilers and lunch-bucket drones, the jungle, beyond inaccessible, seemed merely a childish dream.

Fanny pointed through the plate-glass window toward a sad-faced capuchin monkey tethered hat-in-hand to an equally dour Italianer's barrel organ. "Maybe you could get his job," she teased.

Among Avigdor's airborne attributes that failed to translate to sea-level was his aptitude for playfulness. "I got already a position," he replied, and was instantly ashamed of having adopted a contrary tone with his beloved. But while the shlepping might foot the bill for an occasional excursion to the nickelodeon or the candy store, he knew perfectly well it could never support a wife and family. So what was the alternative? Should he apprentice himself to his father and look forward to a future paved in infant foreskins? His distaste for the profession aside, he was aware that inflicting the bloody sign of the covenant on newborn pishers earned the *mohel* little more than a dubious local prestige. He supposed he might join the legions of cutters, basters, and pressers that swelled the district's sweatshops, but even these occupations required a modicum of skill, let alone the fetters they imposed on the worker. Or—and here Avigdor had a vision of trapezes and mid-air arabesques above cheering crowds,

"Maybe I could join a circus?" he proposed.

"Maybe," responded the girl with a coquettish wink, "my papa will give you a job."

[

] The two families met in the rabbi's stuffy chambers in back of the Beit Emunah sanctuary on Stanton Street, where a heavy-lidded Rabbi Iskowitz officiated over the signing of the *ketubah*, the marriage contract. The Bronfmans and Podhoretzes were courteous to one another, though both families were clearly skeptical about the alliance. After all, their children, barely out of diapers, had bypassed traditional channels in their haste to pledge themselves to one another; and while Fanny was a good girl with a practical nature, Avigdor had only recently shown signs of overcoming a lifelong fecklessness. As they toasted the occasion with thimblefuls of Kiddush wine, Reb Bronfman repined with a shake of the head, "Amerikaner kinder," upon which Mr. Podhoretz placed a hand in sympathy on the dandruff-dusted shoulder of the *mohel*'s gabardine: "At least we robbed from the marriage broker his fee, eh Bronfman?" Their wives—respectively moon-faced and fruit—assured each other that this was how things were done in the New World, where tradition was trumped by something called love.

For all his giddy emotion, Avigdor was uncomfortable with the businesslike atmosphere surrounding the contractual arrangement; while on the other hand he was pleased to be regarded as a person of substance, a grownup if you will. He felt a measure of gratitude toward his prospective father-in-law—he couldn't find it in him to call him Leon, nor did Mr. Podhoretz invite the familiarity—for offering to take him on as an employee in his shop. True, his salary would not amount to much more than his shlepper's wages, but Podhoretz also owned some rental property on Rivington Street and had promised to provide the newlyweds an apartment, rent-free, as a wedding gift. It was a tiny apartment in a dilapidated Old Law building, but even for that Avigdor was thankful, since its condition somewhat salved his feelings of being in the merchant's debt. Still, he was a little breathless from the speed with which events had proceeded: Was he in fact about to swap his secret life for a domestic one he was wholly unprepared for? But the important thing, the thing to remember, was that he'd found his *bashert*, his fated one; that, astonishingly, Fanny had made up her mind to accept him, albeit with some reservations.

"You got potential, Avi," she assured him, poking a forefinger point-blank in his solar plexus, "but you got yet to be a man." Which estate seemed to preclude his simian hijinks.

On strolls past the East Broadway shmoozeries or along the 2nd Avenue rialto in the weeks preceding the wedding, she allowed him certain liberties, but always at a price. The held hand required the promise of some newfangled appliance or, say, a Brussels carpet; the pecked cheek a baby boy. As he listened to her recite the plans for the wedding —echoing her father's anxiety over the rent for the hall, the cost of the catering, the bridesmaids' bouquets—Avigdor felt again his sense of having entered into a business transaction he'd experienced in the rabbi's chambers. He longed for spontaneous displays of affection, the heated embrace that she would return with a fervent will, her "surrender"—though he wasn't entirely sure what that would entail. But mostly he contented himself in the knowledge that it was her appreciation of his animal grace that had won her; she understood that he was not your garden variety Orchard Street son. So Avigdor kept his passions in check, though it seemed to him dishonest that he should have to suppress them. Also he resented how, the more time you spent on earth, the more the earth's ills flocked about you. The papers harped on the events of the day: the war in Europe, the threat of Spanish Influenza, the lynching of Leo Frank. Such incidents from the so-called civilized world had not much concerned him in his days aloft, but now they infected him as if contaminating his blood with lead.

He and Fanny went one night to the picture palace on Grand Street, where they saw Douglas Fairbanks in *The Thief of Baghdad* leaping from onion dome to minaret, and Avigdor felt the charge along his sinews that announced his impulse to soar. He missed the days, already growing remote, when he'd longed for the girl with such keen devotion from an airy distance. ("His thoughts were of the beautiful white girl; they were always of her now. The apeboy knew no god, but he was as near to worshipping his divinity as mortal man ever comes to worship.") He needed to see his Fanny that way again, from a vantage clear of the poison creepers of commitment that had begun to hamper his limbs. So he climbed walls and vaulted over airshafts and alleys onto her roof, where he lay across the skylight above her landing waiting for a glimpse of his betrothed. She emerged that very evening from her family's flat with a pair of her girlfriends, while her fiancé, feral instincts in play, regarded her through a pane whose dustiness lent a halo to her ginger head. And again he wanted to snatch her up and carry her off without ceremony: The ways of these white men, these Jews, were not his. Watching as she and her friends disappeared down the stairs, he was impervious to the groaning of the window frame (which might have been the rutting of pigeons) as its slats sagged under his weight, then collapsed, so that he plummeted willy-nilly onto the landing below, shattering his leg.

[

] At the wedding he leaned on a crutch like some crippled beggar invited out of charity to partake of the feast, as the veiled bride encircled him seven times. Over her finger he placed a silver ring, purchased on credit, that would often see the inside of pawnshops in the coming years; then he nearly lost his balance while trying to lift a leg to stomp the goblet before he settled upon smashing it with his crutch. During the catered meal that followed the ceremony, the wedding bard cut capers that seemed a deliberate mockery of the acrobatics Avigdor had once performed so effortlessly overhead. The spidery *badhkn* in his boxy skullcap and tailcoat made crude references to the groom's wooden third leg and lampooned his father's profession in the style of the boys at school: "Reb Bronfman was careless on the job and got the sack." A three-piece orchestra serenaded the company and the bard did a kazatski, the mother-in-laws a *mekhutonim à deux*, but the groom was unable to dance. Fanny had insisted on the goyish tradition of a honeymoon, so they took a train to the Catskills Mountains where they could not afford the price of a hotel. They stayed in a rundown bungalow colony whose noisy neighbors made of the place a lumpen annex to the ghetto itself. There Fanny tried her hand with mixed success at cooking, while Avigdor, graduated from crutch to mahogany cane (the same he'd once hooked over telephone wires), hobbled about the yard gazing at the dense forest that blanketed the mountains. Then he bounded up a slope, grabbed hold of a low-lying limb and, hoisting himself into the upper branches, swung from tree to tree until he was beyond the observation of anyone in the known world. Having thus imagined his flight, the bridegroom concluded that undomesticated nature, which he looked upon for the first time in his life, was rather forbidding; whereas Fanny's freckled pink and alabaster body under her modest blue gown—a place she now welcomed him to without conditions— was home.

He ate her rubbery farfel, listened to her dreams of pier-glasses and carpet sweepers, and entered her bed with a trembling gratitude—and by winter the stem of her waist had begun to swell with the ripening fruit of their union. By then Avigdor had become more or less accustomed to working in his father-in-law's shop. It had not been an easy adjustment; retail sales demanded of the clerk a healthy measure of convivial talk, which Avigdor did not come by naturally. The ladies, mostly zaftig wives grown heavy with the cares of their middle years, had to be coaxed into feeling comfortable when purchasing intimate garments—garments whose very nature had at first given Avigdor acute distress in handling. He would have liked not to handle them at all, to perhaps offer them to the customers on the end of the snatch-pole used for retrieving out-of-reach merchandise. But Mr. Podhoretz, textbook in his methods, told him in no uncertain terms that he must learn to "seduce" the ladies into purchases. The word made Avigdor's skin crawl. But in the end the son-in-law overcame his discomfort and learned to present the corsets and corset covers with deft fingers that tickled the ladies as if they were wearing the garment he teased in his hands. He cultivated the appropriate patter (". . . your patent bust improver modeled on the one by the famous Venus de Milo . . .") and displayed the more compromising items, such as abdominal supporters and uterine trusses, in a manner requiring the utmost discretion. In the end, his clientele warmed to the young man with his stringy muscles grown slack from want of exercise and his pronounced limp; for his leg, improperly set, had never truly mended. By the time the child was born—a difficult birth that injured the mother, precluding any further offspring—Avigdor had made himself a virtually indispensable assistant to his father-in-law, whose largess he had more than repaid.

Taking partial credit for her husband's satisfactory progress, Fanny proudly declared one evening as he slouched into the apartment, weary from the day's labor: "You're housebroke, Avi," and Avigdor had to pause to remember a time when he was not.

The boy, Benjamin, named after Fanny's zayde (who'd died of dysentery during the passage from Hamburg), was himself an anaemic and often sickly child, doted on by his mother to the exclusion of almost everything else. Before Benjy's conception, Avigdor and his wife had gamboled like young animals in their conjugal bed, whose galloping incited the neighbors below them to bang on the ceiling with brooms. In their transports, they'd attained heights from which they were granted an angel's-eye view of their canoodling, their hilarity approaching a dangerous pitch. Sober-minded by day, at night Fanny could be adventurous in ways that shocked and delighted her husband; but once she'd become pregnant, adventures ceased, as she concentrated her energies on the child that filled her womb—which no longer had room for anyone else. Avigdor of course honored her humor; it was after all only temporary; he worshipped at the shrine of her melon tumescence. But after Benjy's delivery, during which the girl had suffered complications that would make intimacy painful in any case, Fanny had no interest in reviving their passion. "If it don't lead to babies, Avi," she stated with a finality that caused her husband's soul to shrink, "it's a sin."

Her body, as if to consolidate her disposition, lost its girlish shape, never again shedding the heft of her pregnancy, while the freckles that stippled her cheeks and chest seemed smeared into blotches and stains. In the meantime, Benjy grew at his unsteady pace, still frail and subject to a cavalcade of childhood diseases. These he endured in his convertible bed in the corner of the crowded parlor, reading Bible stories and later the novels of Baroness Orczy and Rafael Sabbatini, leading the cosseted life his mother facilitated. She was protective of him to a degree that seemed sometimes to protect him even from his father, who adored him as well—though he nourished an anticipation that the boy's reading would lead eventually to notable deeds. To Avigdor's private dismay, his son was also an acrophobe, who shunned the fire escape for his studies and threw tantrums when his parents tried to take him onto the roof to sleep. As a consequence, the family was confined on summer nights to the furnace-like atmosphere of an apartment cluttered to nearly impassable with its Windsor range, davenport bed, and Brunswick Vibrating Shuttle sewing machine; for Fanny would have her distaff accessories. Then she would have a larger apartment ("I got a *hashek* for a real home, Avi") and had begun to extol Brooklyn as the Promised Land. To please her, Avigdor took his wife and child on an excursion out to Brownsville by subway to inspect the mushrooming subdivisions in their uniform lots. Such a move was not out of the question; Podhoretz's Foundation, thanks in part to Avigdor's good offices, was prospering. Mr. Podhoretz had bought the failed haberdashery next door and knocked down the wall between them, expanding his premises as well as his inventory—which now included a new line of queen-size vests and bloomers, and fancy French underwear. Then just as Avigdor was about to close the deal on a two-bedroom duplex in Brownsville, a series of calamities befell his family.

They started when a pair of two-bit extortionists in their fedoras and pencil-stripes began dunning Mr. Podhoretz for protection gelt. Edged out of competition with the local bootleg syndicate, the thugs had fallen back on strong-arming East Side shopkeepers, and were naturally attracted to the thriving garment mart with its increased stock in trade. But Leon Podhoretz, a stiff-necked man of commerce, a landlord and wise investor whose son-in-law's yeoman service permitted him to contemplate an early retirement, remained obstinate in the face of threats. Avigdor, however, was worried, worry having become a recent avocation. The Stock Market had crashed, and the old ghetto, in its proximity to the epicenter of the collapse, was especially rocked by the seismic shudder. Pleased with their Yankee-style speculations, Mr. Podhoretz along with his brethren of the Kaminsker Landsmanshaft had lost their shirts, but despite Avigdor's counsel to the contrary, his father-in-law still pooh-poohed the underworld menace. The fire that consumed the Podhoretz gesheft spread to the businesses that flanked it on either side, so that a great gray cavity like a meteor crater smoldered in the middle of Orchard Street. The property was of course heavily insured, but the insurance company protested the owner's claim, alleging arson, which was epidemic on the Lower East Side. Thus began a lengthy period of litigation that exhausted what remained of Mr. P's savings, while his unemployed son-in-law was forced to apply for jobs that he was eminently unsuited for.

With his lame leg bedeviled by various -itises that flared from activity as from an infestation of fire ants, Avigdor was officially handicapped. Nevertheless, he made the rounds of the local shops, limping on his walking stick, canvassing situations that had dried up in any case in a rash of layoffs. He turned out faithfully for the pre-dawn shape-ups (which now attracted multitudes) in Seward Park and at the fish market in South Street, where his disability precluded his selection for work. A little relief came from an unlikely quarter, since Reb Bronfman's profession turned out to be Depression-proof, and his destitute son, beyond humiliation, had no choice but to accept his papa's handouts. He used the pennies to purchase from a Delancey Street wholesaler tin cups, potato mashers, and shoelaces, which he peddled, in the absence of a pushcart, door to door. But the competition was stiff and few had the wherewithal to buy; never mind that the drag-of-foot-peddler, appearing with his sack like a troll out of a grandmother's tale, did not present an appealing countenance. While he might scrape together enough to keep the family in bad herring and stale farfeloons, he continually failed to make the rent they owed under the building's new ownership, since Mr. Podhoretz had had to sell off his holdings. For that, Fanny had to take in sewing, restoring spent gathers and orchid folds in worn knickers, stitching needle-run lace to the hems of old petticoats, demonstrating a talent that who knew she had for rejuvenating second-hand apparel. Still, they lived week to week in jeopardy of being dispossessed. Then Reb Bronfman, despite a flushed face that some took as a sign of health, dropped dead of a stroke, and Avigdor's fretting over the fate of his bereaved mother supplanted the grief he might have spared for the *mohel*.

With his wife, he discussed his intention of moving the Widow Bronfman into Rivington Street, where her piecework operation combined with Fanny's furbelow trade would comprise a regular cottage industry. But Fanny pointed out that this was a physical impossibility.

"Tahke, so she can have the closet we ain't got?"

But even as he understood there was no room, Avigdor resented what he perceived as his wife's selfishness. Selfish? She was taking in work by the bushel without complaint, bartering for cracked eggs in the market, sometimes returning home with a chicken under her dress that her increasingly dumpling anatomy helped to conceal. All this she managed while shielding her delicate Benjy—whose diet consisted mainly of milk of magnesia—against the depredations of hard times. If he harbored any lingering spite on account of her frigidity, Avigdor was not aware of it, since his chronic fatigue (and her dowdy figure) had neutralized all carnal thoughts; and besides, a second child in these circumstances would be catastrophic. Still he accused her: "Fanny, a heart you ain't got!" But when the tears started in freshets from her eyes, Avigdor wept along with her, and his mother—who had no wish to come between husband and wife—accommodated the children by passing away herself, death in those days being an option of easy availability.

In his distraction, Avigdor remembered Shaky Gruber, the friend of his youth, with whom he hadn't communicated in over a decade. Gruber had become a floorwalker at Wanamaker's Department Store, a sharp dresser with the haughtiness of one gainfully employed while the rest of the country waited for F.D.R.'s alphabet agencies to save them. At first Gruber mistook his diminished old chum for a panhandler, until Avigdor, who'd staggered up to him outside the store at the corner of Broadway and 8th, identified himself. "Guess you don't do much running through the jungle these days," quipped Shaky, though Avigdor didn't seem to know what he was talking about. Once he heard his old friend's appeal, however, Shaky Gruber tugged his lapels and made noises like he might have an inside track; and while he promised more than he could deliver, he was ultimately able to secure Avigdor part-time work as a stockboy, for which the petitioner embarrassed the floorwalker by kissing his hand. Most of the labor went on behind the scenes, on the loading dock and in the stockrooms where the merchandise was sorted and stored—sometimes on shelves that involved climbing ladders upon which Avigdor experienced bouts of vertigo, to say nothing of the constant aggravation in his leg; but often he was called on to move garment racks through the various departments of the mammoth emporium. Then the freight elevator gate would open like a mouth debouching him into gilded halls lined with jewelry in glass cases, aisles of mechanical toys and luxury items in galleries overlooking a cathedral-size atrium. It was during one of these forays, while rattling through Ladies' Furnishings, that Avigdor happened to spy a sales girl at a loss for words before a customer who insisted on returning an "underbelt corselette."

"The thing makes me look in my chemise like I'm wearing a canary cage," she complained.

"I'm s-s-sorry, madam," stammered the sales girl, evoking a clearly much rehearsed phrase, "but store policy prohibits the return of discount items . . ."

Looming over the diminutive girl, the woman was demanding to see her supervisor when Avigdor, without thinking, abandoned the garment rack and trundled forward to volunteer his expertise. Later on it would seem to him that he'd stepped from a towering height into a void.

"Excuse me," he said, "but you have every right to complain. However, the new Corslo-silhouette, which it's just in from Paris that I have samples of on my rack, offers a combination of bust bodice, hip belt, jupon, and pantaloon—the fabric so flimsy if you eat a grape it will show. We have them in satin and apricot crêpe-de-Chine . . ."

The salesgirl stood open-mouthed as the stylish lady listened attentively to Avigdor's shpiel, then she recovered herself enough to protest the stockboy's temerity only to be shushed by the customer. Actually stomping her foot in indignation, the girl was further chastised by her supervisor, who'd come from behind a counter upon witnessing the scene. A matronly woman squinting through a tiny lorgnette, the supervisor had sized up the situation, and having determined that the crippled stockboy, albeit a male but otherwise innocuous, was the better spokesperson for their unmentionable merchandise, promoted him on the spot, and dispatched the inept salesgirl to the bargain basement. And that was how Avigdor found a safe harbor in intimate apparel, just as the Japanese bombers demonstrated to the nation that no harbors were safe.

But even then he felt uncommonly snug in his new situation, where he remained unruffled in the presence of the ladies who sometimes teased him as they might have a eunuch with whom they felt perfectly at ease. He was a *balebos*, a householder and provider again, and it wasn't until his bookish son Benjy received his conscription notice that Avigdor's worries, briefly dormant, were recalled to life. This was soon after the Bronfmans, having waited their turn on a long list of intensely vetted applicants, had moved into an apartment in a recently completed housing development near the East River. The apartment had two bedrooms, steam heat, a tiled bath, and a balcony with a view of the Brooklyn Bridge; and though the news from Europe was dire, it seemed to the Family Bronfman that they had arrived on a friendly shore after a storm. Their son, still prone to infirmity, had just earned his high school diploma and was being courted by colleges looking to fill their Jewish quotas with whiz kids. Vain of his academic accomplishments, Benjy was coy in fielding their invitations, having yet to decide on a particular area of study; for he'd excelled in every subject in the curriculum other than phys ed. The apartment was full of his awards and citations, and his parents' pride in his achievements was a place where they still found common ground, though they sometimes differed in their ambitions for the boy: Avigdor imagining he might build rocket ships and cure pestilence while Fanny preferred he take an easeful seat on the Supreme Court. She was concerned however that the stress of high office might tax his feeble constitution. Given his continued poor health, it had always been assumed that, even in wartime, the boy would be deferred from the draft. He was a special case and it was unthinkable that his fate should be cast among the rank and file. Then it seemed even more inconceivable that after his induction, rather than assigned to some administrative (if not counter-intelligence) desk, he was sent instead to the front, where he was shot by a sniper in the snow-deep forest of the Ardennes.

Now, thought Avigdor, there was nothing left to worry about; the worst had happened. Now there was only his trying to imagine the magnitude of the fear his son must have known in the chaos of battle, and as it turned out he was very good at imagining; it was an exercise that caused the chronic pain in his stiffened leg to resonate in his heart. Then the fear, assuming volume and weight, would come to occupy the spaces where the boy had been, supplanting the ache of missing him and the regret over having neglected him when he lived. Nothing on earth was untainted by it; naked fear emanated not just from the Bomb or the Reds or the execution of the Rosenbergs, not only from the evidence of a continent *toiveled* of Jews, but from the diaphanous fabrics he handled in the emporium and the doll-like women who bought them. It emanated from the coffee-skinned strangers who'd begun to invade the old neighborhood. By the time the fear had subsided enough for Avigdor to notice her, his wife had languished too long in the bed from which he'd banished himself. From the first he'd resented the way she hoarded all the sorrow, leaving him to absorb the dread, but in time the situation started to seem like a fair enough bargain. It was only when her body (which in wasting away had reverted to its original spindliness) began to fail her that Avigdor wondered why, though he no longer loved her, he should be so afraid of her passing. Nor did his apprehension die with her, when after a regimen of pills that left her sleepwalking when she wasn't prostrate, Fanny finally gave up the ghost—or was it that the ghost she'd become surrendered the heartsick Fanny? In any event, the world now seemed almost too frightful a place to visit anymore, notwithstanding Avigdor's fear of being alone.

His old friend Shaky Gruber tried to remind the shop clerk that the world was wider than the blighted Lower East Side. Shaky himself had made a killing through shrewd investments in the post-war real-estate boom and had moved his family into a house on Ocean Parkway in Brooklyn. He came into the neighborhood on Sundays to buy delicatessen, when he would deign to treat the sad sack Bronfman, not much stouter these days than his own walking stick, to cheese blintzes at the Garden Cafeteria. Grown venerable in his prosperity, Shaky would assure Avigdor that the earth was still full of a number of things.

"Such as," Avigdor humbly conceded, "the murder of a young President and a brand new war—or is it just the continuation of an old?" For the shop clerk caught only vague references to such things between episodes of *Mr. Ed* and *I've Got a Secret*, and reruns of *The Honeymooners* on the snowy screen of his rabbit-eared TV.

Shaky dismissed his friend's rotten attitude with a harrumph. "You must've accumulated what, maybe a decade's worth of vacation time? Why don't you make a holiday?"

"Where would I go?" wondered Avigdor, whose whole life, come to think of it, was circumscribed by the vanishing ghetto. The journey by bus from Grand Street up to Broadway and 8th was far enough for him, thanks all the same. (He'd since curtailed his junkets to a home for the aged in Greenwich Village, where Fanny's little sister, grown up and married to a doctor, had installed her parents—for the Podhoretzes had made it clear they regarded their son-in-law as somehow complicit in their daughter's demise, a judgment with which the son-in-law guiltily concurred.)

"I dunno, Bronfman." Shaky stopped chewing, one varicose cheek stuffed with blintz. "Visit the Fiji Isles, go to the moon. Maybe you should get in with the Chasids that got a shuttle service between East Broadway and paradise . . ." He was alluding to a community of fanatical Munkatsh refugees who had taken up residence down the street, their little shtibl sandwiched between a bodega and a Puerto Rican social club. "If you don't want a woman, you can get religion instead."

Shaky himself was a big shot at a showcase temple out on the Parkway, and he recommended that Avigdor get involved with a local congregation if only for the sake of fellowship. Avigdor respectfully rejected his advice out of hand, prompting Shaky to ask, "Why do I bother?" Then he stopped bothering and more years passed bringing more universal enormities, some of which bled uncensored into the shop clerk's companion TV. Meanwhile Wanamaker's had changed hands, though Avigdor, as much a fixture as the model home on the furniture floor, managed to hang onto his job; but his increasingly clunky demeanor no longer inspired confidence in his clientele. Moreover, he'd grown uneasy with recent trends in the undergarment industry, squeamish in the face of their vulgarity. So when it was not so subtly suggested that he'd outworn his usefulness, he took the hint and retired on a modest pension; he rented a small apartment in a lower-income development and became for all intents and purposes a shut-in.

His television, however, remained a poor filter for the incursions of history, and even *Bonanza* and *The Beverly Hillbillies* were haunted by images of torched villages and cities in flame. Then the retiree, harried from his isolation, would find himself toiling along once-familiar streets: such as East Broadway, where, in lieu of the talkers' cafés and Yiddish journals, there was tropical music even in winter, and where the Chinese had commandeered a beachhead in the old Forward Building. On this particular early evening, in a sudden blue flurry that rivaled the staticky reception on his TV, Avigdor heard issuing from an eroded fieldstone townhouse the sounds of inharmonious prayer. He hadn't been in a synagogue since his dead papa had circumcised his son with a palsied hand in the vestibule of the Stanton Street shul, its doors since boarded up. But shivering in his threadbare overcoat, he told himself he was only seeking warmth rather than heeding some primordial call. He trudged up the steps and pushed open the door of the Munkatsher shtibl, surprised that no one prevented his entry; because it seemed to Avigdor that he should have been forbidden what he then witnessed: A *minyan* or more of Chasidim, like a crowd of black mantises, their forelegs resting on each others' shoulders, shuffled in a circle about an old man who stood on a stepladder (in place of a *bima*), hugging the sacred scrolls. With his thin beard curling like smoke from a lamp, his narrow face lifted in ecstasy, the old man maintained a precarious balance on the ladder's middle rung. "*Kadosh, kadosh . . .*," warbled his disciples, raising their raucous singsong a decibel or two as their rebbe ascended another step. Their voices swayed the chandelier and caused plaster to waft down from the ceiling, as the rebbe, in his gymnastic rapture, mounted the ladder's summit then stepped further onto an invisible rung. Was Avigdor dreaming or did the holy man, his white-stockinged ankles a visual echo of the Torah finials, hover in midair an instant before plunging into the arms of his disciples? It was in any event the moment when the retired shop clerk, having seen more than enough, fled the roomful of lunatics.

Safely returned to his apartment, he switched on the television set, which as luck would have it was on the blink. This was no great loss, since the thing had recently become nothing more than a cabinet of proliferating horrors, but left to his own devices, Avigdor, still trying to catch his ragged breath, realized that he had no devices left. There was little to distract him amid the sparse furnishings of his compact abode, scoured as it was of any mementoes of his marriage—which made the small shrine of his lost son's books, on their shelf atop a wheezing radiator, so conspicuous. Avigdor could not remember the last time he'd read a book, nor had he ever been tempted by these, which were mostly dry academic texts. But among them were also a handful of dog-eared novels that Benjy had abandoned in early adolescence: adventure sagas by Delos Lovelace and Jules Verne, a volume by Edgar Rice Burroughs entitled *Tarzan of the Apes*. Taking the latter tentatively in hand, Avigdor could feel his follicles tingling, though he couldn't at first have said why; but when he opened the book and perused a random passage ("None more craftily stealthy than he, none more ferocious, nor none who leaped so high into the air in the Dance of Death"), his heart beat like a clapper tolling sobs from his shallow breast.

Collapsing into an armchair, he concluded, "Whatever time I got left, it's wasted on me," and thereupon resolved to end his miserable life. Months passed, however, before he was able to stir himself to the task. The bones of his crooked leg seemed as if replaced by a fiery brand, which did little to assuage the chill that pervaded the rest of his meager frame; so it wasn't until a soft morning in April that he felt mobile enough to put his plan into practice. He nibbled some toast dipped in tea, bundled himself in his overcoat despite the warm weather, and began his halting progress toward Orchard Street, obeying a sentimental impulse to locate his childhood tenement and fling himself from the roof.

The building was still standing, its dim stairwell still dense with a palimpsest of odors that included, beneath a veil of peppery spices, an ancient cabbage stench. The water-stained walls were riotous with spray-painted graffiti like prehistoric glyphs on the walls of a cave. Having slogged to the head of the stairs, his lungs and joints howling,

Avigdor nudged open the unlocked door, inhaled a deep draught of noxious ozone, and fell into a coughing fit. The brick bulkheads were also emblazoned with gang insignia, the defunct water tanks with Day-Glo portraits of murdered boys. As the cripple made his way between the rotting frames of untended gardens, he was aware of trespassing, of perhaps being watched by the tribes that oversaw these heights. Exhausted past his capacity for being afraid, however, he approached the parapet and, with the aid of his cane (which he relinquished thereafter), hoisted himself onto the knee-high wall, its width broadened by an ornamental molding. He stood totteringly erect and thought he could see, beyond the skirmishing antennae and huddled towers, continents swarming with ignorant armies butchering their own. Their distant cries mingled with those of the immigrant merchants shmeikeling cheap leather goods in the street below.

Then a memory insinuated itself into his weary brain: of being taken as a child to the East River wharves by his parents on the Jewish new year, where he was instructed to toss his fledgling sins in the form of breadcrumbs into the murky water. Could a person release the burden of his years in the same fashion? he wondered; but Rosh Hashanah was months away and Avigdor could not at any rate imagine how to discard his sins exclusive of himself. So, as a breeze fluttered his coattails and bussed his cheek, he stepped from the ledge and dropped like a stone. But no sooner did he find himself plummeting toward the pavement—which was rushing up to slap him into oblivion—than he realized that the wounds of past decades were nothing compared to what he'd suffered at the hands of the mountain apes Bolgani and Kerchak. Instinctively he snagged an electrical cable with the same strong arm that had slain the brute Terkoz, and felt his body whipped into a sudden jackknife from which—once he'd adjusted himself to the empty air—he unfolded into an impeccably executed swan dive. He caught hold of a wrought-iron signpole that jutted above a shop and swung around it, hesitating at the apex in a momentary handstand, enjoying his view of the world turned upside down. Then he spun in a giant revolution once, twice, three times before letting go, confident that in flight he would find something else to grab hold of . . .

] Toward Lithuania

I came to his house every Friday, supposedly to teach him English. At first I was convinced he hated the language, he spoke it with such an unrestrained violence. His w's came out like g's, his j's pure "sh"— "shust shoking," he'd say after pronouncing something particularly bad. I might have sworn he refused to conjugate his verbs as a protest against the English language—against its relative power, or its importance, or its ubiquity. But something in the insistency of his mangled speech, the rapture with which he sputtered out his own personalized grammar, suggested that something else was going on. And maybe because I was new to teaching, or because I felt similarly driven to beat my head against a Spanish-speaking world I could hardly understand, I relished his jumbled diction, sat rapt even in the role of teacher and rarely, far too rarely, corrected his mistakes. "My wife, he be home," he'd say when his much younger wife came in the door. "She be good gooman," he'd go on, switching pronouns back-and-forth, changing genders midstream.

I'd come down South after my father had gotten sick and passed. It had always been something I intended to do, but never enough, never really. My father had been born in Argentina and he never spoke well of the place, never visited, never planned to see the country again. Whenever someone—a hapless visiting cousin, a new friend, a delivery boy— mentioned anything about the land of his birth, he'd launch into a bitter, hour-long dissertation on its problems, its innate dishonesty, its history of violence and unrest. And yet somehow, I'd grown up certain something was waiting for me there, something I needed to learn, or absorb, or reject. Not that it stopped me from making excuses not to go; I'd gone almost everywhere else I could think of before my father's last surgery, when I finally ended up in Buenos Aires just in time for the dead heart of winter, a few months before I turned 28.

On our first Tuesday class, Elías told me he'd been studying English for twenty-five years. I told him, as directed by the institute I worked for, that I'd been teaching for three. "Ah, and your Spanish?" He asked me, in Spanish. The institute owner had told me to lie: that if Elías knew I spoke a word of Spanish he'd never break off its wide, smooth boulevards to bump and skid onto the unpaved English streets. But with me he was cooperative. I told him I'd spoken it sometimes with my father; later it came out that my father was born in Buenos Aires, and Elías often spoke to me—quasi-cryptically—about what it meant to be an emigrant, an Argentine, or both. What I never mentioned was that my father had been expunging Spanish from his vocabulary, erasing Argentina from his speech, for about as long as I'd known him, that my father was so indifferent to the idea of me visiting Buenos Aires that I'd waited until he was gone to make the trip.

I'd arrive at Elías's flat in the Once district at 6 P.M. sharp, and by 8 I'd be downstairs, where the weak winter sunlight had given way to darkness, and the busy commercial streets had emptied of all but the shopkeepers shuttering their storefronts, sounding the heavy rumble of metallic black gates. I liked it up there in the world Elías kept for himself, though I hated the coming and going and made up my mind each week on my way there and on my way home to quit. The pay was bad, too— just under $10 an hour—and I most certainly wasn't helping anyone learn English.

What else did I do that winter while I was in Argentina? Where else did I go? With whom did I spend my time? Of course, I'd taken up with some expat friends, fellow wanderers and searchers—a miserable bunch on the whole, always pining to run off toward the next excitement, or to bump into a compelling reason to not. I'd been seeing an Argentine girl, too, but we'd arrived at a point where there was sex and comfort, but not much else. In her eyes—and she saw me pretty clearly—I was a First World Lost Boy: enough cash in my pocket to fund a walkabout, but not enough to lay concrete down under an adult life. I was 27 going on 27 going on 27, and she knew that, even if I was just starting to catch on.

If I thought that Argentina was going to provide me with answers, was going to show me the outlines of a route on the secret map of life, I quickly was disavowed of this notion. Still, I spent my days walking the streets looking for evidence of my father, pacing neighborhoods he'd possibly inhabited, studying the facades of buildings he might have walked by, if not entered at some point. He'd lived in Once—that much I knew from the family lore. My grandfather had come to Buenos Aires from Lithuania when he was sixteen. My father once told me, when we were lost in Queens, that his father could find his way anywhere in Buenos Aires with ease because, as he put it, he'd been there when the roads went in. And so I walked those roads, and I looked for him, and it rained some days, and others it was just cold, and all I saw were people living their lives, navigating sidewalks that were too narrow, ducking across city streets choked with zigzagging taxis, climbing on and off loud, lumbering buses. And they were Argentines, and my father, all of a sudden, somehow, was not.

It was on one day in particular, toward the end of my time as Elías's ineffectual teacher and as an unofficial refugee from adulthood, that a wild convulsion of rain erupted over Buenos Aires and the unforgiving chucking left me stranded at Elías's for a good hour after our usual lesson time had passed. It was already late August by then, a time when everybody back home would have been fleeing the city, trying to escape the heavy blanket of summer, to suck in a little hot air before Fall swept in.

In Buenos Aires, you would never have guessed people were sweating on the other side of the world: everyone there seemed to have burst into a crazed pursuit of shelter. Wrapped tight in scarves and plastic jackets, they flooded and then deserted the streets, heading, I assumed, to their respective homes to gulp at hot drinks while hugging each other around open gas stoves and space heaters. I'd been relieved to head to Elías's that day; my apartment didn't have proper heating and I appreciated being able to hide from the rain and cold in the worn coziness of his crowded flat. And when I would arrive, he'd always have coffee waiting for me: the bitterest of Argentine blends, and as black as I'd ever had. He couldn't drink much himself because of a stomach ulcer, he'd remind me, while gulping it down with abandon.

That day, I'd actually prepared a lesson plan. I was convinced that I was going to teach him something: travel vocabulary, as it happened, and the present continuous tense. It was a lesson inspired by the events of his life: His wife had just left on a business trip—like he'd been, she was an important doctor, a cardiologist, and she'd been summoned to speak at a conference in Manhattan. And so after I proposed a list of verbs (pack, drive, board, fly, arrive), and we reviewed a list of sentences (I'm packing my bags; he's driving me to the airport), we got to talking, Elías and I, about the United States, and about the city of my birth, New York. I was done teaching, but he kept on in English. I imagined he must have felt on a roll, and I said nothing to interrupt. Outside, rain was smacking so hard on the street and against the window that I had to lean halfway out of my chair to hear Elías butcher his insoluble cuts of my maternal tongue.

"There was time, I do tell you, when even my wife wanted for us to go there—to be Yankee," he was saying. "Her brother, he arrange for me to be a job in the Queens. I went to United State with my wife then, to be with his brother and to make a interview, but I couldn't smile, I couldn't."

Sitting deep within the gray folds of his living room couch, Elías, who was into his seventies, gave the impression of a shrunken *padrino*, a shriveled godfather holding tender court over a sole, silent supplicant. His small, stubby fingers, speckled with gray hairs, hugged the sides of his round belly, and as he spoke he drummed them on it.

"We spent many night passing from shit-hole to other hole—to apartment, from a bar—and every night I thought it beautiful, sure, this is. But we would view this brother, my wife and me, and would drink the *mate* and view the football for all 24 hour, the *parilla*, the meat, the newspaper *Clarín*. Obsessed with this, with Argentina, yes? But just the things. He had changed, but half-changed. *O sea*—he was always looking for himself away, back over here."

I knew the details of this immigrant existence—many peripheral Argentines had befriended my father and lingered, half-ignored, at his side through the years. I'd always known Argentina that way: as a vague memory not particularly my own.

"I was admissible for this job," Elías was saying. "This one and other one in Israel also, believe it or don't. Though we did not visit to that promised land. In those times in *la Argentina* everyone was shit himself. There was crisis, inflation, insecurity, criminals—the Jews they ran to Israel, *italianos* to *Italia*, *españoles* to *Espain*—and everyone was break my balls for medicine. I went and I really considering. My wife was pressing too; *uy*, how he press.

"And so then of course I had this moment, a very real New York moment," Elías went on. "I went with the brother to the Blue Note. You know it? The classy—no, classical—club in the Village. And meanwhile waiting in line we get thirst. We needing *café*.

"So we go, brother and I, to a corner, to a *kiosko*, and we converse to a Israeli man, this other Jew. Yes, and *I* was talking. So you can imagine: I am with my English, this *argentino*, this *sudaca* beast, and she is this man, this thin little man from—I dunno, *ponele*, Tel Aviv—and I am to buy *café* and he is to giving it me." Elías pushed a puff of laughter out through his lips. It appeared, as steam, on his glasses.

"And I is asking for this *café* and is talking to this Israeli, and he is say: Oh yes, *Argentina*, Maradona, etcetera etcetera and I say: How is it that you have come here? Was it too much for you the unrest, the exploding? And this Israeli man you know, he look down at the *café* like he want it dead and does not laugh.

"And this brother he look at me, *a ver*, he say in the eyes: Are you crazy? You sonofabitch! He does not want me to ask strangers, maybe. But I want know someone, you understand? And this is the thing I ask him: Are you happy? Why don't you return? Why stay here?

"And the Israeli, he put down the *café* and he start to twist on top. He look at me, big like, dog-like maybe, I see his teeth, you understand? And there is nothing friendly, *entendés*? He says: because I am contaminated, I am at home, I am not at home: I am contaminated. And meanwhile he open me the *café* and *la espuma*, the fuzz, it went all over, down the counter, on my pant—it been knocked, is that clear?—and he, *oopa*, crack into laughing, you see? Not fun laughing. This is fear. And the brother, she look to me to say in Spanish, *boludo*, and she pick up the *café* to try to give apology. There is *café* on my arm, on my leg. But there is in the Israeli and in this brother something and they look up at me both until somehow the laughter that was angry becomes sweet and water drips from their eyes like *café* and we are nowhere else, just laughing and laughing and laughing."

We sat there for a time in silence—a whole minute, perhaps. I glanced over at Elías. His glasses had fallen onto the bridge of his nose, and he was looking up at me over the tops of his lenses, squinting. I thought of something my father had often said: that for Jews nationality is an accident of birth. I wondered if that had made him feel less out of place, though he'd never had much use for the Jewish community and never spoke of feeling anything but comfortable where he'd ended up. I wondered what Elías would have thought of my father, and if my father would have had anything more to share with him than the Israeli.

Then outside there was a loud crack as a tree, or something like it, snapped and went down. Honking cars, a siren, the faint sound of men yelling; we got up to stand by the window and gaze down at the ensuing commotion. It made me anxious, the storm, the recklessness of it, its apparent anger, but Elías had picked up his coffee and taken it with him and as we stood there next to each other looking out at the blackened smudges of people and cars he lifted the cup to his mouth and took a series of deep swigs.

Across the street, we could barely make out a light post, bent at the middle, sloping toward the ground across the entire *avenida*. On the other side, where it seemed to touch the street, it was on fire, lit, or so it looked from our height and angle, like a huge candle. Suddenly, it felt too hot in the apartment, stuffy. Under my shirt, across my chest and on my lower back, sweat spread out its thin sheet. From Elías's eighth-floor window, I could normally trace my way through Buenos Aires's fanned streets all the way back to my flat—it was one of his apartments' greatest charms—but obscured by the storm, implicated by its bad-tempered destruction, the city looked like any other place.

"I did not take the job," Elías eventually said. It seemed an obvious thing, and redundant, and yet he sounded almost unsure. "And so this mess remain my mess." He gestured toward the men below who with the aid of the downpour and buckets were putting out the flame, and then at the city that we could hardly see stretching out behind them: the modern apartments and the French-style boulevards, the unfinished shanties and the dirt *pasillos*, the people staying dry, and those, further out, who couldn't. I stood there and I looked, but all I saw were smudges of light and darkness. I was ready for the rain to stop, ready to head home, already imagining climbing into a taxi, up the stairs to my apartment, under the sheets. "More *café*?" Elías asked. I shook my head no.

When I think about that evening now—the strange, wild weather, Elías's heavy diction and the odd tale he told—I sometimes put my father in Elías's place, and cast myself as some sort of distant, Argentine nephew. Or, it's my grandfather telling the tale and the clumsy Israeli is my dad. It helps me get some perspective, maybe; helps me narrate it as if the experience itself were important, not just the way, being there then, I felt.

Truth is, that night, when I finally left, I walked under the angry sky and couldn't, for the life of me, find a cab. My glasses, dripping, had to be removed and I made my way without seeing much. Instead, I just set out like my father: toward one place and away from another. Perhaps that was the only way, or the easiest way, or what struck him as the healthiest way for his son. Toward Lithuania, toward Argentina, toward New York.

] The Florida Sunshine Tree

Beleaguered by teachers, parents, and fools—by which he meant Hebrew teachers—Sandy Levinson stepped outside the Law. It wasn't an easy step to take, but it wasn't as hard as he'd been led to believe. Everyone, he realized, was closer to the edge than anyone thought. In his case, the boundary lay between the Levinson yard and the Keller property, delineated by a line of feathery mimosas that led down to the Atlantic.

Despite zoning guidelines that discouraged fences to give the illusion of greater expanse to all of the homeowners along Jupiter Beach, the lots were actually quite small except for the Keller spread, which took up no less than four properties in a row due south of the Levinson ranch as well as one to the north that was used for guests. And Hank Keller, a.k.a. The King of Toxic Waste, whose privately held company disposed of everything from hospital sharps to nuclear fuel, had made it abundantly clear to Sandy's mom that if she ever felt like cashing out, she need look no farther than next door for a ready buyer.

"Hmpf," Renata, born Renee, Levinson snorted. "Just because the man has all the money in the world doesn't mean that he can have my little slice of the sea."

In fact, what she really desired was Keller's estate, or at least the right to sell it through Levinson and Wellington, the real estate agency she had founded with a nonexistent aristocratic partner fourteen years earlier. Renee from the Bronx did well in south Florida, timing her training to the hard market of the mid-nineties and then booming with the oughts. Credit was tightening these days, but beachfront property was always at a premium.

In her signature lime-green Corvette, Renata drove clients to her various listings, and when she brought along a matching lime-green handbag, that was the signal to make the deal or clear out. Other, more flexible buyers were waiting.

If the handbag remained at home, however, it meant nothing. Literally, no sale.

Sandy's father, Mike, lived over in West Palm and ran a juke box rental concession that required spending most of his time in bars that ranged up and down the coast about the length of Renata's domain. Sandy spent alternate weeks at his mother's and his father's homes, but both Levinsons worked so hard that he was often left alone to pilfer shots from their liquor cabinets and watch videos and masturbate and contemplate the consequences of his lifestyle. According to the rabbi who taught him tradition and morality Tuesdays and Thursdays from 4:00 to 6:00 P.M. at the Stern Academy for Jewish Studies, there was a God, and we knew him—rather perversely if you asked Sandy—from the grief he'd given the Chosen People over the millennia.

First, God teased Adam and Eve with the Tree of Knowledge of Good and Evil. "Why," Sandy asked, "didn't God put that tree someplace else? Why didn't he put a fence around it?"

"Because he's God," inadequately answered Rabbi Posnow, whom the students called Rabbi Porno behind his back, as he advanced through Genesis to chronicle divinity's torturings of Noah and the forefathers Abraham, Isaac, and Jacob.

Worse, the suffering of the ancients didn't compare to historical atrocities that were also a part of Stern's curriculum. In the Middle Ages that meant the Crusades and the Inquisition. In the early modern era it meant expulsions from nearly every country in Europe except those in which the Jews were finally murdered in the twentieth century.

Sandy wasn't into the Holocaust as much as some of the other Stern students whose grandparents had numbers on their arms, but he knew his own grandparents' earliest years in Russia as well as he knew the Palmdale Mall.

Both of Sandy's grandmothers died when Sandy was a baby and both of his grandfathers died within weeks of each other in the previous year, lung and pancreatic cancers, which was totally unfair. As Sandy dressed in a blue suit to attend the successive funerals, he felt a baffled rage that such nice people—always with candy, always with presents, always with stories—should be gone. Just like that, gone.

"Hide and seek?" Zayde Max said once when Sandy urged him to play. "You think it's a game. Try hiding from the *khoppers*." *Khoppers*, Sandy knew from frequent repetition, snatched Jewish boys from the streets of *shtetls* and sold them into the Russian army.

"Ach, you think you had *khoppers*?" Zayde Nate upped the ante. "Your *khoppers* in Minsk were amateurs. Our *khoppers* in Smolensk jabbed swords into beds to make sure no one was hiding."

Whether *khoppers* really existed or not, Sandy wasn't absolutely sure, but he'd had nightmares about them since he was five. So when Rabbi Posnow arrived at that era of Jewish history, it was the first time Sandy paid attention to the small man with a thin goatish beard whose short-sleeved yellowish white shirts bore the faint scent of sweat.

"Yes," Posnow regaled the Hebrew school class of bored eighth graders, "the Tzar's men kidnapped young Jewish students and put them into the army for 25 years. The lucky ones died. The unlucky ones stopped being Jews."

Sandy thought the latter might have been luckier than the former.

Posnow added to his litany of misery. "There were pogroms, organized riots, in which *shuls* were burnt, the Torah scrolls violated."

Again and again, the Rabbi's priorities struck Sandy as ridiculous. Scrolls, *shuls*: Posnow emphasized the physical accessories, the handbags as it were, of Jewish life rather than any personal, intellectual or—god forbid—spiritual dimension. Still, the stories had a gruesomely compelling power. In a way, they kept his beloved grandfathers alive.

"The Tzar's men wrote a book called *Protocols of the Elders of Zion*," said Porno like a summer-camp counselor telling a scary story around a cookout with frankfurters and blobs of marshmallow seared over an open flame. "It claimed that Jews were plotting all the evils of the century."
[
] The elders of Zion. Sandy imagined his two *zaydes* playing cards on the patio of his house on Jupiter Beach back when Renata and Mike were still married. Max suggested, "Let's have an oil crisis."

"Better yet," Nate, as usual, went further. "How about we start some global warming."

"Excellent idea!" Max cried. "And I've got gin."
[
] "But worst of all," Porno prepared the boys for yet another terror. Sandy assumed it was something to do with candles or *yarmulkes*, but

for the first time the rabbi surprised him. "Worst of all," he relished the suspense, "was the blood libel."

Maybe it was because the phrase echoed the title of his favorite computer game, Cloud Bible, in which multiple contestants in different countries vied to establish the most successful religion, that Sandy sat on the edge of his seat as the Rabbi went on. "They said that Jews slaughtered Christian babies to mix their blood with *matzoh*."

The allegation was on the face ludicrous for culinary if not moral reasons, yet the repercussions were so vast that Sandy wondered: What if it was true?

After all, everything about Jewish life in Eastern Europe staggered. Take the *khoppers*. Or the Tzar himself, an outsize figure impossible to imagine in the contemporary world, like a pharaoh. More mundane, and therefore more extraordinary, Sandy's grandfathers were constantly telling him how they didn't have computers or cell phones when they were young. Max and Nate, who generally agreed on nothing, both claimed that there were no malls in Russia. "Malls?" Max scoffed. "There weren't even stores."

If so, how did they get stuff? And without cell phones, how did they talk to other kids? And without computers, how did they buy advance tickets to movies?

"Movies?" Nate sneered, "We didn't have no stinkin' movies."

Nothing that defined a typical American adolescent's life existed in Russia. The place was simultaneously the stuff of Sandy's most intimate dreams and as foreign as Mars. It was impossible to tell what was real and what was the product of a fevered imagination.

Sandy had been weaned on lox and cream cheese on poppy seed bagels for Sunday brunch and pastrami sandwiches from Wolf's Deli in Boca for Saturday night dinner before movies at the Cineplex in Del Rey, but his father ate cheeseburgers in his bars, and his mom ate crab salads despite Rabbi Porno's prohibitions, so he didn't fully understand the difference between sacred and profane tastes. What, he began to wonder, if blood was the ultimate Old World flavor that had been denied in the New World?

Sandy left the Stern Academy that evening in a contemplative mood. Lost in his own cloudy Bible, he biked toward his mom's home by way of Sunrise Park, idly taking in the toddlers and their nannies around the sand box and the local kids whose parents were either nonobservant or non-Jewish and were, therefore, lucky enough to not have to attend Hebrew school. Some were tossing a pink Spaldeen while others played tree tag. The game was a local favorite, its rules passed from one generation to the next. Sandy himself was adept at the leap between two grand beeches at a perilous ten feet from the earth.

"Yo, Levinson!" shouted Deborah Blitzstein from the thicket of copper-colored leaves. He knew that bray well. Though Deborah's parents were modest people who owned a tiny store in Palm Beach that sold music boxes—indeed, they were like two delicate figures spinning around in one of their products—their daughter was appropriately nicknamed The Blitz. She clamped her thighs around the trunk of the beech tree and started hoisting herself up after some other child who'd been given a head start. "It's a new variation, Levinson," the Blitz called out, "Get the goy."

For a second, Sandy's dreams and the reality of the playground mixed together in his head. Then he caught a glimpse of bright reddish hair camouflaged in the tree. Several branches above the Blitz was Suzy Keller, daughter of the King of Toxic Waste. Sandy had known Suzy since they were in kindergarten, but had recently grown tongue-tied whenever they met at Jupiter Junior High or on the beach by their adjacent residences. Worst of all was when Suzy asked him about Hebrew school or Jewish holidays.

He remembered his grandfathers' final Passover. Despite the divorce, Renata and Mike agreed to celebrate together for Sandy's sake. He was helping his mother lay out her best, lime-green china on three folding tables that had been set up in the den, which was the only room large enough to contain the multitude of cousins expected that evening. Two ceremonial plates, one silver, one enamel, were placed at either end of the table so that Max and Nate could officiate simultaneously. Sandy was thinking that he'd probably sit midway between the elders and allow their prayers and songs to come to him in stereo when Suzy appeared at the plate glass door to the patio.

Sandy went to the door and placed his hand on the glass. Suzy set hers parallel to his on the far side. He opened the door, but no further touch occurred. "Hi," he said.

"Hi," she replied, and a pause that seemed to last an hour ensued. Finally she continued, "I just wanted to see what's going on."

"It's a seder."

"I know. I wish we could have one."

Was it possible that this paragon was actually jealous of the bizarre rituals of his tribe? He loved his grandfathers, but was too conflicted about Jewish identity to understand any potential appeal it might have to a non-Jew in a 95-percent Jewish community. Here the outsiders were insiders. "Um, it's like a party, but . . ."

"With all this wonderful food." She gazed longingly at the table arrayed with *matzoh* the texture of cardboard and nasty raw parsley and hard-boiled eggs steeping in salt water and horseradish guaranteed to burn through The Terminator's stomach lining.

"It's just . . ." Sandy started.

"Oops, I promised that I would babysit for my brother," and Suzy was gone.

[

] Now Suzy clambered from branch to branch as Deborah set out after her. Sandy half stood on the ground, half sat on his bicycle seat, watching the show performed by one lithe little monkey and one hairy gorilla. But as he watched, the apparently solid branch from which Deborah was reaching out to tag Suzy cracked and gave way. The zaftig Jewess crashed onto the petite heiress and the two of them hit the ground in a tangle of limbs both fleshy and arboreal.

Debbie immediately stood up and dusted herself off, but Suzy remained still.

Sandy leapt off his bike, letting it, too, clatter to the ground, and dashed forward. Suzy's eyes were open, but so unfocussed that she must not have understood what happened. Then her eyes blinked as they examined the sky where a branch had been, and she gazed along her belly, along her thigh, to her knee, and screamed, "Blood!"

A rosy blush on her knee darkened by the second and then started dripping.

Before Sandy could think about what he was doing, he put his mouth to the wound.

The whole event couldn't have taken more than three seconds, but a world was created and destroyed. The taste, maybe more so the texture of blood on his lips, in his mouth, flooded every fiber of Sandy Levinson's being, and he understood the nature of his own blood flowing through his body, and he pursed his lips to draw more of the vital human fluid through the shredded skin on Suzy's knee as she moaned with unexpected pleasure and then, reconstituted, shrieked, and kicked him away.

"What?" He hardly realized where he was.

Deborah, standing arms akimbo, called out to anyone who could hear, "Sandy Levinson's a vampire!"

[

] By the next day, half of Jupiter Junior High School knew the story. As a group of girls passed Sandy in the hallway, one said, "Thirsty?" and the others snickered.

And a ninth-grade thug slapped him on the back, laughing, "Try a little higher than the knee, fella."

Sandy was a solitary, never an outcast, but neither a popular kid, so he was easy prey to sick teenage humor. Even the teachers seemed to know that he had done something strange and gave him leeway in the hall. Wherever he went, from algebra to world history, someone welcomed him in a lugubrious Romanian accent.

There was no way out; he would remain the butt of jokes until another loser made some gruesome faux pas. Only then would the world of J.J.H.S. forget Sandy.

"How was school?" his mother asked that evening in the ritual pretense of caring for her child's education.

To which Sandy gave the adolescent response from time immemorial, "Fine."

Likewise, his dad the next week asked, "How's everything?"

"What's with this? Suddenly everyone is so damn attentive!"

"Whoa, cowboy. I was just asking."

"You really want the truth? Everything sucks."

His father should have known better, but he couldn't resist. "So I hear."

It was the final insult. Sandy stormed out of the house and hopped onto his trusty bicycle. He pedaled across the causeway from West Palm, past the precious shoppes on Worth Avenue and northward on the corderoyed Boardwalk without any real idea where he was going. No one understood him except his tragically dead grandfathers. He looked up at the cloud formations and thought he discerned profiles of Max and Nate. He looked out at the ocean and the shape of the waves recalled Nate and Max.

He biked on, leaving the Boardwalk and cruising up the coast road that led to his mother's home, noticing the signs with her name on the lawns of various houses for sale. But Sandy had left his dad's house without eating dinner and he was ravenous. The hunger gnawing at his belly was stronger than the shame. He wasn't running from the shame; he was running to the hunger. Turning a last familiar bend in the road, there was the object of his craving.

Between two carved stone pillars spanned by a curving metal gate lay the cobbled driveway to the Keller mansion, hidden by a row of gigantic eucalyptus trees. Somewhere beyond those trees, Suzy Keller probably sat on a white leather couch, scabby knee tucked under her bottom, flipping channels on a plasma TV. Perhaps Hank Keller or Suzy's mother was there, too. Perhaps there was a gardener trimming the pachysandra on the terrace or a housekeeper fluffing up bedding, a cook frying bacon or shucking oysters or some other goyish dish. Somewhere in that house also lay Suzy's baby brother, Ethan.

Sandy had seen ten-month-old Ethan only a few times, once when Suzy lay him on a blanket on the beach while she unstrapped her bikini top and lay flat on her incipient chest, once when Sandy and his mom bumped into Mrs. Keller on Worth Avenue on their way to the Blitzstein music box store to buy a present for a client Renata was wooing. As far as Sandy could tell, Ethan was, like all babies, an undifferentiated blob of flesh, rather, Sandy thought at the time, like a loaf of white *challah*.

Sandy passed the pseudo-Spanish hacienda built in the twenties, left his bike under the lanai at the Levinson bungalow, and wandered out to the mimosas. Then he crossed the line.

[

] Could anyone see him traversing the yard kept brilliantly green in spite of the Atlantic's briny spray? He didn't know. An arched French door that gave onto the private beach was ajar. A television somewhere emitted a laugh track, so Sandy tiptoed up the marble staircase.

"Is that you?" a female voice asked, and he froze, but whoever had spoken wasn't curious enough to pursue her inquiries, and he continued. To the left of the wide landing was a broad hallway to a single large door. To the right were about half a dozen doors. Assuming that the single door led to the master suite, Sandy walked in the other direction. How he found the nerve, he couldn't have said, but forbidden knowledge would not be denied: Ask Eve.

First, he opened a door to a linen closet the size of his bedroom.

Ranks of puffy towels were arrayed in a spectrum shifting incrementally from pure white and pale yellow to deep indigo. Then he opened a door to a hall bath as large as a kitchen. Then he discovered a bedroom that must have been Suzy's, decorated with a pink Aubusson rug and matching lace-canopied bed and hand-stencilled designs in a frieze under a cathedral ceiling. Wedged into the frame of a heart-shaped mirror over a vanity covered with scores of make-up and nail-polish bottles were several dozen photographs. Most showed Hollywood boy stars, but one shocked Sandy. It was his own picture, torn from a copy of *The Echo*, Jupiter J.H.S.'s yearbook.

He could retreat now, he knew, and perhaps ask Suzy to a movie. He could be a normal person if only he suppressed his thirst for blood, Christian blood, the blood that sustained his ancestors before they lost their nature in the Goldene Medina. By now he was shaking. Like Noah told to build an ark, like Abraham told to smash his father's idols, like Moses told to let his people go, Sandy Levinson had a mandate from God.

Two more doors remained. One led to a family media room with enough electronic equipment to outfit a network news center, and the other contained nothing but a bassinet and changing table. Inside the bassinet, surrounded by a dozen stuffed animals as large as he was, lay a sleeping child.

Sandy lifted him and the infant's eyelids fluttered, though he remained asleep. How to do this? Where to do this? The sinner didn't have the forethought to arrange a proper altar for the necessary sacrifice in his own garage, or perhaps on a pyre by the sea.

The only question he didn't ask was why. That was obvious. If *khoppers* were real, and pogroms, expulsions, and inquisitions, if pharaohs and tzars and popes and kings and prime ministers and all the anointed, appointed, and elected leaders of humanity had nothing better to do with their power than torture a nation of scribes and tailors, then who could begrudge the tiniest, tastiest bite of recompense.

Tucking baby Ethan under his arm like a warm football, Sandy made his way back along the endless Keller corridor, down the magnificent Keller staircase, and out the Keller arches to the vast, green Keller sward. It was a good hundred yards from the end zone in which he had apparently intercepted the baby ball to the safety of the mimosas.

A hundred yards in the other direction, a Latino gardener wearing a straw hat knelt in a loamy patch where he tenderly hand-planted a row of tulip bulbs. The gardener's back was toward Sandy, so he presented no danger, yet Suzy or her mother or perhaps The King's mother-in-law visiting her wealthy daughter from Indianapolis or whoever had asked "Is that you?" might glance out a window at the precise moment Sandy was most vulnerable.

"Nu?" Max's voice came to him.

Nate added, "When isn't a Jew vulnerable?"

Crazed with thirst, or just plain crazed by the pain of the ages, Sandy ran across the open yard to the shadowy line between properties. There, he found a private thicket in which the mimosas were densest and sat the baby down and examined his pockets for a tool appropriate to the task.

Unfortunately, he had forgotten to bring a pocket knife. All he had was a wallet with his school I.D. and $7.53 in cash and a credit card that his mother insisted was for use "in emergencies only" and a ticket stub he'd paid for with the credit card when he and Louis "Beef" Wellington —no relation to Renata's imaginary partner since Beef's family's original name had been Wallechinksy—skipped Hebrew School one day to see a movie at the Palmdale Mall. What else was there? A neat stone with red veins and a fold-out map of the county bus lines and a feather from the nearby Hallaconda Bird Sanctuary and a button that had fallen off a sweater during a nippy day the previous November. In his breast pocket he had a pencil and Bic pen, the kind where a tube of ink ran up a hollow plastic shaft.

Max and Nate's tales of resilience under totalitarianism had taught Sandy that you used whatever was available in a given situation. He unscrewed the nib attached to the tube from one end of the pen and a tiny blue plastic cap from the other end. Then he used the point of the pen to puncture Ethan's wrist.

At last, the passive baby cried, but Sandy placed his hand over the child's mouth until he was quiet. Then he inserted the plastic cylinder in the pulsing blue vein, like a straw into a milkshake, and he drank.

[

] By the time the police arrived, Sandy lay sated in his bedroom with matching Colonial oak desk, dresser, and headboard. His mother had arrived earlier along with the sound of sirens and more flashing lights than the Date Palm Disco on Route 1. Renata and three serious men wearing brown suits knocked on his door. "Huh?" he murmured as he struggled to rise from a dream of two little boys named Max and Nate fleeing from *khoppers*.

"It's important, honey," Renata said.

"In a minute."

The detectives didn't tell him what was already headline news on the local TV channel.

"These men want to ask you some questions."

"Um, sure." He wiped his hair, still wet from the shower he'd taken before collapsing in bed, off his forehead.

The men stood with open notebooks, two of them holding hollow-core Bic pens like the one poking up from Sandy's breast pocket. One asked, "When did you get home?"

"Um, maybe an hour, two hours ago."

"Did you see anything?"

"I . . . I don't know what you mean."

"Son, we're investigating a disappearance next door," this a modest understatement since the Palm Beach County coroner's van had already removed Ethan's lifeless body while the rest of the Kellers took the Toxic Waste company plane to their weekend house in Bermuda.

"Did you see anything unusual?"

"I don't think so."

"Anything at all may be helpful. How did you come home?"

"My bicycle. It's under the lanai."

"Any trucks next door?"

"There's always trucks next door."

"What sort of trucks?"

"Construction, I guess."

"You came directly inside?"

"No, I went out back and did my homework on the patio."

"What sort of homework?"

"English, math. Some from Hebrew school."

"Can you see onto the Keller's property from the patio?"

"A little."

"Did you happen to glance over there?"

"I might have."

"Please, son, it's very important. Did you notice anything at all?"

"Well . . ."

"Yes?"

"I'm sure it's nothing."

"Let us be the judge of that."

"Really, all I saw was a gardener."

"A gardener?"

"Yeah, doing some work under the trees."

"Could you tell what sort of work?"

"Gardening."

"What was he wearing?"

"Um, jeans I think. And a straw hat."

"Anything else? Could you tell what sort of implements he was using? Could you tell if he was working hard or taking a break? Could you tell if . . ."

"No, I just caught a glimpse out of the corner of my eye and came in to take a nap before dinner."

"Thanks, son. If you think of anything else, don't hesitate to call."

[

] The gardener, an adherent of Santeria, was arrested the following day, and in the weeks leading up to his trial nobody in Jupiter could talk about anything else. Most of the conversation was either voyeuristically appalled, "Can you believe it happened in their own backyard?" or subtly appalling, "We've got to do something about immigration." But one day, again after Hebrew school, when Sandy biked up to his house, the Blitz was waiting for him. "Hey, Sandy."

"Deborah."

"I was in the neighborhood, so I thought I'd stop by."

"Hi."

"Is that where it happened?" She pointed to the row of trees, less well tended since the Kellers left Jupiter Island for a semi-permanent escape to Bermuda.

"Yeah."

"Can you show me?"

"Um, sure." Sandy hadn't been out to the mimosas since "it" happened. The ground was packed flat from the footsteps of a hundred detectives and reporters. A strip of forgotten yellow police tape was tangled in a root. "Here."

"Here?" the Blitz repeated.

He nodded.

"Y'know, Sandy, I was thinking about that day in the playground."

"What day?"

"The day I fell out of the tree with Suzy Keller, and you . . ."

Sandy waited for the accusation like a Jewish child hiding under a feather mattress waiting for the *khopper*'s sword. "I . . .?"

"Well I'm sure that creepy gardener did it, but, you know, it doesn't seem accidental that . . ."

The girl built like a tank held his fate in her hands. He knew it, and he knew that she knew it, and he could barely keep himself from dropping to the ground and clutching her massive legs to beg for mercy.

Yet rather than wield her power, the Blitz was absurdly coy, twirling a clot of kinky hair around her forefinger and tilting her turret-shaped head to the side. "We . . . ell." Sandy couldn't meet her eyes. He looked down at the ground that had absorbed baby Ethan's blood.

Deborah continued, "The way you were . . . the way the police claim the gardener . . . I couldn't help but wonder . . ."

Kill me now, he thought, and shut his eyes to avoid the death sentence. Put me in jail for 25 years. Maybe I'll stop being a Jew; maybe it will stop the craving. He was so lost in doom that he didn't notice the soft metallic click of his belt unbuckling and the softer metallic gasp of his zipper coming undone. Only when he realized that the Blitz was no longer standing but kneeling in front of him, and that as he had taken one liquid of life so was he giving, giving, giving another, did Sandy understand that he was going to get away with his crime. He looked up at the mimosa leaves that hid him and the Blitz from God.

[

] Renata got the listing. She sold the former Keller estate to a Jewish banker from New York.

] Remittances

I hear it everywhere, and this morning I finally read it in the English-language daily I buy each morning at the kiosk on Tel Aviv's Ben-Yehuda Street: Jewish is *in* in Germany. An enterprising brewery in a small town in Bavaria is making the first officially kosher beer in the old Reich, called King Solomon ("the beer for the wise," the brewmeister says), even though all the beer in Germany is already de facto kosher. Hops, barley, yeast, malt—these are the only ingredients, the article says. So King Solomon's kashrut certification is a redundancy, a non-necessity. But the brewmeister wants it, he tells a reporter, because things Jewish are hip in Germany these days. The populace, especially the young, are drawn to them. King Solomon will make for good business.

When I tell this to Arieh he sneers. This disgusts him, he tells me, even though his grandparents' wretched personal history also once disgusted him. This was before Israel's Official Embrace of the Holocaust. After decades of a barely disguised silent national shame—*how could they let themselves be led like sheep etc.*—the country is finally able to look these old people in the eye. Have a little sympathy. It wasn't always this way. When Arieh was a kid, people used to tell the crones at the beach with numbers on their arms to cover themselves up.

But now this latest news from the Deutschland makes him ill. He gets up from the table and tells me to stop reading the English-language dailies and learn better Hebrew already so I don't have to read that kind of drivel.

"I think it's probably in *Ha'aretz* too," I tell him, collecting the coffee cups from the table and carrying them to the sink. "They cover the same things, you know." Which I know because my paper is just an English translation of his.

"Well, I don't understand how anyone can call that newsworthy." He takes his plate to the counter. Shells of three hard-boiled eggs jostle on the glass. He eats like a kibbutznik—boiled eggs, half a dozen skinny cucumbers, a tomato, thick bread and salt—even though he's lived his whole life in Tel Aviv. "Enough already with Germany. We've been obsessing about them for sixty years. Who gives a shit what they think of Jews now? Who gives a shit what they think of anything?"

"It has the fastest-growing Jewish population in the world," I call to him on his way to the bathroom where he'll brush his teeth before heading out the door to work. He's fastidious that way. Likes to have his teeth brushed, hands washed, hair combed just so before he walks out into the muggy soup of the street. It's the *yekke* in him, his German-Jewish ancestry. Though of course I won't tell him that. "All those Jews from the FSU," I call. "The second language in Berlin is practically Russian."

"Same as here," he calls back from the bathroom, the water running. Instinctively, I glance out the kitchen window at my neighbor's balcony. The Russian cleaning woman is beating a small rug on the railing. Puffs of dust billow up like little genies. All the people in these buildings employ Russian women, Tanyas and Irinas and Galinas, to clean their apartments; they're shocked to hear I clean ours myself. *It's not exploitation,* they tell me in their excellent college-level English. The Russians were engineers or physicists or dentists back in Moscow, but if they don't speak the language they can't find work. *Think of it as giving an illiterate immigrant a job.*

At that, I usually smile and end the conversation. They could just as well have been talking about me.

[

] I met Arieh my third week in the country and latched onto him like glue. My image of volunteering at a leafy kibbutz redolent with citrus groves had run up against reality when a sharp-tongued bureaucrat in a windowless office next to the Tel Aviv bus station informed me that the only spaces available were in a collective in the desert where I could work eight hours a day in a plastics factory. I chose to politely decline and found myself a room in an apartment on Allenby Street with two other Americans. One was thinking of entering a women's yeshiva and finding God, whom she had not been able to locate in L.A.; the other had burned out in high tech in Boston and was working under the table as a waitress in a vegan restaurant on the beach. It was in the restaurant where I'd seen the ad for the room.

"It'll just be temporary," I told the waitress, Mia. "While I get myself together."

"That's cool," she said, sipping her lemon-eucalyptus tea. She was on a break. The waves slapped the sand behind us. "So what have you been doing 'til now?" She was trying for casual but I knew she was appraising me. I was a total stranger and there was probably something about me.

I opted for a half-truth. "Dropped out of grad school. Social anthropology." Which was basically accurate. I'd been required to withdraw after the so-called incident. It wouldn't have looked good for the university—Ivy League, big name faculty, reputation to protect.

Mia flashed a smile. She was skeptical. But there was a tacit understanding among us English speakers; we had to help each other out.

She gave me a key and I prepaid a month's rent and moved in the same day. The other roommate, Elisheva, though that wasn't her real name, which was something embarrassing and Californian like Arden or Cassandra, was almost never there, checking out the religious scene. Mia got me a job chopping vegetables in the back of the restaurant. It wasn't bad. No one bothered me, and I walked the beach when I was done.

But then one day Elisheva came home from one of her Torah-for-Beginners classes and told me someone in her group had seen me outside the apartment and recognized me. That he remembered me from New Haven and had heard I'd been involved in something violent and terrible. She could barely get out the words. By then she was wearing long skirts and praying three times a day. She didn't want my messy past seeping into her newly purified present. Mia, on the other side of the table, went pale.

It was late in the afternoon. I hardly knew them. I said nothing and went to my room, leaving them in the kitchen frantically whispering. That evening Arieh came to the restaurant for a quinoa pilaf and salad, and when he asked me if I wanted to go out and get a coffee after my shift—I was covering for a waitress who'd called in sick; Arieh told me later that I seemed interesting—I packed up my stuff from Mia's apartment and went home with Arieh and never went back.

[

] With Arieh off to work I finish cleaning up—the Russian on my neighbor's balcony has gone inside to continue her labors—then take the bus to the Interior Ministry on Kaplan Street to carry on in my lurching pursuit of citizenship. After almost three years in the country, Arieh has convinced me I need to do this, not because I need the work permit or the tax breaks on a washing machine, or because, like the Ethiopians or the Argentinians or the Iranians or, lately, the French, I am a Jew from a country that won't especially want me back, but because I need to make a commitment to a new life so that I can let the old one go. Zionism—he offers, amateur psychologist—as therapeutic intervention.

The waiting area is surprisingly empty. Immediately I wonder if the workers are on strike, because the waiting room is never empty. But it turns out it is simply my lucky day. I have gotten there at exactly the right time, Irit, the official assigned to my case, tells me when I shamble into her office and sit down; I was hoping for a long delay so I could once again try to persuade myself that this is a good idea. I've just missed the morning rush, Irit tells me brightly, pulling my file from a silver mesh holder on her desk. Irit is neat, organized, efficient. She likes pretty things and has been, she's told me, to Venice and Paris, to Prague and Istanbul and Barcelona, though not to the United States. The Pacific coast, the redwood forests, the ribbon of highway, like from the famous song: have I been to these places? I haven't, I tell her, and she *tsks tsks*. Americans don't explore their own country, she doesn't understand this.

"*Tov*," she says, wrapping up the small talk. "So did you finish the paperwork?" She squints at her computer screen. "No. I see you have for me one more form."

It's the one asking about criminal history. Charges, arrests, convictions. Arieh has typed up a long explanation in Hebrew and carefully stapled it and all the official documents to the sheet: the hasty trial, the successful appeal, prosecutorial misconduct, damages for wrongful imprisonment. Even an apology from the State of Connecticut. I'd wanted to bring in the papers smudged and wrinkled and dog-eared so that their condition might cause my application to be ignored, so that maybe Irit wouldn't read it. Never in my life would I turn in papers like that, not even a request to a professor for a conference; always everything was meticulously typed and clean and respectful. Because once upon a time I was a promising student at a famous university with a great future. But this morning I wanted to bring a mess. Arieh wouldn't let me. *You are going in there with the truth. You have nothing to hide. You should be proud.* Proud. I rustle through my bag and find the pristine manila envelope. Palms damp, I hand it to Irit.

She swivels in her chair and sits back, opens the papers onto her lap. I look out the window at the bougainvillea trailing on the façade of the building across the street. Someone has told me the vine is a parasite, always growing on something else; that despite its lush purple and pink blossoms, it's an uninvited guest. Under the giant blooms, a pair of Filipino women are walking arm-in-arm. They are here taking care of the elderly, thousands of small Asian men and women pushing ancient Jews in wheelchairs, helping them with their walkers in the coffee shops. They are exceedingly patient, exceedingly kind. I once read in the English-language daily that thirty percent of their countrymen leave their homeland to work—in Dubai, England, the United Arab Emirates, Israel—and send back their earnings. Remittances. The government in Manila encourages it. It's the only way to make their economy work. It's also what allows the Filipinos to stay here, the ones who like it. The price of admission, they call it. If they can't pay, they have to go home. On Saturdays, their day off, beautiful happy couples stroll the promenade by the sea and buy ice cream.

Irit has put down the papers. I glance back at her. She is resting her chin in her palm, thinking. I look at the wall behind her head and register nothing. It is unbearable to me that she has read it, that now she knows.

"*Tov,*" she says finally. Enough. Finished. She takes up her mouse, clicks a few times and watches the screen. There is nothing further to discuss. She will recommend that they approve my application, she says. There is just one more hurdle. Sign-off from her superior. But approval will be Irit's recommendation. *Give me your tired, your poor, your wretched masses yearning to go free.* The Israeli Law of Return says that anyone with a Jewish parent or grandparent—same definition as Hitler's—is enough of a Jew and has the right to become an Israeli citizen. Certain limitations apply. Killing a fellow Jew in self-defense is not de facto one of them.

"The next meeting with my superior is at the end of the week," Irit says, poker faced, all business, but later she will go home and tell her husband about the young woman who was in her office today. Thirty years old, a murderer. But justified. He could not imagine what the creep did to her. Yale University—has he heard of that? Like Harvard except in Connecticut. Irit folds her hands on top of the file. Behind the crisp professionalism I detect a slight crack in the veneer, the faintest catch in her voice. "We'll do the best we can. I call you when it's over."

[

] The Russian from my neighbor's balcony is sitting on a ledge outside our apartment building clutching an overstuffed plastic bag that contains slippers and a housedress, things she wears for cleaning. A cracked black vinyl pocketbook is tucked in beside her.

"Everything all right?" I ask in my rounded American Hebrew. It's nearly noon and feverishly hot. I've never seen her sitting outside before.

She opens a palm and says something fast in Russian. A tiny Star of David glints on a thin gold chain around her neck. Apartment three, floor two, she manages in Hebrew. She has a customer in my building. But why is she outside? I fish for my keys. Does she not have a key? I mime, holding them up. Nobody home?

Correct, she nods. Nobody home. Brassy gold caps glint on two of her upper teeth. So maybe she wasn't a mathematician or astronaut in the Mother Country; maybe she's from Uzbekestan or Kazakhstan or one of those other long-ridiculed stans, but, still, I find her cleaning-person status distressing. I don't like it, no matter what my smartly dressed Tel Aviv acquaintances say. *This is how it is. Our parents and grandparents were once immigrants too. They did their share of dirty work. Now it's someone else's turn.*

"*Cham m'od,*" I say to the woman in my simplest Hebrew, fanning myself to demonstrate, in case she hasn't learned even the basics. Hot out here. "Would you like to come to my apartment for a cold drink?" I throw back the imaginary contents of an imaginary glass and make pretend drinking noises.

She tips her head, uncertain. She doesn't want to stand up her employer. But her employer is not home, and someone has made a mistake. Either the Russian has a key and forgot it, or the Israeli forgot about the Russian. I'm suspecting the latter because people don't let out keys around here just like that.

I perform a series of gestures to get across that I will write her employer a note and leave it on her door. Then she can come in out of the heat.

"*B'seder,*" the woman says. All right. She will come. We take care of the note and walk the stairs in silence. In Arieh's apartment I bring her a glass of orange juice mixed with seltzer. She likes this, and I pour another despite her protests. Refreshed, out of the blinding sun, she's quite attractive, about my mother's age. She even looks a little like my mother, who comes from a long line of Russian Jews.

She waves away my offer of something to eat, folds her hands and looks around. A husband? she inquires. Do I have a husband?

No, no, I tell her. Just a *chaver*. A boyfriend.

She nods. "And you?" I ask. "Husband?"

"Ach." She waves away the question. From a mélange of Hebrew and grimaces and hand motions I deduce that the husband was no good, that he came with her to the country but soon disappeared, leaving her with a problem daughter, a son who got into trouble, and, apparently, a couple of grandchildren. She lives in Bat Yam and is tired all the time.

What did she do back in Russia? I ask, pushing a plate of grapes in her direction.

"Ah." She makes a broad smile. "*Direktor,*" she beams, and takes a grape.

"Director? You ran a business?"

Vigorous head shakes. *Bizness.* Same word in Hebrew as in English. No, no, not bizness. *Direktor.* She moves her hands like a symphonic conductor.

"Musical director?" I imitate the conducting, sing a little *la la la.*

No, no. She floats her fingers toward her face and holds her head high. Her hands are reddish and raw from detergents and scouring powders, but they are also graceful and expressive. Then I see it: comedy and tragedy, the famous thespian masks.

"Ah, theatre director!" I say, as if we're playing charades. "Dramatics!"

"*Ken, ken!*" Yes, yes! "*Shekspeer. Shekhov. Bernid Sho.*"

"You directed Shakespeare? Bernard Shaw?"

She tips her head, smiles. The actor taking a bow.

"Wow. That's some change," I offer in English. "A theatre person and now you're cleaning houses for rich Israelis in north Tel Aviv."

She smiles—I know she didn't understand—and murmurs something melancholy in Russian.

"And here?" I ask. "You are also a director here?" because there's a huge Russian community, surely they put on plays and other entertainments.

She sighs. She is too tired, she says. She is telling me in her mix of tongues that it is not possible. That no one can work all day cleaning houses and then come home at night and inspire a fleet of desperate actors. That you can't feel fresh and energized after taking three buses to the city, then three more home, then coping with your difficult off-spring and needy grandchildren. I don't understand a word but I am certain this is what she's saying. Life is full of burdens. Full of mistakes, losses, regrets. But—and this doesn't have to be said—it's better here than it was back there.

A knock at the door. We glance over. We both know who it is. The Russian sighs again and begins to collect her bags. The slippers, the housedress. The carriage turned into a pumpkin. Art, its pulls and potent demands, has vanished. She's the cleaning lady again.

"Oh, Janine, thank you, I got your note!" The Israeli in her stylish pantsuit and impossibly high heels and perfectly dyed blond hair is breathless. "I feel terrible keeping Tanya waiting." She pokes in her head. "Tanya," she says, loud, in Hebrew, as if the Russian were hard of hearing, "I got tied up in traffic! Stuck behind some Arab with a horse-drawn wagon, if you can believe it! Crazy Tel Aviv!" The Russian pulls herself out of the chair, exhausted though she hasn't even begun, and follows her employer out the door.

[

] Arieh's grandparents never told anyone their story. Who wanted to hear it? Enough already about the death camps, the forced marches, the children shot in the streets, the mutilated women. Arieh's Israeli parents didn't want to know, his friends' parents with their identical histories didn't want to know. Nobody wanted to know. Enough, the country of wishfully amnesiac Jews declared, and insisted the newcomers change their names. Kaminetzky became Kedem, Perski became Peres, Rubitzov became Rabin. Heroic Hebrew names to get rid of the taint. Enough of the bent-over sheep-to-slaughter. The survivors were given their dim depressing flats, their shameful reparations, their new and improved last names—Ginsberg to Gidon, Mayerson to Meir—covered up their forearms and said nothing.

[

] It was the surgeon in New Haven who gave me the idea to go to Israel. He'd just come back from his first trip. *Changed my life*, he said. He was making small talk to relax me. I was on my back on the vinyl table in a blue paper gown, legs spread, a pre-op exam. The ER doctors had done the best they could under the circumstances, but there was no getting around this. He apologized for the pain.

"Ever been there?" he said from down near the stirrups. They were covered in yellow golf club socks, the kind with little fringed balls on the ends, to warm up the metal. His big-chested, no-nonsense nurse stood beside him trying not to gasp at what she was looking at.

"Mmm," I murmured, eyes squeezed shut, counting breaths. Six, seven, eight, nine.

"Oh? When?"

"Trip after high school. Another. In college." My mother's idea. We took two ten-day tours with women's groups where all the ladies were widowed or, like my mother, divorced, where I was the youngest participant by twenty years and where I developed an interest in anthropology.

"They've taken in people from all over the world," the surgeon said. "Kosovo. Chernobyl. Darfur. Survivors of everything. Went with a mission of doctors. Blew me away, to tell you the truth."

A cool washcloth settled on my forehead. I opened my eyes. The nurse. She'd migrated to my end of the table. She was a tough cookie, a matron with a New York accent who would violently disapprove of the profligate behavior and stupendous failure of judgment that got me in this situation in the first place, a woman whose kids knew exactly where she stood and who tolerated no back talk. She took my hand and said the exam was almost over and that the man whose head was between my legs right now was the best gynecological surgeon in the state of Connecticut. And that she hoped that whoever did this to my insides would be strung up by his balls.

From southward by the stirrups, a soft reprimand. "Mary, that's not quite protocol. There's a police officer outside, Ms. Bloom is in the custody of the state."

"Sorry," the nurse said, perfunctory, unconvincing. Then she squeezed my hand and brought a fresh cloth to my burning face.

[

] Arieh calls at three to find out how it went this morning with Irit.

"So are you Israeli yet? Because if you are, you have to get a fierce haircut and start wearing overly tight jeans."

I laugh a little. One of the things Arieh says he likes about me is my determination not to hide my American-ness. In three years in stylish

Levantine Tel Aviv, I've kept my frumpy grad student Birkenstock wardrobe and still eat a little salad at midday and a big hot American dinner every night.

"Now it goes to the supervisor," I say. "Irit will let me know."

"*Tov.*" He's relieved. He thought I might not go through with it. "Tonight we celebrate," he says, decisive. "Because you turned in the papers. We'll go to the port, have a beer, some good food, listen to some music."

"Okay." I want to say *But first we stay home and make love.* But I don't. Because that's not exactly what we do. The surgeries were successful—the externals were repaired anyway—and the doctor assured me it was allowed, but I'm afraid it's going to hurt, even now, after five years. So some things Arieh and I don't do. He says he doesn't mind. It could be a lot worse. Look at what's here, he tells me when we're walking down Rothschild and someone is pushing a twenty-year-old with no legs in a wheelchair, or we pass a girl in a café whose face is striated purple. That's how it is. A tough country. Casualties of a war-ravaged life. For Arieh, my condition is a shrug. No penetration? We'll work around it. No childbirth? We'll work around it. We have a running joke. *Your father in Arizona with his third wife never contacts you? We'll work around it. Iran developing a nuclear bomb? We'll work around it.* It's not the Israeli way to stew or mull. Better to be practical. Move on. *Gamarnu.* Finished.

"This is a good thing, Janine," Arieh says. There's noise in the background, people waiting for him to get off the phone. He works for a software company, a start-up like in Silicon Valley. Dress code jeans, hours 24/7, no one there over thirty-five. "Even if they hold up your application for awhile, you'll be glad you did this."

"I will?" I say, and then remember the reporters camped out on our lawn, the constantly ringing phone, the smarmy ghostwriter who wanted to write my book, my exhausted mother telling them all to go away, the calls she tells me she gets even now. Even the contrite letter from the Yale dean sitting on Arieh's dining room table inviting me back. *Surely you understand, initial legal proceedings, university policy.* "Okay, maybe. Yeah, maybe I will."

[

] I'd met him in the dean's office at the end of the spring semester, a meeting for selected students about fellowships for the fall. He was in economics. His Yale recommendation was from a former Secretary of the Treasury, a friend of the family. Prep school, Princeton, a well-connected Jewish pedigree, parents who were hot shot lawyers in New York. A little chit-chat. Then out for coffee. There was something about him from the start. An edge. I liked that. I'd always liked men who were a little tough, a little mean. Maybe it was the absent father. Maybe it was because, with them, you knew what you were getting. Unlike with the sweet ones, who could turn on you and suddenly ignite.

We didn't waste a lot of time. He wanted to go to his dorm because, he said, he had a suite to himself and I'd be impressed with his house-keeping. I thought it was a joke. It wasn't. He was very orderly. His desk was neat and the bed tightly made; the rug looked newly vacuumed. *I like women to be surprised when they come here. They think men are slobs, I like to prove them wrong.* He made it sound like he was a progressive, a feminist; that he would never expect a future wife to do all the cooking and cleaning. A line that was bound to please. This was, after all, New Haven; we were all equals there.

He brought a chilled bottle of wine to the bedroom. It was obvious he picked up a lot of women. Who didn't? I'd had my share of hook-ups. Maybe more than my share. After some cursory talk we lay down and he tested the waters. He was trim but strong, athletic. A kiss, some strok-ing, unbuttoning, then a hard grab at my wrist, pinning it down. A little rough play. He turned me over and pressed my shoulder blades into the mattress, then pushed at my buttocks, shoved his hard cock in the space between. I could feel the urgency, the need. After a minute, I eased out and climbed on top of him, felt the stiffness of him, the throbbing demand. *Not yet*, I murmured coyly. *You have to wait your turn.* I thought he'd like that, thought he was into prolonging things, stretching out the tension.

But something was off. A darkness washed over his face. Maybe it was my taking control. Maybe he didn't like being told to wait. *Trouble delaying gratification*, a psychiatrist testified at the trial. The house-master of his dorm had referred him months before, some of the other students were disturbed. *He could become enraged. We discussed strate-gies. He discontinued treatment.* I was on him, moving up and down, and then I felt it, first a stab, then a sharp burning, the pain, something trickling out of me. Then he was on top of me, doing something down there with an instrument, his other hand over my mouth to muffle the screaming, and I saw the crazed wolf in his eyes—*shut up, bitch. Just shut the fuck up.* He was pumping up and down, all the while moving the instrument, the sheets flooding, a gleam of sick joy on his face, and I knew that I was going to pass out. That I was going to bleed, bleed to death.

He stopped, finished, and slid halfway off me onto his side, exhausted, a wet bloody blade trailing across my stomach, and I understood in my delirium that this was my only chance. That a depleted man, a man whose procreative force has just left him, is a man without defenses, a window that might last only seconds. I made myself lift my arm and pulled the knife from his clammy hand, and with a final reserve of strength before I lost everything to darkness plunged it into his chest because that's what was closest and that's what I saw. His perfectly muscled smooth chest, the chest of a swimmer or a wrestler, of a magazine ad. *It's my fault*, I thought in that flickering instant. *I should have known, should have expected something like this one day. It's my own fault.* Then he fell over me and everything went black.

[

] Arieh has arranged a little surprise party for me. Lev and Galia who live upstairs are at the restaurant, along with Doron and Ronit from Arieh's job. Doron and Ronit have recently crossed the line and gone from being work friends to lovers. Everyone in Israel thinks it's crazy to put self-imposed romantic limitations on office relationships like we do in the States. *If you can't sleep with your co-workers, who are you going to sleep with? We're a small country. Once you rule out relatives and your friend's lovers, there's no one left.*

We order wine. Everyone raises their glasses. To Janine, they toast in enthusiastic English, who finally turned in the application. Who will soon become a citizen! They say they are post-Zionist, that the world's Jews should live wherever they please and shouldn't be made to feel guilty if they want to stay in Chicago or Sydney or Toronto. These are hip, left-wing, secular Tel Avivis. They've been to university and traveled all over Europe, South Asia, the Far East. The raison d'etre of Zionism is over, they say; there are enough Jews in Israel now. The problem isn't getting more Jews to settle the land; it's working things out with the Palestinians so that everyone can peacefully co-exist. Still, it makes them happy when someone from America wants to join them. It cheers them up. A person who's not being persecuted, not fleeing, not broke, wants to come live there, in tiny isolated Israel? They are touched, moved that I want to cast my lot with them and their constant wars and labor stoppages and broiling khamsins and claustrophobic boundaries. Even with my bad Hebrew.

"It's a burdensome process, no?" Lev says. He and Arieh and Doron went to high school together. Ronit and Galia were in the same class in law at the university. Everybody knows everybody. Which was why Arieh was interested in me. I was new. Unrelated. A refreshing change. My past was irrelevant. *Who here doesn't have a past?* he told me once. *I never shot at someone I wasn't supposed to in the army? My grandfather never killed anyone to get off a German transport?*

"Not so bad," I say. "A lot of forms."

Galia rolls her eyes. "Bureaucracy. You probably had to fill out everything in triplicate, and then they sent you to ten different offices and none were open on the day you showed up, right?"

I tip my head. Arieh says it's been surprisingly streamlined.

"Good, then," Doron says, smiling. He is handsome, an Israeli from central casting. Dark hair, dark eyes, neck veins like cello strings. "Nothing to worry about. One, two, they'll approve you." He takes a sip of wine. Ronit leans her head on his shoulder. Arieh says the relationship won't last, that Doron changes lovers as often as others change shampoo brands. "I mean, if they let in all those Russian mafioso with criminal records as long as my arm, they're certainly going to let in you, a nice Jewish girl from Connecticut who just didn't want to finish her PhD."

Ronit smiles dreamily on Doron's shoulder. It's a mild barb, not meant to insult. I'm such a good girl. The Americans are all so squeaky clean. They come here full of idealism, eager to improve society with their three hundred years of democracy and can-do spunk and sympathy for the underdog. They come with advanced degrees and a passion for recycling and the latest ideas for improving the status of women and bettering the state of public education. They bring small fortunes and sometimes big ones and the habit of wearing seat belts and waiting patiently in lines. They're good citizens who obey the rules, and worldly Israelis like Doron and Ronit and Galia and Lev find them likeable and amusing and sometimes admirable but always naïve.

Under the table, Arieh squeezes my knee. I can tell he's trying to formulate a response—*Actually, it's not so simple. Actually, she's bringing some serious baggage*—when the waitress arrives with the free appetizers the place is famous for: little dishes of olives, Turkish salad, marinated chickpeas, roasted beets, cubes of potato in mustard sauce, the mandatory tehina and hummus. She distributes six plates, sets down a basket of steaming pita, asks if we're ready to order.

"Order?" Lev says, then makes a little whistle. "We haven't even looked." Ronit lazily moves off Doron's shoulder. Everyone opens their menus. I leave mine untouched. It's in Hebrew and today of all days I don't feel like asking for the ones they keep around for tourists, the ones in routinely butchered English.

The waitress hovers. "It's on me," Arieh tells the others, waving away their objections. "Because," he says, still scanning the menu, "it's not easy to decide you want to become a citizen of another place. That you're going to leave the richest country in the world, the most powerful country in the world, and come here." He keeps his eyes on the menu but his hand is on my knee again, as if to hold me steady. "It takes guts to go where you can't speak the language or get a job or find your way if you get lost, or don't have a single goddamn relative or old friend or anyone who knows you longer than ten minutes, and where the population is so fucking on edge they're killing each other on the roads when they're not asphyxiating themselves with cigarettes and meantime walking around with a superiority complex as big as the Mediterranean. I wouldn't have such guts, and neither would any one of you, and you all know it."

The table has gone silent. The waitress is looking at me, her mouth slightly open. Arieh orders. Salads, plates of schnitzel, smoked eggplant. Beers all around. Then he glances at me, gives my leg another squeeze. The others make awkward smiles.

[

] King Solomon, I read in the next day's paper, is running into problems. It seems the kashrut certification is not guaranteed, despite the brew's ingredients. *We wish the business well*, one Yitzchak Moskowitz, Berlin's chief rabbi, has told *Ha'aretz. But the question is: can a beer that's being manufactured in a plant where in 1939 Jewish slave labor made spirits for the S.S. ever be considered kosher? Can all sins be thusly erased? Certainly we'd like to move past our dark history. But using the Jewish culture to turn a profit in Germany seems, how shall I put it, obscene. There is a limit to how much our people are willing to forget.*

[

] Tanya's employer is at the mailboxes in the lobby. The cleaning woman, she tells me, has been fired.

"Don't ask," the Israeli says, pulling out envelopes. "She's been stealing. That's right. For months. My friend across the street? Merav? I feel terrible. I sent Tanya there to clean and, boy, did she ever. Cleaned her right out. Jewelry. Cash. Cameras. Even a credit card. We turned it over to the police. The woman's claiming her husband went back to Russia and is blackmailing her, demanding hush money." She shakes her head. The blond hair swings like a thick curtain.

"Hush money?" I ask. "For what?"

"Who knows?" She works a catalogue out of her box. "That's the Russians for you. Half of them were into shady dealings before they came. Or they're not really Jewish but saying they are. Some of them will be paying off people back there for the rest of their lives so they can stay. I hate using stereotypes, but you have to admit it: most of them are liars and thieves." She turns to me and smiles. "What we really need are more Americans. You obey the law, you don't drink. You people don't even smoke. So now we'll have a Filipino come clean. Not as good but at least they're honest."

Back upstairs the phone is ringing. Irit, from the Interior Ministry.

"Janine, I'm calling unofficially. Your application is going to be approved. You won't hear for three, four weeks, but I saw my supervisor this morning and she told me. So why make you wait, okay?"

"Okay." Irit goes on with details, specifics. I half-listen. A ceremony, family and friends invited, very moving, sometimes held on Masada where the Zealots held out against the Romans. Or maybe it will be at the Ministry, for convenience. Tax benefits for five years, foreign income exclusion for ten, a preferred rate on a mortgage, I should call if I don't receive anything in the post, good luck, *baruch haba*, welcome to Israel.

We hang up. I start to call Arieh with the news, though I know he'll say he's not surprised, that they weren't going to turn me away, but still, something has caught in my chest, something huge and pressing waiting to exhale. But as I punch in his number I glance at my neighbor's balcony. A young dark-haired woman is awkwardly soaping the sliding glass doors. She can't reach even halfway up the glass, and looks from this distance tiny. Tiny and fragile and uncertain. The Filipinos are excellent caretakers but not such good cleaners. They are small and delicate and sensitive, and I am suddenly afraid she won't last, that she won't have any remittances to send home. That she'll have to go back.

The doors are covered in suds. It will take hours to wash them off, dozens of trips back and forth to the kitchen sink with the bucket, gallons of water to get rid of the residue so that her employer will be satisfied. And even then the tops of the doors will not be clean. She is struggling with the rag, standing on tiptoe on the rickety stepstool, trying in vain to expand her reach in hopes of earning something, anything, and I put down the phone, unable to stop watching her, desperately wishing I could go over there and help so that she can pay what she has to. Send back what they demand. Do what she must so that the people here won't make her go home, and will let her stay.

] Leo's Squid

Jerry and Leo were nearing forty when the Events Coordinator for *Goliath's Harmonica* tracked them down. Jerry, in Massachusetts, was home to take the call. Leo, in New York, was on a date with a sociology professor who specialized in the effects of hip-hop culture on small towns in Eastern Europe. He'd been hoping—in vain, he soon discovered—that she would have a sense of humor about her work. At quarter past ten he returned home and headed for the kitchen to kick off his shoes and have a glass of wine before bed. Life was supposed to be good for divorced men in the city. He was removing his corkscrew from its elaborate leather case when he noticed the flashing light on his answering machine.

[

] Neither twin had ever read *Goliath's Harmonica*. The Events Coordinator gave them access codes so they could browse through the online archives while they considered his proposal, and they were soon immersed in the culture of twenty-something Jews cultivating a certain mix of sloppy stylishness and eclectic knowledge. They read about Margalit Havari, an Israeli-born poet with a collection called *The Desert is My Favorite Cunt*, and Saul Berkowitz, a retired train conductor who was the brother of a prominent rabbi but was himself best known for his extensive collection of Supremes memorabilia. It did seem that Jerry and Leo had a place somewhere in this world. They'd spent a few post-college years touring small venues across the country as Mossad Mickey, a comedic singing duo founded on the premise that they were secret agent wannabes. Fake moustaches; banter full of inflated, ridiculous spy jargon; songs with names like "Temptation in Tehran" and

"That Was My Fake Identity—My Real One Would Blow Your Mind." The fact that they were identical enhanced the joke—was probably responsible for more than half their bookings.

[

] They decided to go. The Events Coordinator had invited them to join a tour of Israel organized by the magazine. Their plane tickets would be fully comped; their hotel rooms partially so. They would be the entertainment—the washed-up, offbeat quirk factor. Jerry and his wife Sarah decided to make a family trip of it; bring the girls along. Leo considered asking the lawyer next door to water his plants while he was away. He came close to asking her several times in the elevator but ultimately decided that the plants were past their prime, stuffed them into Hefty bags and tossed them down the trash chute.

During the months leading up to the trip, the twins received regular mailings from *Goliath's Harmonica*. There were itineraries, and revised itineraries. There were votes for excursions to the Galilee versus the Negev. There were also T-shirts with the *Goliath's Harmonica* logo, which they were instructed to wear to the airport. The T-shirts were orange, and the logo was a drawing of a large hand with a miniscule harmonica cradled in its palm.

Jerry called to say that his daughters had insisted on wearing their kid-sized shirts immediately. They were already covered with tomato sauce.

"Not a bad logo, right? Sarah likes it."

Leo glanced at his own T-shirt, sitting in its plastic wrap on the kitchen counter. If he and Marina had still been married, there would have been two shirts. She would have taken a knife and slit the packaging on hers with a look of cool concentration, then shaken it out and held it in the air at arm's length.

She would have said, "This clothing is peculiar, I think."

[

] Marina was a Ukrainian computer scientist with fine bones and long, straight, dirty blond hair. She and Leo had been together for a total of fifteen years—nine of dating and six of marriage. Their dorm rooms were next to each other sophomore year at college, and he'd often found himself sitting cross-legged on her carpet at the end of the day. She didn't talk much. She responded to his jokes with quizzical looks. On her bedside table was a black and white photo of a balding man with glasses and an enormous, slightly off-center bowtie.

"Is that your grandfather?" Leo asked during one of his early visits.

Marina got up and brushed her fingers against the cheek of the man in the photo.

"No!" she said, laughing. "He is Vladimir Horowitz! The piano player!"

She was never nearly as amused when he was actually trying to make her laugh. She was distant, inscrutable, nimbly evasive. One night she decided that he should stay. She stood and stripped swiftly down to her underwear. Her legs were pale and lean. Her panties were white cotton, with something illegible—a designer's signature, maybe?—scrawled across the waistband.

Jerry met Sarah Aliza Weinstock that same year. Sarah was all breasts and freckles. She was an architecture student down in New Orleans, visiting Columbia for the birthday of an ugly cousin of whom she was fiercely protective. Jerry met her at a party and that was it. All he would talk about.

Sarah Aliza Weinstock had dropped out of an anthropology class because the teacher was a white woman who wore bone necklaces and gushed about the month she'd spent living with her *Zulu brothers and sisters*, who were *some of the most dignified people she had ever met*. Sarah Aliza Weinstock had designed an addition to the White House for one of her classes, and she now used the model to store her stockings and underwear.

Sarah Aliza Weinstock was hoping to come up north for grad school.

[
] Leo joined his brother on one of his many trips to New Orleans, and brought Marina along. The debauchery was not to her liking. She leapt over piles of puke with an affronted sort of precision.

"The birds are sick in this area," she said, pointing at a mangy pigeon. "See! Like a rat."

Jerry and Sarah weren't listening. Sarah's tight T-shirts and frizzy hair had Leo's brother looking crazed—his hands and lips were on her in the street, in cabs, in restaurants. Leo considered ending it with Marina but turned toward her instead. She was a cool, square room at the end of a hallway. She was a small white envelope waiting for him to slip inside and seal himself in, and so he did.

] At the airport, the orange T-shirts were easy to spot. Jerry, Sarah, and the girls were there already and Leo walked toward them, filled with sudden loathing for his luggage set. Most members of the *Goliath's Harmonica* group were a few years out of college, by the looks of it, and had well-worn backpacks at their feet that screamed of lustful, pennilessly decadent trips across Europe. Leo's nieces had small pink suitcases on wheels. On Leo's own shoulder was a neat, cylindrical tote in charcoal gray, emblazoned with a pattern of black abstractions that looked a bit like seahorses. Somewhere in the bowels of the airport, heading toward the plane, were two more matching pieces. He'd carefully packed them all the night before, crossing the arms of his long-sleeved shirts over the torsos as though arranging the limbs of corpses.

"Leo!"

Was he imagining it—

"My twin in sin!"

—or had Jerry developed the habit of talking to him in an over-amplified voice, as though his muted marriage, his divorce, his child-lessness, had rendered him deaf and dumb? Leo set down his depressing seahorse tote and kissed his nieces. They were six, four, and two now, and smelled like jam.

[

] On the airplane, he was relieved to find himself seated next to two group members his side of thirty: a pair of lesbians with mismatched names. Glen had long blond curls, and a turquoise necklace resting crookedly atop her breasts. She should have been named something softer. Sissy, maybe. One of those names that was so sweet it was almost a joke. Lila, meanwhile, was short, with cropped hair and expensive-looking track shoes. They'd both done freelance work for the magazine —Glen had taken the photos accompanying a series of articles about musicians, and Lila had done some web design.

"Tell him about that hippie sitar-player on the farm," Lila said.

"Oh, he wasn't so bad."

"He wanted you to shoot him nude! I'm telling you, those old hippies think they can turn us. They think they're so *in touch*—like their dicks are some kind of magical Peruvian rain sticks or something."

Leo had been adopted several months earlier by a pair of lesbians, at a wedding he'd attended alone. He'd danced with the plainer one several times, and the prettier one once. Now, he leaned back in his seat and prepared to sum himself up in a way that was just sad enough, just funny enough. He decided which tragicomic dating stories to tell.

[

] The group arrived at the hotel in Jerusalem just before midnight. Everyone else stumbled off immediately in search of their beds, but Leo was overcome with the need to make sure the handling company had delivered his guitar intact. He lingered at the reception desk in the cavernous marble lobby, arguing with a succession of hotel employees about the existence of the guitar, his right to claim it, and the outdated photo on his passport. By the time he had the familiar black case in hand, the room was deserted. His footsteps echoed as he followed a surly, middle-aged bellhop into the elevator. A cigarette poked out of the bellhop's vest pocket, and the outline of a pack showed through his trousers. He raised his eyebrows impatiently and motioned for Leo to press the button.

Up on the ninth floor the hallway stretched out before them, endless, smelling of stale, recycled air and shampooed carpet. When, at long last, they reached the door to Leo's room, he gave the bellhop an over-sized tip and carried everything inside himself. Then he propped his guitar against the wall opposite his bed, ripped the sheets down hungrily, and threw himself onto the mattress.

[

] *In eighth grade, Erica Cohen and Melissa Reinhopf wore matching dresses to a birthday party. They were white, spaghetti strap dresses, with a floppy yellow flower sitting at the bottom of each V-neck. Erica sat between Melissa's legs and allowed her friend to brush and stroke her hair, twisting it into a French braid. They kept saying it,* French braid, French braid. I want a French braid. Yes, I know how to do a French braid! Wow, thanks, you make the best French braids. *They were silly and maddening and beautiful.*

This was when the truth about the twins had already begun to push its way out of the ground, an abstract sculpture rising up between their mother's tulips. They hadn't invited it, this twisted form, weighty and solid, growing taller each day. They didn't quite understand it. But there it was, looming. Their difference. They still slept, in those days, with their guitars at the feet of their beds, standing sentry in parallel. They still woke within seconds of each other, spoke with rhythms and inflections that belonged to both of them but no one else.

But Jerry was looking at the girls in their matching dresses like they were something he might be able to have. Maybe. Maybe they would laugh at him, or maybe they would let him brush up against their shoulders, lean in close to ask them questions.

He would try.

[

] Leo woke alone, picturing Glen and Lila naked. It was just limbs and tangled sheets, but it was them. His lone guitar regarded him reproachfully from across the room.

[

] At breakfast, the Events Coordinator addressed the group. He was a tall, wiry kid, with a head of black corkscrew curls that looked like a wig from a biblically themed high-school play. The general effect was that of Samson before the weightlifting—or one of Joseph's brothers, maybe.

"In the morning, we'll check out some standard, touristy places," he said. "Then, later in the day, we'll do it *Goliath's Harmonica* style."

Leo sipped his weak, lukewarm hotel coffee. The Events Coordinator used the phrase *Hidden Jerusalem* several times.

"To paraphrase our monthly column," he said, "we'll be meeting a *Legend No One Knows*."

[

] At four o'clock, they all stood sweating outside the apartment of Boaz Livni. In the early years of the State, he'd been the muse for a female painter named Dina Berman. She'd painted him nude, in Technicolor. The scenes and poses were surreal: In one painting, the muse stood in a field strewn with dried-out onions, strumming the tines of a rake as though it were a musical instrument. In another, he sat on a sofa with a pineapple between his legs. Berman was a source of controversy in Israel—some considered her the artistic voice of the country in the fifties and early sixties; others thought her work hedonistic, her talents questionable—but no one had known the identity of her muse until an arts reporter tracked him down several years after Berman's death. The Events Coordinator had handed out copies of the exposé article and color images of some of Berman's better-known works in the bus on the way over. He'd seemed giddy, as though he were leading the group on a covert mission to meet an exiled monarch.

[

] The door was opened by a mousy woman in a long skirt and dirty tennis shoes. She nodded curtly, and led them inside. The apartment was small and dim. There were some cookies set out on a coffee table in the living room, on a series of yellowing lace doilies. Boaz, stooped and liver-spotted, with his shirt tucked neatly into his slacks, regarded the group with confusion. He turned and spoke softly in Hebrew to the woman in the tennis shoes.

"Mr. Livni was expecting schoolchildren," she said in a faint British accent. Who was she? Daughter? Lover? Eldercare attendant? No explanation was given. There was a small hole near the armpit of her white button-down blouse. "Last year a school organized to send some students for a visit." She gestured at a pile of worn children's books sitting next to the cookies. "He read to them."

The room smelled faintly of urine. The Events Coordinator stepped forward and extended his hand. At some point during the course of the hot morning, he'd drawn his Samson hair back into a little stump of a ponytail, and Boaz gazed at him with suspicion. An honor, the Events Coordinator said. An important place in history. Amazing paintings. Boaz's companion did not translate any of this, either because the old man knew enough English to understand it, or because she didn't think it worthwhile.

"When that article came out, it must have been like Deep Throat!" The Events Coordinator persisted. "After all those years, revealing yourself . . ."

This the woman in the tennis shoes attempted to translate, with a wrinkled brow. Boaz wrinkled his brow as well, and held a hand questioningly to his throat.

"Sorry," the woman said. "His throat? We don't understand."

[

] Eventually, the former muse salvaged the situation for himself by flitting his bleary eyes around the room until they landed on a couple of attractive female *Goliath's Harmonica* readers. He motioned for them to come over and they sat down at his feet, arranging their limbs in lithe, yoga-like poses. He leaned forward to examine the beaded necklace one of them wore, the embroidered collar on the other one's shirt. Grinning, he plucked the reproductions of his youthful, naked self from the girls' laps and held them in the air.

"I am here," he said, pointing first at the pictures and then at his chest.

[

] Back at the hotel, Jerry knocked on Leo's door.

"That was weird," he said, walking straight to the window.

"Yeah."

"Some of those paintings are wild, though. You ever seen them before?"

A beam of pinkish, early evening light fell through the drapes as Jerry parted them.

"No."

"I'm really glad we came, man. It's your first trip, isn't it? Since—"

[

] When you got divorced, everyone told you to travel. Distance and diversion; colors, spices and women . . . Leo could understand why it seemed like a good idea. But he hadn't done it. He had gone, instead, to Jerry's house. They'd turned the den into a bedroom for him. There was a pullout sofa, and an ugly but extremely comfortable brown velour blanket. He'd stayed for almost three weeks, drinking tea each night from a mug that said *Tot Tunes: It's Never Too Early for Music!*

[

] "Your view is better than ours," Jerry said now, turning from the window. "We've got the parking lot." He walked toward Leo's guitar, rapped lightly on the case with his knuckles. "Want to practice tonight? When the kids are in bed?"

Their first performance for the *Goliath's Harmonica* group was scheduled for the next night, and Leo had been on the verge of suggesting a practice session himself.

"I can't." His brother looked surprised. "I have plans."

[

] As soon as Jerry was gone, Leo went in search of the lesbians. He knew their room was between his and the elevator, and he thought he might remember the number. Lila came to the door in a towel. Her hair was wet, slicked back—it made him think of handsome young guys in Mafia movies. He hadn't realized just how short she was. Her collarbone looked nice.

"It's Leo!"

Glen stepped out of the bathroom in a green dress, slipping an earring into her ear.

[

] Tucked behind a hedge of fragrant bougainvillea was the only restaurant in Jerusalem that served seafood. There was an air of conspiratorial defiance to the place; the waiter gave them long smiles and too much eye contact as he rattled off the list of profoundly unkosher specials. Leo had never liked slimy, quivering things on his plate. After perusing the whimsically translated English version of the menu, he ordered the only item that was breaded.

The outdoor patio where they sat was almost empty. There were candles lit on all the tables, but only one diner aside from Leo, Glen, and Lila—a Filipina woman sitting alone, popping slippery gray things the size of chicken nuggets into her mouth. The waiter came and went, touching the tabletops, rearranging silverware and flowers. Lila ordered a bottle of wine, and then a second. It was beginning to feel as though they were in a play about an eternal wait for seafood. An evening breeze, smelling of saltwater and bougainvillea, pressed itself against their hair and skin. The Filipina woman paid her check and got up to leave. She was short and compact, with wide shoulders and a busy way of walking. She smiled at Leo.

"Come have some wine," Lila said.

[

] Her name, her Filipino name, was a little tricky. She told them to call her CeCe. She had been in Israel for five years, taking care of a sick child.

"Soon he will have seventeen years." She wrapped both hands around the bowl of her wine glass as though it were a coffee mug, and drank quickly. "But his mind is like a baby." She shrugged. "He loves me. So I am not leaving him."

She had a husband overseas, in America. He'd worked for a while at a nursing home in Bet Shemesh, then heard from a cousin in New Jersey about a job.

"This certain man in America made promises." She shrugged again. "And my husband, he believed."

By the time their food finally arrived, Leo was tipsy enough to experience his surprise as something profound. The ground had shifted beneath him. Something was wrong. There was a small octopus on his plate.

He summoned the waiter back. "Breaded," he said, too loudly. "Crumbs? Fried?" He had pictured calamari; something he could pretend was onion rings. The waiter fetched a menu and leaned over Leo's shoulder, pointing at the item he'd selected.

"Ah. Bread."

"Right. See? This isn't breaded."

"Bread, yes." The waiter indicated three soggy beige lumps on the rim of Leo's plate. There was a sprig of parsley on each lump.

"Sweetbreads!" Glen laughed. "It must be some kind of seafood interpretation of sweetbreads."

Leo waved the waiter away, defeated. CeCe reached over him and began to cut the tentacled object he'd ordered. It jiggled under her knife.

"See?" She took a forkful into her own mouth. Her lips glistened. "Mmm. You try."

[

] With a belly full of slime and alcohol, Leo felt more like he'd had a series of toxic martinis than like he'd had a meal. He stepped out onto the street without looking, and Lila pulled him back. The four of them were headed toward the hotel. Someone had said something about the bar.

"Are you sure it will be open?" Leo asked, for the third or fourth time. "Doesn't it close at ten or something?"

"It'll be fine."

"Isn't it late?"

Glen and Lila exchanged looks, and Glen pulled CeCe ahead. He was drunk, but he finally saw it. They were giving him more time with her; with CeCe.

Did he want her? He watched her walking side by side with Glen. Her calves were solid, and her back was remarkably straight. She was about five years older than him—or a year or so younger; he couldn't tell. She was good at feeding people. She wore red Capri pants and a sleeveless black tank top with a polo collar.

Yes.

He did.

How he loved his lesbian wingmen! Lila, hard-bodied little animal.

She could outrun anyone, he was sure. And Glen with her soft, soft ass, swinging around under that green dress. He loved her and her jewelry.

[

] When he woke the next morning, CeCe was standing naked by the window, the hotel bathrobe pooled at her feet. His body remembered everything—the warmth was still there in his sinews. It was as if he'd been given a pounding massage, then all the healing steam baths in Eastern Europe, and then a fuck.

He walked up behind her and crossed his arms over her belly. The curtains were still parted a bit where Jerry had opened them, and down below a group of young Hassidic men rushed across the street in a pack, their swinging arms and pumping legs creating the impression of a single, roving organism. He leaned down and nuzzled the back of CeCe's neck. She rocked her pelvis a bit, and he slipped a finger inside her.

"Someone was knocking," she said, rapping the air with her fist. "A man with your same face."

Leo stilled his finger, waiting for her to continue. She shrugged.

"He went away."

] Sovereignty

I am the envy of womankind, or so my friends proclaim. When the twins turned one and I was nearly forty, my husband gave me two gifts: antique amethyst earrings from the turn of the century and a trip to wherever I chose.

Which is why I find myself, alone, in a taxi that strains up the last hill to curve into Jerusalem. I walked out of the airport woozy from the half-sleep of the plane into a clamor of waiting relatives—not mine—and drivers calling out directives in such a cacophony that all I could say was "Jerusalem?" again and again until one of them beckoned me decisively into his car.

I pried sweaty fingers from my suitcase, handing it over, and held myself upright, away from the plastic of the back seat.

"No water?" said the driver, giving me an unopened bottle. "Every one here need water. Your first time, yes?"

No.

Can it be me, rising out of the desert into the rounded hills, bare when I knew them, breasts of hills, now glittery with thousands of lights?

The windows open suddenly. These inhabited hills are unfamiliar, but the air is a perfume I know—elixir of cypress and stone, lavender and rosemary.

I have not been to Israel for twenty years.

Ha-melekh daveed, I tell the driver. When I lived in this city as a student, I certainly did not stay at the King David Hotel. But I am a grown-up now, mother of two, I remind myself. For seven days I will not be an appendage to infants or the list-making counterpart to a frazzled, sleep-deprived husband. I am, astonishingly, by myself.

Can there be anyone more ecstatic than a woman who closes and locks her hotel door to gaze upon an empty room, a bed of pressed, turned-down linens and bounty of pillows, with the guarantee that no relentless cry will drill through her brain for an entire night?

In a new silk nightgown, unstained by spit or clutching hands, I walk to the window and part the curtains. There lies the city in her magnificence. Below me, the garden of the hotel, and beneath the garden, the terraced valley. I lift my eyes to the evening light of Jerusalem, gleaming tips of domes and cupolas. As I stretch my arms euphorically above my head, the last filaments of day ease from the sky.

Whose body is it? I think, turning toward my reflection. My breasts, ornaments of desire, utilitarian fuel pumps, are returned to my sole possession. I am going to take a long bath, without interruption.

Ahava bath gel, spilled unstintingly, becomes a voluminous, milky foam into which I sink with an audible sigh. Two pink-brown dots poke through the bubbles, like a naughty Victorian postcard. Since I became pregnant they've changed color, I observe for the hundredth time. Now they are off duty.

I turn through the hotel magazine, its pages dampening, comparing myself to the twenty-year-old models in tourism ads. It took a year to lose the weight of two babies, my body swelling to unprecedented oriels and cambers, like the ship of a foreign land or a building from another era, and then, infinitesimally, over three hundred and sixty-five days, deflating until I recognized its pristine, tended guise.

As of this birthday, I will formally attain middle age. But I am so elated by the reemergence of my self that I feel uncannily young, as if I am newly arriving from the exile of my American life to this unknown city.

Where, on the first night, as I wandered through leafy streets, purposefully and then truly lost while looking for something to eat, I met him, the one who guided me out of the alleyways, brown beret on his shoulder, gun at his back, Gilad, who became, effortlessly, my first love.

Suddenly I'm starving. I walk dripping wet to the closet—no one is watching—and enfold myself in the luxuriant robe of the hotel. Lying on the bedspread, I scrutinize the room service menu, salivating over food I do not usually eat.

I can order anything.

I can eat as slowly as I please.

I can sit without moving for the length of the meal.

A delicious languor suffuses me, not the bone fatigue of working motherhood, but the soothing flush of the scented bath and the vista of inconsequential choices I can make, an inner landscape as seductive as the one beyond my window.

At the door, my husband, a baby in each arm, said goodbye extravagantly. "Do what you want and spend whatever you like."

I pick up the phone, but the appetite stirred by the menu is one the King David room service cannot satisfy. I want street food, hummus and *ful*, like the plate I shared with Gilad at Abu Shukri, where he showed me how to rip steaming pita and scoop up the savory paste, feeding me, and I him, until we were barely able to walk back to his room.

I know I should sleep, but my heart is awake, the city expectant, intimate. I put on my favorite jeans and exult in the ease with which I can zip them up. Turning on the radio, I am prancing around the room in my tank top and Fryes, a rock 'n' roll mama in the city of David.

But when I leave the hotel, the air on my bare arms is biting, and I need to return for a jacket. Hesitant, retreating, I ask the concierge: "It's okay to go to the Old City at night?"

He looks at me as if I'm crazy. "Alone? No, madame," he says gravely. "I cannot advise it."

Instead, he directs me downtown, where I can get pizza or hummus; it's not too late.

Not too late. Not too late. My feet chant as they make an unnatural clatter on the darkened road. I used to walk everywhere, reveling in the shelter of overhung pathways, narrow staircases linking the tranquil streets, no one in sight, the peace of Jerusalem.

I want to be fearless, to stride with self-contained delight. But the emptiness tonight is menacing. My body remembers exactly where to go, but until I reach the outdoor cafés, the street musicians, I'm consigned to a Jerusalem of shadow and solitude. Behind me, in the jeweled light of the hotel lobby, are clusters of polished French mothers and their languid daughters, rotund Israeli diplomats, bellhops lingering. But around me is silence, piles of rubble and springy weeds between the dimmed, prosperous buildings, the city a palimpsest.

Racing forward, I come to the maze of tiny lanes that open to the plaza. I am forty and timid, but at every corner I meet myself, girl of bewildered hopefulness, Gilad bent over me, my face raised to heaven.

His language: The way his throat shaped the letter *resh*, grounded, nothing like the effete way we said it in New York, or his delicate *lamed*, my fingers in his mouth as I tried to learn how to say it from inside him. *Ohev otakh ba-laila*: Even when he told me he loved me, I imitated the sounds, determined to master them.

In the years after Gilad, whenever I was between boyfriends, I would fall asleep by imagining my hands on either side of his face. I could summon the bones beneath his caramel skin, flecked, transparent eyes searching mine, asking something of me I was not prepared to offer.

No American boys looked like Gilad. All-night training hikes and impossible, immediate orders from his commander were responsible for a body whose muscles could be named as if Adam himself were the model. Like many an American girl before me, I lied to my parents, skipping classes to be with him, prone, for whatever minutes either of us could salvage.

Panting up to Kikar Tzion, I want to eat the past, take possession of it so that it will never abandon me. I am looking for him, the boy-man who did not understand half the words I spoke and could not get enough of my body.

Now there are couples tangled in each other, expressive faces rapt in conversation, a girl's hand thrust into a boy's back pocket. Where is she, the girl I was, ardent, intrepid, convinced of an unbound future in which sorrow and disappointment would abate to nothing? Believing each dawn, eternally, in transformation.

There is a soldier approaching me. His stride, the cock of his head, eager, inquisitive: I am rushing toward him, tossed through time, hastening to Gilad, when I see at the edge of my consciousness a scurrying ghost.

Convinced someone is shadowing me, I turn to confront him.

An older woman, desperate, is looking directly at me.

"Who are you?" I demand, hands on hips, as she imitates me, mocking.

She is wearing my jeans. I am looking in the mirror of a closed boutique.

Delusional. Demented. Deranged. Thank God no one can see me. I am laughing out loud on Ben Yehuda Street.

The musicians, wary, stop their play.

I want to stand in the way of the still-approaching soldier, bring him into my house, unbutton his shirt tenderly, urge him to rest while I make him food so tempting he will not return to his unit. I want to bathe him and anoint his skin, wrap him in newly washed sheets while I sing to him of protecting angels, Mikha-El, Gavri-El, Uri-El, Refa-El. And above us, above all, securing his safety, Rachamim, God of a mother's ferocious, implacable mercy.

Even if Gilad were here, on my bed in the King David Hotel, to which I have fled by taxi, thrusting against the revolving door to jab the elevator button, fling myself, still clothed, beneath the covers, reaching for the phone; even if his right hand were on my breast, his left cradling me, I would not be young. And Gilad would be—how can I not have seen it—a gray-haired father, too old to serve.

I have a tiny daughter and a son. My heart is a wilderness, terrible as an army with banners, cruel as the grave.

"I want to be alive while I'm alive!" I cry out to my husband across the Atlantic, in the middle of his work day.

"Of course you do," he says gently. "Who doesn't?"

] The Liars

I was twenty-six years old and not, perhaps, as mature as I should have been. I had been sheltered from most of life's hardships, except for the sickness and death of my father ten years earlier and even that I had not yet registered as anything other than the kind of loss it was simply required, in the British manner, to suck up and move past.

I was staying in Jerusalem with Y. Ravny, who everybody called "Ravi." He was an Israeli poet, recently turned fifty, with a solid reputation, although, to his chagrin, perhaps more as a scholar and translator than as a poet. His poems, laconic, guarded, literary, cleverly allusive, were not universally admired. I had met him in 1974 while I was (officially) studying for my D.Phil. at Oxford. Unofficially, I was a fool for love, a habitual drinker and doper, a bit of a fuck up. Worst of all, among the dirty veils of illusion on offer to ambitious youth, I had plucked the mask of a promising young poet. I wore it with pride, although my output and talent were incommensurate with self-assurance.

Ravi had spent ten years editing what would become the seminal scholarly Oxford edition of Hebrew verse from biblical times to the present. Toward the end of his labors, he had grown nervous about some of the English locutions used in the Introduction, for although he was American-born and had lived on and off in the United States for many years, Hebrew had been the first language in his New York Zionist household. He enlisted my help for some minor editing. I was honored, although I couldn't help thinking that Ravi's professed weakness in English was a bit of a pose: a political maneuver to assert his Israeli identity. For my re-arrangement of the syntax in three of his sentences I received a generous thank you in the Acknowledgments to the anthology, but a bigger reward awaited me: an invitation to spend Passover in Jerusalem.

I was in awe of the poet's set-up, which seemed to have sprung unaltered from my own generally distorting but vivid romantic imagination. The Ravnys' old stone house was halfway up a sloping street in Abu Tor, a sleepy neighborhood off the main road to Bethlehem that still featured open space between the homes: small areas of high grass and rocks bordered by eucalyptus trees and scattered with wild flowers. Outside the basement apartment at 10 Silk Street, an old woman fed scrawny chickens in a broad courtyard. At the side were stairs that led to a roseate iron door adorned with a raised pattern of nippled dots in small circles: music, a Boccherini cello concerto, issued through the open windows, while sunlight flowed in the opposite direction. A German Shepherd, Dag, roused from his mid-afternoon stupor on the top step, barked like crazy in the garden.

"It's a snake." Ravi said calmly, pushing open the door and looking over into the garden, "He's found a snake."

A snake in a poet's backyard! What could be better? Well, a "difficult" artist wife with the almost-beautiful looks of the truly beautiful for starters. And there she was, Avital Arbell-Ravny, disappearing down a serpentine path at the foot of the garden in the direction of her rented studio. Ravi watched her skirt two huge, green garbage dumpsters that blocked her route, and I watched too, trying to make my gaze neutral and impatient. Avital was not the first wife of course, or even the second, but a woman only a few years older than myself. On this burning afternoon, her long black hair was piled in an uncharacteristically prim bun on top of her head. At three o'clock the previous morning, jet-lagged and sleepless, I had turned in my sofa-bed to watch her walk naked through the book-lined study that had been assigned to me for the night. She had crossed in thin light through to the kitchen and returned a moment later holding a glass of water before her like a candle. Her breasts were heavy and full, the curve of her thighs illuminated white and scarred in a sudden shaft of moonlight. Travel can truly broaden the mind.

Ravi stood framed by the doorway in an oblong of light that seemed to represent the transcendent space to which his poems aspired. From my point of view, everything about him was perfect. He smoked, and coughed dramatically. His voice had a tenebrous roughness calibrated by two packs of TIME (the cheap Israeli cigarette) a day. Even his hair, raked high and back like the head of a stiff paintbrush soaked in grey, seemed to bespeak the life of art, if only because it revealed a daunting Shakespearean forehead. To complete the picture there was the man's history of personal heroism, rarely alluded to by the poet but readily available if you wanted to take a bus ride to the British Council library in the Terra Sancta building and peruse, as I had, accounts of the Battle for Jerusalem during the Israeli War of Independence in 1948. Y. Ravny, twenty-three years old, and recently arrived in Palestine after working two and a half years in Paris at a home for the displaced children of Holocaust victims, had joined the Haganah. Within months he was lugging a Beza machine gun to a rock outcropping near Sheikh Jarrah ready to give his life in a do or die attempt to hold back the Arab Legion. He had taken out one armored car and damaged two others. The tiny force to which he belonged had lost more than half its men but, through a combination of luck, guile, and astonishing bravery under fire, had emerged victorious. Behind the rock next to Ravi his closest friend lay with his head sundered as if parted by a meat axe.

Sitting in the incongruous English atmosphere of the library—a woman in a straw hat was returning two novels by Iris Murdoch—I thought of Yeats's lines in memory of his doomed friend, the Renaissance man, Major Robert Gregory: "Soldier, scholar, horseman he. / What made us dream that he could comb grey hair?" But Ravi *had* lived to comb gray hair; and he had maintained his military bearing. He walked with shoulders back and chest puffed out, as if by standing straight he could put behind him the entire bent and crooked history of the Jewish Diaspora.

A week went by. At night there were small social gatherings around a coffee table in the front room. The local visitors, who would arrive around nine, materialized in the house without knocking, and frequently, I understood, without having been invited. Everyone enjoyed this studied informality, the appearance of spontaneity and looseness. Thrillingly, to my apprehension, the guests were invariably from the worlds of art or literature and this fact erased the awkwardness I felt when the conversation inevitably drifted into Hebrew, and I was left grinning and nodding my head to the unknown music of the language. On Friday night, an English couple, the husband a painter, the wife a poet, came for dinner. Like me, they had been in the city for a week.

Both their names were familiar to me: They were British culture figures from the second, or maybe third tier—not the American heavy hitters—Edmund Wilson, Robert Lowell, Bob Dylan!—whose visits to Jerusalem Ravi had so amusingly described to an entranced crowd in the snug of The King's Head in Oxford. For this was 1975, and the big-shot foreign writers who, in the aftermath of plucky Israel's victory in the Six Day War, had made the city a must-see stop on the travel itinerary—like Paris or Florence—had, after war-machine Israel's Yom Kippur triumph, abruptly scattered to be replaced by lower profiles. Israel, as Lowell himself told Ravi in a letter, was back "on the wrong side of the stockade."

Avital, wearing a long, white, embroidered Bedouin dress, refilled the olive dish. Ravi topped up the whiskey glasses. The delights and truancies of language were his favorite topics for discussion. There was much talk of etymology and definition interrupted by frequent forays into the study to check dictionaries for the root or meaning of certain words. My compatriots loved it. And so did I, theoretically anyway, or until I realized toward midnight on this ritually insecure Sabbath evening (there were no candles, no braided challah) that I was profoundly, unutterably, and completely bored.

Across the street in a small stone house surrounded by scented pines lived a young couple, Ilan and Michal Delisboa with *their* German Shepherd, Kush. Ilan, whom I had met briefly on my first walk up dusty Silk Street, had departed to serve the annual two months reserve duty in the army mandated for all Israeli men over the age of twenty-one. Left alone, his wife, a kindergarten teacher with a neo-hippie style—peasant shirts, jeans, wrists heavy with silver bracelets—came home, bought groceries, tended her garden, walked the dog, made dinner, listened to music and danced by herself in the couples' sparsely furnished living room. Walking Dag shortly after sunset (slivers of singed orange peel in the sky), I had paused to watch her on two consecutive evenings as she moved though half-shadows thrown by a dim, shaded yellow bulb. Her long, dark hair flapped over her face like a scarf. I had no clear picture of her features. I had only seen her on the street from a distance. She might have been the ugliest woman in the world (although of course something told me that she wasn't) and yet, in the ten years of focused sexual desire I had experienced since my sixteenth birthday (twelve to fifteen had blurred around brassieres and breasts) I had never wanted to go to bed with anybody more. It wasn't only that Michal represented a counterpoint to the tedium at Ravi's but also her symbolic status as an ur-Sabra (the cactus fruit, spiky on the outside but with a mushy pulp, from which all native-born Israelis took their collective nickname) magnetized me: She was the unattainable Israeli beauty, a Jewish forbidden fruit, tastier, I was sure, than the ripe split figs I had filched from Ravi's kitchen to eat while walking his dog. And then, early in the morning after the first seder, a festive, subversive poets' and artists' seder of wine and song with much comico-scholarly undermining of rabbinical nonsense, I saw her close up. Of course she was beautiful, with the Tartar features that some Jewish women own because willingly or unwillingly their ancestors rolled in the hay with neighbors from the Caucuses. I approached with Dag and she with her dog. The dawn unfolded like a bolt of pink cloth across the sky. "Shalom," she said, but the curse of Moses' hot coal was on my tongue and all I could do was stammer, smile hello and hope that our respective leashes would become entangled, but they didn't.

While I dreamed of having an affair, Ravi was in the midst of one. After he had toured me around the bars of Jerusalem (we drove in his tiny Renault from spot to spot), he would drop me back at Silk Street, then take off again for his 2 A.M. to 5 A.M. shift. Avital slept through her husband's nocturnal wanderings, or perhaps she didn't. But if there was anger, it was well hidden from me. If drinking and carousing kept Ravi happy, then so be it. She was, after all, an artist herself, and aware of the struggle. She knew in her bones Wordsworth's dark summary: "We poets in our youth begin in gladness; / But thereof comes in the end despondency and madness."

On the first Friday morning after Passover had ended, Ravi asked me to meet him at Kadosh Brothers, a three-table patisserie and coffee shop on Shlomzion Hamalka Street behind the Post Office. I arrived at eleven o'clock, the appointed hour. Ravi was already there, nursing an espresso. He was not alone. Michal was beside him. Did she have her hand on his knee? If so, she quickly removed it. Before I could properly digest the scene, Avital arrived. She came through the door in a light raincoat and wearing a red beret. "So," she said, addressing Michal while unbuckling her belt. "Are you fucking my husband?" What followed was denial and evasion, imaginative riffs and explanations, good and bad poetry, tears and confusion. I felt my cheeks burn. I was being used. I had been brought along to act as a firewall but I was getting scorched myself. It began to rain, warm fat drops that we had prayed for only days earlier. Ravi ordered a slice of cheesecake. Michal left. For a while, husband and wife held hands. The world had shifted but it had not been rocked off its axis.

I had one more week in Jerusalem. I moved out of 10 Silk Street and into a cheap hotel near the Damascus Gate. At night I made my own way around town. I saw them everywhere, the liars; at the Khan night club down by the railway station where at 3 A.M. the local hookers drank black Russians, smoked, and shaped their guttural Hebrew into love hearts, at the Piano Bar on Bezalel Street, whiskey soaked, their arms around each other, and, for the last time, one chilly dawn, the sky hung with orange lanterns, in the market at Mahane Yehuda when a truckload of parsley edged forward to reveal the lovers in a small café, the two of them in earnest conversation, hands clasped, heads inclined, and faces marked with the desperate looks that say "This is the end."

All gone, all gone: Ravi, Dag the dog, Avital, the house on Silk Street, presently a playground, the whores down at the Khan, the jazz men from the Piano Bar; my sweet Bohemian Jerusalem, city of honeysuckle and betrayal, and all that is left are her dusty skirts, as if she was merely Tel-Aviv's shabby Orthodox auntie, custodian to one of God's many homes, the one He no longer visits.

] Come on Zion Put Your Hands Together

South through the desert. Crossing and re-crossing the green line like a child's toy on a spring. Through the windowpane's glare, the rockscape: shuddering with speed.

A dry spiced heat from the vents, the smell of the desert. On the wheel of the flimsy rental car, his hands.

August 2000.

In their years of shared travel—airport security and currency-exchange kiosks, potholed roads and crowded conference rooms with chain-smoking translators—it had been the place, the only place, she'd been certain they'd never go.

He was Palestinian by birth, British by citizenship and principle. He hadn't set foot in Israel or the territories since boyhood—he'd seen no need to visit, he knew oppression and how it dragged the mind backward. She was a Jewish Londoner, atheist, undeterrable in her activism. It was these facts, along with the fierce honesty they were known for, that placed them at the top of their field. Corporations, foundations, offices of foreign governments called for Almasi and Reed Mediation Consultants when conflicts became intractable. Ahmed Almasi and Karen Reed made their name by listening vigorously; instigating or calming as the situation required; infusing in combatants a stamina built on the belief that if one simply had the strength to keep talking, differences could be resolved. They taught this faith in Bosnia, Rwanda, Ireland. Knowledge of the other was possible, they maintained, only when one dared take taboos head-on. If this principle did not persuade and if all else failed, they let be known their personal stories. Her grandparents: Dachau survivors who spoke nothing of the camp, only reiterated to their granddaughter that the world was a battle for freedom. His parents' suffering under Israeli rule, up to the day the older cousin he'd worshiped had been murdered and they'd fled. The accusation was false; the cousin had not collaborated. Had simply served coffee to the two Israelis waiting for their car to be repaired.

So, Ahmed told the stone-faced adversaries, he understood oppression. And how it shrank one's worldview to a pinhole. What he did not say, though to Karen's ears the conviction thundered beneath his speech: He knew enough to sever his life from it all.

Where race was at issue, Almasi and Reed made a point of shocking with their own level of comfort. This coffee tastes like piss, he declared during one break at a Brooklyn mediation. The food had been provided by a kosher caterer. She said, I apologize on behalf on my people. Reparations will be required, he growled. Gathered around the pastry table, the participants in the Black-Jewish dialogue looked bewildered, then relaxed visibly.

Between themselves, Ahmed and Karen had an agreement: They did not take Israeli-Palestinian cases. They no longer discussed in detail events of the Middle East. Their hopes for the region were identical but when they took up the topic they inflamed one another. They'd endured trans-Atlantic hauls on which their voices rose over a shared newspaper, other passengers glaring in the tight confines of the tin can bearing them over the ocean at an impossibly slow speed; they'd arrived, sapped, at the far shore's blaring airport and the conclusion that their differences were matters of inflection. They'd learned, in the manner of a long-married couple, to provoke and to trust. Above all, to trust. Once a limping white-haired woman at a Sidney reception had singled out Karen. Identifying herself as a member of the hosting organization, the woman lilted, We've covered everything. So you don't have to worry. I know you Jews hate to pay the bill. Before Karen had absorbed the remark, Ahmed rose and informed the woman that she was to leave. A crowd gathered. It's always the sinned-against who walk out in protest, Ahmed said. But that's wrong. The racists are the one who need to leave the party. The woman left, but not before receiving a further blast of Ahmed's fury. Tears made rivulets in the woman's face-powder. Ahmed watched the limping retreat of her broad figure. Drink in hand, he stared stonily out the window before shrugging off the incident.

Ahmed in an argument was a wolf shaking its prey long after its neck was broken. He had an implausible, impossible personality for a mediator; he strode past niceties, brushed straight past the tiresome process of building trust, and made for the delicate heart of things in precisely the way they were taught not to. Fellow students in the training sessions where he and Karen had met had skirted him as they would a predator contained behind a zoo fence they didn't entirely trust. Ahmed, in turn, had underscored his separateness by skipping as many sessions as possible. Only once had Karen seen an instructor, bristling in his tie and carefully rolled sleeves, confront him. *The only reason this is tolerated is the unique perspective you bring*—even as Ahmed stared the instructor down from across the conference table. Karen liked to tease that Ahmed had had to partner with her because she was the only one willing to work with him. But in truth there had been no one else she'd considered approaching for that first mediation they'd undertaken together, and over the years their partnership had succeeded where others failed. There was something about Ahmed that people trusted, after their initial shock at his directness—as though they sensed he would not abandon their fight until every last injustice was addressed. Karen, too, trusted his anger, and matched him principle for principle—censuring a Jewish co-panelist at a Washington convention who denigrated the quality of Palestinian literature, not relenting until she'd brokered an apology, along with a pledge from the organization to invite a Palestinian poet to open the following year's conference.

She was not above goading him, and he condoned her raciness with a puckered half-smile. On a long-ago panel, someone had asked her to comment on the latest problems in Arab-Jewish relations. She said, He snores. Her intimate knowledge of his snoring was, in truth, gleaned from one lone experience. But let the audience imagine. They weren't lovers; they were more.

Now they were lost. On double lanes of blacktop, ancestral routes, they shot southward without landmark. At a roadblock, they were hailed by an Israeli soldier who squinted past Ahmed to Karen and found in her freckled skin and blue jeans justification for a lazy wave. She opened her mouth to ask directions but Ahmed was already swinging the wheel, narrowly skirting the cement blockades.

"These rentals aren't allowed in the West Bank," she reminded him. Not with their yellow Israeli license plates, beacons for trouble.

He didn't answer. The long loop south condoned by the rental company would add forty-five minutes to their travel. He was going to drive them through the West Bank.

"At least let's stay on the main road," she said.

For the first time that morning, Ahmed assessed her with a long look. "You've gone native."

"Special for the occasion." She touched the silver hamsa at her throat, a birthday gift from David. Call it a good-luck charm. She felt the need for luck, though when she asked herself what luck would be her mind went silent. The silver chain around her neck was weightless. Every curve of the road unleashed a heavy feeling in her gut that declared itself, incrementally, to be nausea.

"Where's your ring?" he asked.

She fanned her bare fingers. "I don't travel with it."

"Too valuable?"

She looked at him.

His firm nod erased any bite the words might have held. When he referred to her fiancé it was always with respect: a tipping of his hat at the boundary of another man's turf.

Her engagement, just three months old, was the reason they were here. Why else would Ahmed have capitulated? They'd been invited to Israel dozens of times before. This time—so he'd said when he phoned her office from Milan—his speaking invitation to neighboring Jordan made accepting the Israelis' invitation only logical. But logic, she knew, was incidental. He'd acceded to the assignment because the two of them needed it.

It would be an easy job. They had only to coach the Israeli team that was mediating a dispute—a stalemate between the Israeli government and a desert community over citizenship rights. The community was made up of African Americans whose desperation in urban Detroit or Washington had led them to uproot their American lives and set up camp in an abandoned absorption center in the barren plains of the Negev. They had rediscovered the spiritual path of their people, they said, returned to their ancestral home. They were the true Israelites; their leader was the messiah; they had established a hierarchy of princes, eradicated all disease, eliminated crime. Etcetera. The other Israelites—the ones with a nation and a flag—didn't trust them to serve in the army and wouldn't grant them full citizenship.

Tomorrow and the next day, Karen and Ahmed would oversee the routine that was the substrate of their lives, the routine that stamped every page of her passport with ink documenting Almasi and Reed's jaunts around the globe: stubborn rhetoric, cultural misunderstanding, a provisional agreement that would be shattered when someone lifted his head and said "You people are corrupt snakes." The vocabulary might vary; the quarrel rarely did. This time she and Ahmed would be mere observers, expected to resolve nothing. They would spend two days coaching the Israeli facilitators for the new round of dialogue between government representatives and community members. Then they'd leave them to sort out the human mess that kept all, each seeker in the long queue of true Israelites, earthbound.

At times she hated everything that did not soar.

Beside her, Ahmed turned on the radio. He scanned past stations in Hebrew, Arabic, and Russian, coming to rest on a treacly English-language pop station. *Baby you're my sun and moon.* For a moment he sang softly with the radio, and though she knew he was mocking the song his voice was low and resonant. Mid-song he snapped the radio off.

The last of the terraced, dry farmland gave way to the rubble of desert. They passed low buildings sporting the spray-painted name of a Hasidic rabbi—handiwork of what she and Ahmed termed the hysterically religious. Political flyers referring to the week's headlines wrapped electric poles—scraps of history blanching in the sun, soon to be torn away. As they drove, the trilingual signs became bilingual. Into these used furniture shops and corrugated-tin farmstands Hebrew speakers were not invited. Then English evaporated as well. Ahmed drove in silence.

By the roadside, a leathery grizzled man in a keffiyeh guided a vine along a trellis. Headscarved woman stood in the shade of a cement bus shelter, the only structure on the empty horizon. Several kilometers on, Palestinian schoolgirls trooped along the verge of the desert in groups of two or three. Traffic was sparse; almost all the cars had blue license plates.

At a junction, Ahmed slowed to a stop. The car idled.

The road ahead continued straight south; another two-lane highway branched east. A sign at the intersection said, in English, "Be'er Sheva" —the city they were aiming for. Its arrow pointed east.

On the gritty plastic of the rental's dash she unfolded their map, and traced the morning's journey with the tip of her finger. Her finger stopped at a fissure, one fine line becoming two. The straight road bore directly down through the desert to Be'er Sheva; the eastern loop was winding and indirect.

"I don't understand why they're directing us east," she said.

Without a glance at her he hit the gas hard, harder than was necessary; the tires spun them forward onto the southern route. "I bought a flat," he told her.

"What?"

"In Primrose Hill."

For a moment she was speechless. "Mr. No-Roots bought a place? Mr. Rentals-and-Hotel-Rooms?"

He shrugged. "Thought you might be interested to know. Nice neighborhood. Parks. It's a small place. But a rolling stone has to slow now and then." He spoke evenly, without looking at her. His eyes were hidden behind his sunglasses.

Her own words: words she'd never expected to hear in his voice.

They rode in silence. After a while she roused herself. "Possibly that sign was meant to steer tourists away from a trouble spot," she said.

"Cool down," he crooned. His face was inscrutable. "They'll see I'm a brother."

"And if they come up on my side of the car?"

"You just tell them you're my girl."

"Brilliant. Then they'll let me go out of pity."

"Racist."

"Egotist," she countered.

"That's it," he sing-songed quietly as he drove. "That's it, that's right. *My girl.*"

She held her breath but he said nothing else. They crested a long hill, passing a woman in an embroidered blouse leading a mule on a thick rope. Was it now merely a joke to him? And why, she admonished herself, shouldn't he be able to let go so easily? She had.

The pace of their conversation, usually exhilarating, exhausted her. She rested her head against the seat and allowed her half-shuttered gaze to linger on his face. His features were sculpted, his eyes black and heavy-lashed. The blue buttoned shirt he wore didn't disguise the rounded, compact muscles of his chest. His rolled sleeves exposed strong forearms. There was nothing about his form that was wasteful, nothing easy. Yet the hands on the steering wheel had a softness that had shocked.

Her body, he'd said that one night, felt like sunlight.

In the past month, he had taken three solo assignments without consulting her.

She closed her eyes and thought with longing of David, breakfasting alone in their flat. Of David on the phone, his patient voice instructing an inmate of his rights. The human heart, David said, had many rooms. He understood her toughness, the conviction that drew others to her just as it had drawn him. He understood the need for control that sent her crying to her balcony the night she first said she loved him: this kind man, this man who was possible. David understood she'd loved others and he needed no details; he needed only to know that, going forward, she could reside happily in the room that held the two of them.

Out of nowhere, from dusty capillaries, traffic. Ahmed downshifted and plied the brakes. A scarred pickup full of car parts and staring teenagers swung in front of them. Karen nodded to the young men, then averted her eyes. Cresting a long hill in a line of sun-baked cars, they entered a town. The road undulated with large unpainted speed bumps. Each trough brought a wave of seasickness.

She could not deny the seasickness. Nor was she ready to comprehend it. She was thirty-six, David was forty-one; they had agreed to start trying upon their engagement. She folded her hands across the flat plane of her abdomen and drew a long breath.

Shops lined the street, their dented metal signs catching the sun and returning blinding reflections. Schoolchildren loped after one another in a game that seemed to involve endless circling around a broken segment of chainlink fence. People of all ages sat on stoops. Men, their figures distorted by heat, fed rubbish into the soundless red flames that lapped the brims of rusted trash bins. Here and there stood pillars of discarded tires.

The traffic slowed, then stopped. The rental car idled. No one seemed perturbed by the delay; the driver in front of them turned off his engine and engaged the parking brake, his teenaged passengers absorbing the jolt wordlessly. She could see the impediment, perhaps fifty yards ahead—a produce truck positioned diagonally across the road, its driver conversing unhurriedly out the window with a young woman who seemed to be making a list. The driver behind them got out and settled against the hood of his van with a cigarette; he was joined by one of the trash-burners.

"Get me a bottle of water," Ahmed said.

She stared at him. His mirrored glasses returned a distortion of her face: narrow and pale. With her, Ahmed always nipped in play, without malice or injury. Surely he was aware of the recent violence?

His silence was strangling.

On any other day she'd have refused. She'd have required him then and there to explain the restless irritability that had been on display since they'd met at his hotel that morning. But instead, without warning, she'd herself turned penitent—as though his every word were an accusation she could not refute.

She stepped out of the car, conscious of her blue jeans and small beaded handbag. Across the way was a wrinkled woman watching the road from beneath a black shawl. Beside the woman, a flimsy table bearing a few dozen guava and apricots and four plastic bottles. Without glancing to either side Karen strode toward her, communicating urgency with her eyes. The woman returned her gaze with an expression of sorrowful meditation. Karen took hold of a tepid bottle, dropped the shekels into the woman's creased brown palm, and received her change. The transaction took seconds.

Back in the car he nodded thanks and unscrewed the bottle's cap. His throat danced as he drank. Before he'd finished, the truck in front of them started its engine. The line of traffic rolled forward. As they descended the hill the town thinned. Traffic dispersed along faint unpaved tracks. The road they were on began to curve crazily, its banks steep and rubbish-lined.

The van behind them was tailgating. Its driver and single passenger— the man who'd left his post at the trash barrel—were upright shadows, heads motionless with concentration.

Ahmed glanced in the mirror. He waved a friendly censure. The driver drew closer; the van was a handsbreadth off their bumper. Ahmed beeped the horn twice. "Sod off," he muttered. The van edged closer, so close Karen braced for impact.

"It's cool baby," Ahmed said to her, and hit the accelerator.

They rocketed forward, the van on their bumper. She glanced at the speedometer and saw that they were traveling over ninety kilometers per hour. The curves wrenched her from side to side. At each turn the hills loomed and spun. Dark patches had appeared on the side of Ahmed's shirt.

Abruptly the van accelerated into the opposing lane and zoomed past, its silent occupants facing straight ahead.

They slowed gradually, coasting down the remainder of the hill. The empty highway leveled out before them but she could not let go the car's handgrip. The rocky world heaved around her. At the brush of her fingertips on his knee—the barest caress against the rough fabric of his jeans—he stopped. She lurched from the car and was sick at the side of the road.

When she returned he put the car into gear and propelled them forward. The muscles in his jaw flexed. He spoke without a glance in her direction, and his voice was brutal, barbed on all sides. "If I lived here," he said, "I'd chase down Jews."

[

] Stuttered dreams. She woke in a sweat. The clock read 4 A.M. and her headache was deafening, magnifying the quiet of the desert to overpowering dimensions. Lying still on the hard hotel mattress, she gathered herself, then rose and swung the window wide. The sky over Be'er Sheva was cobalt. She inhaled the dusty pre-dawn air and watched a date palm, eight stories below, shift in the breeze. Its rustle reached her faintly. In her bag she found a peach and, biting into its hard flesh, lowered herself in her underwear onto the wicker chair.

Where had she read this: One carries the thought of one's beloved like a camera on one's shoulder, recording life in order to bring it before him.

For years she'd carried Ahmed thus. Every shocking folly she witnessed, every human welter or slow swimming toward light, was fodder for his wicked debriefing. Everywhere she found treasures to share with him. With other men she'd sue for her desires, spell out her wishes; with Ahmed she made only barest mention of them. For years she was in love with a hard man without demanding anything of him. He'd told her—he told everyone in earshot—he didn't do possession and he didn't do that relationship shit. Flings only, thank you kindly. She didn't try to alter him. She was proud of that—of not trying. An older woman had once said to her: When a man tells you something about himself, believe him. The biggest mistake women make is not believing.

He said he didn't want children.

"Nor do you want brats getting needy on you," he once instructed her. "Watch out for all those men who're after you, the instant they succeed they'll just want to breed you. Then you'll be dropping babies and all you've worked for will go to shit." Everything about how she'd shaped her life, in fact, affirmed that she didn't want children. Only, she did. She told Ahmed so quietly, without need for argument. He did not argue. A rolling stone has to slow sometimes, she'd said.

He'd looked at the world and made his bargain. His only loyalty, he liked to say, was to truth. He'd made himself nationless to preserve his own mind and heart and soul. He'd made himself a lonely man.

When she met David at that dreadful dinner thrown by her cousin in Finchley—the dinner she'd thought would never end until she spied a stranger's bemused smile and the evening was lit with absurdity— she'd seen the life she wanted. Stepping toward it was no renunciation. Yet she could not deny the feeling of giving up something prodigious, ir-reducible. Some audacious magic she and Ahmed asserted in the world.

Below her window, a first bus rumbled past. Four twenty-five A.M. A few cars began crossing the empty intersections. The blue's fierce vibra-tion had stilled without her noticing. A few birds took measure of the paling sky, then abruptly went mad with chirping.

She dialed David's office and pressed the receiver to her ear while his voice, deep and patient, instructed her to leave a message.

"Sweet," she said. "It's twenty-five past ridiculous in the morning, even earlier in London, and I'm crazy to hear your voice. I'm okay. I feel a little sick. Want to talk to you, love."

She set down the receiver, her throat tight. Her own voice rang in her ears; the naked, unguarded tone she used with David. At length she turned from the window and surveyed the hotel room. Ahmed's native habitat. She took in its comforting sterility: the television clicker; the over-stuffed pillows; the wet-bar they consulted on difficult jobs and the constancy of its answers—gin for her, vodka for him. With a soft smile she recalled her family's shock at each thing Jewish girls didn't do: drinking with the men, braving war zones. Traveling the world with a Palestinian. Early on in their association, her certainty that she'd one day be Ahmed's lover had lit the hours with a reckless elation. But that had changed, reshaped into something deeper. Was it hubris to believe she might have convinced him? She knew she could have. She knew he loved her; she could have dared him to make good on what they both knew. But as she got to know Ahmed she saw she loved him with a strength that was outside the usual. She could never do the thing that would doom the bond between them.

During the years of their partnership he had women. She liked them without ever meeting them. When they told him off she laughed at his indignation. For her and her alone were the small gifts: the way his voice broke when she woke him with a phone call at midnight Singapore time—the fissure in his *Hello?* a moment's weakness, a moment's candor.

Only once they'd crossed the line, choosing to cross it in full awareness and not drunk, choosing to without debate or discussion and after years of saying they would not. They broke their own rule out of contrariness, out of inevitability, out of absurdity, out of a necessity to claim, possess, cradle; out of something powerful they chose not to name. Then he left for Australia. They spoke on the phone but his voice seemed to warn her from the shoals of dependence. When she saw him six weeks later, it was as it had always been. She flirted with him; he told her daily without word or touch how he appreciated her, mind and spirit and body: more than her most ardent suitors, whom she rejected one after another.

One night when she'd known David only a month, some inconsequential thought had nudged her at the verge of sleep. She opened her mouth to call David's name in his dark bedroom, and the name that formed on her tongue was Ahmed's. She felt it escaping her and swallowed it just in time. The next evening she sat through an urban charities benefit concert, mulling while the children's choir sang. Next to her sat David, and beside him his friends—Jewish, professional, politically astute, fond of discussing the morning paper and their intrusive in-laws. The sadness that washed her was unanswerable. The beauty of this glowing wooden balcony could not compare with the knowledge of defying gravity—of arguing a mile high with an ocean spinning below you.

She had no doubt of her choice. Before her lay a life she wanted more than she feared it. Yet while the choir sang and the audience nodded its approval, she allowed herself to think of Ahmed. Of sitting with him at a student bonfire outside Helsinki, silent. Of the few words they spoke to one another; each utterance significant, each cutting the cold air, everything between them fraught.

But there came a time when a woman had to evaluate her scorched-earth romantic policies.

With David she was argumentative, she was kind, she was grateful; she sank into his arms with the joy—yes, joy—she found in easing up for goddamn once. They touched as often as they spoke. They shopped, scheduled, chopped vegetables. A tactile life. A life among her own. In David's features she took familial comfort. Mornings she traced his handsome forehead with the tip of one finger, kissed his eyelids when they fluttered.

When she'd told Ahmed of her engagement, he's said nothing. She'd risen from her chair at their conference table. "You and I have always . . ." she hesitated.

He stood. His face was filled, for an instant, with the same fury she'd seen him turn on the unseeing whose hatreds betrayed all hope. "Don't—" his voice dropped low "—understate." He left. The next day he sent her flowers, an act so out of character she stared for a half hour at the single word on the card, trying to comprehend. *Congratulations.* Later that week she saw him get out of his car and stand for a moment as though undecided. When he turned for their office, he carried himself with grim fatigue—like a man who'd caught himself in the mirror and been shocked by what he saw.

He'd traveled extensively the following weeks. When he returned, he was his usual self.

Now in the room next door an alarm clock shrilled. Some moments later, a pounding on the wall. "Wake up," Ahmed called. "Even bloody Christ rises in these parts."

"We'll have to put the lid on tighter next time," she called through the wall.

"You can't stop a righteous man," he countered.

"I've been up since dawn." She stood, her head light with thirst. "Poisoning wells, you know," she continued bravely. "Killing Christian children. Got to get up early to stay ahead in this game." She stopped there. Normally she would continue goading until one of them forfeited and retired to the shower. She would add a warning, normally, not to wear those bloody sunglasses again, he looked like a pimp. Instead she fell mute. Afraid of his hurt.

[

] By the roadside, a cluster of sheet-metal lean-tos. Their roofs, ragged plastic tarps, inflated with the wind of the car's passage. She watched four asses gallop across the highway ahead of their car. Near a small city of low buildings in the middle of endless desert, an Orthodox boy in a black hat crossed an intersection, prayer fringes dangling from the base of his white shirt, talking into a cell phone. The variegated madness of this country.

Ahmed wore black shirt, black pants, mirrored glasses. She couldn't gauge his response to the Israeli mediator, who'd met them at the hotel and now sat behind Karen, gripping her headrest as he spoke. The man was friendly, respectful, efficient in his briefing: This settlement of African Americans believed themselves to be descendants of the original Israelites. Some had gone so far as to declare that the Jews were imposters; an abundance of Jewish Israelis had readily reciprocated the compliment. Nonetheless, most of those involved acknowledged, however reluctantly, that improved coexistence was necessary. There were matters in urgent need of resolution: Citizenship. School accreditation. Housing rights. Loans.

At the gate of the community they were joined by a second Israeli mediator, and by a girl who looked to be about eleven years old. *Your tour-guide*, she announced, and without awaiting a response turned and led them across a dusty courtyard. Dozens of children, their skin ranging from charcoal to pale coffee, milled about in clothing sewn of brightly patterned cloth. Their parents, young women and men, crisscrossed the compound, speaking English with the accents of inner-city America. None appeared to be over the age of fifty. The girl directed them in a staccato voice. More than 35 people in a house, she enunciated. Personal sacrifice, individual desires surrendered for the whole. They passed two boys building a go-cart, one using a rock to hammer a nail. They passed one cluster of buildings on the blanched desert plain, then another. Karen strayed toward one of the low concrete buildings; with a hard grip on her arm, the girl pulled her away.

A man in his forties joined their party. With a flourish, he led them to a doorway and unlocked it. In his home, he said, they would learn about the community's social structure. They entered a crammed but neat set of rooms crowded with women and an assortment of children. On the wall of the entryway, a family photo. With a smile the man pointed out the images of his three wives, two of whom now stood behind Karen and Ahmed and the mediators, offering glasses of cool water; the third wife, a young woman with a lovely heart-shaped face, knelt in a corner of the room, wrestling a shirt over a child's head. Turning back to the photo, Karen counted eighteen children in addition to the wives.

"What has made us strong," said the man, a lanky, handsome American, "is we've aligned ourselves with a common thinking." As he droned on about the community's princes and ministers and priests, Karen scanned a second framed photo. In the photograph, a teenaged boy was presenting a wrapped gift to a chocolate-skinned man in his sixties, white-robed and white-capped, standing tranquilly with hands clasped before him. *Most holy one of Israel*, said the inscription at the photo's base, *we present this to you and pray that it find honor in your sight.*

Their host noticed Karen's focus. "That's our father," he said.

"The messiah?" asked Ahmed evenly.

The man answered with gravity. "He is, for us, the Messiah in this particular dispensation of time."

When the man had turned away to say something to his wives, Ahmed's brows arched above his sunglasses. "And when the big guy croaks?" he whispered to the mediator nearer to him. The man shook his head in agreement: It was the kind of setup where you could imagine a mass suicide.

Their host detailed the achievements of the community, from its beginnings in an abandoned absorption center, through the years of reconstruction. Now they had a dance studio. A health center. The boys studied trades, the girls domestic virtues. He himself had left the United States on a personal search, aware of something radically wrong with the world. He'd sacrificed a large income, he said, to live in this desert outpost. Ahmed, removing his sunglasses, shot a look at the man's three wives, and Karen heard the smirk as clearly as if he'd spoken it: *Sacrifice?* But the silent commentary had not been for Karen; Ahmed had directed it to the mediator, who suppressed a chuckle.

The young wife with the beautiful face and warm, bright eyes settled on a stool and gestured Karen to a folding chair beside her. Karen perched on its seat.

"We call this Heaven on Earth," the woman said in a soft voice. "Your former self has to die to get here." Now and again as she recited her speech the woman raised a hand and touched Karen's shoulder. "Do you know what it's like, sister, to finish high school into drugs and no hope? I know you can imagine, sister. There was nothing to hold me there. Then I heard about this community. My spirit opened. I came here to embrace my heritage. My children are safe here."

The woman's face radiated a vitality Karen found disquieting. Despite herself, she felt a craving for each return of her touch. She indulged a fantasy: This woman knew whether there was a life even now taking shape inside her. She held the possibility like a breath she was afraid to expel. For a dizzied instant, she understood these people's longing to be among their own. For roots. She wanted to open her mouth and speak to this woman about the bone-weariness of resisting partisanship. She wanted to set down her cup of water and confess; speak of the years she, Karen, had spent living a life of openness with no room for the blind loyalty of home. The very life she was now . . . wasn't she? . . . rejecting. She wanted to ask: Had she chosen right?

Which was better? To subsist on the pure oxygen of principle—to devote oneself to being a bridge, to devote one's life to a love without children, without comfort? Or to succumb—to choose one's own tribe, to shut the windows on parts of the world in order to stay warm?

She thought, desperately, of David. She thought: There are important issues in London, too. She'd been offered domestic speaking contracts in the past, a mediation schedule with light travel. She could manage light travel with a child.

Without warning, nausea surged, making her frantic. Ahmed watched her coolly from the wall. For weeks he'd been unstitching himself from her—she'd felt the links slip, one by one. The woman, still speaking, looked concerned. Karen's thinking blurred. She could not distinguish one thing from another thing, a right choice from an abdication, boldness from flight.

"Is this a cult?" she interrupted. Without realizing it, she'd risen to her feet. Ahmed, standing by the room's small window, gave out a derisive laugh. The glance he let fall on her was cold and full of anger. His eyes bored into hers.

With effort she broke from his stare. Her question merited derision— she knew better than to engage this conversation. It violated every bit of her training and experience. She forced herself to ignore Ahmed and the Israeli mediators and the husband and the other wives, all now silent.

The woman smiled gently. "Most people," she said, "think of a cult and they think of Jonestown. You must know: Jonestown wasn't suicide. It was murder. Those people were injected with a poison, my sister. The C.I.A. did it."

Outside, she took a coffee break in the sun. She strolled to the settlement's gate, the eleven-year-old girl trailing her in mute suspicion. The road outside the gate petered out a hundred yards past the compound. Beyond the end of the road, silhouettes of three camels made their way across the rocky horizon, led by a figure in Bedouin dress. The image was seductive; she stared until they were gone. She lit a cigarette, then stubbed it out, angrily, on a fencepost. Her head pounded.

In all these years, she had not asked herself how Ahmed felt. She had taken him at his word with pious strictness, reinforcing his determination not to be recruited by anything or anyone. She'd left his isolation unchallenged, had patrolled her own feelings until they'd relented enough for her to fall in love with someone else.

Now she saw that she had excluded the possibility of Ahmed's changing.

Sentimentalism counseled that in some alternate universe she'd always be as she was at this instant: an atom traveling the universe without constraint. A spirit refusing limitations. A Jewish woman in love with a Palestinian. This was a lie. There was only one story of a person's life. She was the woman turning her back on Ahmed. She, with her large stable family, who for years battled alongside Ahmed only to return to her flat—she'd never wanted to acknowledge it—keen to phone her sister and find relief in mundane gossip; while he slept, halfway across London, on the narrow shelf he'd carved for himself. She'd told herself he'd rejected their relationship. In fact it was the other way.

He had come here for her. He had ventured back among roots he found poisonous in order to communicate something to her, some wordless message more powerful than any confession. It was for naught. They no longer had ground on which to meet.

[

] "It's the kingdom of Yah, y'all."

Deep, body-shaking amps. Sitting in the front row of the compound's auditorium, Karen felt her heart struggle to preserve its own rhythm.

"Anybody that's been redeemed, raise your hand!" The woman on stage was astonishing. Head wrapped in gold lamé. Stylish, charismatic. Ebullience personified. The auditorium bounced with her physical energy. Here, in this hall in the middle of the desert, was one of the best performers Karen had ever seen. The woman's smile was fantastic. Her voice turned sweet, passionate. "Children, its about you, babies," she cried. Her voice enveloped the hall with the opening lines of "Redemption Song."

This sort of concert was staged here every few months, the Israeli mediators had informed them. The team's appearance would be noted, and would pay off in goodwill at tomorrow's sessions.

"Emancipate yourselves." The song rose from the tiered rows behind Karen. The crowd numbered in the hundreds. Everyone except their group was singing along now. The only other white woman in the hall stood entranced in the center of the audience, her palms turned up to catch the divine presence like a fine drizzle. The room was ecstatic. People rose and danced in place. Karen could feel the audience's emotion, a tide surging toward the stage: pain, longing, joy. And a rich, voluptuous relief she recognized. She'd seen it in her grandparents— German Holocaust survivors who grew pink-cheeked and spirited only in the company of fellow refugees. She'd felt it herself: the sheer physical release of belonging.

The singer gathered the audience, she harvested their applause in her arms. "Come on Zion put your hands together!" The hall swelled once more with gratitude, and this time Karen joined in, and the applause was dizzying and pure and had she ever heard a singer more deserving?

The woman was joined on stage by a full band. The music this time was a commanding, pulse-jolting soul. Midway through the song, Ahmed leaned into Karen and said something, his shoulder warm against hers. His voice was lost in the amps. He repeated himself, his breath brushing her ear. As she strained uselessly to make out his words, a sharp, vertiginous hope flooded her. Did he, too, feel the pull—the ache rising all around them? The heavy beauty of the desire for home?

He took a pen from his pocket and scribbled on his notepad, which he passed to her. Through the dark she made out the words: *Fucking lunatics.*

Intermission was called by a whip-thin, frenzied emcee.

"Let's get some air," said Ahmed.

The eleven-year-old girl stood with them. From nowhere, their host of the afternoon and his bright-eyed wife joined. Karen felt herself led along the aisle, the wife's gentle touch on her elbow. The crowd moved slowly up the incline toward the rear door, which someone had propped open to admit a breeze. Suddenly there was a commotion. Behind them the crowd knotted. Then, abruptly, the aisle cleared, the throng splitting as if by magic from the base of the auditorium to its heights. Karen was shoved to one side, ferociously, the girl's hands jamming into her ribs. She hit the wall and fell to the floor, landing on her tailbone so hard tears formed in her eyes. Looking up, she saw a man in a white robe passing inches from her: the messiah proceeding serenely up the aisle, adults and children scrambling out of his path.

She checked herself; nothing broken. Yet she was too shaken to stand. Breathing deeply, she conquered the tears but could not stop the heart crying inside her like a child's.

Reaching blindly, she took hold of his wrist. At her touch Ahmed startled like a deer. She couldn't see his face; the crowd was milling once more and her head drooped with fatigue. Her fingers queried the soft warmth of his skin.

He took her hand.

He will not abandon her. There are some things that do not alter. There are hearts that do not waver. He has always been a truthful man and he will always be so to her. It is this she loves about him as he picks her up from the floor and for a moment steadies her, before letting go. His hand is honest, its clasp electric with grief.

] The Lunatic

I went on to have the good things, the good life promised to me. I went to college, got a decent job, got married. Later, my husband and I would have two children, and we would buy an apartment, the second floor of a brownstone in Brooklyn Heights where we still live. It was in the time between, after we were married but before the children were born, that I came home from work one evening and found my husband watching television, hunched forward, intent on whatever it was on the screen, the way he otherwise watched television only during the World Series.

"What's so interesting?" I asked.

"Not interesting. Terrible. Yitzhak Rabin was assassinated," he told me. "One of those right-wing Meir Kahane crazies. Shot him."

I sat beside my husband on the couch and watched what looked to be a celebration; Jews cheering a murder. Jews, but not Jews, the way the snake-handling Holy Rollers aren't Christians the way Episcopalians or Presbyterians are Christians. The crazies. The lunatic fringe. The television camera panned the ecstatic crowd, and there he was.

"Stanley," I said, as if it were no surprise at all.

"Who is Stanley?" my husband asked.

"That one," I pointed. "There." Stanley was holding up the right corner of an Israeli flag. His other hand was clenched into a fist and raised, as if in victory. As if he'd won a war or a game. "I went to high school with him," I explained the peculiarity of my knowing such a person.

[

] Printed on a sheet of lavatory-green paper beneath the headline that read YEARBOOK!!! was the assigned day and twenty-minute slot when we were to be excused from class to get our pictures taken. For the year-book. The high school yearbook. Franklin Pierce High School, where less than half the students could identify Franklin Pierce, but so what? To know that he was president from 1853 to 1857, where would that get us? Our lives were already just right; we had everything our parents wanted us to have, and our futures were practically ordained, destined to be more of the same. I got Friday at 10:20, a stroke of luck that would spring me from physics class with Mr. Banner. Physics was as interesting as lint, and Mr. B didn't exactly have a personality. Also on the sheet of bathroom-green paper was a list of suggestions for photographing well, how to look our best: powder your nose, take off your eyeglasses, sit up straight. For their yearbook photos, boys were urged to wear a dark sports jacket, a white or light-blue shirt, and a tie.

I twisted around in my seat to look at Stanley, and I tried to picture him wearing normal clothes.

Stanley. A name from my father's generation or worse. And it wasn't just his name either. Everything about him was wrong or off or weird and Jewish. By Jewish, I mean different Jewish. Not the way I was Jewish, or even some of my friends whose families were more religious than mine. Families who went to synagogue on the holidays and the girls got bat mitzvah, which was something I didn't even know existed until Mindy Zuckerman had one and it was a Hawaiian luau theme. Then I wanted a bat mitzvah too, but my mother said, "You'll have a Sweet Sixteen." The way Stanley spoke, he made English sound like Hebrew or Yiddish or some other Jewish language, and he talked with his hands and he shrugged his shoulders like a grandfather instead of a normal person.

That year, on the first day of class, when I turned to see who was sitting behind me in home room, I'd assumed that Stanley was new to our school because I'd never seen him before. By all rights, he should've stood out in the crowd. The boys at my school, even the super-geeks, wore what was practically a uniform: blue jeans or khaki pants and T-shirts or button-down oxford shirts. But there was Stanley all decked out in camouflage pants and a flack jacket and combat boots like he was some kind of survivalist nut. But when I asked, "Are you new here?" he made some old Jewish man face and said, "No."

Even with the G.I. Joe costume, Stanley was one of the invisible. Which was not the worst thing in my school, to be invisible. It was not the lowest rank. Social hierarchy was complicated and there was some overlap and periodic shifts but mostly it was clear-cut and fixed. The uppermost echelon, they were the athletes, guys who were like gods, and their girlfriends. The bottom, they were the kids everyone else tormented for fun.

I had a few quasi-friends in the upper-echelon category, but one thing that positively and officially kept me on the outside looking in was that I didn't have a boyfriend. Those girls all had boyfriends, and most of them were having sex. If I had a boyfriend, I definitely would've had sex with him.

On his YEARBOOK!!! sheet of paper, Stanley was doodling. Stanley had long eyelashes. I was a big doodler, too. Flowers, mostly. Also, the cube that was three-dimensional. Long eyelashes, and his eyes were green, and shaped like almonds except bigger than almonds. His mouth was full and wide and I was on the fence as to whether it was a good mouth or a weird one. His hair was weird, for sure. Copper-colored. Not usual hair. As far as I could tell, he didn't smell bad but I had this idea that he might.

He looked up at me, and I shifted my gaze from his mouth to his YEARBOOK!!! paper, as if that's what I'd been looking at all along.

Stanley's doodles were of fighter jets dropping missiles.

"When do you get your picture taken?" I asked.

"Never." He spread his hand over the sheet of paper, the first step to crumpling it into a ball.

"You're not going to have your picture in the yearbook? Why wouldn't you want to be in the yearbook?"

"For what should I want to be in the yearbook?"

"Because," I said. "It's a keepsake. To remember high school. You know, the best years of our lives."

Stanley said, "Feh," or some kind of old-man word like that.

It did occur to me that on some level I found Stanley to be cute, and I banished the thought.

He was not acceptable for a boyfriend, or even as someone to know.

It was for no reason, really, that I would sometimes turn around in my seat to look at him, although I did often consider if it were possible to turn him into someone acceptable, the way Henry Higgins redid Eliza Doolittle in the movie *My Fair Lady*. Different clothes. Different hair. A new name. Those times when he caught me looking at him, I pretended

I had a reason: Did he have an extra pen I could borrow? Are we supposed to answer all the questions at the end of the chapter? Are we having a quiz on Friday? And, I asked, "Where did you apply to school?"

"I didn't," he said.

"To college, I mean."

Aside from the expected preoccupations—boys, girls, sex, sports, clothes, parties—we were now, in our senior year, obsessed with college. How did we fare on the SATs? Where had we applied? Would we get into our top choice? Which was our safety school? Despite not knowing or caring who Franklin Pierce was, everyone, all of us, including the not-smart kids, in my high school went to college, even if to community college. Once in a while we'd hear of someone dropping out, but always we went in the first place because what else was there to do?

"I'm not going to college," Stanley told me. "I'm joining the army."

"The army?" The year before, we, America, went to war in Grenada, which caused embarrassment far more than it stirred up national pride. "Why would you join the army?" Who joined the army?

"Because I'm a Zionist." Stanley said, and when I didn't say anything he said, "The Israeli army."

"Oh, that army," I said, as if it made a difference, which as far as I was concerned, it didn't.

The summer before, Sandy Slotnik went to Israel to work on a kibbutz. Her parents actually had to pay for that, for her to work, as if picking peaches on a kibbutz were the same as water-skiing at Camp Schlomo-Oneida or a Teen Tour. Some of my friends took Teen Tours to Israel, but the army? Who would pick the army over college?

Not only did it provide the way out from under the parental thumb—parties and sex whenever—college was about our future. It was not for the love of learning that we kept up our grades. Good grades got us into the better schools. Better schools led to better jobs and better jobs led us home, to the life promised. We joined the swim team and the debating society and the French club for the same reason we did volunteer work as Candy Stripers or at that home for the retarded children: College admissions committees took note. Not to go to college was to choose to be a loser all your life. Plus, as I understood it, the Jewish religion practically required that you go to college.

By all reason, Stanley's plan to enlist in the Israeli army should've meant shit-all to me, but instead, I cared. A lot. I wanted him to go to college like everyone else.

At our lunch table—our table having been claimed by my group of friends the way explorers will claim territory with a flag—some of the girls ate tuna fish packed in water, not oil, brought from home in Tupperware. Tuna and sliced tomato—no bread or mayo. Also, there were two thin girls who ate chocolate chip cookies for lunch. Although unspoken, the tuna fish girls wished the cookie girls dead. The tendency to put on weight was shameful, as if Eve ate not the apple from the Tree of Knowledge, but a Reese's Peanut Butter Cup from the Tree of Fat. I was in the middle of the two extremes. I could've stood to lose a few pounds, but not so much that I had to bring the dry tuna fish from home. The cookie girls had boyfriends.

"You know that guy? Stanley?" I asked.

No one at our lunch table knew Stanley.

"He sits behind me in home room and in history class."

"Is he the one in the army clothes?"

"That's him." I popped open a can of Diet Coke. "He might be kind of cute if he dressed normal, don't you think?" I said, all tra-la-la, as if I just happened to notice.

No one agreed that Stanley would be kind of cute if he dressed normal.

Sandy Slotnik said, "He's a lunatic."

Leslie Davies said, "He has weird hair."

Barbara Green said, "He smells."

"He doesn't smell," I said. "He just looks like he smells."

"Fuck the lunatic," Barbara Green pushed her sandwich aside and leaned in, as if to gather us around her. "Never mind him. I have big news." Barbara's big news was that—are you ready, she said—the night before, she'd had her first orgasm. Barbara was one of the thin girls. "It's like dying and going to heaven," she reported, which didn't really give me anything specific to take away from the discussion.

"Like eating chocolate?" Leslie Davies asked.

"No," Barbara said. "It's like your insides go all fluttery."

Fluttery; with that, I imagined Stanley kissing one of my breasts, which was not what I would've picked to imagine but there it was. Fluttery.

Maybe it was more than occasionally that I turned around in my seat to look at Stanley. Maybe in home room and history class, I was all the time turned around until the history teacher would tell me to face front. In home room, the teacher paid no attention to us as long as we weren't destructive to the furniture or windows. Mostly, Stanley didn't notice me looking at him because he was absorbed with his doodling of exploding missiles; also he drew pictures of machine guns. His drawings were very realistic.

Where were Stanley's parents, I wondered? Why aren't they insisting he get a college education?

"Are your parents upset?" I asked him.

"Upset about what? For what should they be upset?"

"That you're joining the army. The Israeli army. It's not even our army."

"Not our army? It most certainly is our army," Stanley said. "Tell me, where are you going should the Nazis come again?"

I considered the question, and I had an answer. "Canada," I said.

Stanley said something in response but I don't know what because he mumbled and it was at the exact moment when the bell rang. He raced from the room before I could collect my books.

The year wore on, and in a way similar to a Catholic girl's calling to become a nun, I came to believe that I was called to save Stanley from doing such a stupid thing as joining the Israeli army. The difference being that my calling involved sex. That was my idea. If I had sex with Stanley, he would change his mind and stay here in America and go to college. Or art school, even. I confess that this wasn't a new plan on my part. The previous summer my family went for a weekend to Lancaster, Pennsylvania where we stared at Amish people. My mother went on and on about how quaint the Amish people were, and I got this idea about having sex with an Amish boy, and how that would get him to run away from his quaint life which couldn't possibly have been any fun.

A good deed, plus killing two birds with one stone.

If Stanley and I had sex, he wouldn't be wearing the camouflage pants and the flak jacket. He'd be naked.

I was convinced of my plan, that it was a fine one, both altruistic and likely to succeed, but how to set it in motion?

The deadline for applying to college had long since passed; in fact, we'd already received our acceptances and rejections. I was accepted everywhere I'd applied, although I didn't apply to any of the top top schools. I went for those a rung below. Like Middlebury, Williams, Bates. But deadlines come and gone was no reason to give up on Stanley. He could enroll in a community college for one year and then transfer to a regular college. Now, a month before graduation, and no closer to saving Stanley than I was back in October, it was a race against time. I turned around in my seat and said, "Hey, Stanley."

He paused mid-doodle, the start of a village engulfed in flames. By all rights, my proximity to the upper echelon and Stanley being so far from it should've resulted in his being thrilled to talk to me. Grateful that I would talk to him, but whenever I initiated conversation, he never acted thrilled. Mostly, he wasn't even polite, which I attributed to his being shy and awkward because teenage girls often attribute obnoxiousness and lack of interest to shyness.

"What do you want?" he asked.

"Meet me after school today, okay?"

"For why?"

"I just want to talk to you for a minute."

"So talk," Stanley said.

"No. It has to be private," I told him.

He shrugged, which I took for a yes.

Because I didn't want anyone to see me with Stanley, who still wore the flak jacket even though we were well into May, I told him, "Wait for me by your locker. Don't leave. I'm going to be a few minutes late. I have to talk with Mrs. Evans about my art project. Something went wrong with the glue." I invented an excuse even though he didn't ask for one. "I won't be long. So don't leave. Wait for me, okay?"

Again Stanley shrugged, and again I took that for a yes.

A day such as that one was, when the sky was blue and clear and spring fever was pandemic, I hung out in the bathroom for the two minutes it took for the building to empty out, for the school grounds to be as deserted as if it were mid-summer or after the apocalypse. The coast was clear, and Stanley was at his locker.

Make-Out Corner was where the new wing of the school, which wasn't, relatively speaking, all that new, conjoined with the original building; a blind spot that got no sun. No grass grew there either, and it was a place for couples to go for a quick grope between classes. Also, it was where you could sneak a cigarette. But on that day, everyone had someplace better to be. Stanley and I were alone.

My back was to the wall. Stanley stood facing me, an arm's length between us. He kicked at loose dirt with his combat boot.

"Aren't you kind of warm?" I asked him. "With the boots and jacket?"

"You think the desert is air-conditioned?" he said, and I guess I had some sort of look on my face, like I wasn't following him because he explained, "I'm going to be in the Israeli army. It gets hot in Israel. Really hot. What do you think? Soldiers wear short pants and sandals?"

I hadn't a clue what Israeli soldiers wore, but I wasn't about to admit that to Stanley. "I didn't say anything about short pants and sandals."

"What do you want from me?" Stanley asked.

"I want you to go to college. Like everyone else," I said. "I want you to have a future."

"I intend to have a future."

"I mean a real future. An education. A good job. A wife. Children. It's crazy what you are doing. We're Americans," I reminded him.

"We're Jews," he reminded me.

"But you don't have to be that kind of a Jew. You can be like everyone else here. You know, have some fun and then a nice life." Stanley said nothing, just stood there except for moving around more dirt with his boot. As if air were fortitude or courage, I took a deep breath and then I said, "How about this? If you stay here and go to college—you know you could enroll in one of the community colleges now, then transfer to a better school—if you did that, I would have sex with you."

"What did you just say?" He was smiling; he had a dimple on his left cheek. I'd never noticed that, the dimple, before, maybe because I never saw him smile before.

"If you don't join the Israeli army, I'll have sex with you." I smiled back at him, and Stanley came in toward me, closing the gap between us. He put his hand on my shoulder, as if to steady me for the kiss to come. I closed my eyes and offered my mouth to him. I felt nervous, but nice. Nice, in that fluttery way, and I waited for the kiss until the impact of a blow knocked me to the ground where I curled up, my arms crossed protecting my stomach, although it was too late for protection.

Stanley, his hand still clenched into a fist, looked down at me and he said, slowly, enunciating with precision, "You stupid fucking cunt."

Then, he left me there, curled up on the dirt, and off he went to have his future.

I stayed curled up on the dirt waiting for the pain to subside. Eventually it did, and then I got up and went to off to have my future, too.

[

] "He was crazy even then, in high school," I told my husband. "A lunatic."

] Homewrecker

My future husband's former wife has a PhD from Harvard, but the phone messages she leaves are lunatic, rambling, grammatically bizarre. These phone messages usually concern the welfare or financial circumstances surrounding her son, Trevor, whose father is my future husband. Trevor lives with his mother in Wisconsin, and all evidence suggests he is a nice child, a sweet child, although a child about whom my future husband has every right to be anxious, since at six years old the child still doesn't speak. My future husband doesn't say much about him except when his former wife leaves a message on the machine about speech therapists and the money to pay for them. "Goddamn kid's still a mute, huh?" my future husband asks, and then looks straight at me, as though I have any more information than this.

My future husband's first wife teaches Russian literature at the University of Wisconsin, a job she loves even more than she used to love my future husband. When it came time for them to make a choice—stay in Wisconsin, where he was going out of his mind, or leave Wisconsin and all that Russian hoo-ha—he took Manhattan, and she did not. Six months later, he met me; a year after that he proposed. He explained to me, during the proposal, that as a man he feels calmer when he's married.

"So well I think I forgot to tell you," my future husband says to me over breakfast one morning, "that they're coming." At first I have no idea what he's talking about, but then I look at the way he's scowling and I get it. He could only be talking about one particular they.

"That's lovely," I say. "When are they expected?"

"Next week. Monday. There's this speech therapist at Columbia. She insists it's necessary." His face is twisted like he's smelling something foul. "She won't drop it."

"I understand."

"She wants Trevor to stay here," he says. "With us. In this apartment. So he can spend time with his dad."

"Oh! That will be fun." Again he looks at me like I've just made a smart-alecky remark, although I haven't. I very much like children. My future husband says this is just a phase.

"This is a no-children building, for the record," he says.

"But there are lots of children in this building." I don't want to be confrontational; however, there are children here. I see them in the lobby, the elevator, the hallways. The doormen give them lollipops.

"I've never seen any." My future husband is slicing up a roll with one of the advanced-technology German knives he brought home from a trip to Frankfurt.

"The older ones," I say, "are at boarding school." Again with the look, and with the knife in his hand he's making me uncomfortable. "Where's Sonia going to stay, do you think?"

"Not in this house," my future husband says, putting down his knife but still glaring. The very topic of his ex-wife makes him crazy; he doesn't like it when I so much as say her name. I am, however, quite curious about the subject of Sonia, and I pump my future husband for information on those rare occasions when it seems like he won't mind. I've gleaned that she's taller than I am. She's an expert on representations of women in Stalinist literature. She has a weakness for designer shoes. Like my future husband, she's a Jew. I know what she looks like because she sent us a New Year's card with a picture of her and Trevor on it, and I got to it before my future husband could find it and throw it away.

"Wherever that woman is staying, it's not here," my future husband grouses.

"So then where?"

"Jennifer," he says, twisting the lid off a jar of jam, "how the fuck is that my problem?" He wipes the lid with his napkin. My future husband is fastidious, and now he's angry, too. I take a hard-boiled egg from the bowl and slice it into smaller and smaller pieces.

[

] After he leaves for work, I put the knife away. I put the rolls and the jam and the coffee maker away. We have nice granite countertops, teak drawers. Ronda will be here later, to do the mopping up, but my future husband has taught me the importance of taking care of messes before they start to take over, and anyway, I like putting stuff back in its place. It makes me feel industrious. I know where everything goes.

After I've swept up the kitchen, I take off my jeans and go to paint my toenails on the ledge of the bathtub. He prefers that I don't paint my toenails at home—he says, "that's what the Koreans are for," but smiling, so that he doesn't sound racist—yet I find a home pedicure to be very relaxing, and anyway, what he doesn't know won't really hurt him. I spread newspaper under my feet and retrieve my secret stash of Pink Pearl from the cabinet to the left of the guest bathroom sink.

My future husband is twenty years older than me. He has always been successful. Even in Wisconsin, where he didn't know a soul and there were no good restaurants, he made a lot of money doing some private brokerage and setting up a satellite office of the hedge fund he works for. He got the university professors investing, made them some profits at a meaty clip, assuming all the while that Sonia would figure out that nothing sucked worse than Madison and let them move back somewhere civilized, like Manhattan. I think he was honestly surprised when she told him that she didn't want to leave. I think he was especially surprised because of the baby.

"I couldn't stand it there, Jennifer," he said to me the first night he came in to the bar. I didn't know what the hell he was talking about, but he was drinking Glenmorangie single malt and when he said my name he smiled. I poured him more, figuring him to be a big tipper.

"I just couldn't," he said. "One more college football game and I would have—"

The thing to know about a man like my future husband is that he was made for only one place, for only one way of living. You can't put an Eskimo in the desert and you can't put a nomad on an island and you can't make a man like my future husband, who doesn't even know how to drive—you can't make a man like that move to Wisconsin. But I believe he tried, and I believe he loved his first wife.

"Jennifer," he said, on maybe the fourth or fifth night he came in. "She really fucked me up, you know that? She made promises she didn't keep."

I smiled a neutral bartender smile and kept the Glenmorangie flowing. Back then I lived in Brooklyn and wouldn't have gone to the Upper East Side for high water, etc., but now I like it here. I'm a hausfrau.

I haven't been to Brooklyn in months, because my future husband doesn't like it there and refuses to go. Owing to this reason I am always aware that his first wife moved him all the way to Wisconsin.

When I'm starting my second coat of Pink Pearl, the phone rings. I cap the polish and tiptoe across the carpet to the phone next to the bed, but I have to walk carefully not to screw up my pedi or, God forbid, the carpet. By the time I get to the phone the ringing has stopped. I check the caller ID. It says: Sonia Bornow, Madison, Wisconsin.

I look at the name until it fades away, and then press a button to make it reappear.

Madison, Wisconsin.

Although it's possible I shouldn't do this, I can't help myself. I'm going to meet her soon, after all. I know that her voice is smoky. Sometimes, when she's really mad, she has the faintest Russian accent, even though she was born in Boston. I have heard her rambling messages, after all. I have heard her curse in languages I can't understand.

Somebody picks up the phone but does not say "Hello," or "Yes?" or "Bornow residence."

"Hello?" I ask. "Hello?"

I can hear breathing, but no talking.

"*P'zhalste?*" I say, which is the one word of Russian I know.

There is more breathing. "Sonia?" I like saying her name out loud, but the person on the other end doesn't respond, and suddenly I think I know who I'm talking to.

"Oh, it's you," I say. "Hello," I say.

Breathing.

"How are you doing?"

The faintest breathing.

"Did you call to talk to your daddy? He's at work right now, but you can talk to me if you want."

Then I sit on the bed and hold the phone to my ear, listening to the child's breathing. I smile to myself. I don't think that liking children is just a phase.

"How are you doing today?" I ask, in a conversational tone that he might enjoy. "How's everything where you are?"

Silence.

"Here in New York it's pretty sunny out. Cold, though. Probably not as cold as Wisconsin."

Silence.

"Your dad and I can't wait for your visit, you know."

Silence.

"Do you know who I am?"

Silence.

"I'm Jennifer."

Then he begins to breathe again into the phone, quick, happy breaths, a little boy's.

I lie back on the bed, imagining his little face, his little hands, his little boy's grin. I happily breathe back.

[

] Over Portuguese muffins the next morning, my future husband tells me that Sonia will stay at a hotel on the Upper West Side, closer to Columbia, but will be dropping Trevor off on Monday morning to have breakfast with us. His therapy appointments are Monday afternoon. My future husband and his ex-wife have discussed this, he says, over e-mail, and he hopes these arrangements are all right with me. "Oh, of course," I say. "Couldn't be better." I cannot tell him how excited I am. I must keep my enthusiasm to myself. My future husband doesn't even want to talk about having any more children. He tried it once, the kid turned out mute, what does he need more problems for? As far as he's concerned, children are for people without anything better to do. We, on the other hand, are going to Fiji in March.

In order to get ready for Trevor's visit, I go to the Toys "R" Us in midtown, the one with the indoor ferris wheel, and I stock up on plastic robots and remote-controlled cars. I buy six stuffed animals, three board games, and, just in case, a Speak & Spell. I go to the pharmacy and buy kiddie shampoo and kiddie toothpaste and a kid-sized toothbrush. And then it occurs to me that Sonia might be a bit flighty—she does leave all those insane messages on our machine—so I go to the kids' boutique on Madison and buy six year-old-sized underwear and jeans and socks just in case his own mother forgets what to pack.

I wish I knew what baseball team he liked. I wish I knew his favorite cartoons.

"May I help you with those packages, Miss Sullivan?" the doorman asks, and this is the first time that he's ever said my name.

"No, thank you, Roger."

We live in what they call a classic six, which means that we have two official bedrooms plus a cozy little maid's room where Ronda sleeps on the nights we need her to stay over. If Ronda didn't have her stuff in the maid's room, I'd turn it into a little boy's room, since my future husband never goes in there and he wouldn't know the difference. I'd put up shelves for picture books and model airplanes, and I'd hook up a video game system with race-car games and Super Mario Brothers. I'd fill the closet with miniature Nikes and baseball caps and baseball jerseys. But circumstances being what they are, Trevor will stay in the guest room, which has beige wallpaper and a queen-sized bed. I wonder if the bed will seem enormous for Trevor, if he'll feel lost in its enormity. I wonder if he will wet the bed, and if my future husband will be annoyed. I wonder if the doorman will give him a lollipop. I never wonder why Trevor doesn't speak.

I sit down on Trevor's bed. It is big and grand, even for a person as old as I am, almost a quarter-century gone.

Before I met my future husband, before I moved into this place, I was formless, rootless. Honestly I was barely a person. I mean, yes, I'd had thoughts about being a dancer, and even now sometimes I get out my shoes and go down to the studio, but back in my full-time dancing days I wasn't making enough money and I wasn't talented enough, really. I knew it. Companies knew it. My future husband, when he first met me, said I seemed to be in the midst of a crisis of confidence. I decided to become confident in him. I grew up in Florida, near the highways, in the endless murky mildewed heat. My future husband has given me coolness and light. He's given me a list of things to do every day and a soft bed to sleep in every night.

I know I will love his son, and I hope that his son will love me.
[
] And then, three days later, they're here. I am wearing the black cashmere T-shirt my future husband got me for my birthday, because he says it makes me look mature and to tell you the truth I'm nervous. He asks me what all the wrapped packages are for in the guest room and I say, "Oh, just a few things to make Trevor feel at home," and he says, "You don't do kids any favors by spoiling them."

The doorman checks to make sure it's okay and then sends Trevor and Sonia on up. My future husband will be late for work because of this and I can tell he's unhappy already. He's checking his watch. "What's taking so long?" And then there's a knock at the door.

"Sonia."

"Adam."

"Come on in."

Oh well Christ, she's beautiful. That New Year's card did her no justice. She's wearing dark sunglasses and a black suit and her hair flows like a rusty river past her shoulders. Trevor is hiding behind her, his face poking out from behind her waist. I am staring at her, and my future husband is staring at his son.

"Hello, Trevor," my future husband says, and there is a quality I've never heard before in his voice. A softness. He goes up to them, kisses Sonia on the cheek, pulls Trevor out from behind his mother. He picks his son up and holds him up high, the kid's sneakers swaying in the air. Sonia looks around the foyer, nodding crisply, like this is exactly what she'd expected. Meanwhile, my future husband has folded Trevor to him and buried the kid in his arms.

"Oh, but she's just a child, Adam," the ex-wife says. She has taken off her sunglasses, and after a moment I realize she means me.

He puts Trevor down and leans down over him, his hands on his knees. "It's good to see you, Trev," he says, and rubs his forehead against his son's.

Trevor is smiling bashfully. He puts his hands on his cheeks.

"I mean really, Adam, she's just a child."

"It's nice to meet you," I say, holding out my hand. "I'm Jennifer Sullivan."

"Sonia Bornow," she says. I wonder why she still uses his last name. She shakes my hand with a forceless grip and a limp wrist. "How old are you, anyway?" she asks. "Twenty-four?"

"Sonia, leave her alone," my future husband says, and still there is a quality in his voice that's alien to me—now it's a quality of familiarity and boredom. It occurs to me that these two know each other extremely well. It occurs to me that Trevor looks just like his dad.

"I'm staying at the Lucerne, on 79th," she says.

"Did you have a good trip?"

"We had to connect in Chicago," she says. "O'Hare's impossible." She is walking into the living room, and we follow her: first my future husband, then Trevor, then me. "You're still on an Eames kick, I see." She sits down on the cowhide lounge.

"I had a decorator." He sits on the couch opposite her. He sounds apologetic.

"And what do you think of all this leather and steel?" she asks me. She stands up again. "Does he even let you do your nails in this palace?"

"I don't—"

"Sonia," he says.

"I'm just making conversation," she sighs airily. Now she plants herself down on one of the chairs I picked out from the museum store. They're expensive chairs, nice and solid, velvet versions of the chairs in a family portrait painted by Degas. I was just moving into this place—we'd been together five months—and my future husband told me that I could have everything, anything I wanted. We'd seen that painting together at the museum, and so I picked the chairs. I knew my future husband wouldn't mind them.

"How's business?" she asks.

"Fine," my future husband says. Actually, I'm pretty sure that it's better than fine, because sometimes I deposit the checks. His bonus this year was more than my father made in his entire life.

"Tomarkin's on the board now," she says. "They cleared him of impropriety."

"You're kidding."

"Nope. He's a *mamzer*," she says. "But a lucky one."

"Tomarkin," my future husband says. "I can't believe he got away with that shit. He must have found an excellent accountant."

"Someone from California, I heard. Sausalito, strangely enough."

"An accountant from Sausalito?"

They are speaking a foreign language. Sausalito, Tomarkin, *mamzer*: I can't tell nouns from verbs.

"And what about Linley?" my future husband asks. "Did he escape without—"

"Christ," Sonia says. "You don't even want to know." Then she stands up again, a jumping jack.

"You don't even want to know," she repeats. "All that money he lost."

"He should have stayed put. I kept telling him—"

Sonia's expression darkens suddenly, like a curtain dropping. "So will you be able to drop Trevor off?" she says, an arch note in her voice. She moves forward three paces so that she is standing over my future husband, who seems queerly diminished. He hunches forward on the couch. She really is quite tall. I didn't know Jewish ladies could get that tall.

"Sonia, of course," my future husband mumbles.

"What?"

"I said, of course."

"Don't of course me," she says. Her voice now has razors in it. "Don't give me your of courses. You haven't even visited your son in two years. You haven't even sent so much as a birthday card. You haven't paid for the speech therapy, I've told you a hundred times how much it costs, you who have all this—"

"Sonia," he says, and I can tell how he wants it to sound, like he's warning her, but it's not working. He doesn't sound the way he wishes he does. He looks older there, thirty years older, hunched over like a gnome on the couch. I am off to the side of the room, tugging on the corner of my cashmere T-shirt. The boy is sitting on the floor near the window. I have lived in this apartment for over a year. My clothing is in the closets. My pictures are in the bedroom. I sleep with my future husband every night, my head on the warm pad of his chest, his legs folding over mine.

"Please," my future husband says to his ex-wife. "Please, let's not do this now."

"You owe me thousands, Adam. You walked out on our family and you owe me, big time."

"Please," he says again, my future husband, the gnome.

Sonia puts her hands on her hips. I can't believe the way she is standing over him, a leaning tower, all black suit and long hair and enormous feet. She taps a toe slowly.

"I couldn't take it anymore," he says, and still there is only emptiness in his voice.

"So you decided to get revenge on me by abandoning your only child?"

"Sonia, I couldn't—"

"By abandoning him?" Her voice is raised. She seems taller and taller, filling up all the space in this apartment.

But it's my hand he holds when we walk through the park. It's my hand he holds when we walk to the movies. He holds doors for me, in restaurants and museums, and he opens the doors of taxicabs for me in the rain. And I have changed for him, gone to galas, given up Christmas.

"I didn't—" Then he stops.

"You know you did," she says. "Blame it on whatever you want, but you know you abandoned him." The kid is hunched over too, just like his father, and oh what I would do to go over there and take him in my arms. Trevor is focusing intently on his shoes. I tug on the corner of my sweater.

"You forced me." He stops again. He looks up at her; he's helpless. "I couldn't stay anymore. I couldn't live with it. You were killing me, Sonia." His voice is quiet now. He whispers, "You were killing me."

"Oh please," she says.

"I couldn't take it anymore," he says.

She doesn't look away.

"You broke my heart. I wanted to be there. I wanted to stay. And you— you broke my heart."

"Adam," she says, sitting back down on the velvet chair I picked out. "I beg you not to be an infant about this. You owe me thousands of dollars. Your son has a speech problem and it takes money to fix it. I will take it to a lawyer if needs be, although I've been reluctant to—"

"You broke my heart," he says.

"You owe me money," she says.

Trevor is playing with his shoelaces now. I had thought I could talk my future husband into more children, maybe, eventually. I thought maybe after Fiji. I thought maybe after the wedding.

"I wanted to stay, Sonia. I loved you. I loved you more than I ever—"

She cuts him off, taps her enormous toe. "Not in front of the children," she says, and looks at us, past us, toward the big glass windows in this Upper East Side apartment that just an hour ago felt like my home.

"Perhaps I'd better—" I start.

"A man who refuses to pay for the medical care his child desperately needs—"

"Sonia—"

"But still has money for these horrible, for these tasteless, for these *1997* chairs—" and here she points at one with that toe.

"Why don't I go somewhere—" But I am lost; there's nowhere for me to go. So instead I find myself backing up and sitting down on the floor next to Trevor. We're in the corner of the room, invisible. We're both staring at our shoes.

"I still miss you, Sonia," Trevor's father whispers. He sounds broken. "We could still—"

"You owe me big-time money, asshole. And that is all." I can hear the Russian accent appear, that accent I know she didn't come by honestly, and at this I want to jump up and say something, that for her to come into this house and call him an asshole isn't right, it's clear he loves his son, it's clear she ruined his life, it's clear he hasn't recovered from it. And this is my house too, by the way. This is where I live now, these are my chairs, I am no longer a child.

But as I'm opening my mouth to speak, my future husband's son looks right at me. He puts a delicate finger in front of his mouth. He smiles slightly. He's still holding onto his shoelace. "Shhh," he says.

So I stay quiet.

] One Good Reason Why Not

Darren's rehab counselor told Marcia it would be best to avoid asking him questions: "Everything is new. Follow his lead." They were letting him out for her 60th birthday, sprung on a chaperoned pass.

He showed up at the bustling Italian place near the end of dinner. They had waited forty minutes before going ahead and starting without him. His chaperone was a stooped man with girlish hands, a stutter, and ancient rimless glasses. Marcia said "Hi, Dare," and left it at that.

Darren said "Hey." Then, with effort, but seeming to mean it: "Happy Birthday."

He and the chaperone sat in the two open chairs, and Marcia tried to bridge the distance with her smile, an open face. She wanted to ask *what held you up?* Or *How are you?* But following Darren's lead made questions—any questions—impossible.

"Awkward!" Nina stage-whispered.

Marcia introduced herself to the chaperone.

"Ar-ar-t-tie," he said, looking her in the eyes. "P-pleasure."

They went around the table, and Marcia's old sorority sisters identified themselves.

"Anne."

"Ellen."

"Linda."

Artie nodded at everyone.

"And I'm Nina," said Nina. "My mother was friends with these ladies. Now she's dead. I like to spend time with them because it makes me feel less motherless." Gayle—dear, dead Gayle—and Marcia had been pregnant at the same time. They had shared an OB, who liked to joke that he could catch one baby in each hand if need be.

Artie grinned, his teeth the same shade of yellow as the crème brûlée. Marcia liked him very much.

Zelig was asleep under the table, splayed face down like he was embracing the whole of the world beneath him: polished marble and sealant and grout and floorboards and joists and cement and earth and earth and earth.

"And who-who-who's this f-f-fine young gentleman?" Artie asked, theatrically lifting a piece of tablecloth.

"This is really not a place for a three-year old," Anne noted for the third time. Zelig had spent the appetizer course running loud loops around the perimeter of the restaurant, shouting his name. Anne had been decidedly frosty with her two daughters, who lived near each other in Irvine somewhere now, coordinating family portraits for holiday cards, stay-at-home-mom pseudo careerists. They were always sending out these relentlessly cheerful mass e-mails with the same discount offers. *What could be better than a keepsake photograph of the whole clan?* Memories Forever, it was called. *Why not give each other the gift of memory this year?*

"Who's he bothering, Anne?"

"There are adult places and children's places, Nina. A nice restaurant at 9:30 P.M. is an adult place. Adults should be able to enjoy adult places."

"Just say he's bothering you. Say 'He's bothering me.'" They were indeed Nina's stand-in mothers, and she baited them accordingly. Artie let the tablecloth drop.

"Are you hungry, sweetie?" Marcia asked Darren, not following his lead.

"I'm fine," he said.

She waved down a waitress anyway. "Can we get another couple menus, please?"

"I'm *fine*," he said again.

Whatdoyouwantforyourbirthday, Mom? Darren had called to ask last week.

Just you! she'd said, overly enthusiastic, not used to this kind of overture. Not used to phone calls or questions about birthday presents. Or being addressed as "Mom," for that matter. Usually he avoided addressing her directly. What did she want for her birthday? She was surprised he knew when her birthday *was*.

Just you: She had meant to say she was glad he was alive, that his existence was birthday present enough. He'd almost died this time. And the time before, too, but this time he was very nearly dead. She worried it came off like veiled criticism: He had failed to kill himself with a dose of recreational narcotics large enough to sate a frat house, and she was glad he had failed.

After dessert, Marcia opened her birthday card. *Signs You're Getting Older: The only names in your little black book have* M.D. *after them. Your back goes out more than you do. You're asleep but others worry you're dead. Happy Birthday!* Signed Anne, Ellen, Linda, and Nina (*under duress*). A year-long gift membership to a dating website for Jews was enclosed. User 163542, come see the possibilities!

"Try it, Marsh," they chanted. "The *internet!*" They were lit from below by sparkling silverware, shiny dessert plates, votives. Who replaced her old sorority sisters with crones? How long had they been feeling sorry for her? Linda badly needed to stop wearing shoulder pads, Anne could stand to change up the perm she'd been sporting since 1982, and Ellen smelled like her four King Charles Spaniels.

Darren picked silently at a piece of birthday cake.

"What do you think, Dare?" Linda always the butchiest of them, with her raspy voice and her broad shoulders, reached over and gave him a shove. "Should your mom give it a go?"

Darren was not one to open up freely. Except for that once, when he had shown up unannounced at her house at eleven P.M., wanting, he said, to "hang"—*Mom, it's like we're bumper cars sometimes, you know? Like, we just bump into each other and then we're off again, and I don't get why it has to* be *that way*—but she realized later that he had been very high that time.

"Yeah, why not." It sounded not very much like a question. He cleared his throat and headed for the bathroom, cloth napkin in a heap on the floor by the leg of his chair. Artie, after a moment's hesitation, got up and followed.

"Darren's *big* into the internet," Nina said, lip in curl.

Darren was in fact fighting overlapping addictions to women and poker and pornography and downers. Strange combination, to Marcia's thinking. "Not uncommon," according to the rehab lady. Darren directed television commercials and was into self-actualization seminars from which he had more than once called Marcia to confess some sordid emotion, asking of her some sort of vague "closure" or "healing." What this meant, Marcia had learned, was that she was to pay money to accompany him to one of these seminars so that he could tell her just how much he despised her before he fell off the wagon again. On the rare occasions Darren deigned to make an appearance at a family function (his grandfather's funeral, for instance), he'd invariably have an inappropriately dressed aspiring actress/model of color on his arm. (*He's got jungle fever*, Nina would sing, shimmying.) The last one, Stacia, tottered on platform heels as long as her calves and simply giggled when asked how she and Darren met, giggled and giggled and giggled. Hence, forty thousand dollars a month at an estate in Malibu with a chef, masseuse, and pool. No insurance accepted. The details were like rocks Marcia had to carry around in her mouth: distasteful, making it very difficult to hold a conversation. It could be worse, though. She could be refinancing her house. Selling her mother's big heavy pearls.

"Thank you so much, ladies," Marcia said. Her smile got the eyes all wrong: squinty. So she halted the smiling, but then her eyes went all botched-face-lift-wide and she just gave up, examined the card on the table. Its thick folded seam looked like a scar.

Ellen signed the check. Anne expertly, without a compact, applied the same pink Chanel she'd been wearing since junior year. Linda muttered again about the internet, the internet, the possibilities, the internet, *a-woman-I-work-with*-and-the-internet!

They gathered for birthday dinners. They took turns choosing bestsellers, half-reading them, then getting drunk and one-upping each other on topics as diverse as daughter-in-law rage and grandchild-precociousness. They were Marcia's friends in the sense that they had been her friends for a long time. But they were not her friends in the sense that they were her friends.

Darren's bathroom run was of course too long and Marcia wondered about the state of his digestive system. Once upon a long while ago she had been monitor and confessor of his bowels, changing diapers and keeping track of the consistency and frequency of his shit. When he returned, trailed by Artie, it was as though he knew what she'd been thinking. He offered a savage "*What?*" as they all got up and headed out to retrieve their cars from the valet. Without eye contact, he barked a second staccato "Happy Birthday" and got into the passenger seat of Artie's decade-old white Lexus sedan. Artie, his eyes shining with apology for all manner of disconnected sadnesses, wished Marcia a "Hap-hap-happy Buh-buh-birthday."

[

] Weeks later, at the computer, fighting the discomfort of the thing, Marcia turned out to be a WOMAN between 60 and 70 in search of a MAN between 60 and 75.

"*Hell* no!" Nina said. "Ask for a sixty-five-year-old and you'll wind up with an inbox full of assholes pushing eighty." Her hands hovered over the keyboard for a thoughtful moment. "So, wait. Here. Look. Good news. You're actually forty-nine. Voila!"

"But—"

"No, seriously, everyone lies. You just have to factor the lies in; it's how it's done. Promise you. Trust me."

"Why? Why."

"Because. Shush."

She was a little curious, truth be told, about the "possibilities." But was her need for companionship so objectively large? Did her friends— did *everyone*—think she was pathetic? Having been dumped by the father of her child had certainly been at least a little pathetic; she had been attempting, by refusing to date over the course of these years, the lifetime since that devastation, to mitigate any further humiliation.

Years ago Marcia went out with a man—a fix-up via Anne's husband Paul—who'd insisted she take off her shoes before she came into his house for coffee. Some sort of Japanese affectation, though the man was a Jew from the Bronx. She had demurred: lymph edema caused her right foot to swell rather grotesquely, and she was self-conscious about it. They had each stood their ground—

"Just leave them right here, they'll be fine, I promise."

"I would really rather not."

"Well, I don't allow shoes in my house."

"I'm sorry, I would just rather not."

"Do you have any idea the kind of filth we track into our living spaces on our shoes?"

—and said their goodbyes on the front stairs. Anne had been furious.

Nina wriggled onto the side of the chair and then over, pushing Marcia off and out of the way. He could be SINGLE, DIVORCED, or WIDOWED, but widowed would be ideal. He'd still worship the memory of his old, sweet, lumpy love. He'd be heartbroken, amenable, eager. None of the sprouted misogyny of the newly divorced; no entrenched quirks of the confirmed bachelor.

"Let's hope for someone who hasn't been alone too long," Nina said. The mouse was like an extension of her hand; she was swift and graceful with it. He should be OVER 5'10, and have at least a COLLEGE DEGREE. "They always tell you not to date someone just out of a relationship, but those guys are way, way easier to work with. Malleable. Men get warped when they're alone too long."

"Everyone gets warped when they're alone too long." Marcia was referring to herself, meant no offense. "Everyone old is warped."

"You're not old."

Marcia laughed. "I'm not young." She had the fleeting thought that she was glad Gayle was dead: It was nice to have Nina around.

"You're the same age as Helen Mirren. Did you see that tabloid bikini shot? Snap out of it."

"You know when your mom and I were in school we had to take typing?"

"Ideal date?"

"Well." Marcia considered. She wanted to abandon the whole idea. Like while putting on gym clothes for her dutiful bi-monthly trek to Lady Fitness: *I can't, I can't, I don't want to, I don't want to, you can't make me.* No, she would not bail. She would Just Do It, as the gym clothes advise. Once there she's always glad she made it to step class after all; she feels robust and unassailable en route home afterwards. This would be like that. "A chance to get to know each other."

"That's implied. Here, okay: 'Dinner, a movie, a moonlight stroll, breakfast in bed.' "

Marcia laughed again. The thought of sex with men from the internet was absurd enough to make moot even the smallest protestation. The thought of *sex* was absurd, internet or no internet. It really wasn't that important as you got older, sex; it just mattered less and less. One dared not say this out loud, however. Especially to a single mother in her thirties.

Nina left at eleven, rousing Zelig from a deep sleep in front of the television. He was disoriented and near-tears as they made their way up the drive.

"Want . . ." he said, trailing off. Whether this was a verb he hoped to connect to himself and an immediate desire or a noun meant to identify the sorry state of being alive, there was no telling.

[

] On visitor's day in Malibu, Marcia wore a cream linen pantsuit and delicate gold chain necklace. She looked, she thought, not at all like the kind of woman whose only son trolled the internet for anonymous sex whilst munching valium.

"We have a wonderful opportunity today," said the counselor, "for openness and healing." Seven residents—overweight, underweight, heavily made up, tattooed, pierced, gorgeous, and Darren—sat next to seven visitors. Marcia saw no sign of Artie. Underweight's visitor—her father, it soon became clear—was a handsome man with a deep tan set off by a thick shock of white hair. Marcia caught his eye and smiled cheerfully—*do I look like the kind of woman whose only son trolls the internet for anonymous sex whilst munching valium?*—but he did not reciprocate. His daughter, it turned out, enjoyed vomit and heroin.

"She never talked about anything," Darren told the group. "My father left and she just refused to say anything. My father died and she didn't say anything. She just sits in her house alone, drinking tea and reading the paper."

The counselor looked pained. "Darren, how about telling your mom about some of the more positive framing we've been learning these last few weeks?"

His shoulders relaxed a little with an exhale. "It was just really hard for me not to have anyone to talk to growing up."

"Darren feels that he was left to his own devices at crucial moments in his life," the counselor translated.

Marcia nodded. "Yes," she said. "I understand."

Darren had a life coach and a therapist and a sponsor and a peer mentor, too. Marcia had sat helplessly at more of these group therapy sessions than she could count. Darren feels ignored by you. Darren feels that you do not hear him. Darren feels judged by you. Excuse me, she did not dare herself to say, but how is it possible to be both ignored and judged? You see? Darren would say to the life coach or the therapist or the sponsor or the peer mentor. You see??

To her frustration, Marcia could not remember the origin of the name Darren. Why had they named him Darren? A name with no meaning, no history, and no real relevance to their cultural, religious, or family heritage. Could it have been because of the television show about that sexy witch and her clueless husband? Dick had liked that show. Had she named her child thoughtlessly? Was that why he was who he was? There was always the *why* with Darren: Why was he Like This? Why was he *Darren*? Linda's daughter Stacey had named *her* daughter Ona. Presumably, as Nina loved to point out, without bothering to look up "onanism" or "onanist."

So the unconsidered name was Marcia's first failure. Then, following the advice of the pediatrician in hopes of getting Darren to sleep through the night, she had allowed him to scream himself unconscious alone in his crib at four months old. Two hours, he had screamed. At the time it had seemed a brutal necessity borne of exhaustion; now the memory made her feel physically ill, and she wanted to hold him, that tiny child.

After an exquisite lunch of homemade ricotta ravioli and pesto under a heavy green canvas umbrella, the ocean hissing sweetly below them, and still no sign of Artie, they said their goodbyes.

"See ya," he told her, smiling his strange, angry smile.

[

] She was surprised to find she loved the internet, loved checking it and checking it and checking it and checking it. She knew this much: In a relationship, she could best tolerate weaknesses she herself did not share. She did not want a spendthrift. She did not want an over-reactor. She did not want someone with low self-esteem. She had recently begun therapy. ("Wow," Darren said. "Only thirty years too late.")

Was it too much to hope for someone with altogether fresh, surprising flaws? Was it too much to hope that it would cost her nothing at all to accommodate those unfamiliar vulnerabilities?

Her first date—screen name: CATCHOFTHEDAY3—was a seventy-one-year-old widower, retired from tax law, an avid fisherman.

"What was your best catch ever?" Marcia asked him, game, over salad.

"A one-hundred-pound hammer-head shark," he crowed, destroying her appetite.

"Wow," she forced. Was that even possible? And what was the point of luring a large animal, mutilating it, hauling it out of the ocean? Recreation? She couldn't have been less impressed or interested. "That's amazing." The meal stretched interminably ahead of her. She drank three large glasses of Bordeaux, started to think about dying, about what it would be like, about the minutes of her life ticking away at this table, with this man. When he pulled out pictures of his grandkids (Emily, 9, Ethan, 6, Max, 2) she felt like her throat was closing up. She felt itchy and hot, like she might be developing some sort of wine-allergy.

"And what about you?" he asked, folding the snapshot back into his wallet, then lifting an ass cheek to replace it. Short legs, a comb-over. "Any grandkids?"

"No," she laughed. She'd meant for it to come out light, uncon-cerned, simple; instead it was a rueful bark, a heavy cannon launched over the top of the third glass, smoke trailing thickly behind. "My son Darren is . . ." She could already tell he didn't want to hear it, or wouldn't hear it right. ". . . has problems."

"Aw," said CATCHOFTHEDAY3. "He's got to grow up sometime!"

Later, in his idling Jaguar in front of her house, Marcia could see the forthcoming attempt at a kiss taking shape even before he turned off the engine. If she listened closely she thought she could actually hear the gears shifting in his head: rusty, ancient, awful. She was embarrassed already, for both of them, but she let it happen anyway. There was no stopping a thing like that. He slipped his tongue between her lips, darted it in and out, lizard-like. His breath was rotten, like he'd never flossed in his life, like not even once.

When she got inside she made herself slightly burnt toast with mar-garine, asked herself quasi-cheerfully if it had been *really that bad*, brushed her teeth for a solid four minutes, put on a freshly laundered nightgown and socks, got into bed with her ancient electric blanket, shivered, and fell asleep.

[

] "I can't do this," she told Nina on the phone after date number two, a widower (LOOKIN4LOVE) who'd teared up when she ordered chocolate mousse because *Ruth was always on a diet; she refused to believe that I thought she was beautiful, but I did, I really did.*

When it had come time for Marcia to relay the facts—childhood in Brentwood, first Jewish family admitted to Los Angeles Country Club, honors English teacher at private girls' school in the valley, only son, no grandchildren, one failed marriage a hundred and ten years earlier, decades spent in blissful isolation ever since, the need to have her own bucket of popcorn at the movies and not have to discuss what she'd seen, the way she prided herself on the ability to go an entire weekend (Friday evening to Monday morning) without speaking one word to a single solitary soul, the birthday/book group, Nina—she had fallen back on "I don't know, I suppose I'm pretty boring."

A wail erupted on Nina's end.

"I swear to fucking God, Zelig, take it *off*. I'm not asking you again." The wailing tapered off to a whimper, then quieted entirely.

"It isn't for me," Marcia said. "This stuff." Sitting with strange old men in large idling cars outside her house.

Nina sighed. "Zelig! *Now*. Marcia, can I call you back?"

"Absolutely," Marcia said.

The phone rang twenty minutes later.

"Okay. We're both sedated and in bed." Zelig, now almost four, was Nina's partner-in-crime, which made even the roughest parenting patches seem like a loopy adventure: stressful, wacky, no biggie in the end. She brought him to music festivals and movies and cafés and restaurants, lived her life just as she always had, only with the little boy in tow. She worked for a record label, did something with rock bands, traveled a lot, seemed to move within a vast network of friends and friends-of-friends, referred to hers as "the life." In the sixties, "The Life" had meant prostitution, but Marcia knew that this association, like most of her associations, was anachronistic. Marcia prided herself on maintaining an insoluble membrane around herself through which nothing as transient and meaningless as slang, as this or that trend, could penetrate. How else to protect herself from ever-shifting tides? Zelig could nap anywhere, Nina bragged. He had slept backstage at a Radiohead show when he was eight weeks old. He had traveled cross-country with his mother in a tour bus at two. "Now. How bad was it?"

LOOKIN4LOVE had teared up twice, apologized profusely, and had seemed, by the time they sat in his Mercedes, even less inclined to initiate some sort of amorous farewell than was Marcia. Which was at once a relief and somehow insulting.

Nina found this hilarious. "I once went out with a guy who gave me a lecture at the end of the night about why he wasn't going to kiss me. He had, like, a power-point presentation. Douche."

It was Nina's favorite insult, though she was too young to remember when women actually did such things, encouraged to think themselves filthy, barely manageable. Marcia had tried muttering it under her breath, in traffic, say, when someone cut her off, but it sounded absurd, brought forth awful sense memories of those awful euphemistic advertisements and that awful sickly flower scent. That same scent on the scratch-and-sniff page of Zelig's copy of *Pat the Bunny*. How shameful to have been part of that generation, too ignorant or compliant to know better. She found herself wishing bitterly that she'd been smarter, or born later. Wishing, really, that she was Nina: fearless and free.

Marcia didn't tell Nina the worst part of the date, that after hearing his dead wife's name Marcia could not stop repeating it to herself until she was finally safely back in her house, alone: *Ruth, Ruth, Ruth*. LOOKIN4LOVE was solicitous and kind, clearly in agony. *Ruth*, she chanted to herself. *Ruth, your husband is a mess*. At parties, in another life, the husbands had talked to the husbands and the wives to the wives. [

] Couldn't we perhaps read something a little more *interesting*? she wondered periodically. They found her condescending. Yes, she thought herself smarter than they. And they understood that. And still: couldn't they read something a little more *interesting*? Her ninth graders were doing more sophisticated literary analyses.

They let it go because they could indulge in a little pity party where Marcia's singledom was concerned, all hushed and consoling. As though it couldn't be a legitimate choice she'd made: peace and quiet and her own bucket of popcorn at the movies and blissful exemption from having to discuss the movie on the way home. They were not at all conscientious about curtailing discussion of their own marriages, their own squadrons of grandchildren, the cruises and cruises and more cruises they were planning now that Bob/Stuart/Jeffrey was retired. She bristled at the sappy shit novels they insisted on reading and discussing in depth; they made endless mention of their happy, healthy families.

And then there was Nina, hanging around her dead mother's friends, enjoying wine and cheese like she was one of them, but given to statements like "there's just no way I'm going make it through my thirties without getting herpes." The women were marginally appalled but more than a little amused. On one adolescent Halloween, Nina had famously removed her tongue ring, dressed up in clean, conservative clothes, straightened her hair, donned control-top pantyhose and beige lipstick: "Me, if my dad hadn't died," she'd said by way of explanation. She was as self-possessed and vibrant, at sixteen, at twenty-five, at thirty-two, as anyone Marcia had ever known.

She couldn't talk to her friends, Nina said. They didn't understand. Their parents were still alive. Their empathy hung on having lost a grandparent or two. She felt freakish and unrelatable, small talk beyond her. She could, she claimed, stand only Marcia's presence, only the book-club ladies, only her sweet elderly therapist. She had crossed over, she said, to the dark side. "I can't listen to my friends whine about how their parents don't understand them," she'd said. "At least the fuckers *have* parents." Nina's father had died when she was seven, of a massive coronary. Then Gayle, fifteen years later, of cancer.

She would come over unannounced, smoke a joint, grow tired and philosophical, stretch out on the couch, and wonder softly: "Can I sleep over?" And then, a few years following her mother's death, Nina had come upon the need for a child like a road-block: no way around it.

"Who fucking cares?" She had said dispassionately one night on a chaise in Marcia's backyard. She had gone off the pill, slept with a no-strings older married friend, and was keeping the baby. Marcia thought this crazy, reckless, and fascinating. Fall had set in and they were wrapped in blankets against the Los Angeles night air, which always seemed so much colder than expected, somehow.

"Nothing ever happens the way it's supposed to and who fuck-ing cares, anyway?" Marcia hadn't been sure what this meant, exactly. Nina looked nothing like dear, dead Gayle but for the exact same hairline—asymmetrical and impossible to wear any way but loose and messy. It had, in their perfect-flip-era early-sixties adolescence, been the bane of Gayle's existence. Marcia remembered a period of time in the spring of 1962 spent unsuccessfully dissuading her friend from hairline electrolysis.

"I mean, why not?" Nina had said. "What's one good reason why not? Money? Life is *life*." She was a special girl, Nina, special from the time she was a tiny: fierce and funny and bossy as hell. Darren, three weeks younger to the day, used to cry whenever Nina came near him.

[

] "No more dinners," Nina declared. "Dinner is way too long. Coffee. Finite. A half-hour. If you like each other, you have the rest of your lives to eat meals together."

So on her third date, Marcia met DRFEELGOOD for coffee, and had something approaching a good time. He was bearish, an anesthesiologist with palms like platters and a Range Rover.

"I know, I know, global warming," he said, first thing, when he pulled up in front of the Coffee Bean and got out of the car. "I know."

"Global *what?*" Marcia said, coquettish. And then, admiringly: "Big car," as though she'd never seen its equal. She loved a cocky bastard. Dick had not infrequently begun conversations with the phrase "The thing about me is . . ." well into their eight-year marriage. As though Marcia were a perfect stranger, only just getting to know him. Enough years had elapsed, enough time had worn away at her memories, and DRFEELGOOD seemed charming.

It was a quick date, forty-five minutes on the nose. Marcia had lied, on Nina's advice, and told DRFEELGOOD that she'd have to leave at six for a dinner party.

"Well, Martha," he said to her, an enormous hand on her back, "you seem like a nice lady."

"As do you," she said.

"I am a nice lady!" he said, and they both laughed, Marcia with a hot flush. He gave her a polite kiss on the cheek and opened her car door. "I'll e-mail you."

"Okay."

Bingo, DRFEELGOOD. The sheer size of him, the way he hadn't seemed nervous or hesitant in the least. She bought a teeth-whitening kit at the drugstore, prepared to dazzle him on their second date. It was an odd feeling, dusty and vertiginous, and she went with it.

But he didn't e-mail, and she spent days analyzing those three little words—I'll E-mail You—with Nina.

"He said he'd e-mail me."

"Sometimes they don't do what they say they're gonna do."

"But then why would he say it?"

"One of life's little mysteries."

"Should I e-mail him?"

"No."

"Maybe he's just swamped."

"No."

Marcia waited a few days, then a few more.

"Maybe—" she'd begin to say, detailing a justifiable reason why DRFEELGOOD hadn't e-mailed.

"Do not e-mail him, Marcia. Do. Not."

So this was dating: open-ended disappointment that wore, if you were lucky, gradually off.

CATCHOFTHEDAY3, however, did e-mail. *I had a wonderful time*, he said. *Would you like to see the new Spielberg film with me next Saturday?*

Marcia wasn't sure. When last she'd been an active dater, a second date had meant some specific thing. Second base?

[

] Nina came over with Zelig and a copy of *He's Just Not That Into You.*

"Grammy Marcia," Zelig said, looking up from his Rubik's Cube. "Look at my nails!" They were light blue and glittery.

"Very nice," Marcia said unconvincingly.

"And my toes!" He kicked off his sandals. Done to match.

"Yes," she said. "Blue."

The "Grammy" was a little hard to take; Marcia felt guilty as the beneficiary of this title. Nina had introduced it from the get-go; what difference did it make to Zelig? But Marcia was not his "Grammy." Dear, dead Gayle was his "Grammy." So he therefore had no Grammy. This seemed like a reality he could and should understand. But Marcia bore the strangeness: Nina needed Zelig to have a Grammy and she, Marcia, was it.

Anyway, Zelig seemed to genuinely like her, his "Grammy" Marcia. And she liked him, too, certainly, though in general felt so out of place and disqualified where children were concerned that it was difficult to relax. It wasn't that Darren was her fault, per se—he'd had, in addition to his disinterested and depressed mother, the impossible-to-impress, largely absent, and eventually dead narcissist for a father—but surely things might have been different if Marcia had loved him more, or better. *Darren feels rejected and abandoned by you. Darren would like to feel accepted for who he is, with all of his faults. Darren feels like you don't really love him.* Darren likes long walks on the beach and dinners out. Darren would like to find a partner, lover, and soulmate. Sense of humor a must.

Nina put in a DVD of the original *Charlie and the Chocolate Factory.* She foisted upon Zelig movies and books and television shows that she herself had enjoyed as a child. He and his mother, then, shared formative influences and references, sang the same songs: Nina ironically, Zelig earnestly.

They seemed—gleefully singing *don't care how; I want it* now! and substituting "Tofu!" in *sing it once, sing it twice . . . chicken soup with rice*—more like old buddies than caretaker-and-dependant. Who knew you could mother a son in such a way?

"Let's go scope out the dudes," Nina said. In Darren's room, everything was exactly the way Darren had left it: plastic wall sleeves full of baseball cards, framed Leroy Neiman print, faded blue and red bedspread, the lingering sense of surely-somewhere-stashed box of pornography, a fine coating of mustiness and old semen on everything but the computer, shiny and lightening-quick, on Darren's old desk.

He had come over a while back to help her set it up, knitting his brow and barking orders at her like theirs was a secret mission, like they were in great danger.

"I need a scissors!" he'd shouted. "Where's the instructions?"

Where are *the instructions*, she stopped herself from correcting.

Marcia was supposed to have been incredibly grateful he'd come over to help her at all; it was a sort of honor, she knew. She was supposed to *validate*, to *support*. She thanked him profusely and tried to compliment him.

"Wow, Dare, you're really wonderful with computers."

He'd glared at her, rolled his eyes, managed a poisonous "whatever."

"Let's see what the deal is, here," Nina said. Marcia perched on the edge of the bed. "What's your screen name?"

"GARBO5."

Nina typed it in and looked up at Marcia, quizzical.

"You know, Greta Garbo: 'I vant to be alone.'"

"Well, no wonder this isn't happening for you. Password?"

But her password was too embarrassing even to share with Nina, so she typed it in herself.

"New message!" Nina crowed. It was from LOOKIN4LOVE, thanking Marcia for a lovely time on their date the week before and for being so kind to him. *I'm realizing that I may not be quite ready to date*, he wrote. *With Ruth's death still at the forefront of my mind, I'm finding it difficult to move on. But it was very nice to meet you and I wish you all the best.*

"Douche," Nina said.

"Mommy!" Zelig yelled from the TV room. "It's the bad part!"

"He hates that 'Cheer Up, Charlie' song at the beginning," Nina explained. "You know? When the mom's stirring the laundry with a giant fork? Scares the crap out of him."

Nina got up to fast forward. There were no other new messages. Marcia scrolled through her measly inbox—CATCHOFTHEDAY3, LOOKIN4LOVE, DRFEELGOOD, and one she'd never bothered responding to (FOOLFORLOVE16) because he'd gone all the way down to thirty (*thirty!*) in describing his sought-after match.

She looked at DRFEELGOOD's initial e-mail: *How about we get together? I'd love to hear more about your job at the all-girls' school! Do they wear uniforms, or what?*

She did a spontaneous search for men between 30 and 40, thinking that she'd do the motherly thing and "scope out" some "dudes" on Nina's behalf.

"Why don't you do this?" Marcia asked when Nina came back into the room. "Look what darling boys." She'd found a couple already who seemed good-looking and charming, not a grammatical error to be found in their profiles.

Nina snorted. "Right." She leaned over and began browsing. " 'I'm looking for my best friend and soul mate!' Know what that means? Erectile dysfunction. Oh: you 'have a great sense of humor,' do you? Then Why Am I Not Laughing? Look at this one! 'SEXYBEAST76'! He's *real* sexy! Yeeow! Let's see how tall he is!" She went on like this for a while. "Oooh, looky here: the thirty-nine-year-old is looking for a twenty-two-year-old! He's probably the nurturing type. Here's a picture of KEVIN-11970 taken *in a bar while he's holding a martini.* Spray tan much?"

"He seems sweet," Marcia protested weakly.

"Marcia," Nina said finally, "these guys are complete douches. Not to mention the fact that they're definitely not in the market for single mothers." She scrolled down, down, then stopped short.

And there was Darren in a series of snapshots: one with a woman cut out (you could still see the side of her face and the swell of an enormous inflated breast—she looked like Stacia, or a Stacia), one with his shirt off, at the beach, the sun glinting off his pectorals as if he had oiled himself, another with a different woman cut out. Nina looked pained, tried valiantly to hold back laughter.

His profile was awful, full of errors and idiocy: *Anybody that thinks they know who their looking for is selling themselves short. Nothings sexier than a lady in stilettos.* She'd had no idea he had even the slightest interest in a Jewish woman. He'd marked his level of observance as "traditional." He'd listed himself as seeking "marriage and children." Marcia was too baffled to speak. She supposed she knew people often represented themselves (even *to* themselves) in ways incongruent with reality. But Darren? J-Match?

Nina quietly stretched out on Darren's bed, examined her cell phone. "You should probably get off his profile, Marsh. People can see who's viewed them, I think."

She was frozen in place, reading hungrily. He liked Vietnamese food? He enjoyed windsurfing? His smile in the snapshots was so nakedly, surprisingly human. Where had he learned such atrocious grammar?

"*Darren* is why I'm not on freaking J-Match," Nina muttered before getting up and leaving the room. Marcia flashed onto a memory of herself and Gayle sunning themselves on loungers in Gayle's backyard in another century, supervising their tiny children in a wading pool, Nina entertaining herself thoroughly while Darren kept shouting to be watched. *Watch me, mommy. Watch me, mommy. Mommy: watch me!* There was a photograph somewhere. She would find it and frame it, remind herself to hope for the best where Darren was concerned, to pity him with motherly patience, penitence.

In the TV room, the Oompa-Loompas were chronicling the demise of another no-good child. Zelig was fighting sleep, refusing to give in, losing the battle.

"Nina?" Marcia called. She found her on the patio, cell at her ear. *One sec*, she mouthed. Marcia sat on the brick steps and looked at the fence, slats chipping around the top, mud-stained down below. It needed painting.

"I'm just going to run out, meet these guys for an hour or two," Nina said, tapping at the phone. A piece of her hair swung attractively down around her jaw in the evening breeze. "I have to pick something up. Do me a huge favor and put him to bed? He's already halfway there." Zelig was all but asleep on the couch, thumb in mouth, his other hand curled by his temple. Marcia trailed Nina to the door, like following a giant truck down the highway, carried along in her wake.

Nina was so improvisational and unworried. "You know what's funny?" She had said to the book club shortly before Zelig was born. "I totally just assumed I'd have a hard time getting pregnant! I'm, like, weirdly proud it was so easy."

"No one thinks they'll be able to get pregnant until it happens," Anne had said wistfully. And they had all nodded, remembering, eyes on Nina's undeniable fecundity.

Now Nina gave Marcia a kiss on either cheek, hoisted her enormous, worn leather bag, and, with a flash of an enormous, joyous silver earring, that pretty lock of hair, was gone.

Zelig woke as Marcia tried to scoop him up off the couch; she wasn't as adept at handling him as she hoped. He was heavy. He began to whimper, then cry, half-consciously registering Nina's absence.

"She'll be back soon." Marcia said.

"Grammy Marcia," Zelig whimpered, holding tight.

She carried him down the hall, switched off the light, laid him down in Darren's old bed and curled herself around him so he wouldn't have to let go. She hadn't been all that physically affectionate with Darren— she had been busy and resentful and unable to articulate why. Hers had been a constant presence, but a distant, unhappy one. You had different things to give at different times in your life.

She stroked Zelig's hair in the shifting glow from the sleeping computer. He loosened his grip as he fell back into sleep. Marcia began to feel sleepy herself, arms full of warm child. Just before she drifted off, she could, with a sudden, shameful degree of happiness, see it perfectly: He would grow to hate his mother, too.

] Midhusband

I was on the cell trying to calm my wife, Kate, while I watched the crowd file into the funeral parlor across the street. Russell Ardbaum, a friend from my high school tennis team, had been forty-three years old, the first from our team to die.

"I need to jet," I said. "I didn't come all the way up here to be late."

Too sleepless to drive, I'd trained north to Albany from Philadelphia earlier in the day. Kate was probably right where I'd left her, in bed, nursing or thinking about nursing our six-week-old son, Drew. I could hear him crying, like a baby pterodactyl. "Sometimes," Kate said, "I imagine throwing this kid against the wall."

She needed to vent and I needed to let her vent, even if I would never say anything like that. I tended to keep my darker thoughts to myself. Maybe because I was the guy. Or because I was almost eleven years older than she was. Or because I was a relatively successful public relations consultant while she was a part-time paralegal who talked about applying to law school "in the future" but had yet to take the LSAT. I suspected she'd planned the pregnancy in order to put off the exam indefinitely. That was, during those high-hormone months, one of the many darker thoughts I chose not to share.

She began to cry and her sobbing had a lower pitch and slower pace than Drew's prehistoric screeching; she sounded like a forlorn swan. It was late spring and even this far north I could feel a sweltering summer drifting closer. I dreaded it. I was more tired than I'd ever been in my life and it was already a struggle to keep the world in focus. A sustained blast of heat and humidity might push me over the edge. I moved the phone away from my ear, but I could still hear Kate launch into her familiar refrain. "I think he's hungry," she said. "I think he's starving."

Long before Drew was born, Kate had convinced herself she wouldn't be able to feed him. She felt destined to be an awful mother and then during our hellish first few weeks Drew lost ten ounces, encouraging Kate to worry more than ever. She couldn't nourish him and she was sure he'd hate her for it the rest of his life, if he even managed to survive, and the failure would drive her to suicide, and there was nothing she could do about it. By his fourth week, Drew was steadily gaining weight, but Kate kept worrying.

Our third and final lactation consultant, a twiggy fifty-something nurse from Paris, talked a lot about the importance of positive thinking. "Picture the rivers of milk that flow within you, sweetheart," she liked to say. On the job, I pitched various kinds of advertising and promotional campaigns, so I had practice telling people what they wanted to hear while showing them images of what they wanted to see. I was happy to reinforce the nurse's message as best I could, even though that morning, on the train, I'd stared at the gold-bright glare of the sun on the Hudson and imagined asking Drew to forgive me for running away.

"Your milk runneth over," I said to Kate. "I'll be back before you wake up tomorrow."

"Fantastic," she said. "Who cares if the baby starves by then."

"You are the Hudson of milk," I said, "the Schuylkill, the Big Muddy, and the Nile, all rolled into one glorious twin-peaked fountain of white, frothy—"

"If I throw him as hard as I can," she said, "what do you think—"

"Stop it," I said. "You're doing a terrific job. When I compare how we're doing now with—"

"I wish I could shoot myself in the head. That might make me feel better."

"Kate," I said. "He's a beautiful baby. You're a beautiful mother." I had more to say, but she'd already hung up.

Which left me in the perfect mood for a funeral, so I walked across the street and followed the crowd into an old, gloomy building that felt haunted by thousands of dead bodies and sad ceremonies. Deep-stained oak—ceiling beams, banisters, floors, walls, pocket-doors—darkened the rooms and as I stepped toward the small chapel I remembered something else that happened on the train. Before drifting into a nap, I'd glanced up to see my mother shuffling down the aisle toward me. She'd died twenty-two years ago at the start of another summer from congestive heart failure, a predictable result of smoking at least two packs a day since age seventeen. Her coughs during her final days made it sound as if she were clawing herself to death from the inside out. She looked blissful and ruddy-faced on the train, though, smiling brightly. I'd been longing to tell her that I, her afterthought son, the accident of her late thirties, had given her a grandchild. Then, just as I was about to stand up and rush to her arms, I blinked and she became someone older and fatter and taller than my mother had ever been, and whoever it was didn't smile at all as she bustled by me.

In the chapel, I rubbed my eyes and scanned the crowd. I saw our midwife, Ali, waving at me from one of the back pews. She'd told me she might make the trip and now my whole body thrummed as she slid over to make room. "Michael," she said. "Join me."

My wife's voice echoed in my mind as I sat down. I knew Kate wouldn't harm Drew or herself, no matter what she said. Actually, the opposite was true: She'd do anything to help him; she'd nurse him for hours, as she had been doing night after night, and the effort of it all was what she lived for, what she'd been looking forward to for years. I cherished the memory of how riveted she'd been at our granola-ish birth classes, the way the other mothers-to-be sometimes sought her advice during the breaks. Still, the constant reassuring I now had to do—of her, of my-self—wearied me even more than the sleeplessness.

Ali leaned close to ask how I was doing. She'd been a godsend for us. She always took Kate's calls and she would stop by anytime during the pregnancy, day or night, and she never seemed to mind hearing the same old worries again. Kate didn't think the baby was breath-ing. The baby hadn't moved in hours. The constant hiccups within her were unnerving. She was gaining too much weight. She wasn't gaining enough weight. She would be pregnant forever. As usual, I believed everything was fine, but my opinion didn't count for much. Nearly everyday, Kate wanted to call Ali and it didn't take me long to stop resisting. Let the woman earn her money, I figured. Getting out of the way was the best thing I could do, though I did always try to be home for her appointments.

The first time we met, she sat by our kitchen counter, her back straight as a board, and told us how she became a midwife. For a while it sounded like a familiar hospital birth story, featuring the typical cascade of causes and effects—fetal heart monitor strapped on which means the woman can't move much which means the contractions don't work as they should which leads to Pitocin which makes the contractions more painful which leads to the epidural which leads to the woman not pushing enough which makes the baby's heart race which leads to a diagnosis of fetal distress and a rush to perform an "emergency" c-section. But Ali was talking about her own sister and that sister died on the operating room table. Her would-have-been-niece died a few hours later in the NICU.

Ali became a midwife with a sober, no-nonsense approach to her job. "A birth is a normal occurrence," she told us. "It's something a woman's body is designed to do. I work hard to help you do it yourself. It's that simple."

We hired her on the spot. We liked how tough she seemed, though we also occasionally joked about her lighter side: She had small, boxy glasses with bing cherry red frames and she often wore a matching thong. When she examined Kate on the couch beneath the largest window of our two-bedroom apartment, that thong would rise up into view. It reminded us of how different Ali was from the midwives we'd read about in Ina May Gaskin's books. Kate read deeply, watched a few homebirth videos, and even talked about becoming a doula if law school didn't work out. I wasn't nearly as interested, but I'd sat through the videos and flipped the pages of the books, staring at the photos. Those *Spiritual Midwifery* women were pony-tailed tie-dyed earth mothers with hippie husbands who'd caravanned cross-country in school buses to found a hospital-free haven in the hills of Tennessee.

Meanwhile, young, wounded, smoldering Ali looked like she could preside over an art gallery in New York City. Early on, I'd noticed her short, angular bangs and her habit of running her hand up and down the fine black hair on the back of her head. Kate thought she resembled Louise Brooks and hoped we'd all become friends, especially after I discovered that Ali and I had both grown up on the same edge of northeast Philly; we'd attended Abington High five years apart. Russell, it turned out, was one of a handful of friends we had in common. She'd delivered his daughter, but after that, she'd lost touch with Russell. And then, during Kate's third trimester, we'd both learned about the brain tumor.

I didn't fantasize about Ali too much during the pregnancy itself. But eventually the third trimester came to an end and there were twelve hours of labor before Kate climbed into the green birthing tub we'd rented. It looked like an oversized, over-padded wading pool in the middle of our living room. I stripped down to my boxers, climbed in behind her, and leaned back against the plastic wall. After each push Kate rested against me. When she let me I massaged her shoulders. Then Ali was reaching into the reddening water, guiding Drew out and up and settling him onto Kate's chest. Time seemed to stop for a moment and in that moment I saw that our newborn baby was waxy and motionless. I leaned forward, thinking I should have listened to Kate's worrying more carefully. The baby wasn't breathing. His eyes would never open. The candles balanced on the coffee table by the couch guttered off black smoke, as if they were about to be snuffed out, too. I stared into our baby's blank, unmoving, shut-eyed face and, for a split-second, I was surprised to feel, of all things, relief.

Suddenly, I'd been handed another chance. I loved Kate and I believed that having a child was an essential part of being human and I didn't want to miss out on that experience. We'd discussed it for two years after the wedding and we were both excited when we started trying and we were even more excited when after five months of trying the pregnancy test was positive. But right then, at the instant of birth, excitement wasn't what I felt. I looked down at the bruise-blue baby and heard only the sound of the murky water sloshing in the plastic tub. Maybe I wasn't completely prepared to be a father just yet. It would be good to have more time to get ready.

I kept staring and waiting and I sank down into my own fears. A dead baby. A divorce. I would die alone, remembered by no one.

At the same time, once again, I was free.

But then Ali was saying, "Everything's fine," and Drew opened his tiny mouth and gasped and wailed away, his cries an answer to the cries Kate had been pushing out for hours. His skin pinked up and minutes started speeding by again and in a daze I found myself cutting the umbilical cord. It felt like slicing into a thick piece of sashimi. Octopus. And before I could get my mind around what I'd just done, I was standing in the bathroom by the sink, holding the towel-wrapped baby to my chest while Kate showered herself off and that's when Ali came up behind me and reached a hand over my shoulder to caress the side of the baby's head and I turned my own head, thinking I'd kiss Ali on the cheek, jubilant, guilty, but relieved in a whole new way.

Either I turned too far or she wanted to give me more than her cheek. My lips landed on hers, which felt dry but pillowy. They vanished in a heartbeat, maybe two, though her open hand lingered on my lower back. At first, in the days that followed, I thought about that kiss the same way I'd started thinking about the handful of women who preceded Kate. Sometimes, late at night, before I drifted off to sleep, I was haunted by montages of memory and fantasy. The scenario involving Ali brought together her thong, our kiss, and a moment a few minutes before Drew was born, when Ali had told me to reach down and stick my finger into Kate's vagina. She wanted me to show her how far my finger went in before it tapped the baby on the head. She'd asked Kate to do it herself, but Kate had refused. "Not my job," she'd shouted. So, Ali had turned to me. I worried about the dirt beneath my fingernail. I worried about poking the baby's soft head too hard. But with Kate's permission I reached around and did what was asked. I showed Ali the bottom line on my index finger's first knuckle and she thanked me. In my fantasies, she sought a different appendage and she wanted it stuck deep inside herself right away. Kate was nowhere to be seen. Ali stripped down to her thong and said, "I wore this just for you."

Ali seemed underdressed. I was wearing a black suit while she had on a much more casual outfit—jeans, a silky gray T-shirt, and a long-sleeved, short-bodied black blazer. The blazer and her black low-heeled mules were her only concessions to the occasion. I was paying too much attention to the narrow line of her bra strap near the neck of her T-shirt when the rabbi stepped up onto the pulpit and asked us to rise. I turned away and tried to concentrate on more wholesome memories. I remembered that after Ali had helped me and Kate settle into bed with the baby, she'd steamed brown rice and broccoli for us. It was close to ten in the evening and I felt no trace of the soft, quick kiss, no lingering guilt over my momentary rush of relief. I watched Ali measure Drew's length and the circumference of his head. Then she took out a sling and weighed him like a bunch of fresh produce. "He's gorgeous," she said. "He's perfect."

Later, after Ali had cleared our bowls away, washed all the dishes, and quietly departed, it was for the first time just the three of us together in the apartment, a brand new family. Kate fell asleep with Drew tucked against her, but I could barely manage to close my eyes. Kate seemed more peaceful than she'd been in months. The skin of her face looked as smooth and unlined as the baby's, as if sleeping next to a new-born was all she'd ever needed and now she could at last truly relax. I watched Drew's miniature chest rise and fall. I still wasn't ready. I couldn't possibly be ready. And yet I felt a sparkling in my lungs I'd never felt before, like a box of matches slowly lighting up inside me with each breath. When I tried again to close my eyes, more matches flared up and it was almost blinding. Was this what people meant when they talked about a third eye opening? Transcendence? I had no clue, but I could not stop grinning.

[

] I'd first learned about Russell's illness not from Ali, but from Gary, my old doubles partner, the only teammate with whom I'd been in regular touch since graduation. He'd sent me a link to a website where Russell posted updates. Gary lived in Boston these days and he had a nine-year-old son, Robbie, who was autistic and a three-year-old daughter, Naomi, who wasn't. Back in high school, Gary was a gifted athlete (varsity soccer, varsity tennis) with a well-earned reputation as a troublemaker. His gruff, fat father grounded him for weeks at a time, but he'd still managed to sleep with at least a dozen of our classmates. Then he was off to Boston University and he stayed there for law school and soon after that he got married and started having kids and that seemed to keep him reasonably faithful and far from trouble.

I spent hours on Russell's low-tech site studying a collection of photos (there he was, pre-surgery, sailing on the Hudson, holding an impressive sunworshipper pose in one gym, working over a speedbag in another) and treatment summaries (surgery, radiation, Temodar, Avastin, Dasatinib). I was still staring at the photos when I called Gary and we talked about planning a trip together to visit the poor guy. We traded possible dates, but Kate and I were a few weeks from delivery and Gary was in the middle of another skirmish with his school district about his son's needs. In the end, he made the trip without me, and then time ran out. After I heard Russell had died, I checked back on the website and watched a video, just posted, of Russell playing indoor tennis with his ten-year-old daughter, Iris. He looked watery and ponderous, as if the final treatment had been to pump him full of fluid and drown the damn tumor. The daughter had done a voiceover for the video. As he labored along the baseline, a sweat-darkened Phillies cap covering most of his shaved head, she tried to sound upbeat. "All is well killing cancer cells," she began, "and my dad is an awesome tennis player. Look at him hustle." Something about the desperate brightness of her voice and the way he winced as he shanked another easy forehand made me decide to attend the funeral. Too little, too late for an old friend, but better than nothing. Plus the idea of a quiet day to myself was appealing. And, of course, there was the possibility that Ali would be there.

But now, sitting and standing beside Ali, I kept looking toward the door, hoping Gary would walk in. I wanted his company. I wanted to see him and talk about fatherhood. My own father died less than a year after my mother coughed her last breath. "I'll console myself on the Cunard Line," he'd told me, and he sounded genuinely excited about traveling through the Panama Canal. "The sea and those great locks. It will put everything in perspective." He'd never been that interested in my life. He'd given in to my mother on the issue of me, so to speak, but he wasn't going to compromise on his daily pleasures. I'd vowed to be a very different father, and yet what would he say if he saw me next to Ali, so tempted, so ready to wander myself? I could almost feel him watching. "There's nothing wrong with putting yourself first," he used to tell my mother, usually on his way out the front door.

As the service ended, Ali touched my arm. "Did you drive here?" she asked. "I'll give you a ride to the cemetery."

We zipped out ahead of the crowd in her silver Audi. She drove like someone rushing to a birth-in-progress while I glanced out the window at the old brownstones lining the street. They had seen much finer days. Had Albany followed Philly's stupid example and bombed out a few of its own city blocks? I studied Ali more closely as she drove and that made me feel better and worse. She accelerated into each turn, her hands loose on the wheel. "Have you spent a lot of time up here?" I asked.

"Just a few trips for work. You?"

"First time," I said. "Looks pretty grim, but I remember reading a great book set in Albany."

"Did the book say that all the people who lived here were funny-looking?"

"Not that I recall."

"Well, then it couldn't have been a realistic depiction of the place."

"It was a beautiful novel, set in the 1920s or 30s, full of ghosts and a poor bum. Before the guy was a bum, he was a baseball player who dropped his baby in the kitchen and the baby died."

"Must not have paid attention to his midwife," she said. "Unlike you."

She slapped my thigh and I laughed, but I also wondered if I'd drop my son or do something equally fatal. Kate was unlikely to carry out her threats. What about me? I didn't explode the way she did. I just stored everything up until one day I was off by myself imagining begging my son's forgiveness while I lusted after the midwife.

At the cemetery gate, a black-suited old man, pale and thin like one of the ghosts from that Albany book, directed us toward a parking lot atop a hill. Ali headed right up the incline, but then turned a different way. "We'll park over here," she said. "We can have a quick drink and you can tell me how everything's going with Kate and the baby."

As soon as she'd parked, she reached behind her seat for her bag, pulled out a curved silver flask, took a long swallow, and offered it to me. "Don't mind if I do," I said, not bothering to ask what it was before following her example. I tasted cold, clean vodka with a hint of citrus. "Kate's driving me crazy," I said.

Ali chuckled and took another drink. "I assumed you found her neediness charming."

I liked the chill of the smooth flask in my hand and I took a longer pull this time. The vodka burned its way down to my stomach while the air conditioner sent a cool breeze into my face. I knew I should rise to Kate's defense, but I was laughing again. I hadn't felt so excited in weeks. "Are you calling my wife needy?" I asked.

"Please," Ali said. "I haven't gotten that many calls since high school."

I wondered what would have happened if we had attended Abington High at the same time. As I searched for something clever to say about that, I glanced out at the cemetery, expecting to see the procession rolling toward us. There was a scene from that Albany book where the bum rides around town in a horse-drawn junk-wagon, seeing ghosts at every turn. He winds up watching his burly ragman boss-driver have sex in a cellar.

"You have that look on your face again," Ali said.

"What look?"

"Like you think something bad is happening and you're okay with it."

"Maybe we should get going," I said.

"Flask's almost empty," she said. "Might as well finish it off. It's the best way to make it through a funeral."

"Or a birth," I said, even though I'd been completely sober for Drew's. I took the last swig, gave the flask back and put my hand on the door.

Ali stayed where she was, staring at the rearview mirror. "You thought your son was dead," she said, "and you were fine with that."

I wiggled a finger in my ear and then started to push the door open. She reached across me and covered my hand with hers. "It's not uncommon," she said. "Don't judge yourself for it. Don't have feelings about your feelings and all that."

Her hand was warm and I could feel its heat as she kept talking. "My sister used to piss me off on a daily basis," she said, "and there are still times I don't miss her a bit. Honest responses aren't always pretty."

When she leaned closer to me, I met her more than halfway. I'd thought of her lips so often they felt familiar now. Her fingers were on my face and in my hair. Then I tried to stop thinking. A few minutes later, I took a breath and said, *"Ironweed."*

She dropped her hand onto my lap. "Is that what you call this?"

"It's the name of that book," I said.

She pressed her hand down. "You, me, and Mr. Ironweed might be more comfortable in the back seat," she said.

I was almost forty-four years old and the history of my sex life was a very brief history that went, essentially, like this: In high school, despite hanging around with Gary, I had zero significant dates and directed my frustrated energy onto the tennis court. UPenn wasn't much better though I did lose my virginity senior year to Melissa Brancher, who found me working on a paper in the stacks of the art library. That seemed to establish a pattern. I've never been popular and I'm shy and I'm on the short side, but the women who want me tend to want me right away. After I split with Melissa, I stayed mired in my orphanhood for a while until a co-worker, Ruth Larsh, fell for me. Then Ruth fell for a different co-worker. And then there was Kate who appeared just as I was resigning myself to a solitary life in perpetuity. Less than an hour into our first date, we walked by a park where I tossed a wayward soccer ball over a fence to a group of young kids. Kate watched the kids dash happily back to their game. "You look like you'd be a great dad," she said.

Looks can be deceiving, as everyone knows. It's the banal truth at the heart of my day job—a truth I'm always working to conceal and exploit. Still, I'd never cheated on anybody. One partner had always seemed like the extreme limit of what I could handle and I felt that more strongly than ever after I met Kate. She was my last, best hope and I couldn't imagine desiring anyone except her. I thought even a whiff of adultery would fill me with guilt, but sitting there with our midwife's hand in my lap I felt dazed and beamy.

Before we could decide about the back seat, I heard car doors opening and closing. "To be continued," Ali said, lifting her hand and sliding out from behind the wheel.

[

] Graveside, my heart skipped a beat when Iris carefully set a bright blue tennis racket atop her father's plain pine coffin. As I watched, a few scattered details about Russell came back to me. He was left handed; I used to forget that whenever we played. I'd lob over his left shoulder and he'd reach up and put it away with ease. He had a black Prince racket. He dated a girl with hairy arms named Deirdre who lived around the corner from the high school. His family went skiing during winter vacations and he usually returned with his face tan, except for where he'd worn his ski goggles, so he looked like a raccoon.

I searched for more memories, but I was too distracted. I couldn't stop wondering if there'd ever been a better argument—a young friend dead and boxed up—for sleeping with a beautiful, willing woman. Meanwhile, Ali seemed unfazed. She whispered to me about the Albanians in the crowd. "The whole town's dysfunctional," she said. "It's unmistakable. I don't know what happens to these people."

"Maybe they're born that way," I said.

"They're not," she said. "I caught Russell's daughter up here, remember? She came out normal and she looks all right so far. I hope she leaves town before it's too late."

A few people turned to glare at us, so we stepped back from the crowd. I glanced again at Iris from afar. What would her life look like without a father? I'd heard her voice on that video and she seemed tough to me. Resilient. She could stare loss in the face and move on, stronger. Ali had that and I liked to think I did, too. Who knew if Russell had even been a good influence on Iris. Maybe she'd be better off without him, which was a lousy thought to have at the guy's funeral. And yet, after my father's death, it hadn't taken me long to believe I was better off.

I felt a hand clap down on my shoulder and I jumped, still thinking of my father. It was Gary. If Ali had seen him first, she might have taken him for another Albanian. She'd point to his pudgy waist and the puffed-up face that made his eyes beady, like he was peering out at the world from deep within a cave. The years had not been kind to him, but I could see the goofy kid in him and I knew he could see the same in me.

"How's the new munchkin?" he asked.

"He's fine," I said, "but the rest of us have been better."

Gary smiled. "Nothing better than kids. Who's your friend?"

"This is Ali. She's a fellow Abington alum. She was Russell's midwife. And she was our midwife, too."

"What do you mean was?" Ali joked. "You're due for another checkup very soon." She rested a hand on the back of my neck and squeezed with her fingers, setting my spine a-tingle from top to bottom.

Gary had been my doubles partner for four years and, apparently, he could still read me. He said nothing for a moment, displeased, waiting for me to explain. I kept quiet and watched the people around us make their way back to their cars.

"We need to go sit shiva," he said.

"Sure," I said. "Of course we do."

"No harm in grabbing a few drinks first," Ali said.

Gary didn't argue with that and neither did I, so I rode with Ali again while Gary trailed behind us. I told her about our tennis heyday, what a fantastic athlete he once was, how demanding his kids were. Then Kate called. She wanted to describe the nightmare she'd had while napping.

"You wouldn't even look at me," she told me. "You said my circulation was poor and we had to amputate my feet before it was too late. You were exactly the same age as the day we first met and I felt ancient."

It was almost five o'clock in the afternoon and I would have bet a year's salary she was still in bed, unshowered and hungry. "That's a terrible dream," I said. "You're not old let alone—"

"I'm so sick of myself," she said. "And I know you must be sick of me, too."

She sounded exhausted, and I could tell some part of her understood she was shutting down, pushing me away, closing herself off, and yet she couldn't help it. Maybe she yearned to be back in the office, dreaming of her law career. Maybe she wanted to be somewhere, anywhere else. Maybe I wasn't the only one having second, third, and ad infinitum thoughts.

I looked over at Ali, who wasn't hiding her efforts to eavesdrop. She probably knew exactly what to say to Kate, but she had a hand on my thigh again. Talking about Gary had dimmed my excitement. Also, though Ali still seemed drawn to me, I had no idea why, and that made me uneasy.

"I love you," I said. "What's up with the Drewster?"

"He's finally taking a nap, thank God."

"Are you still in bed?"

"Remember all those people telling us our lives were going to change forever?"

Ali's hand climbed higher up my thigh and she whispered, "Metal-plant returns."

"I remember," I said, pushing Ali's hand away.

"I don't know if I like it," Kate said. "It's too much. I left a message for Ali, but I haven't heard from her yet."

Ali pushed her hand back where it had been. "Paging Mr. Steelroot," she whispered.

"I hear what you're saying," I said. "It can feel so overwhelming."

"Oh shit," Kate said. "He's crying again. I've got to go."

We were driving through Washington Park, a few green Olmsted-inspired acres at the heart of the downtown that must have been the pride of the city. The brownstones bordering the park looked stately and well-kept and we also passed by a boathouse, a small lake, and an enormous statue of Moses using his staff to bang water out of a pile of rocks. An odd moment to commemorate, if I remembered the story correctly, but it could have been a comment on how this particular Moses found himself stranded in Albany, just a few hours upriver from the promised land of New York City.

Ali watched me struggle to slip my phone back into my pocket. "Why didn't you tell her I said hello?" she asked, removing her hand.

"I wanted to tell her," I said.

"But?"

"I also didn't want to tell her."

"Must prove we're good for each other," she said. "The midwife and the midhusband."

When I'd boarded my first train hours ago, I'd been longing to relax. I wanted to spend a day without feeling like a parent to two children, one big crier and one tiny screamer, both inconsolable. But being around Ali was beginning to make me feel childish myself, and that wasn't relaxing, either. "Is this what midwives do?" I asked. "I didn't see anything about seducing new fathers in the documentaries."

Ali shrugged her shoulders and smiled. "These days I'm not a real big fan of people, with the occasional exception. Just a straightforward girl, as you know." And with that, her hand returned to its now-familiar location. I tried to think of cold, icy places that existed somewhere in between adultery and fidelity.

The bar resembled the funeral parlor, a dreary place with dark-stained wood and little light. I ordered a martini and fled to the bathroom, which was even drearier. The air was heavy with urine, mildew, and shit. It was the smell of an open grave, repellent, even though it was also the completely human stink of life. There was no mirror on the wall. I looked at the silvery surface of the hand-dryer and tried to convince the smeared reflection of my face that an affair was simply another part of being human. So what if the experience led me to be alone once again. I'd never asked to be an orphan, but I was used to it. How many times had I already been on the verge of leaving? Whatever the total was, it was still on the rise.

When I returned to the table, Gary and Ali were well into an animated conversation. "It's just a job," she was saying. "I'm good at it, but I'm allowed to be sick of it, too. Reach down and grab your baby. Reach down and grab your baby. Every goddamn day. What about the things I'd like to reach out and grab?"

Gary was shaking his head. "I don't see how that kind of attitude is fair to the parents. It's definitely not fair to the babies."

"Are you serious?" Ali asked. "Didn't Michael say you have an autistic kid? Is that fair to the parents? Is that fair to your precious babies?"

"A misanthropic midwife," Gary said. "Maybe you need a vacation."

I cleared my throat. "I see you two are hitting it off," I said.

I picked up my drink, took a few sips, and sat down, but Gary stood up abruptly. He looked at his watch and chugged the rest of his pint. "I'd love to spend more time sympathizing about overworked midwives," he said, "but I need to swing by the house now if I'm going to get home at a reasonable hour." Then he turned my way. "You want to ride with me on this leg?"

I glanced at Ali. "I've got a few calls to make," she said. "I'll meet you there." She was still sitting in her chair and talking on her cell when we walked away.

[

] "Tell me I've got it wrong," Gary said in the car. "Tell me you're not sleeping with her."

"It's good to see you, Gary," I said.

"I don't know," he said. "Might be better not to see anyone."

I turned around to check if Ali was behind us. She wasn't. "What do you mean?" I asked.

"Look at us," he said. "These are our lives and soon we'll be just as dead as Russell. You're doing what you're doing and your baby's not even two months old yet, right?"

"I don't know what I'm doing," I said.

"Who the fuck knows what he's doing?" he said. "Not me, that's for sure. But with the midwife?"

"Anyhow," I said. I guess I'd expected a little understanding, some reassurance. Gary was starting to sound like his father.

"It's just that I remember how we were," he said. Then he sighed and his voice lost some its edge and the familiar sound of my old partner thinking aloud made me feel younger, filled with some meager measure of potential. "I didn't see us getting so lost."

"What did you see?"

"I should shut up," he said. "It's your life."

"I want to hear it," I said.

"I'll sound like an idiot."

"Some things never change," I said. He smiled. "Seriously," I said, "tell me."

"I thought we'd be good people," he said. "Good husbands. Good fathers. We'd stay healthy and teach our kids to play tennis. Our families would get together every so often. We'd meet up at father/son doubles tournaments."

It was a nice vision. Now we were driving away from the city into the countryside, where streets were named for lakes and parks and hills, spacious split-level houses with their sloping lawns and long driveways instead of the rowhouse-packed downtown. Gary drove more slowly. "I guess we didn't turn out that good," I said, as if there still might be room for doubt.

"Well, I know I didn't, and you're not looking too upstanding at the moment."

He parked behind a line of cars, but we stayed in our seats, staring out the windshield, the air conditioner still running. "My turn to sound like an idiot," I said.

"Go ahead."

I took a breath and then let out another thought I hadn't shared with anyone. "I feel like I didn't sign up for this and I might not be cut out for it. Maybe I'd be helping everyone if I just stepped away."

"Of course," Gary said, as if I'd described the most normal feelings in the world. "Correct me if I'm wrong, though: I bet your wife is the one driving you crazy these days. The kid is fine, right? Even at their worst, the kids are more than fine."

Drew *was* fine. Most of the time he cracked me up. Even the pterodactyl crying was kind of funny when it ended. "You're not wrong," I said, looking for Ali's car again. "The truth is I can't get my mind around any of this. The baby, the mood swings, the midwife—"

Gary tilted his head back and spoke up toward the roof of the car. "You know my situation," he said. "And there were plenty of days I would have happily taken the kids and let my wife go live on her own. I would have had a second kid right away, but only with a different wife. Or no wife. Has Kate—it's Kate, right?—been sobbing and weeping and threatening suicide or murder or anything like that?"

"All of the above," I said. "You're going to tell me that passes, aren't you?"

He punched my shoulder, just a tap, but enough to remind me how much fun it had been to be Gary's partner. All I had to do was play consistently and Gary would put away shot after shot. When we were really clicking, nothing felt better. In those moments, we were an unbeatable team.

"No one will ever want to hear your version of the birth story," he said. "I can tell you that. And remember all the fuss about the woman who said she'd throw her kids in front of a bullet or a train to save her husband? Everybody was outraged, like it was unforgivable to think such a thing, let alone say it out loud. But you know the truth?"

"Go ahead," I said. "Please tell me the truth."

"I'd bet my house that woman's husband often feels exactly the opposite way. He'd let that woman take the hit in a heartbeat. Save the kids and watch her go down."

"That's awfully bleak," I said.

Gary thumped his hands against the steering wheel, as if I'd offered further proof of his theory. "It sure is," he said. "And I'll tell you something else. That woman herself sometimes feels exactly like that husband. Exactly like you and me. One way or another, one time and another, we all want to escape."

"Escape," I said. The last time I attempted a heart-to-heart with my father, we were about to drive to his condo so I could help him pack away my mother's things. We'd just met with his life insurance agent to review my mother's will. "That couldn't have been pleasant for you, Dad," I said. Sarcastic, but at least I was trying.

"Every day in that hospital," he said, "that cute leggy nurse filled my mind. I wanted to kiss her so badly. And that's not the half of it."

Right up until the very end, he could surprise me with the same old thing.

"Don't look at me like that," he said. "I don't care if you understand. I thoroughly enjoyed wanting her so much." A few weeks later, he used the inheritance to finance his final cruise.

"It's getting stuffy in here," Gary said. "Should we go inside?"

I wasn't in a hurry to see those mourners again. "Why don't we sit a little more," I said. "It's good to talk."

Gary looked at his watch. "I guess I've got time," he said. Then he reclined his seat a bit. "Did I tell you about that last visit with Russell?"

I shook my head. "I wish I could have been there."

"He wanted to play doubles. He and his daughter against me and my son. It was a ridiculous idea. Robbie doesn't play tennis. He doesn't really play any sports at all. But I figured Russell should get what he wanted."

I watched the mourners filing into the house and thought about what Russell wanted. This couldn't have been it. What did I want, besides a good night's sleep, another drink, and an untroubled wife? For a moment, I hoped Ali was only late because she'd stopped to re-fill her flask. "So," I said, "tell me what happened."

Gary sighed again. "When I take Robbie out to the courts, he's more interested in the water fountains than anything else. Occasionally I'll get him to swing a racket in the direction of a ball and then he'll try to smash it as hard as he can. Still, we met up at some courts near Russell's house and I thought maybe Russell and I could hit for a bit, for old times' sake. Robbie, though, he took one look at Russell and started crying. He wouldn't let up. We couldn't do anything to stop him."

"You'd already told him about the tumor?"

"I tell him everything," Gary said. "Usually doesn't matter."

"But he knew something was wrong?"

"He knew everything was wrong. Your enchanting midwife might see him as a funny-looking kid, but—"

"Let's not talk about her," I said. "I haven't slept with her yet, by the way."

"Did you say 'yet'?"

"Anyhow, what did you guys do when Robbie kept crying?"

"What did we do? We tried not to be unbearably sad. We talked about our kids. His daughter's a sweetheart. She took Robbie for a short walk and Russell and I lobbed the ball back and forth for fifteen final minutes."

He noticed me searching for Ali again. I couldn't help myself. "A midwife who's never had children," he said. "And she's never wanted any?"

"She has her reasons," I said.

"I bet she does, but it's still odd. My kids are the best thing about my life by far."

"Did you feel that from the start?"

"Not right away," he said. "And definitely not in the first three months. After that, though, it built up fast."

I nodded, unsure what to say next.

"Don't look now," Gary said, "but here she comes."

I saw Ali lock her car and start walking toward us. I tried to stretch out, as if that would help me decide what to do. I rolled my shoulders forward and backward then slowly turned my head from side to side. "I feel like I've been in a car all day," I said.

"One more thing before she gets here," Gary said. "This is about whatever the hell it is or isn't yet between you two. The whole scenario reminds me of picking up my bags at the airport."

"Really?"

Gary was speaking quickly, rushing to finish. "Don't you ever think about grabbing one of the other bags? I'm always curious to take an extra one home, see what's inside, and what are the chances of getting caught? No one ever checks and there's plenty of chaos. If someone questioned me it would be easy to claim it was an honest mistake."

I could hear Ali's shoes scrape against the asphalt.

"I don't do it," Gary said. "That's all I'm saying. I've never done it. I take my own bags and I go home."

Ali tapped on the window. She puckered her lips at me.

"I can't tell you what's right and what isn't," Gary said. Then he laughed. "Either way, it's your funeral."

[

] Inside, Gary paid his respects and we said goodbye, vowing, as usual, to stay in touch. By the time he was gone, Ali was out of sight. A buffet of cold cuts had been set up in the living room and I went over to fix myself a sandwich. I tried again to focus on Russell himself, dead and gone, but there was so much I didn't know. I hadn't delivered his child. I hadn't played tennis with him weeks before he died. I didn't even know why he'd moved to godforsaken Albany in the first place. I wanted to remember things he'd said to me or what he'd dreamed of becoming or what he might have thought about his life. Had he been faithful? Fulfilled? What were the things he wished he'd done? What did he long to undo?

There were a few bookshelves near the buffet and I noticed *Ironweed*, a thin volume squished between the bible and the dictionary. Maybe it occupied a similar place of honor in houses all over Albany. I tried to remember how that book ended, but I couldn't.

If I hadn't had the plate in my hands, I would have taken the book from the shelf and flipped to the final pages. Instead, I took a few bites of sandwich and then watched a hunchbacked man enter the room. He opened his tattered briefcase and passed around small prayerbooks. Eventually he cleared his throat and asked everyone to join him in a short service. Iris stood beside him. It was the closest I'd been to her all day and she looked taller than I'd imagined from Russell's webpage. She also looked more fragile, as if a tennis racket would be hard on her thin wrists. She was wiping tears from her eyes. At home, when Kate and Drew were lost in their crying jags, I could barely breathe until I'd found some way to soothe them. Then when they were quiet, I walked around the apartment braced for the next descent into tears. I was near enough now to notice that Iris was weeping, stifling her cries with short gasps. I wanted to comfort her, but it wasn't something I could do. I would have had no idea where to begin.

The service kept circling back to the Kaddish. It's a prayer I should have known by heart. Traditionally, I should have recited it three times a day for eleven months after each one of my parents died. Iris continued weeping, but she didn't miss a word. The second time the hunchbacked man led us through it, I began to utter the prayer more forcefully— *Yisgadal v'yiskadash sh'may ra-bo*; Glorified and sanctified be God's great name—and then Ali was standing beside me. "Oh yeah," she whispered. "That god. He does phenomenal work."

Without thinking, I shushed her.

"You're devout all of a sudden?"

I kept following along in the prayerbook. I hadn't sat shiva for either one of my parents. My father set aside an afternoon for my mother, then he had her cremated and took her ashes with him to the Panama Canal. Since he died on that trip, I'd arranged for his ashes to be scattered in the same general area. It seemed fitting at the time, the easiest way to be done with it, once and for all. As the Kaddish came around again, though, I was thinking that I must have been an idiot then. Maybe I remained an idiot. Still, I was beginning to understand that you needed to mourn properly. That didn't mean I knew what it meant to mourn properly, but I should have at least scattered those ashes myself. I should have done much more than that. If you mourn wrong, you're bound to do many other things wrong, too, or so it suddenly seemed to me.

I could feel Ali standing by my side, waiting. I guessed that she hadn't sat shiva for her sister or her would-have-been-niece and I didn't think she was likely to share in my revelation, but she did keep silent for the rest of the service. Then, after the final "amen," she said, "There are some interesting rooms upstairs. Let me show you one."

I didn't respond right away. I watched people return the prayerbooks to the hunchbacked man. He placed them carefully back in his briefcase. The ritual seemed to have released some tension among the assembled mourners. The rooms filled with conversation and the occasional burst of laughter and I realized this was the cheeriest place we'd been all day. I glanced at Iris again—she was leaning into her mother now—and I thought I caught sight of Russell in her brown eyes. Those were the same eyes that would shine out from his raccoon-face when he returned from those ski vacations. "How was the trip?" I'd sometimes ask him. "All right," he'd say with a shrug, acknowledging his good fortune even as he asked not to be resented for it.

He knew he was lucky back then—lucky for the trips he took with his parents, lucky to be left-handed, lucky for his ease and grace on the court—but he was nice guy about it. Now I was standing in his beautiful Albany house and he was six feet under. Maybe he'd always suspected all his luck came at a cost. I looked again at his daughter and hoped that wasn't how it worked for him, or for any of us, and before I turned away, I wished Iris the best luck in the world.

Then, with the Kaddish still humming through my head, I followed my midwife once more. She smelled clean and crisp, like her vodka. We climbed the stairs, turned down a hallway, and walked past several rooms before she opened a door. The luxurious bathroom we entered was nothing like the cramped bathroom in our apartment. I imagined Ali helping Iris get born in this bright white clamshell-shaped tub and then I thought of Kate and I could still hear the echo of her cries. There she was, naked in that rented green tub in the living room, doing what I could never do.

Ali made a show of locking the door behind us. "You look like you're thinking too hard," she said.

She was right in front of me, leaning against that door, and in that big bathroom I longed to believe I was living a big, extraordinary, lucky life with room for whatever we might do together. I wished I could be a good husband and a good father while Ali and I fucked ourselves into oblivion, here, there, and everywhere. I wished I could do all that and know that Drew might stand beside his mother and say Kaddish for me for at least a few days when I was gone. I could hear Ali breathing, but in my mind I saw Drew. I saw him growing older—a toddler, a teenager, a college kid, and a forty-something-year-old dad—taller than I am, wiser and stronger.

Ali stepped out of her shoes and moved closer. "Tell me what you want," she said. "I want to hear you say it."

I wanted Drew, throughout all the stages of his life, to carry good memories of me.

Though the lights weren't on, the many mirrors kept the bathroom bright. I couldn't look at Ali anymore and I didn't want to look into those mirrors, so I stared down at the floor and its small white tiles.

Kate might forgive me a trespass or two, but it would cost me dearly for the rest of my life, and our love would grow less full, instead of the other way around. Also, Drew would never forgive me. How could he? That must have been what Gary was getting at with his baggage-claim talk. It would someday be my funeral and my family, whatever family I'd made, would be standing graveside. I stepped away from Ali, closer to the window, and I kept my eyes down. "I think I can tell you what I want," I said.

"Good."

"I want you to call Kate," I said, "and—"

Ali laughed. She took off her jacket, folded it, and set it by one of the two sinks. "You'd like me to be the one to tell her?" she asked. Then she took another step toward me. "I suppose I could do that," she said.

"I want you to call Kate," I repeated, forcing myself to go on, looking back up toward her eyes. "And I want you to help her understand that all this worry and struggle is ordinary."

Ali crossed her arms below her breasts and shook her head. "I felt something," she said. "I could swear I did."

What would it have been like to know her during high school? Maybe she would have broken through my shyness. "It's not like I'm not tempted," I said.

She kept staring at me and I tried to hold her gaze. "Doors open and doors close," she said. "And then we die. So I say why not, while we can?"

"What was your sister's name?" I asked.

"Let's not go down that road," she said, running a hand through the hair on the back of her head. "Can't we just stay in this moment?"

But I stayed on that road. Her sister must have been younger, other-wise I might have known *her* at Abington. That sister must have been the very first baby in Ali's life full of babies. Ali might have been like a second mother back then, changing diapers, holding bottles, reading books, singing nonsense songs late at night and early in the morning. Even my own inattentive mother must have done some of that for me. "I'm sorry," I said. "I can't."

"Fine," she said and, stepping back, she unlocked the door.

I was able to look closely at her again, now that I'd said no. I figured that to her I was simply a diversion that wasn't going to happen. I expected a cutting remark or two. She opened the door and turned away from me, rubbing a palm into one of her eyes.

"It's back to work for me," she said. "As always. You'll probably need to get a cab out of here."

I told myself that whatever sadness she felt wasn't about me. "I'm sorry," I said again.

"Just go home," she said.

I hurried out of the bathroom, down the stairs, toward the front door, and in my mind I was apologizing all the way.

[

] It was too late to catch a train south from Albany, but there was Greyhound to Manhattan and New Jersey Transit to Trenton and then SEPTA to 30th Street Station in downtown Philly. Along the way, I looked in every seat, in every aisle, on the other side of every window, and I saw all the kids I could have had if every thought of sex or attempt at sex had led to procreation. Those poor kids were all funny-looking in their own unique way, shades of me and my parents and those exes and Ali and Kate and our imperfect ancestors, all versions of Drew, but not Drew.

As I traveled home I began to understand what was going to happen next. And Drew, my son, I knew, I just knew, that your mother would be waiting for me there in our bed, down the hall from the living room in which she gave birth to you, and she would be even more tired than I was, but she would find a way to smile when I walked in, which was far more than I deserved, and she would say she had a feeling I wasn't going to spend the night in Albany, and in this moment that I'll remind you about too often when you're older, she holds you up in the air, ready for me to take you in my arms. I can't describe for her where I've been and what I've seen and what I've done and haven't done. I can't even begin with that yet. But I can tell her I've been thinking of her all day. I can listen to her tell me you refused to take a nap and you kept gnawing away at her nipples and now she winces each time you feed and this whole situation seems absolutely impossible, truly absurd, and she can't stop missing our old life.

"I understand," I say. "Sometimes I miss it, too."

Then I look at your peaceful face. Your tiny open hands.

"He's beautiful," I say.

You're awake, but you're also close to sleep. It could go either way and I brace myself for more of the pterodactyl, but you look over to me and your eyes disappear into mine for a heartbeat and then your eyelids drift the last millimeter closed and your breathing steadies as I lift you up and bring you to my chest. I feel your whole body relax into me.

"Shh," I say. "Daddy's home."

Your mother pats the space on the bed beside her. "I talked to Ali," she says.

I stand there, swaying back and forth to keep you calm while my pulse races. I know Ali's capable of anything. Who isn't? But I picture her outside of Russell's, alone in her car, making the call, sad and angry and devoted somehow, mourning as best she can while she goes on with her life.

With you in my arms, I take a breath and sit down next to your mother. "What did she say?" I ask.

My wife leans close to whisper in my ear: "She told me the second baby is always easier."

] The Porchies

It started with Grace. Andrew was heading back to Philly for the summer to work at his father's carpet-cleaning business. None of us could figure out why, but he seemed determined. Perhaps carpet cleaning runs in the blood. My theory was he had a little action going on back there he didn't want us to know about for fear that we'd tell his girlfriend. It was good thinking on his part. Not that we were malicious people, but, considering the amount of alcohol we consumed on a weekly basis, someone was bound to let it slip, and eventually it would trickle back to her.

Whatever the reason, Andrew was not going to be around and we needed to find a sublettor. Or, rather, he needed to find a sublettor. The rest of us couldn't give a shit if no one lived in Andrew's room and Andrew had to pay his share of the rent while he wasn't even there. This option, however, defeated the purpose of Andrew's plan to live rent-free with his parents. So, Andrew was determined to find someone, and we were determined that whoever he found not be a complete and total loser. So, really it became a group project.

There were two major obstacles. First and foremost, was the condition of the house. It wasn't entirely our fault. The house was a shit-hole long before we moved in. Our landlord was a big man named Big Frank who was rumored to have organized-crime connections. The upkeep of our pad was not his main concern. One time the front door fell off and it took him a week to put it back on. Neither (and this is why we got the house) was he concerned with the fact that we crammed seven people into a house zoned for four by stashing beds in tiny, windowless rooms in the basement. Actually, this is an exaggeration. Only one room was windowless. Unfortunately, this room was Andrew's, and to even call it a room would be unfair. Truth be told, it was a closet, and no one in his right mind would live there by choice. That is, no one except for Andrew, who loved it because it stayed dark enough for him to sleep all day.

The other obstacle was us. Our kitchen had been infested with flies for about three weeks (dating back to about a week after the last time anyone had done dishes.) A week and a half prior to our subletting attempt, the power had gone out when we forgot to pay the bill. Out of sheer laziness we didn't get it turned back on for ten days. During that time all the food in the fridge went bad and began to smell. Eventually someone, I think it was Donnie, just couldn't take it and mailed the check. The power came back on and we sort-of cleaned the fridge. By sort-of, I mean we tossed all the meat with the exception of one pack of hot dogs that Mike F. claimed wouldn't go bad. The meat was gone, but the smell lingered on, and wafted out the window along with our chances of finding a remotely sane sublettor. Or so we thought.

Although the kitchen was the worst room, it barely took the gold over the living room, with my room, perhaps, being a close third. But you get the idea. Let's just say that we wished the flies were the only creatures living there. But, alas, these stories must wait for another day. After all, this is not a story about the house, or even us, but one about the Porchies. And, as I said, it all started with Grace.

Here's what happened. Every potential sublettor who came and looked at the house never came back. I couldn't blame them. Andrew, sensing failure, and being the crafty guy that he was, put an ad for the room online. This was before Craigslist and roommates.com. His assumption was that someone in another state might be moving to Boston, desperate for any room, see the cheap price, and hop on board. Because this person would be out of state, he or she wouldn't have a chance to look at the room before entering into a contract. Sure enough, a week later, a small Asian girl was unpacking a blue Ford with Florida plates.

Grace accepted her windowless fate with no hint of emotion. Quietly, over the next two days, she moved in. Not once did she mention the smells coming from the kitchen or the stickiness of the floor. In fact, unless you were paying attention (I was), you might not have noticed her at all amidst the trash, clutter, and revolving cast of guests and girl-friends who breezed in and out of our door each day, stepping lightly to avoid sleeping people on the floor as if they were landmines. Someone once overheard the neighbors say, "they live like Mexicans in there." We recited the story to our friends with pride. Far better to be Mexicans than white, middle-class college kids.

Aside from the seven rent payers we had three "Extended Stay" guests. These were people who'd shown up one day and never left. The first and longest-standing of these guests was Johnny T-Rabs. T-Rabs was a friend who'd failed out of school a year prior to his stay on the couch. After failing, he'd disappeared back to the Bronx for a while where he lived with his mom and sold dime bags off his bicycle. He was a funny guy, half-Dominican, with young–Bob Marley dreads and a penchant for dry sarcasm. After some coaxing we convinced T-Rabs to come for a visit, unaware that he would never leave.

T-Rabs was not obtrusive to our lifestyle. He watched TV all day and hand-rolled cigarettes. He had no income and survived on scraps of people's leftovers. We all liked him.

About a month after T-Rabs, we got the junkie sisters. The junkie sisters were younger, also failed out of school. They slept with my housemates in (unwritten) exchange for room and board. No one minded them either, mostly because they were good looking and walked around in towels or otherwise skimpy apparel. And they fucked Dan and Jay. They both chainsmoked and got high a lot. I don't think either of them ate food. It was T-Rabs who coined the nickname, and it stuck. Once again, however, I have lost focus. What I'm getting at is that we were a happy family before Grace came along, and that Grace was very small, and it was easy to disappear into the windowless room in the basement out of sight from the madness, and beyond the general concern of the roommates.

I tried to help Grace move in. I carried things from the car, offered to go to Target. That kind of thing. She was fairly unreceptive, though not unfriendly. It wasn't that she was cold, just aloof.

Grace was an utterly plain-looking girl. She wasn't unattractive per se, she just didn't stand out. Her skin was terrible—dry and acne-scarred. Some guys don't mind that, but to me it's always been a turn-off. I like a girl with soft skin.

The point is that my interest in Grace was far from sexual. At the time I was still convinced of my love for Annie, a girl who'd blown me to Jimi Hendrix' Star-Spangled Banner before heading back home to California for the summer. I entertained fantasies of driving cross-country and showing up at her doorstep but I knew I didn't have the balls and that she probably wouldn't care anyway. Instead, I spent my time writing awful love letters that went unanswered. She thought they were creepy, but I didn't know that, and still clung to the belief that my West Coast surfer girl would return, tanned, and into my arms, come September. It was probably, in fact, because of my ongoing infatuation with Annie that I turned my attention to Grace instead of a romantic prospect. That Grace didn't want to have anything to do with the rest of us didn't bother me. I was happy to watch her life from the wings, hearing her phone conversations through the vents that connected our rooms. It gave me something to do.

I didn't have a job that summer because my father had died a few months earlier and left me a lot of money in his will. Cancer. It wasn't a pleasant year. Like Grace, I spent a lot of time disappearing behind walls. I started watching reality TV, particularly Survivor. I became engrossed in the race for survival: the backstabbing and manipulation; the strategy, the sheer will, temerity, and luck that it took to survive. I lost touch with my friends. Until Annie came along I spent most of my time alone. I passed my classes because my teachers knew about my dad and felt bad for me.

I met Annie when I was drunk. I don't remember what I said to her or she to me, but we made out. I decided she was beautiful. She had gone to all-girls Catholic school and wore a tiny silver cross around her neck, though she claimed to be an atheist and hate her parents. For me, a Jewish boy with a dead father, and a child of the spiritually devoid East Coast suburbs, there was something remarkably alluring about the way she wore that cross, secretly, beneath the clothes that I was now allowed to remove. Or maybe it just reminded me of a Billy Joel song. When she slept I fingered the cross and whispered I love you just to see how the words sounded as they came out of my mouth.

This was a week before school ended, not an ideal time for budding romance. We spent the week together drinking wine and fooling around, eating Thai food in my bed. I thought we had a beautiful connection. I thought we were soul mates. I don't think Annie knew this, but it didn't matter. She was leaving in a week. I drove her to the airport on a Saturday morning. We made out for a while in the car, and I had a feeling it would be the last time.

Once school ended and she was gone, I went back to my lethargy. I didn't want to get a job and didn't plan to. The problem was, I wasn't sure what the alternative would be. I figured Donnie and I could go fishing on the weekends and I'd watch a lot of re-runs during the day. Maybe get some reading done. At night I'd drink and sit outside with no shirt on. I got bored of it within a week but by that point there was no turning back.

Summer in Boston is slow and humid. The students leave and the heat smothers you. If you don't have AC you're fucked. We didn't. We did have a system of fans, but they only worked if you were standing directly in front of one. I spent a lot time pacing from fan to fan and thinking about Annie. It was too hot to sleep, so I'd get up early and smoke cigarettes on the porch with T-Rabs. We'd watch our neighbors leave for work. They would get in their cars, sweating in their short-sleeved dress shirts and ties. They looked at us and I knew they hated us. Sometimes we'd drink Pabst or Bloody Marys, but usually it was too hot for drinking. We didn't talk much, which was okay with me.

The junkie sisters never hung out with us on the porch. They hogged the TV, which annoyed me because they didn't even pay rent. They always watched weird girly crap too, like house-decorating shows. I thought it was funny because I couldn't imagine either of them ever decorating a house. Usually they'd fall asleep in front of the TV and I'd come in and steal the remote. They were often up all night doing coke and ecstasy, so by the time it cooled down in the afternoon they tended to pass out. The rest of the house went to work during the day. Except for Grace. She stayed in her room and talked on her cell phone to someone I guessed was her boyfriend.

In one of our brief interactions I asked Grace why she came to Boston. "My boyfriend lives here," she said. Soon I would meet him.

In the meantime I did more of the same and nothing happened. My mother called me crying several times, insisting that I come home for the summer and spend time with her and my brother. She wasn't taking my father's death well. In March she'd popped a handful of Valium and had to get her stomach pumped. They said she just wanted attention, but I was pretty sure she was going for the full monty. Still, I couldn't face a summer at home with my self-medicating mother even if I knew it was best. Let my brother deal with it, I thought. Eventually I stopped answering her calls when I saw her name on the I.D.

[

] Donnie and I went fishing the last weekend of June. (Grace had moved in on June first.) We had wanted to go before, but he was working in a lab and kept getting stuck going in on Saturdays. No one else came. Dan and Jay spent their weekends fucking the junkie sisters; Mike C. went to visit his girlfriend in Connecticut; Mike F. sold hot dogs at Fenway; and T-Rabs never went anywhere. "Keeping an eye on the house," he'd say.

Donnie's parents had a cabin in the Berkshires that they never used. They were a slightly older couple, and kept the house around for their kids. That was the type of people they were and I liked them for it. One summer Donnie had a huge party for July Fourth and I fondled Tessa Bacler in a docked canoe on the shore. It was the same canoe we used for fishing. It made me smile to think about it, probably one of the reasons I liked fishing so much.

This isn't one of those stories where going fishing reminds me of my dead father and I get all sentimental and shit. He wasn't really an outdoor guy; he was more into watching sports on TV. I learned to fish at summer camp when I was twelve. If anything, fishing made me nostalgic for girls wrapped in towels wearing their bikini tops in the dining hall to show off for all the older boys.

We didn't catch much. I liked drinking beer with Donnie and shooting the shit, cooking hot dogs over the fire. "What do you think of Grace," I asked him. "Who's Grace?" he said. It was understandable. Donnie worked a lot and it was hard to keep track of everything that went on in the house unless you were there all the time like me and T-Rabs.

During the day we swam in the lake and played one-on-one Wiffle Ball. It felt good to move my body again after all that time on the couch. I liked the way the wind felt when I took my shirt off.

The drive home was peaceful. I slept and Donnie drove. I'd wake up and catch glimpses of the mountains, hear pieces of oldies songs coming from the radio, then fall back asleep.

When we got back it was drizzling. There were three guys sitting on the porch (it was covered), drinking Budweiser and eating pizza. I was still half-asleep and wasn't surprised that there were strangers hanging out in front of our house.

"Hey," I said. I lit a cigarette.

"What's crappening?" one of the guys responded. He was a funny-looking dude with a goofy, fifties-style flat-top haircut and a big beer gut. He looked about our age.

"Who are you?" Donnie said. He was tired from driving and slightly on edge.

"Chill," the dude said, "I'm Jeff, Grace's boyfriend."

"Oh," I said, "I'm Ben."

"I'm Donnie," Donnie said. "We live here."

Jeff's friends introduced themselves. They had thick Boston accents, no "R"s. Probably townies, I thought.

Donnie and I went inside. The dudes stayed on the porch for another couple hours, drinking. I thought it was strange that Grace wasn't out there. Eventually the two guys who weren't Grace's boyfriend left. Jeff came in and went down to Grace's room. He gave a nod as he walked past. "Gonna get laid," he said, and smiled. When he was gone I asked T-Rabs, "What's the word on that guy."

"Townie," T-Rabs said.

"He asked me what's crappening," I said.

"Bizarre," T-Rabs replied.

[
] I tried to listen to them talk in Grace's room but they had music on too loud. They were listening to Korn or some other teenage mall music. I wanted to ask them to turn it down but requests of that nature weren't generally considered appropriate in our house. Everyone was expected to put up with any disturbance.

I had trouble falling asleep because of it and because I'd napped in the car. I lay awake imagining Grace and Jeff fucking and then trying to block out the image by thinking about Annie. At this point I could hardly remember the details of her face. I thought for a moment about my mother and figured she was probably up too, or else sedated by drugs and snoring loudly. I tried not to dwell on it. Instead I imagined floating in Donnie's lake on my back and looking up at the clouds shaped like strange animals from a fairy tale.

[
] It was still raining when I woke up. Jeff was gone. Unsurprising, considering it was two in the afternoon. When it rains I can sleep all day, especially since I went to bed so late. I watched TV for a while with

the junkie sisters and drank a cup of coffee. T-Rabs was asleep on the couch. The rain made it feel like a Sunday and for all I know it could have been one. In fact, it probably was.

By five-thirty the sun was out and Jeff and his buddies were back on the porch drinking Budweiser and eating pizza. I didn't say anything. No one did. They came back the next day too and then the next day and the next. Five-thirty each day and they were gone by 9, 10 if there was a Sox game because they listened on a portable radio. On the fourth day I invited them in to watch the game with us.

"No," Jeff said. "We'd just stink up the joint." He talked like he was in a greaser movie.

"Okay," I said and went back inside.

"What's the deal with those dudes," I said to T-Rabs."Porchies, dude," he said, "just Porchies.

After a week the Porchies were commonplace. Aside from T-Rabs and I, the housemates were too busy with their lives to pay attention. I watched them through the window for a couple days. I enjoyed looking at Jeff even though I couldn't hear what he was saying. He was very animated when he spoke, constantly waving his arms and moving his body. When he laughed the undulations of his gut were mesmerizing and the fat around his cheeks gave his face a cartoon look.

The other Porchies weren't as interesting to look at. Al was short and blonde with wavy hair and big arms. His muscles were big but ill-defined; the type you get from manual labor rather than weightlifting. He also did a lot of talking, though his face was more somber when he spoke, his features more distinct. Steve, the third guy, was the scrawny one. He wore wife-beaters and had a large tattoo of eagle's wings between his shoulders. He rarely spoke and seemed to drink more than the others.

I made a habit of inviting them in but they never accepted. Every day when his friends left Jeff would walk past us on the way to Grace's room and say something about the fact that he was about to have sex. It was different each time, and it became a part of the day I anticipated. Once he said, "It's fornicatin' time," and the next day, "Get ready for the horizontal tango." Then he'd walk by us with a grin that turned his cheeks red, and disappear into the basement.

"That's disgusting," one of the junkie sisters would inevitably remark. No one could disagree.

I never got used to the teen-angst music coming from Grace's room at night and I couldn't stop picturing them having sex. I wasn't sure which bothered me more: the insomnia, or the image of Jeff's stomach bouncing to the music as he took Grace from behind. Probably what freaked me out most was that I was even thinking about it in the first place. Eventually I started buying sleeping pills from a British guy down the street.
[
] July fourth came shortly after the arrival of the Porchies. We decided to have a party. I was glad. My brother was coming to town for the weekend and I wanted to show him a good time. I figured his summer had to be pretty shitty dealing with mom. He deserved to let loose.

Derek showed up an hour before the party started. He looked worn out. He was still in high school and it must have been a lot to handle. We sat on the porch drinking and smoking until the guests arrived. We talked about the new Wilco album which we both thought was amazing, and how there was nothing good on TV in the summer. I asked him if he'd been to any Sox games this year but he hadn't. We couldn't talk about the big stuff, but that was okay. No one had to say anything; we both knew. It was good just sitting together.

Eventually the guests arrived. Parties in summer are a whole different scene, comprised of a melting pot of stragglers: townies, people's high school friends, neighbors; basically, whoever's around. It's usually easy to get laid because things that happen in summer don't seem to be a part of real life. Still, I didn't feel like trying, although I'd pretty much given up on Annie by this point. She hadn't responded to my letters and I knew it was because they were weird.

I hardly recognized anyone at the party. A bunch of Mike F.'s Fenway friends were there, and Mike C.'s girlfriend had shown up with some chicks from her hometown. Some frat dudes from down the street came as well as some hippies from the next block over. Everyone was getting along fine, mostly due to the two kegs of cheap beer and large quantities of marijuana being smoked in the living room. At some point the Porchies showed up. They weren't usually around on weekends. I had invited them but assumed they wouldn't come. When they arrived they took their spot on the porch and proceeded as if it were just another night. They didn't have pizza this time but they still brought their own beer.

The Porchies had a lot of company. The porch is a popular spot in summer, especially during parties. People like to smoke outside and mingle. I watched for a while from the window as drunk people talked to them. Jeff seemed to make the drunks laugh easily.

I didn't spend the whole time watching the Porchies. I'm not a stalker or anything. I walked around for a while, mostly to and from the keg. I talked baseball with Mike F.'s Fenway friends and said hello to people I hadn't seen in a while. Mike C.'s girlfriend introduced me to her home friends. They were cute and younger and I thought I could probably make out with one if I wanted to, but I knew I didn't have it in me and I remember feeling like I'd never have it in me again. This turned out to be untrue, but at the time I had trouble speaking to girls whose eyes did not carry a hint of death between the pupils and the whites. Say what you will about the junkie sisters, but they had it. Maybe they had too much death in their eyes. I don't know; it's a difficult distinction to make.

When I went back to the window I could see Grace out there sitting on Jeff's lap. She was holding a beer and looking up at the streetlamp like it was a full moon. She seemed content. Her mouth was curved slightly upward in a gentle smile. It was a secretive smile, almost embarrassed, but clearly present as she kept her eyes fixed on the artificial light and let Jeff bounce her on his knee as he blew smoke rings into the humid air.

I felt an arm around my shoulder and immediately knew it was my brother. It was strange to feel another person's skin against my own; his red cheeks inches from my face. I thought this must have been the first physical contact I'd had with another human being in a long time because I'd forgotten how natural it felt to have another person's hand clapped against my body.

"Who is that guy?" Derek asked me.

"Jeff Porch," I said.

"Pretty weird," he said, "He told me he was gonna shove a tube of toothpaste up my ass."

"Sounds about right," I said. "I think he's a good guy though."

"Tell that to your neighbor," Derek said.

"What?"

"Your neighbor, that guy called him a douche and then said he fucked his daughter with a corn on the cob."

"Shit," I said.

I looked at Jeff. He was smiling; a beautiful goyish grin.

I didn't ask Jeff about the encounter with our neighbor. Better not to know, I thought. The party wound down. People left, drifting out the door slowly, lingering in the doorway to say goodbye, or else disappearing hand in hand to a patch of grass outside because it was still warm and the neighborhood was quiet. I didn't notice when the Porchies left, just that they were gone. I could hear the music coming up from Grace's room. My roommates were gone too and I guessed that most of them were also getting laid. Even T-Rabs was nowhere to be seen.

Derek was passed out on the couch. Even in sleep he didn't look peaceful. His breath was heavy, and his legs kept kicking, trying to bend into comfort on the too-small couch. I grabbed one of the blankets that T-Rabs usually used, a worn-out red one with a Coca-Cola logo sewn into the stitching. I placed it on my brother with light hands, knowing I wouldn't wake him, but trying to be considerate anyway. "Get some rest," I whispered.

I wasn't tired, but I was wasted and figured I should get some sleep. When I got down to the basement I could hear the music really loud. Grace's door was open about a quarter of the way. I wasn't sure, but I thought I could hear some pants and moans mixed in with the heavy bass and screaming vocals. I edged closer to the door just to check it out. Fuck it, I thought. I peeked into the opening. Their bodies were obscured. All I could see was Grace's head from the side, tilted back over the edge of the bed. She was making the same face that I saw her make on the porch, only this time her eyes were closed and her lips were slightly parted to reveal a front tooth biting hard on her bottom lip as she gave that smile. She was biting so hard, in fact, that a thin trail of blood dripped from her lip, over her chin, and down the nape of her neck. Grace kept smiling with her eyes closed, her head swaying slowly to the beat of the music.

[

] When I woke up my brother was gone. T-Rabs was back in place on the couch and wrapped in the Coca-Cola blanket. Grace changed her contacts in the bathroom with the door open. She was wearing an orange bathrobe with pink dots. I looked away. I felt like leaving the house but couldn't think of anywhere to go. I didn't want to just walk the streets; it was way too hot for that. What I wanted was a destination but I couldn't think of one. Instead I did my usual fan-pacing with headphones on. I avoided the Porchies for a while after July fourth. When they were on the porch I'd hide in my room listening to CDs. I wanted to write but I'd given up on writing to Annie and didn't know what else to say.

July moved slowly. Donnie was busy with work and couldn't go fishing. I had trouble keeping track of the rest of my housemates. Their lives, once so entwined with my own, had become a mystery I wasn't interested in solving. T-Rabs was still around and we hung out a lot, staring into the television in the hope it would bring us with it into the land of palm trees and police drama. I liked T-Rabs because he never asked about my problems and didn't expect to be asked about his. He was unhappy in a way that I understood. I don't know what spawned it in him, but it's a certain type of sadness that paralyzes you in front of the television or the fan, chains you to the house like a prisoner condemned to the fate of boredom.

The junkie sisters were the same, and the more I began to realize that, the more I despised them for it; despised them for the fact that they were human beings beneath the shell of intoxication and indifference. To me, they didn't even have names.

They did have names, of course. Louise (Lulu) Dupont and Sarah Grossman. They were both blonde. Lulu was from Louisiana and of Cajun origin. Sarah was a Jewish girl from North Jersey. I assumed they both came from money because neither of them worked but they could always afford drugs. They were attractive enough—skinny and pale, if that's the look you're going for. But, they had those vacant eyes that scared me a little bit, though I was pretty certain that mine were the same. Towards the end of the month, Lulu's mother came. T-Rabs and I were on the porch when someone pulled up in a Ford Focus. It must have been a rental. A tall woman came out. Her blonde hair was stringy and pulled back so you could see where her cheeks had been lifted to converge with her eyebrows. You could tell by the way she walked that she had once been beautiful. She stood up straight and marched to our door.

"I'm looking for Louise," she said calmly. "I was told I might find her here."

"Lulu's inside," T-Rabs said.

Mrs. Dupont looked through the window. Lulu was sitting on the couch with a cigarette between her fingers, staring into the television. I looked at Mrs. Dupont's face and it was almost like a reflection. Because of the drugs, I suspect, Lulu's features had aged prematurely, and, combined with her mother's surgical modifications, came a striking similarity. The eyes were the same. For a second I thought Mrs. Dupont might cry at the sight of her daughter through the window, but she fixed herself, pulled her shoulders back, and remained stoic as she walked through the door to do what she'd come to do.

"How'd you find me?"

"I called your roommate. She said you were probably here."

"I'm not going with you."

Mrs. Dupont was standing in front of the TV. I could see Sarah attempting to peer around her at the screen. Lulu put out her cigarette.

"You can't stay here forever," Mrs. Dupont said.

It seemed to apply to all of us. She was looking around, noticing the broken windows, fast-food wrappers, discarded beer cans. They were things I hadn't thought about in a while. Mrs. Dupont leaned over and turned off the TV. You could hear the fans humming.

"C'mon Louise," she said. She grabbed her daughter's hand and pulled her limp body from the couch like a puppeteer might tug the strings of a marionette.

"Get your things," Mrs. Dupont said, "We'll have to fumigate them."

Lulu tossed a few scraps of clothing in a backpack. As they were walking out she said to me, "Tell Jay goodbye." I never did. He never asked about it either.

Once Lulu was gone Sarah didn't last long. I saw it coming. She hardly watched TV anymore. She started putting on makeup and getting out of the house during the day. One day she never came back. No one was sure when, but I'd say it was the last week of July.

She probably found another guy to fuck, maybe even a house full of guys like us. Another place where she could watch television and put powder up her nose without the guilt of seeing sad mothers come to rescue their daughters, and without the sadness of not being rescued herself—a sense of abandonment that no one could fix, but would be easier to ignore on a different couch in a different room. We weren't special. Boston is a young person's town and was littered with houses exactly like ours. If she was smart she found a cleaner one.

T-Rabs was the next to go. I sensed he was incomplete without the junkie sisters. He rarely spoke to them, and didn't seem to like them all that much, but they were his in a way that no one else could touch. Lulu and Sarah shared Dan and Jay's beds at night, but their souls were on the couch, and the couch was T-Rabs' territory.

He gave more warning than the others. It was a couple days after we noted the permanent disappearance of Sarah. We were all sitting on the porch drinking. It was the first time the whole gang had hung out together in a while. The Porchies had already left, but even Grace was there, nursing a beer in the corner. It was one of those nights in August when you can still go shirtless at midnight. We all did except for Grace. I noticed how pale my own body looked compared to the tanned skin of my roommates. Donnie sat on the steps lighting candles and then dripping the wax onto his bare forearm. Mike F. tossed a baseball up and down in his hand.

"Think it might be getting time to head on out of here," T-Rabs said. He liked being cinematic.

"Is that what you reckon?" Donnie replied.

I wanted to tell him to stay, but that's not the kind of guy I am, and it wouldn't have mattered anyway.

T-Rabs stuck around for a couple more days. He and I watched the street in the mornings like we used to. On Wednesday he walked to the T and was gone.

"Take care of yourself," I told him.

"No doubt, bro," he said.

We stayed friends for a while, a few years. I didn't see him much, but we'd have drinks if I was ever in New York, talk about who we'd seen and shit. He still lived with his mom and was in and out of jobs. One of us would always bring up the Porchies.

"Remember Jeff Porch," T-Rabs would say.

"Yeah," I'd reply. "He asked me what's crappening."

We'd laugh for a bit and mutter, "Jeff Porch, dude, fucking Jeff Porch." One time, when I called, his number was disconnected. I never tried it again. I was married at the time.

I do remember Jeff Porch though, who was still around after T-Rabs left. After all, this is a story about the Porchies, so it's only fitting that they were there until the bitter end (which, inevitably, was not so far away.)

After T-Rabs left I was bored and started to watch the Porchies again through the window. I still remembered the blood squirting from Grace's lip, but it seemed less embarrassing now that the house was emptying out and the summer dying down.

Eventually I joined them on the porch, bringing out an extra chair from the kitchen. They didn't seem to mind my presence, but I didn't feel included either. I didn't join in when they recited (as they did every-day) the inscription on the Budweiser can (*"This is the famous Budweiser beer. We know of no brand produced by any other brewer which costs so much to brew and age. Our exclusive Beechwood Aging produces a taste, a smoothness and a drinkability you will find in no other beer at any price . . .*). But I did listen to the Sox games on their radio and make comments, and I did sit and drink with them.

I was surprised at how little they talked. For some reason I'd imag-ined their conversations to be interesting. In actuality they were at least as boring as my own discussions with T-Rabs or the junkie sisters. Jeff talked a lot, but he didn't have much to say. Mostly he swore and made sodomy threats. Al, I learned, was a communist. He worked in a Coca-Cola factory, and was big into unions and conspiracy theories. You would think this would spark some good discussion, but, in truth, his rhetoric was no different from that of the kids in my sociology classes whom I'd grown to hate for their self-righteousness. I guess Al was more deserving of his beliefs; he was, after all, an actual member of the proletariat, but I still found him boring, and none of his friends paid attention when he spoke.

"I'll Castro your dick off," Jeff would say. He had a habit of repeating jokes. Steve didn't talk much. I kept my eyes away from him for the most part.

Jeff would still make his pre-sex announcement before heading down to Grace's room, but it was awkward because I was the only one he was talking to. I could sense that he felt superior to me in a way, because he was having sex while I was confined to pace the halls and stare into the television.

One day Jeff was the only Porchie to show up. It was the second week of August and I wasn't feeling ready for the upcoming school year and the return of life to the city and campus. He was sitting on the porch by himself doing an Axl Rose impression and trying to light a match on his belt buckle.

"Hey Jeff," I said. He continued singing, "Take me down to the Paradise City where the grass is green and the girls are pretty," playing air guitar for my benefit. I grabbed a beer out of his case and lit a cigarette.

"Hey Jeff," I said, "how come Grace never hangs out on the porch?"

"Honestly," he said, "she's just shy. I don't make her stay in the basement or anything. She's just not that into partying like me."

"I see," I said.

"I'm gonna head down there. I guess you know what I'm gonna do."

[

] The next day there was a knock on the door. When I opened it Big Frank was standing with his arms crossed. I hadn't seen him in ages, but he didn't seem thrilled about the reunion. He handed me a piece of paper. Without looking, I knew he was kicking us out.

"I have to evict you guys," he said. "Jimmy from next door's been complaining. Said someone's been harassing his daughter, threatening her. Been going on for a while now. Jimmy's an old pal of mine and he said if it doesn't stop he'll call the cops. I don't have time to figure out which one of you fuckheads is causing this problem and I don't care either. I can't have any cops coming here. You knew that when you moved in. I expect you'll all be out by the end of the week."

I didn't have a chance to respond, and I didn't want my kneecaps broken. Frank left me the piece of paper and walked back to his car.

[

] I was the last one to pack up and leave. Dan and Jay had moved all their stuff to some other friend's house and were staying there until they found a new place. Mike C. said peace out and went to stay with his girlfriend for the rest of the summer, which is where he wanted to be anyway and now he had an excuse to go. Mike F. was from Acton, just a quick drive down Route 2. Donnie left in the morning while I was sleeping. He had work at the lab. I think he was going to stay with some friends around town also.

No one said goodbye or anything. Everyone knew they'd see each other soon when school started.

I helped Grace load up her jeep in the same way that I'd helped unload it at the beginning of the summer. She didn't have much stuff.

"Where you heading?" I asked her. I assumed she was going to Jeff's.

"Florida," she said.

"What about Jeff?"

"Don't think I'm really invited. Besides, these things end sometimes." She didn't seem sad.

"I guess," I said. I watched Grace drive away and remembered her face as blood dripped from her lip. Some people might think it was surreal, but to me it felt like the only real thing I'd seen all summer.

I looked at the house. It wasn't really empty. We decided to leave the furniture because it was shitty and falling apart and no one had a car big enough to take it. There was trash everywhere, a sort-of "Fuck You" to Big Frank. Literally. Dan and Jay had spelled out "Fuck you" in beer cans on the living room floor.

I didn't have much to take. Mostly just a bunch of clothes and CDs, and the TV from the living room. I carried it out to my car and then up to my room in the house I grew up in, which I began referring to as "My mother's house." I watched a lot of TV when I got home, for hours, days, weeks. My brother and I would drink beer on the porch sometimes.

I hardly saw my mother. She stayed in bed most of the time and when she got up her nightgown would be slipping off one shoulder and her hair would be all crazy and her eyes were barely open so I didn't even want to look. "I'm glad you're here," she said a couple times, which was strange because it didn't even seem like she noticed I was there, but she put her hand on my forehead and ran her fingers through my hair like when I was a kid, and I knew she was being honest.

I started stealing her pills. I thought they might help me relax, which they did. They gave me a numbness that stopped the feeling I had when I paced the halls listening to loud music. It was a feeling like I wanted to smash windows with my fist and run down the highway screaming with my shirt off and one hand raised above my head. With the pills I could sleep and I lost my appetite, which was good, because no one ever cooked in that house anyway.

I didn't go back to school in the fall. I couldn't seem to get it together. Dan, Jay, Mike F., Mike C., Donnie, and Andrew got a new house on the other side of campus. I went over there a couple times at the beginning of the semester. It looked just like our old house. There were people hanging out that I didn't know, mostly younger girls. After the second time I thought people were looking at me funny like they thought I'd gone crazy or something, so I stopped going back. It was probably nonsense. We'd had a lot of friends on "hiatus" from school before. I don't know why I thought I was special.

I'm not going to get sentimental and say it was "The summer that changed my life," or anything like that. It wasn't. I've had worse summers since, and certainly more fucked-up ones. The next summer I was in McLean's hospital in Belmont talking to doctors about why I took all those pills in the first place and why I wasn't gonna do it again. I could have told a story about that—about all the crazy people I met there who were probably more interesting than Grace, Jeff, T-Rabs, and the junkie sisters combined.

[

] After rehab I went back on pills then back in rehab then drinking then sober. I've had jobs since then that I've quit and one's I've been fired from. I have a job now like the ones my neighbors had when I watched them sweat in their cars, and when I look at myself in the mirror it's with the same hate that they looked at me with then. I've had relationships too, good ones and bad ones. I was married for a while but she left me because I really did want to have kids but every time I thought about it I pictured my son—really a younger version of myself—pacing the halls with headphones on and stomping his feet to the beat of some angry fucking music.

My brother got married too. I was the best man but I got drunk and punched a waiter in the face for reasons I can't explain, but were somehow related to a shortage of pigs in blankets.

I watched his marriage dissolve more quickly than my own, though I don't know why because I knew Derek was capable of so much love, far more than me, and I was jealous of that and then sad because it didn't matter in the end.

Our mother died at sixty-five of cancer, fitting, as she'd always wanted to die for him. I wouldn't be surprised if she'd willed it on herself. At the funeral Derek and I stood over her stone and as the rabbi was talking Derek said, "she's happier down there," and instead of feeling trite it just felt true.

[

] I saw Jeff Porch one more time after the summer. It was the end of fall and the wind was blowing in New England fashion, which is a euphemism for unbearable. I had been at school signing the necessary papers for my semester off. I was walking back to the T and trying to light a cigarette, but failing because of the wind. Not giving up I stood there repeatedly flicking the lighter until my finger burned with cold and friction. Someone came up behind me.

"Twat's Up," Jeff said. I gave up on the cigarette and put the lighter away.

"I'm heading home," I said. "What are you up to these days?"

"Going to California," Jeff said, "San Diego, California."

"Sounds warmer than here," I said.

"I heard at the zoo there they have a two-headed snake," Jeff said. Right then I knew that he would make it to California, and that I never would.

] The End of Anti-Semitism

I'd always done well in English class until the eighth grade, when Mrs. Taborsky distracted me with the paisley swirls of her bold print scarves. In Detroit's northwestern suburbs, no one ever wore scarves indoors, especially if it wasn't winter, unless you wanted people to think you were a bohemian.

On those rare days when Mrs. Taborsky wasn't wearing one of her scarves, I found myself mesmerized by her purse, a woven twine bag decorated with faux seashells like a fishing net and its lime green Mondale for President button, or her fire engine red plastic raincoat, or her sea-foam-colored, zodiac-studded suede boots. Then there were her classroom walls, festooned with glitter-speckled rainbow letters that spelled out messages like "Reading is possibilities!" which contradicted my thorough grounding in grammar in English class the year before, when I'd received an A+.

Mrs. Taborsky was new to the Solomon Schecter Hebrew Academy, and there were rumors she owed her position to her soon-to-be exhusband Rabbi Taborsky, who led the largest conservative synagogue in our suburb. Our family went to a smaller, less-fashionable shul, but we'd visited the Taborskys' synagogue for a couple of bar mitzvahs, and I remember watching her nod calmly in the front row during her husband's sermons, her smooth brown hair pulled back in a chignon and crowned with a tan cloche hat that bobbed gently up and down.

But when she came to our school, Mrs. Taborsky's hairdo had transformed into a Whitney Houston-inspired nest of orange-highlighted frizz that spurted out of her head like a fountain. Her lips were sealed in frosted pink lipstick and her eyes and cheeks were outlined in swaths of vivid pink, as if she expected someone or something wonderful to turn up shortly: perhaps her new job at the private Jewish school where I'd been a model student for years—until she and her crazy ways came along.

Because for the first time in my life, my grades in English class were plummeting below the failing mark. I knew how to ace a spelling test, fill in a grammar worksheet, or answer a reading comprehension question from a textbook. But how was I supposed to succeed at Mrs. Taborsky's peculiar assignments, which she explained were not about traditional learning? Suddenly, instead of turning in essays, we kept "free-writing" journals, in which we had to reveal our feelings. Grammar was gone, in favor of "helpful hints." No more spelling bees either; now we had "Words Equal Power!" jam sessions in which we were expected to leap out of our chairs to boldly proclaim the power of language. Worst of all, book reports were replaced with "literary responses."

For our first literary response, Mrs. Taborsky had us choose partners and dramatize scenes from our favorite books. While the rest of the class eagerly teamed up to chat about props and costumes, I sat alone at my desk, even after Mrs. Taborsky said, "No one wants to buddy up with Alan? No one?" A more experienced teacher might have forced someone to join me, but apparently Mrs. Taborsky had read somewhere it was best to let students work these things out on their own. "Here's an opportunity to be creative and attract a partner to yourself for next time by letting out the real you," she advised me. "Let yourself go! There's no such thing as right or wrong."

Oh, yes there was such a thing as wrong, as I learned while portraying *Anne of Green Gables* in an orange wig that resulted in the whole class laughing and me running out of the room in tears. When I came back, Mrs. Taborsky offered a meek smile, as if she were one of those kids who was just on the cusp of being popular and didn't want to risk losing cool points by evincing her sympathy for me in public.

"I think I know what happened back there," she told me later in the hallway. "You were trying to be someone you weren't. Next time, let out the real you."

I knew better, and planned to keep the real me under tight wraps for our next response, in the form of a diorama. It should have been simple enough. I turned an old shoebox of my mother's into a garden populated by tiny stuffed animals that sat on doll furniture and ate off doll plates for *The Wind in the Willows*. But even before Mrs. Taborsky came into the room, her son Mark, whom the school had seen fit to place in our class, helpfully pointed out that I'd used a woman's shoebox, which apparently, in conjunction with my *Anne of Green Gables* costume and my awkwardness in gym, served as incontrovertible evidence that the "real me" was a secret cross-dresser.

I immediately chucked the whole thing into the garbage. Better to take another zero than be known for weeks as a prepubescent trannie.

"I sense you've got so much bottled up inside," sighed Mrs. Taborsky after the rest of the class had rushed out to recess. "We're all waiting for you to let it out."

But Mrs. Taborsky was dead wrong. No one was waiting for me to do anything.

Thankfully, our next "response" was more private. Instead of having us read a book, Mrs. Taborsky wanted us to write our own short stories. Finally, I knew just what to do with a Taborsky English assignment. In fairy tales, you always read about princesses in need of rescue. My idea was to write about a handsome prince who needed to be rescued, in this case from his evil father. For the hero of my story, I chose a not-conventionally-handsome-but-attractive-in-his-own-way court scribe who would help the unloved and neglected (and most importantly dashing) prince escape from the castle where his evil father was holding him prisoner. Then they'd run away together to the sea.

Did I mention there was a prize involved? The author of the best story would be invited to participate in an all-day writing conference at the local community college. That meant he would get to miss an entire day of school (or as I thought of it, "hell") to be in the company of other serious-minded book lovers where he belonged.

I was a cinch to win.

Every day after school, I shut myself in my room and worked on my story. I spent hours on the loving descriptions of my fair prince's golden-brown locks of hair, the silken sheets of his royal bedchamber, as well as the salty winds whipping off the sea and spraying over the joyous faces of the prince and his beloved rescuer.

I showed the final product to my mother, who said she was impressed by my lack of grammar mistakes. I suggested showing it to my father, but the anxious look on my mother's face and the way she said, "He doesn't really know about those things," made me decide not to. I gave a copy to my sister, a high school senior, which she never read. Finally, the morning my story was due, I read it aloud to her as she drove me to school.

As my sister dropped me off, she gave me her review: "Isn't it a little . . . ? I don't know, but do you think other guys write things like this?"

I slunk out of the car and crumpled the story into a ball.

Yet one more zero.

I told myself I didn't care about the contest. Anyway it was clear the whole thing had been rigged from the start when the winner turned out to be Mark Taborsky. We had to waste several minutes of class time listening to him read aloud from his masterpiece, titled "The End of Anti-Semitism":

When it happened, the first thing I thought was, I can't believe it. This isn't happening.

We still lived in a different suburb then, one that was mostly non-Jewish. I was about to board a bus headed for summer camp with my non-Jewish friends, expecting fun and games, a summer of swimming under the sun and campfire songs and toasted marshmallows. I didn't worry if the marshmallows were kosher or not.

The doors opened, and we were all crowding eagerly onto the bus, but the woman in the driver's seat held out her hand, not to welcome me, but like a crossing guard stopping traffic. She said, "Wait your turn, Jew."

The other kids listened closely, as if Mark had just told them that a fire-breathing dragon had landed in the parking lot.

The words burned me, like someone had thrown a fistful of stones in my face. My cheeks turned red and I stepped back, stunned to be singled out like that from my friends. I put my hand over my heart and touched the gold star hanging from my neck . . .

Mark glanced down at the heavy diamond-studded gold star around his neck, no doubt a bar mitzvah present from his father. All the boys in my grade had them except me because my father felt it was inappropriate for a boy to wear jewelry.

. . . That's how she must have known! I realized for the first time how different I was. Suddenly, I understood all the stories I'd heard but never really paid attention to, of Jews from all over who'd been persecuted because of their simple religion. Why was I different? What was wrong with me that this woman had called me this name? I was confused and also very sad.

My parents complained to the camp, which refunded our money and fired the bus driver, who turned out to be a poor single mother living in a trailer park or something of that nature, which was probably why she'd never met any Jews before.

Now I go to a private Jewish Day School and while I will miss my non-Jewish friends, I feel more comfortable knowing that at least here nothing like that can ever happen again.

But what about the other Jews who don't go to private Jewish schools? That is why when I grow up I want to be a lawyer and work for the end of anti-Semitism, so that nothing like what happened to me can ever happen again. Because it is the kind of thing that can lead to another Holocaust.

When Mark looked up from his paper, the entire class burst into applause. I joined in too, but only because I didn't want anyone to think I was a self-hating Jew. There wasn't a single moment in Mark's asinine story half as meaningful as my scene in which the scribe threw open the door to the prince's bedroom and declared, "Take my hand, fair prince. For you are free, and you and I shall never be parted!" Still, Mrs. Taborsky was clapping and beaming as if her son had just discovered America.

The trip to the conference was wasted on Mark, who had no need to escape school. In the half-year he'd been a student at Hebrew Academy (part of Mrs. Taborsky's deal was free tuition for her two boys), he'd accumulated more friendships than I'd had during my entire life, probably because he knew all the right movies to see and sports to watch and video games to play as well as the right things to say about them (like "Sweet!" with the "s" pronounced as an "sh," ergo "Shweet!"). He could hit and throw and catch balls. He had a turned-up nose and golden-brown hair like the prince in my story. Also, it helped that he was a spectacularly unkind person. He took particular relish in mocking different students in class with crude insults that always seemed startlingly original, though they generally amounted to the same thing: girls were sluts, and boys were girls.

I was in love. Somehow I believed Mark's cruelty was born of some unexpressed psychic pain that I could coax him to reveal if I could just get the two of us alone. My first opportunity to test my hypothesis occurred a month after Mark had won the writing contest. Mrs. Taborsky chose the two of us to travel to the gym storage room to return some orange traffic cones she'd borrowed to illustrate the perils of run-on sentences. I'd found the demonstration confusing and undignified, but everyone else seemed to enjoy it, especially Mark, who while posing as a semicolon, tripped up three different boys with his Air Nike sneaker while muttering the magic words, "Flying faggot!" One boy indeed went flying and, while Mark watched with a satisfied smirk, almost sliced his forehead on the edge of a desk. "Careful with the horseplay," Mrs. Taborsky called out nervously from the board, her chalk squeaking out a dependent clause.

As I clutched my share of orange cones to my chest, I kept pondering the miracle of walking down the hall by Mark's side. Think of something to say to him, I kept telling myself, but my mind went blank until we disappeared into the dusty-smelling storage room, and I mustered the courage to ask, "How was that conference?"

Mark, busy shoving a sack of red rubber dodge balls and some field hockey sticks under a shelf of out-of-date prayer books, snarled, "What conference?"

Just then I hated him. He didn't deserve everything he had. Like a father who loved him and showed him how to throw balls and a mother who encouraged his so-called writing talent. And a God who'd given him such beautiful eyes.

"Oh, you mean that writing thing?" Mark went on. "Boring."

He was pure evil. Pure . . . boy. Anything that didn't involve the possibility of physical injury was boring. And those of us who were more sophisticated in our tastes were girls. "Boring, how?" I asked.

"Just boring," he replied with his usual eloquence.

"I was wondering," I said, trying not to choke on my own words, "was there anyone there who wrote a story about a prince who needed saving?"

"No," he said quickly.

"You know, in the fairy tales, it's always the princess who needs saving. So I thought I'd write one where it's the prince who needs saving. I could show it to you. I mean, since you won the contest, you must know something about writing, right? If you want to read it. It's good. At least, I think it's good."

"Why didn't you win that competition?" he asked. "Everyone knows you're the smartest kid in our grade. Probably the smartest kid in school."

Flattered, not by the compliment to my intelligence but by the fact that he knew something about who I was, I mumbled, "I didn't win because I didn't enter."

"Why not?"

I shrugged. "I just couldn't think of anything in time. Your mother . . ." It felt thrillingly naked to refer to Mrs. Taborsky as his mother, "always gives us these stupid creative assignments."

"Shut up about my mother, you faggot," he said.

So there it was, my punishment for committing the sin of whining. My father had always taught me (when he talked to me) never make excuses, never pose questions or whine. Never ask for anything. Follow the rules. Everyone gives you rules. Just follow them and you'd get what you want without having to humiliate yourself by asking for it.

But what about the situations when there were no rules to explain how to get what you wanted? When what you wanted couldn't be asked for? Like what I wanted from Mark then, which somehow he'd deduced without my asking. Because though the orange cones were successfully put away, we were not leaving the storage room. Mark was blocking the door. He asked me, "Have you ever done anything with girls?"

I told him I had.

"With who?"

"Whom, not who," I said on instinct, then came up with a name: "Adrienne Cohen." Adrienne had been my babysitter when I'd required the services of a babysitter.

"Never heard of her. How do you know her?"

I thought fast. "I saw her outside once, standing on her lawn. I thought she was cute. So I asked her if she wanted to go record shopping at Harmony House sometime."

Mark burst out laughing. "You're lying," he said.

"Honestly," I said.

"No one says, 'honestly,' " he said. "You're lying."

"I told her to meet me at Harmony House."

"No one meets anyone at Harmony House," he said, the flicker of a smile playing at the corners of his lips. "Tell me the truth. I'll have so much more respect for you if you say, 'Mark, okay, I was lying. I never asked anyone to meet me at Harmony House. I don't even know anyone named Adrienne Cohen.'"

"I really do know her," I said. Unfortunately, my voice cracked.

"So what did you do with this Adrienne?" he said in a vaguely threatening tone.

I shrugged.

"You didn't do anything."

"We frenched," I said.

"What does that mean," he said, giggling a little. "We frenched."

"Aren't we done here?" I said. "Can't we go?"

I tried to reach past him for the door, but he grabbed my hand, then put it on the front of his pants. He rubbed it there. "Did she do this to you?"

His jeans felt rough and, in the place where I was rubbing, very full. How had he guessed about me? I'd worked so hard all these years to disqualify myself, to hide behind the sidelines.

"Don't let go until I tell you to stop," he said. "Or I'll tell everyone you're a fag."

[

] Something came over me during the next months. I got very quiet, even surly. The kids in school who never noticed me noticed it. Even the crowd of dimwitted, unattractive boys who let me sit with them at lunch in exchange for help with their math homework noticed I wasn't smiling stupidly as they discussed TV sitcoms I hadn't seen.

My sister who drove me to school noticed it, and asked why I acted so grouchy all of a sudden in the mornings. I said it was because I was stuck sharing rides with a self-absorbed jerk. Michael, my oldest sibling, noticed it too when he came home from college to announce his engagement to a former cheerleader. "Oh, I hoped so!" was my mother's ecstatic reaction. Her hands flew up in the air, then caught the cheerleader's face in her hands. "We're taking you both out for a steak dinner!"

Is that what she'd have said if I'd told her I was jerking off Mark Taborsky in the gym storage room? "Oh, I hoped so!"

"How about you, squirt?" Michael asked me. "Aren't you excited to have a new sister?"

"What difference does it make?" I muttered, then thought of something I heard Mark Taborsky say a few times. "Women are all the same, anyway. Sluts."

Michael's smile vanished.

He and his cheerleader got an even colder reception from my father, who said he refused to be seen in public with Michael because he'd recently pierced his left ear.

"It's no problem," my mother said. "We can celebrate right here. I've got leftover spaghetti. I can heat it up in a few minutes." On the stove, she meant, not in a microwave. My parents were suspicious of microwaves, computers, and cable television.

So we ate leftover spaghetti to mark my brother's engagement, my mother, my sister and I in the kitchen, my father in his study with the door closed, Michael and the cheerleader in the living room with all the lights off, only the blue aura from our television glowing on his tear-stained cheeks.

For our next literary response, to *A Tree Grows in Brooklyn*, Mrs. Taborsky asked us to write a reflection about family, and so I described the celebration of my brother's engagement. Oddly enough, I finally received my overdue A+ on it, and I could tell Mrs. Taborsky now regretted choosing her son over me to go to the writers' conference earlier that year. She called my parents to tell them they had a budding writer on their hands, and that was when I hoped they might finally notice what was different about me.

Instead, my father asked why I'd made him the bad guy. "I'm not that bad, am I?" he asked, trying to sound as if he were making a joke.

My mother said my story was well-written, not a single grammar mistake, but there was something sad in her eyes when she said it, as if she were sorry there were no grammar mistakes.

My brother Michael read it too, and said what was I talking about, no such thing had ever happened. He said he hadn't cried over something as silly as leftover spaghetti.

Mark Taborsky promised to read my story, but when I asked him if he had during one of our meetings in the storage room (it was the only place he acknowledged my existence), he said no.

"Why not?" I demanded.

"I don't know anything about English," he said.

"What do you mean? Your story won the contest."

"Only because my Dad wrote the whole thing for me." He spit on the floor. Mark was the kind of boy for whom spitting was as natural an act as breathing. "I didn't even care about that stupid bus driver so much. My Dad was the one who made the big deal. He thought it would make a good sermon."

I thrust a copy of the story at his chest. "You read this, or . . ."

Though I didn't say what I would do, he could easily imagine. I'd finally figured out that it took two people to have sex, and that I had just as much to reveal about him as he had about me. Actually, he had more to lose. He had friends, even a girl rumored to be his girlfriend, though he swore to me they never did anything together, that she'd once tried doing what I did all the time and was a complete bitch about it. "She just sort of touched me once and then acted all proud of herself," he said. "Like she wanted me to give her a cookie or something. Being with you is so much easier."

"Really?" It came out involuntarily. Usually I tried to act blasé around him.

"Yeah," he said, with strange tenderness. "I mean, it's amazing. You're more into dick than my own girlfriend."

He used the same tone a week later when he told me, "So I read your story or whatever. It's good. Really fucking good."

"Thanks," I said, blushing.

"Is your dad really like that?" he asked.

"Worse," I said. "What about yours?"

"He tries to buy me off. When he divorced my mom, it was like Hannukah every day. But he doesn't know me. You know? He's this big important rabbi. He thinks he's a celebrity or something. SuperJew or whatever."

"Can I ask you something?" I said. "Why do you do things to people?" He didn't seem to understand. "You know, like trip them or call them names or treat them like shit. Why do you do that?"

"Because it's fun"

"But why?" I asked. He couldn't answer. "I wish I understood you."

"I don't fucking understand myself," he said. "You really are like a girl."

"Why?" I asked, horrified.

"Because you want to talk so much before doing anything." He unzipped himself. "Here. I wore these for you." He meant my favorite pair of his underwear. Red, silk, low-cut, soft. I felt genuinely moved by the fact that he'd thought of me, hoped to please me in some way.

"What's up with you today?" he asked when we were finished. "Did you get a haircut or something? You seem different."

Everyone was telling me that all the time now. The only people who didn't seem to notice I was different were my parents.
[

] It was spring. One day at recess, I didn't feel like standing outside in the outfield and hoping no balls would fall my way. Instead I hid in the library, which was usually deserted when the weather got warm. That was when I saw Mrs. Taborsky standing at the end of a shelf of books on Jewish Values (the section no one ever bothered to go to). She was looking out the window at the little kids' playground, and crying.

I was too shocked by the spectacle of a blubbering teacher to sneak away. Even in eighth grade, teachers didn't seem to be the same as people.

Then she noticed me. "I'm sorry," she said, dabbing her eyes with one of those colorful scarves, but I didn't know why she'd apologized.

"It's okay," I told her. I cried all the time.

"What have you got there?" she asked.

I blushed as I held up *Anne of Green Gables*, which I was reading for the tenth time. Not a boy's book. Thankfully, Mrs. Taborsky did me the courtesy of not stating the obvious. "I loved that whole series when I was young," she said. "I always wanted to visit Prince Edward Island."

"Me too! Did you ever get there?"

She shook her head and smiled in that adult knowing way.

"I was busy with other things," she said. "I had kids. You'll see."

But how would I see? Who would ever consent to be impregnated by me? And then I had the strangest realization: that in some way, Mrs. Taborsky was my mother-in-law. In fact, someday she might become like my real mother-in-law. Mark and I would eventually outgrow our storage room and maybe in college we'd move in together, share an apartment like good friends. And I'd cook for him, even though I didn't know how. I'd make his bed. Or our bed? There was so much I could do.

"You must be a good mom," I blurted out, overwhelmed by my feelings for Mark.

She seemed puzzled. "Really? I mean, thank you. That's a very nice compliment. What makes you say that?"

"Because your son . . ." I couldn't finish. Not without arousing suspicion.

"He's a good kid, isn't he?" she said, tearing up.

Actually, even I had to admit that though Mark was a lot of things, "a good kid" was not one of them. Only that morning, he'd made a girl cry by telling her she was as ugly as a rug-munching dyke. He regularly stole milk from the cafeteria and books from the library to deface them with messages like "Reading sucks my kosher wiener," and "This book for kikes only." He'd stepped on Ronnie Cohen's hand on purpose to win a ball game. And he was almost single-handedly responsible for the committal to a mental hospital of a troubled Israeli teacher who had a weak command of English and even weaker command of dealing with smart-alecky students.

"Don't tell anyone you saw me here," said Mark's mother, leaving the library.

"I promise, Mrs. Taborsky," I said.

"After today, it's not Mrs. Taborsky anymore." She patted my shoulder and moved past me and into the hall, toward the forbidden territory of the teachers' lounge.

[

] No one was very surprised on the last day of school when Mrs. Taborsky announced that (A) she was now Ms. Schwarz, and (B) she wouldn't be with us next year because she was moving to California to teach art.

After her announcement, during which many tears were shed and many promises to "K. I. T. 4-ever" were made, I bumped into Mark on purpose in the hall and whispered, "Meet me." But he didn't show up in our usual place.

I tried the experiment again later that day. "Meet me."

But he said, "What are you talking about, faggot?"

I panicked for a second. What had I done? Why was he betraying our secret in public this way? But then I realized that he wasn't referring to the things we'd done together in the storage room when he said "faggot." It was just a name he used for kids who were weaker or less popular than he was.

I resolved then and there to learn what to do with a ball, and to stop reading books like *Anne of Green Gables*. And above all to stop writing fairy tales, stories, essays, even grocery lists. Who knows, I might have kept to those resolutions had I not found, on the last day of school, a note mysteriously tucked into the back pocket of my jeans. As I un-folded the looseleaf notebook paper, I immediately recognized Mark's handwriting:

So I guess I won't see you anymore. I hear they have gangs in the schools in L.A., with guns, and if you're Jewish, you'd better join a gang if you want to stay alive because they're really anti-Semitic there. Anyway, you write good stories. You should write more of them. Sorry if I was an asshole to you sometimes. Just know, I didn't mean it. But this isn't a love letter or anything.

Bullshit, Mark Taborsky, I thought, reading the note again and again until I knew the words by heart. This is a fucking love letter if I ever saw one.

When I got home, I ignored my mother's offer of fresh cupcakes and went straight to my room, where I opened my notebook. And I wrote: "Mark Taborsky was the meanest, saddest, best-looking bully in our class. He didn't know it, but he was also my friend . . ."

] Things That Are Not Yours

Dear Masha,

You ask me the eternal emigrant question, "What do I need to bring to America?" In fact, your question really involves three questions: "What will I need?" "What is better to bring to the U.S. for economic, or some other, reasons?" and "What will I want once I'm there?"

Thank you. We immigrants love to answer that question. After some time, we get an almost physical craving to give advice. The kind of advice I hate the most (and crave the most to give) consists of sentences in future tense, describing what will happen to you step by step, based on the advice-giver's prior knowledge that she for some reason finds universal. Remember how you enlightened me about sex and then marriage? "First you're going to feel a slight burning that will soon grow into a real pain." "The first month will be okay. The second you start to get bored. By the third you're thinking about a lover, whom you will take by the middle of the fourth month." That's exactly the form of advice I'm going to use now.

On your last day in Moscow you will still be packing and repacking. There will be six bags on the floor, of the exact size and weight allowed by your airline, two for each of you (even though you complain how infantile your son and your husband are, and how they spend all their time playing computer games, from the airline's point of view they are adults, so they are entitled to two bags). Three red passports on the bookshelf will have blue Russian visa stamps, which read: "Leaving for a permanent residence." You are not just leaving Russia, you are leaving it permanently. You're not coming back. Isn't this a quintessential Jewish experience, to pack for a new place, for a strange place, knowing that you won't come back? Isn't this what Jews have been doing for centuries? But right now the historical significance of this act of packing is lost on you. You don't think about the fate of the Jews, you think about the fate of your very tangible everyday objects, and how their fate depends on their physical dimensions. Some can prove too heavy, or too long, or too inconveniently shaped to make a journey to the new land.

Six hours before your flight. Five hours. Four hours. The question of what goes in those bags will be still open. Doubts, regrets, indecision. If you add something at the last moment, you'll inevitably wreck the weight balance, and you'll have to take something out in order to restore it. The crystal vase with the *Happy Anniversary* engraving, which you've just taken out to replace with *The Selected Letters of Fyodor Dostoevsky*, happens to be of greater weight than the addition, so you'll have to think of something else to add so as not to waste the precious space. You will add blue and white salt and pepper shakers. They will turn out to weigh too much. You will have to leave one. Which one? You can't leave either of them. They are salt *and* pepper shakers, not salt *or* pepper. In the end you will leave both of them out and add a collection of authentic wooden spoons, which will inevitably turn out to be either too heavy or too light . . . The process will go on and on.

What is essential? What can you do without? What has more value? How do you determine the value? There will be countless letters scattered on your desk, letters from your relatives and friends who had left Russia permanently and have been living abroad, letters opened, read and reread. My letter will be just one of many. Lines and lines of advice, often contradictory, will buzz in your head, driving you crazy. Bring pots, pots are expensive here. Don't bring any pots, their weight "outweighs" their value. Bring cast-iron skillets, you can't make proper pancakes without them. Bring good woolen slippers with leather soles and fur trim, you can't find them here. Don't bring any clothes, our clothes look ridiculous. Bring woolen socks, American socks feel and look funny. Bring everything woolen. Don't bring wool, moths will eat it by the end of your first week in the U.S.

Bring anything that you love, anything that means something to you, even if it is heavy, useless, or devoid of value. I'm sure you will find these words in at least one of your letters. They will annoy you, they will make you angry, they will make you ashamed for all your petty concerns about pots and woolen socks.

Jews from the previous generations had it easy—they knew what the things were that they couldn't leave behind. They packed their Torahs, their menorahs, their mezuzahs. They were persecuted for their beliefs, but at least they had their beliefs to sustain them. What do you, a Jew brought up in the religiousless Soviet Union, have to sustain you? Through departure, through loss, through knowing that you'll never come back?

You would like to believe that you are the kind of person for whom the emotional value of things has the most importance. So you'll clear a little space in your bags for that mysterious category "things that you love," and then you'll fill the space in a guilty rush. The heavier, the bigger, the more useless is "the thing that you love," the more satisfaction it will give you to pack it.

My mother packed the huge, awkward, cheap tea set, with teapot, cream pitcher, and sugar bowl that resembled forlorn Chinamen and Chinawomen. The set used to stand in our mirrored sideboard for most of the year, and I thought of it as the Chinese Royal family imprisoned in their massive glass palace. My mother took the set out only when guests came. The Chinamen looked morbid and resigned as she carried them to the table and mercilessly beheaded them to pour sugar or tea leaves and boiling water in.

I took my childhood collection of dolls that relatives and friends were supposed to have brought me from their foreign trips. Two dolls were my favorites. One was a hand-painted clay figurine of an Indian woman in a silk sari, with a long, real-looking braid and bright jewelry. The figurine's clay right breast had fallen off during the long journey from Bombay to Moscow, and my uncle (I think it was my uncle who had bought the doll for me) brought it to me separately, wrapped in his handkerchief. It took me the better part of the day to glue the breast back on. Another favorite doll was Japanese. My father brought it to me from his last trip before he died. The doll wasn't delicate and exquisite, as you would expect a Japanese doll to be. It wasn't even a girl. It was a blond boy with vaguely Oriental features, made from some soft plastic, who squeaked when you pressed on his tummy. For some reason I'd always felt protective of this doll and wouldn't let anybody press on his tummy.

There we were. The bags packed at last. The Chinese tea set safely placed on the bottom of one of the bags, the forlorn Chinamen carefully wrapped in pages of *Pravda* with pictures of Yeltsin greeting the happy

Russian people. My dolls in the middle of the other bag—each wrapped in a woolen sock, the breasts of the Indian doll tightly taped to her body. Ready to leave.

What is the first thing that jumps at a person as soon as he finds himself in a new territory? Unfamiliar scenery, the twitter of a foreign language, signs that don't explain anything but seem to muddle the meaning of the world? If the signs were in your language, it wouldn't have occurred to you to dissect the names of the places and look for the meaning of each part. The words *Sheepshead Bay* read off a highway sign wouldn't have sounded sinister, wouldn't have evoked the severed head of a sheep swimming in the bloody waters of a bay. You will feel uncomfortable, but you will keep saying to yourself, "It's all part of the journey. The journey will be over soon. I'll get to the place."

I can't predict how much time it will take you, but eventually you'll realize that the settling into a strange land is a journey, too.

Your first apartment will be the apartment of your relatives or friends, people who receive you in their home and keep you there until you find a place of your own with mixed feelings of annoyance at your presence and the satisfaction of having done a good deed. People to whom you will always feel both gratitude and resentment for forcing that feeling of gratitude on you. Their apartment is the first place you will enter once you get out of the cab from the airport. Their apartment is your promised land, the end point of your journey, as you will mistakenly think then. There, you will have your initial encounter with the things that are not your own. Your generous hosts will lavish them on you. They will let you use their beds, their linens, their towels, their soap and soap dishes to put that soap on, their plates, their forks, their spoons, their TV, their objets d'art, essential when the conversations get stuck—you can always revive them with "Where did you get that beautiful vase?"—their framed photographs to gaze on when you're lying in bed unable to sleep, and their brand-new yarmulkes and mezuzahs to puzzle you. "What is that?" you will ask, and they will explain, feigning amazement at your ignorance, even though just a few years ago they didn't know what a mezuzah was either.

Your own things, the lucky few that got chosen to make the journey with you, will be still lying in the darkness of your unpacked bags, some carefully wrapped, others serving as wrapping. You will wonder if any of the porcelain Chinamen are broken. You will wonder if the tape on your

Indian doll's chest is still in place, but you won't let yourself wonder for long. "It doesn't make sense to unpack now, when you'll move to your own place in a matter of days," your relatives/friends will suggest, reminding you not to get too comfy at their place. They are right, it doesn't make sense, especially when you remember the amount of time and craziness the packing took. You will agree with your relatives/friends. For the time being you'll have to make use of their beds (too soft or too high for you), their linens (too stiff or too slippery), their soap (having the wrong smell), their forks (tines too big for your mouth), and their stupid, tacky "objets d'art" (What idiot could spend money on something like that?), their yarmulkes to vent your feelings about your relatives' newly acquired piety ("Oh, they just wear them when they come to get their free gefilte fish at the JCC!").

You will be longing to unpack, and you will start dreaming about that new, empty, slightly mysterious apartment devoid of strangers' things. The long-awaited moment will come at last, most likely a little sooner than you'd expect, a little sooner than you'd be ready to be on your own, and you'll be standing with your bags on the threshold of an empty apartment, your own apartment. Well, not your own of course, the landlord's, but it won't matter as long as you fill it with your own things. But the long-awaited thrill will fade as soon as you realize that you'll have to buy some essential furniture. You'll buy a mattress, a mattress frame (a bed-frame can wait), a Formica table, a couple of plastic chairs, and a lamp at a cheap furniture store run by recent Russian-Jewish immigrants who will seem so prosperous to you (they have their own business!) All these things will be of the poorest quality. You're not going to live in this apartment for long, it's your starting point, you'll have a better apartment soon, and then you'll get better things and discard these. The things that you bought will perceive that you don't care for them. They have ways. They sense it in your lack of attention, in your failure to fix them, to clean them, to dust them, or worse—in your pushing dust under them. They will feel betrayed, and they will betray you in return. They won't become your own. They will just stay transitional, faceless objects, and they will give you as little comfort as they possibly can. The bed will hurt your back ("What on Earth do they make these mattresses out of?"), the lamp will bend at the wrong angle and hurt your eyes, the rickety kitchen table won't let you enjoy your food. What's worse, these new objects won't become familiar. They won't disclose their peculiarities. You won't know what to expect of them, and they will use your lack of knowledge against you, breaking or giving way at the most unfortunate moments. I won't even describe to you what happened on the occasion of my birthday, when our kitchen table decided that the array of food we set on it was too much for its delicate constitution.

You will soon see that there are many ways to add to your belongings for free. There will be relatives and friends, whose apartments are crammed with things they don't want, with furniture that they find uncomfortable or tacky, with clothes that are either too small or out of style, with vases and salad bowls received as unwanted gifts. They don't have the heart to just throw those things out, they are waiting for you. And you will take their junk, you will take everything, gladly, enthusiastically, greedily. They are good things, they are better things than you will be able to afford, and you won't be acquiring them forever. Just for the time being. You won't have any obligations. You will know that you'll discard them as soon as you want, when you'll be able to buy better things, or even sooner, when somebody wants to get rid of better things. By the way, I have this stupid vanity table waiting for you in my garage. A perfectly nice table, cherry wood with a large mirror, that came with our new bedroom set. To tell you the truth, I don't see the point to vanity tables, a perfect waste of space, in my view. I always put on my makeup on the bus ride to work. So will you. You won't use the table, but you will be happy to have such a nice thing (cherry wood, mirror) for the time being.

You will finally unpack your Russian bags about a week after you move into your first rental, but you'll find that even though you've been longing to unpack them for such a long time, the things you brought won't make you happy. First of all, you won't know where to put them. We didn't know where to put our Chinese tea set. In our Moscow apartment, it had stood in the mirrored sideboard reflecting the soft light from the window or the lamp's yellow flicker. In our new apartment, there was no place for it, except on the bottom shelf of our kitchen cabinet, behind canned peas and blue spaghetti boxes. It stood there gathering dust until we bought a house, where as it turned out there wasn't room for a sideboard, so the tea set went even further down—to the basement—to spend its days among other objects for which a place couldn't be found. And if you wonder what happened to my doll collection, it got lost. No, not physically lost, but lost on the shelf among the Barbies, which my daughter decided to add to the collection. The Barbies with firm plastic breasts—no fear that those will ever fall off.

Garbage piles on the sidewalks will be another source of enlarging your collection of things. Oh, don't wrinkle your nose! Garbage piles here are not what you imagine them to be. We immigrants think of them as collections of gifts for which the givers failed to find recipients. We treat them seriously. At first we approach them like archaeologists digging up historical artifacts—we learn to distinguish their value and discard the unwanted ones, we strut around the piles with a pensive expression in our eyes, we pull the things out, we examine them carefully: "Does this TV have anything inside it?" "Are there drawers somewhere in the pile next to this gorgeous chest of drawers?" "Is this keyboard compatible with my computer?" We find elaborate ways to deliver our finds up to our apartments. We use toddlers' strollers, shopping carts, hands of the willing neighbor boys. With time it becomes more like a sport, passionate and addictive. We are not ashamed to be seen dragging the things off the garbage piles, we are proud. "You wouldn't believe what I found yesterday!" we brag to each other. Eventually, as your long-awaited financial success comes at last, and you no longer need to search for things in the garbage piles, you'll find that it is very hard to stop. You'll find that it is almost impossible not to look when you pass a garbage pile, not to marvel at the wonderful cupboard you see there, not to ponder ways to take it with you. You'll talk of your garbage picking time with nostalgia, you'll actually find yourself more reluctant to discard the things you found than the ones you bought or received as gifts. I'm writing this sitting on a chair I found in a garbage pile nine years ago. I don't know why I'm still keeping it, the chair is big, chipped, and ugly, but it has something about it, probably the memory of excitement I felt when I found it. "Dema, look! It's cherry wood, I'm pretty sure it is. Okay, so what, if it's not, it is still wood, and look, it has all four legs!"

You won't feel the same way about the new, nice things that you will eventually be able to afford. They will just stand there, massive, glossy, impressive, exuding the expensive smells of wood polish and leather. They will bring you joy only at those infrequent moments when you have new visitors and you take them on a tour around your house. At other times, your new things will annoy you, mostly because you can't enjoy them, even though they are perfect and expensive and chosen by you according to your own taste. There is nothing wrong with them, and if you don't like them, there must be something wrong with you. Sooner or later you will discover that there being nothing wrong with them is exactly what is wrong with them. They will lack imperfections, they will lack scratches, dents, chipped-off paint. Your new sofa will lack a funny way to jam sheets when you fold it. Your new chair won't greet you with a creak when you sit down. Your new bookcase won't have the words "Larka-piggy" scratched on the side by your older brother. Lacking imperfections, your new things will lack character and history.

Your discovery will make you turn to yard sales and garage sales. You will buy things that seem challenging or puzzling. You will buy that weird iron pot with a wire net on top and a carved wooden handle, or a cone-shaped, three-foot-tall bottle with a long, narrow neck, whose purpose nobody, not even the owner, will be able to explain to you. You will buy a vase because of a crack in it, you will buy a book because of a suspicious stain. You will find yourself looking for traces of history, even if it is the history of strangers, even if you don't know it, even if you have to make it up.

But back to your question. What should you bring? I could tell you that it doesn't matter, but you won't believe me. I know you won't, at least not now. So, I would suggest that you bring cotton blanket cases, woolen socks, and a couple of cast-iron skillets—you can't make proper pancakes without them.

] A *Bisel* This, a *Bisel* That

I, Myron Gerstler, age 46, was born in 1963, the year that JFK was shot. My late Grandma Ida believed that this led to my lifelong passion for social justice. It's true that while my teenage peers were out all night, getting high and dancing to disco, I preferred staying home and listening to Grandma Ida's records: Woody Guthrie, Paul Robeson, and Theo Bikel, with whom she swore she'd once had an affair.

For the past 25 years, I've been book editor of *The Promised Text*, the monthly independent Jewish newspaper "for progressive Jews, their friends, and everyone else." Secular and left of center, we at *The Promised Text* pride ourselves on carrying on a tradition whose time may have come and gone for most folks—but not for us. *The Promised Text* was founded during the tumultuous sixties by a Brooklyn-born socialist, a lucky, brilliant bastard who married into left-wing Hollywood money. These days, it would be fair to say that we're a *bisel* old-left, a *bisel* new-left, a *bisel* Zionist, a *bisel* first-, second-, and third-wave feminist—in other words, *a bisel this and a bisel that*, just like Grandma Ida's recipe for blintzes.

[

] Bespectacled, with slightly thinning hair, I'm still in decent shape, thanks to my regular Saturday morning basketball game at the Y. Weekdays, in my worn blazer and jeans, I occupy a musty, book-crammed cubicle in *The Promised Text*'s small, rented offices in midtown Manhattan on the third floor of a building that's known informally as "The Low Rent Indie News Building," owned by a former journalist, now a Harlem-based landlord whose sympathies are "100 percent against the man." In addition to us, his tenants include *The Post-Stonewall Sassy News; The Afro-American Pulse; Leftie Latinos; Hip-Hop Jones; Poetry and*

Politics; The Bronx Soccer News; Fat City: The Newspaper For Large Urbanites; Esperanto For Everyone; The Disenfranchised Village Voice; and more.

For decades, despite the occasional petty squabble, bout of professional envy, and love affair that ended badly, we've all been mingling, schmoozing, and meeting for lunches, dinners, and beer at bars serving heaping corned beef sandwiches and all-you-can-eat rice-and-bean platters. Black, white, brown, Jewish, Christian, Muslim, gay, straight, and transgender—a *bisel* this, a *bisel* that—we read one another's articles and essays, and attend our children's bar and bat mitzvahs, *brises*, *quinceñeras*, communions, Seders, Kwanza celebrations, memorials, and funerals.

[

] Since the old socialist's death two years ago, I work for Rosa, his Harvard-educated daughter, aptly named for Rosa Luxemburg, who's as dedicated to *The Promised Text* as he was. Most recently, I gave a mixed review to a memoir by a 25-year-old Yeshiva boy whose affair with a blonde *shiksa* caused him to attempt suicide and become an atheist, and a favorable review to a novel about a 62-year-old Jewish lesbian and the nine-year-old boy with special needs whom she adopts from Ethiopia, and a negative—but fair, I believe—review to a chirpy self-help tome by a jovial, bearded psychotherapist whose goal is ". . . to help readers to lead a good, blissful Jewish life!"

Every review I've written, whether favorable, unfavorable, or mixed, has engendered at least one letter from a reader. Sometimes the reader calls me "brilliant," sometimes "stuck in a didactic socialist time warp," sometimes "not aware of what *real* Judaism is for Jews who believe in G-d, unlike you!!!" and sometimes "too damned Jewish!" In truth, whatever they say makes me happy for the simple reason that they're reading *The Promised Text.*

Next month, however, *The Promised Text* will publish its final issue, and those letters will stop coming, and I will join the massive ranks of the unemployed. We ran out of money, due to heavily diminished sales, equally diminished advertising, and the loss of the last of the old socialist's money to the Ponzi scheme of a sociopathic Jewish billionaire.

So, at last, we're in the mainstream: Many newspapers are dying, not just the out-of-fashion indies like us, but also the major dailies. In our manic-paced world of cyber-rants, cyber-raves, listservs, networking and gossip sites, and innumerable instant, unpaid, unedited blogs, there's no room at all for us dinosaurs of print and paper.

[

] In a midtown bar known for its hefty lunchtime corned beef sandwiches and endearingly crabby, elderly waiters, I sit at a table with a handful of my cronies from The Low Rent Indie News Building. The lights are dim, and a soundless TV is turned to a station showing rat-a-tat music videos featuring scowling, muscular African-American men and bikini-wearing women of all colors.

"It's all over for us," I say, peering into my beer, continuing a conversation we've been having for months in this same bar. "It's over for our *medium,* and it's over for our *message.*" I shake my head, thinking about the fate that awaits me in a mere month: unemployed and probably unemployable, desperately hanging on to the same rent-stabilized apartment in Brooklyn in which I've been living for almost as long as I've been reviewing books for *The Promised Text.*

"Things are so grim, I'm on Prozac," agrees Ethel Samura, staring gloomily at me, her leather hoop earrings swaying as she speaks. Managing editor these many years at the hanging-on-by-a-thread *Afro-American Pulse*, Ethel sits directly across from me in her red, black, and green dashiki, her hair intricately braided and piled high on her head. Once a size 6 and now more likely a size 14, she's still a knockout. Divorced twice, rumored to have been Huey Newton's lover, she's dedicated herself to two things: raising her sons and *The Afro-American Pulse.*

"Hear, hear," says Marcus Jeff, a former member of the hip-hop group, *'Cuz We Good!,* and now a meticulously careful proofreader at *Hip-Hop Jones,* a newspaper born from a Bronx storefront back in the seventies, whose mission is to write about nonmaterialistic, nonmisogynistic, progressive hip-hop and to bring it to a wide audience—"to the masses," one might even say. Sadly, *Hip-Hop Jones,* like *The Promised Text*, has run out of readers, advertisers, and cash, and has just one more issue to go.

Across the table, Dalit Goldlust sighs loudly. Dalit is Israeli-born, kibbutz-raised, unibrowed, and recovering from breast cancer. Her cubicle is the one next to mine at *The Promised Text*, and her articles about the intersection of culture and politics in the Middle East never fail to dazzle me. Jutting out her strong chin, she says, "I for one do not plan to document my every burp and fart online . . ."

Jake Shapiro, at the table's far end, giggles. A college senior, Jake is *The Promised Text*'s part-time intern. Right now, over his Diet Coke, his heavily lashed blue eyes sweep the table. "Well, I have some good news! *Jewish Tell-All*—it's a *website*," he hastily adds, in case we don't know, "is *hiring* me to blog for them about 'cool Jews,' you know, like Kabbalah-loving movie stars and rapping Lubavitchers."

None of us respond with the congratulations he must be awaiting. Instead, I stare even more morosely into my beer and think about how we at *The Promised Text* have done what we could in order to survive . . . a *bisel* this, a *bisel* that . . . We've published fewer issues, shrank margins, fonts, and graphics . . . discontinued our column on "creating secular Jewish rituals," discontinued our crossword puzzle, feminist advice column, and film and restaurant reviews, until there was less and less text, less and less content, less and less reason for us to exist.

It's Nina Sanchez who finally does the right thing. Thirty-five years old, pregnant and a lesbian, her family had disowned her when she bravely came out as a teenager in Mexico City. Nina has joined us for lunch today even though *Leftie Latinos,* the newspaper for which she'd been writing ever since she moved to the States, closed its doors three months ago. Nina lifts her glass to Jake and offers him a hearty *"Salud!"*

And then the rest of us lift our glasses to him, and over the top of my beer, I gaze around the table at Nina, Dalit, Marcus, Ethel, and even at Jake, and I realize that no matter what happens to any of us, whether or not we ever find work again doing the thing we love, whether or not newspapers and rent stabilization and bars with cheap beer all go the way of manual typewriters and mimeograph machines, whether or not our once-revolutionary/perhaps now hopelessly out-of-touch ideas cease to matter to anyone but us, the truth is that right here and now, I am happy because I am in *my* promised land.

] The Yehudah Triangle

Yehudah Ben-David was not your ordinary hyphenated Jew. His actual name was Jerry Bender. But by the time he enrolled in college he had changed it to something more suitable for a Roman chariot racer or a Hebrew slave. Yehudah Ben-David was the kind of name assembled from the scrapheap of history, one that recalled the desert Jews of Sinai rather than those who now wandered the suburban shopping malls of Shaker Heights or prowled the pulsing discos of Tel Aviv.

Having a name like Yehudah Ben-David was the mark of Cain for anyone hiding as a Hebrew. Of course, no one would have ever accused Jerry Bender of that. Jerry may have been hiding, but never as a Jew. Yehudah Ben-David was not his birth name, the one sanctified before God. God, after all, would not have approved of the Chosen People turning their names into vanity plates. At his *bris* on Miami Beach nearly fifty years ago Jerry was welcomed into the tribe of Irvings, Sauls, Abes, and Chaims. Apparently, those names were not Jewish enough for him.

In the modern world a name so blatantly evocative of the Old Testament leaves nothing to the imagination. One doesn't need to superimpose a skullcap and a beard, a shepherd's staff or even a slingshot. Whomever has such a name isn't likely to ever hear, "Oh, forgive me, I didn't realize you were Jewish," or "Christ, I never pegged you for a Jew!"

Actually, Yehudah Ben-David was a walking billboard of Jewish geography, a patsy in any game of word association, a calling card that invited torment, like tossing blood into an antisemitic shark tank.

It wasn't as if the Bender family was unfamiliar with ethnic hatred. Jerry's parents were Holocaust survivors. They knew the lethal consequences of being Jewish, and could well imagine the consequence of being *too* Jewish. Just because they were damaged didn't mean they were delusional. A Jew could never be immunized against prejudice; certain truths could never be taken for granted. All the scientific research linking the Jewish DNA with disease was of little concern to the Benders. Cancer wasn't the problem; it was all that genocide in the gene pool that was the real death threat to Jews.

Nor did the Benders believe in sanctuary. Miami Beach—and America, for that matter—was just another temporary layover on the turbulent, migratory flight pattern of the Diasporic Jew.

And passing oneself off as a native Jew, not a misfit Belgian or a decorous Canadian but a rugged Israeli with a Promised Land address, was even worse. Israel nowadays was subject to an even shabbier stereotype than American rudeness, German humorlessness, or French snobbery. The Israelis were widely perceived as the new Spartans—not the People of the Book but the bazooka. The Gladiators had moved their operations from Rome to Gaza. And with it an ancient blood libel received a new transfusion, no longer involving rabbis and the making of matzo, but IDF soldiers spilling the blood of Palestinians.

It was quite a stretch, actually, from the wretched skeletons of Auschwitz to the hulking commandos at checkpoints in Jericho. But that's what the world wanted to believe. Traveling with an Israeli passport or advertising an Israeli name had become a death wish, just a notch lower on the risk meter than drawing a Mohammed cartoon. Given the biblical backstory, and that Zionism had become more radioactive than romantic, no one could quite figure out why Jerry Bender would swap a perfectly acceptable Jewish name for one that would bring an immediate halt to any roll call.

Truth is, Yehudah Ben-David wasn't trying to blend in or bend over or simply rise above the prejudice. He was, apparently, looking to run right into it like a Jewish kamikaze. He offered himself up as kosher guinea pig, testing the breaking point where hatred goes haywire. All those rough, guttural vowels swirled in a Petri dish like an *aleph-bet* soup. And so he doubled down on his identity, dialing up his Jewish profile to a name even more amplifying.

In sixth grade he gave himself an alias. He refused to answer to Jerry Bender and insisted that his teacher, Miss Kennedy, call him Moshe Dayan, the Israeli general. He even wore an eye-patch. In Miami such a retro-pirate look was regarded as a bold fashion statement and not as a way to get in touch with one's inner-Sabra.

All the Cuban children in the classroom laughed. Their families had only recently fled a *generalissimo* decamped in Havana. And they couldn't exactly locate Israel on a map, although they were quite certain that it wasn't anywhere near Key West. Miss Kennedy, a freckle-faced Irish Catholic from Queens, wasn't amused by this Miami Beach–boy pretending to be the conquering general of the Six-Day War.

So she marked Jerry absent while he carried on as Moshe Dayan, basking in all that Sephardic bravery until his parents had been summoned and he was sitting beside them in the principal's office.

"We can't very well have children going around switching their names," Dr. Lichter, the school's principal explained. He was stout with a deep tan wedged within wrinkled skin, wire-rimmed glasses, and wiry silver hair. "What if every child tried to do that? Think of the administrative headache that would cause. Children should simply go by their real names. I don't even approve of nicknames," he admitted.

The Benders were busy conjuring a nickname for the principal. As a family they took an immediate dislike to authority. For them, anyone in a stiff uniform or who traded on a title deserved a cold shoulder.

Sally Bender wore a rose-printed dress and a straw summer hat, an outfit more appropriate for a polo match than a school visit. Despite the "No Smoking" sign in Dr. Lichter's office she was lighting cigarettes faster than she could smoke them—furiously, like an unhinged machine about to break down. A pile of ash gathered beside her flip-flops, Florida footwear that was both tinder and emblematic of her state of mind.

"Jerry," his mother began, "what's the point of pretending to be someone else? You can't run from who you are."

"Listen to your mother, Jerry," the principal applauded, although something about these Jewish refugees frightened him, "she is very wise."

The child's mother shot the principal a disapproving look. She didn't like being interrupted.

"It won't help, Jerry," she continued. "Whoever is looking for you will find you. There are no good hiding places anymore. It is all lost."

Dr. Lichter, cautiously, was about to say something, but he noticed the numbered tattoos on the forearms of the Bender parents—made possible by the sleeveless protocol of South Florida—and recoiled. The grotesque always stands out in a tropical paradise. The unsightly is an unexpected sight. As a math teacher by training Dr. Lichter was usually drawn to digits. But not this kind of arithmetic. He was shocked to see numbers put to such a monstrous use—long division that shortened the lifespan of an entire race. And so he remained quiet.

That suited the Benders quite fine. The poor principal was getting a quick lesson on darkness, the kind that even the sunny skies of Miami could not cure.

Jerry looked at his father, who was staring out the window as if he had never entered the principal's office in the first place. Jerry gazed out the window, too, searching for whatever now held his father's attention—not that it much mattered. Even if they both fixated on the same spot it wouldn't make them connected. Father-and-son moments in the Bender household were often best experienced through silence. It was a design flaw in the bond—but one, arguably, of necessity, a kind of natural selection for those who had survived selection in the camps. Words didn't come easily to Nathan Bender. He wasn't a man of few words. He had all the words; he just saw no point in speaking them.

But he did enjoy the ocean, which was a novelty to someone from Warsaw who spent his teenage years hiding in the forests of Hungary before entering manhood in a death camp. The ocean was vast and the air salty and clean. There were no chimneystacks or guard towers in sight. The low-hanging clouds over South Florida, when darkened, were filled with moisture and nothing else. And the impressions left in the sand were impermanent—life affirming and untraceable.

Nathan Bender liked to take his son swimming—well, at least his version of swimming. They would march into the warm, lapping water and drift into the waves like deadwood. Sometimes they would come across the purple oceanic colostomy bags known as man-of-war. These stinging creatures never frightened Nathan. He was, after all, a man-of-genocide, a much higher grade of horror. What had already infected him was well beyond the healing powers of a tetanus shot vaccine.

Even when Jerry was a small boy he waded into the ocean without his father holding his hand. It's just how these family swims were done. The wintry Atlantic would gather force, with its foaming white caps like rabies on the high seas. The waves would topple the boy and yet the father never feared that his son would drown, and never reached out to pull him from the water, either. The boy was required to be buoyant. He needed to be able to shake the salty water from his eyes and ready himself for the next swell. The family ethos always expected another. The waves would keep coming like a neighborhood bully until the father declared that their swim was over.

Nathan Bender was an absent father although he was fully retired and always around. His absence was elsewhere, not unlike his mind. He walked everywhere and in no apparent direction, guided by a compass that had lost its magnet. His hands were always clasped behind his back, walking slowly, as if off to his own execution.

Jerry Bender imagined himself an orphan even though he was the prototype of the Bender line—the mop of blond hair, the short knob of a nose and pointed chin all set provisionally on his face, as if these features were removable parts, easily disassembled for when it was time to break camp and move the Diaspora to a new location. His cheekbones were alpine high. And his blue eyes, wide and round, looked as if they could pop out at any time, the kind of watchful stare that was more mindful of surroundings than of making a good appearance.

The Benders did not acquire their parenting skills by reading Dr. Spock, the baby doctor. If they had received any tips, it was more likely from that other Spock from the same era, the emotionally detached and distant Vulcan, who also came from another planet.

Space travel was very much in vogue when Jerry was a child. There were Popsicle sticks sold in the shape of space capsules. Model kits that once featured planes and trains now erected launchers and rockets. And on TV there was *Star Trek*, *Lost in Space*, and *My Favorite Martian*. Faraway planets and time travel fired the imagination; the potential for human transformation was suddenly in the air, right beside the stars.

In changing his name, Yehudah Ben-David was hedging his bets. He pitted his future against his past, simultaneously moving backward and forward in a kind of box step that boxed him in even more. All those steps and yet he didn't get very far. Except that one time, when, as if blown out of a shofar from Cape Canaveral, Yehudah Ben-David was beamed up and away from Miami Beach, forever.

[

] We stared at the colliding rivers that came to a rest in New York Harbor. Islands floated like lily pads, the geology of New York City resembling a game of three-card monte. From the air, Governor's Island, Ellis Island, and, of course, the island of Manhattan—along with Liberty Island and Staten Island—looked like a forgotten chess match, the pieces no longer in play. But from the water there was little doubt that at least on Manhattan the games had already begun.

If you closed your eyes and allowed the wind and tide to pull you in, you might not realize that you were about to enter an asylum for liars and schemers, smooth operators and silky confidence men. Even the regular artists were con artists. What else could you expect? Manhattan was stolen from the Indians for $24. A city that starts out with such a colossal swindle can never be trusted again.

The Statue of Liberty, with its grim, copper smile, held up an out-stretched lamp as a warning to the unwary, the last sign before exiting the crosscurrents of the harbor. Today Governor's Island (originally known as Nut Island) sits abandoned like a ghost town; Ellis Island is a museum, and Manhattan is where the world comes seeking riches and re-invention and often ends up with a studio apartment and a slogan that never came true.

A century ago, immigrants were taken to Ellis Island for processing upon entry into the New World. These huddled masses of steerage stench would survive a TB scare and then a name change before reaching Manhattan, their final destination. Years later, new arrivals would get processed without the Ellis Island stopover. The new custom was not to make them wait, just line them up, fire the starting gun, and let them race.

I was born on Manhattan. I know how things work on this island. I'm at home on these streets. My family prides itself on always being alert, on not being scammed or caught flatfooted. We're good in a crisis, and that's why we're perfect for New York.

I was just a kid on 9/11, but my school was near the World Trade Center. When the planes hit the towers and everyone believed that the world was coming to an end, I scooted out of class and started running uptown—away from all that smoke. It's the first rule of our family: Smoke is not your friend. We don't have much use for fire drills because we don't need to rehearse. At the first sight or smell of smoke, we're already somewhere else.

I could hear my teacher, Ms. Kennedy, screaming at me, the sound of her voice screeching like the thousands of new ghosts that would soon haunt our island.

"Sarah Ben-David, get back here this instant! You can't be outside alone! It's not safe!"

But I was long gone.

I've been riding subways since I was in middle school. I keep to myself, not attracting attention. It's best not to look like an easy mark. The suckers end up buying a piece of the Brooklyn Bridge or the Empire State Building, or losing their money in a game of three-card monte.

When my friends went off to college towns to see how the rest of America lived—the farmers and the country folks, the ski-slope operators and the coastal beach bums—I simply moved uptown and enrolled at Barnard, where the smart New York girls became co-eds without having to leave home.

Where else should a Jewish girl go? Where else would a Jewish girl want to be? Where else could a Jewish girl feel safe?

My father and I stared into the murky water, this mixture of Hudson and East rivers that mirrored the bi-racial melting pot that existed on dry land. We Ben-Davids don't assimilate so well. Ours is not your usual American family saga. We didn't sail into this harbor in hopes of finding freedom and opportunity. We were just looking for a place to breathe.

My father is the son of two Holocaust survivors. My grandparents had numbers on their forearms. Fortunately for me those tattoos don't get passed down on the family tree like having high cheekbones, a long neck, or a crooked smile. You can inherit genes, and it's nice to inherit heirlooms, but a numbered arm is a generational fluke, a freak accident with low odds of ever being repeated. But then again, you never know.

Had my grandparents come through Ellis Island, the customs officials wouldn't have known what to make of them. They weren't just foreigners; they were true aliens.

And they were far too cunning to stay in New York. My grandparents moved to Miami where the local population suffered from sunstroke and were too dehydrated to harm them. That's where my father was born. But he wouldn't stay long. He was drawn to New York, where everyone else answered to an alias, too.

We stood at the southern tip of Manhattan and stared out onto the horizon, locking eyes with fathers and daughters across time who traveled by boat, arrived seasick but desperate to set foot on the Golden Land.

"Turning 50 in a few months," I said. "Way to go. Does that qualify for longevity in our family?"

The afternoon sun, flooding in from the west, lit up my blond hair like Lady Liberty's torch. My blue eyes absorbed the light with a squint. My father's hair, also blond, and his eyes, equally blue, radiated and pulsed like a spinning siren.

"No, it's still just middle age," he replied without looking at me. "It's not that great an achievement."

"What, are you feeling old?"

"I was born old. I came out of my mother's womb with sand in my hair, like one of the Jewish patriarchs."

"Miami Beach sand?"

"No, Sinai sand."

"Well, get ready then, because you're going back. The shofar has sounded; you've been summoned. You excited about the trip?" I wondered but already knew the answer. "We're leaving in a few days. Our bags are packed and everything."

"Yeah, but fortunately we've packed light, don't forget that," he said. "We're just tourists. We're only in Israel for a few days. We're not making *aliyah*; we're not settlers answering the call."

"That's true, but it's a shame we're not," I said. "We're wasting such a great last name in New York. In Israel we'd be rock stars; we'd be on the fast track to citizenship. And we'd fit in so great with the *Haredim*."

"No, we wouldn't. We don't have the look, and we don't have the faith. And we love New York too much to ever consider leaving. I can't believe we're off on a vacation. I haven't left this island in years."

"Well, you won't be here on your 50th birthday," I said. "We'll be celebrating in Jerusalem."

"I have a bad feeling about this birthday bash at the Wailing Wall. It's symbolic of something; I just don't know of what."

"Think of it as a double affair: Your daughter's bat mitzvah and your birthday—both on the same weekend."

"Way too much sensory overload. I'm getting dizzy; I might fall into this river. It's like we're trying to give the Israelis something to cry about—I'm turning 50, and my London-based daughter, who I never see, is having her bat mitzvah."

A large orange ferryboat cruised past us, followed by a blanket of squawking seagulls overhead, all Staten Island bound. Another ferry set sail for Red Hook crowded with thrifty shoppers looking to furnish their apartments at IKEA. A Swedish export known for its self-service and easy assembly now sits in the borough named for the Dutch town Breukelen. Nothing was ever meant to be permanent in the New World.

On the other side of the harbor, a speedboat painted with fangs and claws carried tourists and glided across the upper bay in a thrill ride that should have been called Disney on the Hudson.

It is true what my father said about Arielle, my half-sister who lives in London. He never does see her. She has grown up without a father. And the same thing is true of Alexandra and Tessa in San Francisco. Of course, it hasn't been that much different for me even though he and I have always lived together. You can be present and still be an absent father; believe me, I know. I have three half-sisters. We all share the same father, and a last name, and, as far as I can tell from the photos, certain physical features, but none of us, including me, actually know our father.

"I spoke with Arielle the other day," I said. "She's very excited, but she's more excited about seeing you than anything else."

His head was down and his right hand clutched his face like a straight-jacket.

"Sarah, I know I've mentioned this before, but probably haven't said it enough. I'm really sorry about the mess I've made. I haven't exactly given you the ideal family life after your mother died."

"Pops, it's okay," I interrupted him. "Let's not even go there. We've got enough going on right now without bringing Mom into it. It was a long time ago," I said, as if my mother's death, when I was two years old, didn't matter to me. The way I saw it, I had it worse than my half-sisters. They never saw their father, but at least they had a mother.

"Truth is," he continued, "family is a joke in our family. One kid in London. Twins in San Francisco. You here in New York; and I'm the one who looks to you for parental advice. It's so fucked up. I've created three of my own lost tribes."

"We're not at the end, you know," I reminded him. "This story has still got a ways to go. I'm in college. Alexandra and Tessa are in high school, and Arielle is having her bat mitzvah. You're only turning 50. You have plenty of time left to get to know your daughters and make it right."

He didn't answer. He didn't have that kind of confidence, certainly not when it came to righting this family ship. Further down the walkway I noticed a man talking on his cell phone while juggling his three young daughters. He was overwhelmed, buying time and some ice cream from a hot dog vendor, yelling into the phone while trying to make change. The girls were bouncing up and down under the spell of a satanic sugar rush.

An NYPD patrolman walked toward us, holding fast to a leash attached to a German shepherd. My father stiffened; he didn't like cops. The dog took a deep long sniff of my father's shoes.

"Good day, folks," the policeman said, but eyed my father suspiciously. My father didn't reply. He felt singled out, profiled in some way, but it was all in his mind. What profile did he think he exactly fit? He had spent his whole life in and out of disguise.

"Everything all right here?" the officer asked.

"Just fine," I replied. "My dad and I are just waiting for the sun to set."

"Okay," the policeman said, "have a nice day."

"Yeah, have a nice day," my father snarled, lifting his visor, which he had tilted down over his eyes. The policeman locked eyes with my father and inched away. Whatever it is he saw made him want to surrender his badge. The dog whimpered. The officer tugged on the leash and they were soon gone.

"After the way I've screwed things up my daughters still want to travel all the way to Jerusalem to celebrate my birthday? It's so hard to believe."

"Well, there's also Arielle's bat mitzvah."

"Of course, the bat mitzvah. That must be it."

"It's funny," I said. "All of your wives converted to Judaism so they could be closer to you and connect with Jewish history. They were anchoring themselves to you, of all people, and to do their part for Jewish continuity. But you're the poster boy for what may be the most Jewish thing of all: Jewish flight. Exodus, all those forced expulsions, the Diaspora always on the move. To be a Jew is to be able to pick up and go, and to be able to leave things behind. We're at our best when we're living apart and in transit. Maybe Israel is just a mirage; I mean . . . it is in the middle of a desert. Think of yourself as a SuperJew, Pops, a true *luftmensch*—always living in the air."

"I'm not sure I like what they've been teaching you over there at Barnard."

"Hey, I didn't learn this in the classroom," I said. "The only teacher I've ever had for this kind of knowledge is you."

[

] I'm knocking on the door of what I thought was middle age and a much younger peer group won't let me in. This isn't the first time this has happened. When you spend most of your life pretending to be someone else, most people aren't all that eager to claim you as one of their own. It's not their fault. I'm not exactly an easy fit—whether it comes to jeans, or genes. I've remained apart. I haven't held on to people very well. If turning 50 leads to reflection, then maybe it's not too late for me. But who knows whether repair is possible at the midpoint of a life already so broken.

I know this much: My midlife crisis isn't ahead of me. It came much earlier. It all happened at birth.

Here's another thing I know: The true measure of manhood is how one stands up to the test of fatherhood. That's a pretty good yardstick, but it's not a great metric for me. The best fathers are present for their children. I've been marked absent for years.

I'm actually quite good at having children. I am Jewish and I know about God's Covenant with Abraham: Jews were required to obey God's commandments, circumcise their sons, and be a fruitful people, and, in return, God promised the Jews their own nation—hence, the Promised Land.

At least I have held up my part of the bargain by adding to the tally of our tribe. Never let it be said that I was the cause of any broken promises. I have four daughters. The Jewish people have their Promised Land. Covenant fulfilled, at least on my end.

Now, I'm not a rabbi or lawyer, but I do detect a slight loophole, a drafting error, a missing clause, perhaps: There's nothing in the Covenant that says that Jews must *parent* their children. All it says is that they must have them. There are a lot of lousy but fruitful parents out there. And in the Ten Commandments children must Honor their Fathers and Mothers—whether the parents deserve it or not.

Maybe I haven't been such a derelict father, after all. I gave my children life; I just wasn't able to face them afterward.

I've spread my seed around liberally, substituting sperm count for quality time. I left my DNA in San Francisco, and in New York and ı, too. Tiny Ben-David footprints appeared in disparate places, ning for their father.

always regarded Mayer Rothschild as a fine parental role model. He ft evidence of himself all throughout Europe by depositing his sons in the House of Rothschild like they were foreign currency. But the sons, and the father, all lived apart, as if the House of Rothschild was more a time-share than a homestead. Mayer Rothschild didn't exactly raise his children. He simply made them rich.

And yet my children are impoverished.

Maybe what I've created is a New Covenant—the anti-*aliyah*. Stay away from the critical mass. There is safety in spreading the risk. Rothschild was right all along: Distance was always the secret weapon for the Diaspora. My daughters are like sleeper cells, surviving independently and with vast space between them. Think about Otto Frank. Trying to hide everybody in a tiny attic—sitting ducks among the Dutch. I've got it all figured out: The Ben-David line will live on, traveling on its own *Kindertransport*—minus the trains.

Surely Jews have a responsibility to replace what has been lost. But we shouldn't lie to the children no matter how desperate and decimated the Holocaust left world Jewry. We shouldn't make false promises about promised lands and safe havens and how things will be much different this time. We don't have any reason to think that. Only fools live in the air—the lunatics and the *luftmenschen*, sharing space with the silly parents who read bedtime stories and promise their children that no harm will ever come to them.

The nuclear family has been nuked. Whatever is loved can be taken away; there are real monsters out there and few happy endings.

We all know what can happen when a parent hands a child off at a train station, or leaves them in a convent or farmhouse without taking a claim check. Those excruciating last looks. The otherworldly grief. What if the child isn't recognizable when returned; what if he's an uncircumcised changeling; what if she is not returned at all?

Maybe I made a mistake; maybe I should have had more children.
[
] The Ben-David twins were a curious breed, and not just because they were of bastard stock. Their mother, Barbara, was from Poland, a convert to Judaism; their father had an Israeli name but had always been

slumming as an American *Marrano*. Oddly enough, the twins were neither identical nor fraternal, but rather paternal: They barely resembled one another, and yet each, in their own way, looked exactly like their father—with their thick blond hair, bracing blue eyes, long arms, and a distinctive chin that placed a nice exclamation point on their face.

Genetics has a way of playing tricks on the human anatomy, or maybe it just compensates for matters of the heart that science can't explain. Alexandra and Tessa Ben-David, disparate twins otherwise inseparable, were actually carbon copies, creepy clones of the father they had never met. Their name was unimportant in identifying who they were and to whom they belonged. They could easily be found without birth certificates, footprints, or even a trail of breadcrumbs. All it took was a glance into their eyes.

Their father always traveled under an assumed identity. He carried himself like unclaimed luggage spinning monotonously on a carrousel. Life's ironies. He didn't realize that the physical appearance of his children would become the smoking gun of his charade. Four daughters genetically designed to blow their father's cover.

The twins left Fisherman's Wharf with its blur of street traffic and smell of fish. Trolley cars tinkled and swayed like toddlers. Seagulls squawked above the weathered docks. The high tide slammed against wooden pilings and rattled the rusty chains. Sailboats navigated the rocks of Alcatraz as the Golden Gate Bridge hovered in the background with its long, swooping cables and humming cars racing in either direction. Such are the frenetic beats of a city trying to keep its mind off earthquakes.

Alexandra and Tessa continued on toward the Embarcadero, where the San Francisco Bay appeared calmer, and the waterfront walkways seemed quieter, as if laid-back Berkeley on the other side of the bay had imposed a new rhythm on its more high-pressured neighbor.

"Let me see if I got this right," Alexandra wondered as she recited her list. "We don't really know our father. He's done almost nothing for us all these years. And we should travel halfway around the world to celebrate his 50th birthday? And the meeting place is Israel, where buses sometimes get blown up and pizza shops are known to cause death—and not because of bad pizza?"

"Yes, that's about right," Tessa conceded.

"You know, he never came to any of our birthday parties," Alexandra continued. "I'm sure he was always invited but I never saw him there, unless he came disguised as a clown."

"Actually, come to think of it, there were a lot of clowns at our birthday parties when we were little," Tessa said.

In birth order Tessa came out second, which is usually the slot reserved for the caretaker. She would have defended her father against any assault—even if the assault was deserved, and even if it came from her own twin. Besides, she'd say anything to convince her sister that this was a journey worth taking.

"We should check the home movies just in case," Tessa added. "He might have been at our birthdays all along and we just didn't know it."

"Yeah, and we sat on the laps of many Santas at Ghirardelli Square," Alexandra said, "but I don't think any of those Nicks had the last name Ben-David."

"But it's Arielle's bat mitzvah, too," Tessa trudged on. "Even if it wasn't his birthday we should all be there for our younger sister. Even Mom's planning on going."

The sun, which in San Francisco is as rare as an Alcatraz escape, was suddenly lost in fog. And a misty chill off the water settled in. The ecological balance of the bay was sending the Ben-David twins a message of foreboding.

"Mom's coming because she wants to protect us from getting hurt, and I don't mean from terrorists," Alexandra said. "That's what mothers do, especially when the fathers are doing the hurting. She's seen this movie before and she doesn't think that the Holy Land is going produce a Kodak moment for the Ben-Davids. And as for our sisters," Alexandra continued, "we hardly know them. We're all strangers who just happen to be siblings. We've only seen their pictures—online. We never even made actual prints. I mean, sure, we all look alike, but so what? We're all half sisters of a phantom father who's probably even a smaller fraction of himself."

"Maybe we can change all that, you know, move the pieces closer together and become a whole," Tessa said. "Remember what Ms. Kennedy said in class the other day: 'Israel is a place where the Jewish people were transformed back into a nation.' Maybe Israel can turn us back into a family."

"I seriously doubt it," Alexandra laughed. "I just hope we don't end up lost in the water. There's no GPS that could ever track this family, and the Black Box won't be able to explain anything about us."

[

] Many people live in the United Kingdom, but it's fair to say that at any given time most are not practicing their *Haftorah*. This is largely true of the Jews of Great Britain, as well, for whom Jewish rites of passage take a backseat to afternoon tea. The British are not comfortable with anything Yiddish. There is no Ellis Island analogue, and the memory of Jews selling apples from pushcarts in the East End of London registers little nostalgia for the days when Brick Lane was not only for Bangladeshis. Tom Stoppard and Harold Pinter, two of England's most celebrated playwrights, are Jews, and Pinter, now dead, was the son of a Jewish tailor from the East End. Neither has Jewish names or joined a synagogue or was particularly sympathetic to Jewish causes. Pinter, in fact, was one of England's leading crusaders on behalf of the Palestinian people.

Speaking of Palestinians, British academics have boycotted Israeli scholars from participating in academic conferences. It's not clear how much has actually changed from the days of Shakespeare's Shylock and Dickens' Fagin. This is probably why the Jews of the UK speak in perfect Queen's English, flaunt their Cambridge accents, and, while tossing down a pint, might let slip a Jewish joke that Mahmoud Ahmadinejad himself would enjoy.

But in a tiny flat on Bayswater Road overlooking Kensington Gardens in Central London, Arielle Ben-David was busy reciting the blessings, practicing her *Haftorah* and the *Parshat* that she was soon about to read for her bat mitzvah—a bat mitzvah that would take place not in Britain, but rather among the ruins of the British Mandate. Arielle was going to test out the *davening* acoustics of the Wailing Wall, chanting ancient Aramaic, a language no one now speaks, while surrounded by her father and sisters, all of whom she had never met.

The Torah portion for that week was *Vayigash*, the story of Joseph reuniting with his brothers in Egypt. Arielle's bat mitzvah was a feminist retelling of this Biblical tale, with a slight twist. This story involved a sisterly reunion, and, like Jacob, but for different reasons, an absent father. And, in another reversal, the welcoming of Arielle

Ben-David into the tribe would take place out of Egypt, and back where the Jews belong.

"Arielle, it's time to go to bed," her mother, Linda, called out from the other room. "I think you've done enough and old Mrs. Kennedy next door is complaining. She's long retired from teaching but still gets up at an ungodly hour. She thinks we might be terrorists. Hebrew and Arabic is all the same to her. I assured her that we're Jews and you're just practicing for your bat mitzvah."

Arielle continued to sing right to the bottom of the page, fearful of losing her place.

"Besides, you're more than ready, sweetheart," Linda continued. "At this rate you know more Hebrew than the chief rabbi of London. Honestly, the man has been knighted, and he's even been made a lord, but I'm not certain he knows a Hebrew word other than *shalom*."

"I can't go to sleep, Mummy," Arielle said, her blue eyes sleepy but inspired, her blond hair wild with curls, and her pink cheeks flushed from all that anticipated family history. Her mother told her that her great-grandfather—on her father's side—had been a famous rabbi in Poland. Arielle's other great-grandfather had been a ham merchant in Arkansas. They sure do package Jews differently nowadays. "I am pretty scared about the bat mitzvah, but I'm mostly excited about going to Israel to see Daddy and my sisters."

Yes, Daddy and the Ben-David Sisters, which sounded like a Motown act from the 1960s, one of those bands that simply couldn't stay together. But young Arielle, on the eve of Jewish womanhood, was thrilled that she was finally going to meet her truly extended family. This was a family portrait long overdue.

Linda waited a beat. As a single mother living in London, a convert to Judaism despite a family trade that had depended on pigs, and someone who once also shared the Ben-David name, this journey to Israel to celebrate her daughter's bat mitzvah and her ex-husband's birthday was slightly surreal.

"We're all excited, Arielle."

"Do you think Daddy will like me?" Arielle yelled out before brushing her teeth. "I want him to like me. If he likes me, maybe we'll see him more."

"He loves you now, Arielle. And coming to Israel, where he's never been, just to be there with you, will be overwhelming—the perfect icing on his birthday cake."

[

] Well, not surprisingly, Yehudah Ben-David never made it to Jerusalem for his birthday or for his youngest daughter's bat mitzvah. Jerry Bender didn't show up, either. The world was awash in broken promises, breached commitments, empty gestures, and solemn words that were never meant to be taken seriously. A promise made in the Promised Land stands no greater chance of being honored.

The El-Al jet landed softly filled with passengers just waiting to kiss the hot tarmac as if God's lips were painted on the runway. Yet, in an otherwise oversold flight, during a time of year when everyone wanted to visit Israel, one seat was unoccupied. Surely there were standby passengers back at Kennedy Airport who would have gladly taken the seat. But somehow 32A managed to remain empty, as if reserved for Elijah.

An American of wavering identity was supposed to have been on that flight from New York. Airport security seemed on high alert for a suspicious character. But there was no threat—at least not that kind. Four girls who all looked alike waited for their father at Ben Gurion Airport, holding flowers, carrying signs, and forming a human wall of sibling sorrow.

"I don't see him," Arielle said, bouncing from side to side trying to inch up to see above her taller sisters."

"I knew it," Alexandra said. She wasn't holding up a sign or carrying any flowers. Instead, her arms were crossed, her hair lapped over her face while teenage steam passed in-between her ears.

"Maybe he got airsick and is throwing up in the bathroom," Tessa wondered.

"Jesus Christ, Pops," Sarah muttered to herself. She had arrived a few days early, wanting to spend some alone time with her sisters. And there was so much of Israel to see, and her father hadn't flagged even a single page in the Lonely Planet guidebook. "It's my fault," she said, with older-sister insight. "I shouldn't have left without him. I should have brought him along with me as a hostage, or claimed him as missing cargo."

"But it's my bat mitzvah and his birthday," Arielle cried. "Doesn't he love us? What kind of a father does he want to be?"

The three older half-sisters stared through the window and wondered why if seas could part in this land of miracles Yehudah Ben-David
could not, finally, materialize as a real father. Sarah considered checking the flight manifest, but knew it was pointless. Neither the flight
path nor the check-in procedure of El-Al had anything to do with why
her father was lost.

The pleadingly blue eyes of the four girls circled the terminal as if
looking to recruit any circumcised Jew among the *minyan* at Ben Gurion
Airport who might agree to serve as their father for the next few days.
Instead they found a Christian youth group of evangelical teenagers
performing a lovely a cappella of *Hatikva*. From the other direction an
elderly woman from Scarsdale screamed with the rapture of an orgasm
at the sight of so many Stars of David.

But nowhere was there an available father to be found.

The Ben-David eyes of Sarah, Alexandra, and Tessa, now foggy with
tears, settled lovingly on their younger sister.

Linda and Barbara, the two ex-wives, looked at each other but didn't
say a word. In this case, parental comfort would go only so far. The
mothers knew from the outset that this family mission was worth a
shot, even if it was never better than a long shot.

El-Al is quite experienced with traveling through time zones, but in
order to transport Yehudah Ben-David a more circuitous route would
have been necessary—one that would pass through time itself, roll it
back, and then freeze the moment right before all the damage had
begun. Of course, that's far too much to ask of any airline, even one with
such a stellar track record of arrivals and departures. Yehudah Ben-
David, after all, was not a typical passenger. He had always been a Jew
in twilight, neither here nor there, the kind of in-between existence that
is far worse than merely being stateless.

On the night of Yehudah Ben-David's birthday, his daughters brought
a cake into the Old City, lit three candles representing the three paths of
his abandoned fatherhood, and sang happy birthday—in both English
and Hebrew. A sharp wind twisted through the narrow alleyways of
Hurva Square and blew the candles out just before the girls had finished
their serenade.

And the next day, on Shabbat, Arielle Ben-David, standing beside her
three joyful and proud siblings, came before the Torah. The Wailing
Wall may have been made of stone, but its heart was not. It had sur-

vived all these centuries and had received the prayers of millions. And, yet, for this particular bat mitzvah, the Wailing Wall wept even more solemnly, spilling real tears that nearly turned the remnants of the Second Temple into a fountain.

Maybe it had to do with all the ghosts that happened to be present as witnesses for this occasion. Invitations had gone out in the afterworld and the response rate was enormous. They came to root Arielle on as surrogates for a family—the entire lost family—that she would never know. Her sisters clung to one another as if they were triplets at the moment right before birth. Linda and Barbara, the ex-wives who until this trip had also never met, hugged each other, too.

And Yehudah Ben-David? Well, he did board a flight on the day his children waited for him in Jerusalem. It's just that he ended up somewhere else, in a place far less holy and historic than where he was supposed to be. He didn't cross an ocean, or even change continents, but his landing was not without its own meaning.

After an absence of over thirty years Jerry Bender returned to Miami Beach. And on Shabbat he marked the day of his daughter's bat mitzvah by wading knee-deep into the Atlantic Ocean wearing nothing but a swimsuit and a *tallis*. He faced east. His eyes were closed and his heart was open. Lost in the water and surrounded by echoes only he could hear, Jerry Bender said *Kaddish* for his parents.

] Money

"Fred doesn't like money," Joyce confided over her third mojito. And then she squinted as if inspecting her husband and this proclivity of his from a distance.

I found the revelation surprising, just as I'd been surprised at her inviting me over in the afternoon, and letting me know in advance Fred wasn't going to be there, and that she preferred it that way. I had assumed there was something on her mind, but money would never have been on my list of possible subjects.

Joyce and Fred had just returned from a lavish week-long vacation in Strasbourg, where they had stayed at a luxury hotel. They always stayed at luxury hotels when they traveled to Germany, France, or Belgium. And they did that twice a year, never off-season and always flying business class. My wife Nathalie and I envied them, but not so much that we couldn't socialize together now and then, and Nathalie would have been there with me, only she was down with the flu. That was another surprise: Joyce not wanting to re-schedule, given Nathalie being ill.

Fred, away at a conference, was a distinguished professor of economics at our university. I couldn't imagine him disliking money, whatever that meant, exactly. Look at the life he lived. He didn't just have an endowed chair; around campus they joked that he had an endowed foot stool as well: a research assistant and research budget which put him in the upper echelons of university life. There was also talk about "family money." Fittingly, he and Joyce lived in a mammoth Tudor house in our Midwestern college town's toniest neighborhood, a house suitable for a family with four children and three dogs, though they had none of either.

They were the kind of colorful people I'd always been attracted to, being somewhat shy myself. Though I'd published enough and gotten tenure on schedule, even my chosen field of American Realism—with a specialty in William Dean Howells—was hardly dramatic. My tiny claim to fame was being the world's leading expert in Howells. That was a continuing source of amusement to my parents who thought Tolstoy and Thomas Mann were worthy subjects of scholarship, but Howells? "Who ever heard of such a person?" my mother loved to say, as if I'd chosen some improbable career, like contortionist or card shark.

I wasn't sure how to respond to Joyce's assertion that her husband didn't like money. But my second mojito obviated the need for prodding, and my hostess settled back in her black leather wing chair and nodded thoughtfully, a narrator clearly on the verge of further exposition.

Though she was tall and lithe, a former dancer with the looks of a slightly dazed and slightly puffy Grace Kelly, the setting of her library gave her the air of some octogenarian in an English club. The large gleaming room was so filled with leather—in the chairs, twin sofas, and the finely tooled editions in many languages cramming endless shelves—that it seemed to creak.

We'd been friends for a few years now, having met at a faculty reception for a visiting scholar. Joyce took my wife Nathalie's hatha yoga class at a local health club, and Nathalie and I enjoyed going out to restaurants with Joyce and Fred better than visiting their morgue-like house. No, it wasn't really like a morgue, it was as if some giant taxidermist had drained all the life out of it and turned it into some kind of mammoth trophy.

"Their place is so grim," Nathalie had noted. "Germanic."

"It's his father's fault," Joyce went on now.

I didn't know much about Fred's late father, except that he'd been German, some sort of industrialist. Given that Fred was sixty-five, it meant that his father would have been of an age to assist the Nazi war effort materially, enthusiastically, and because I liked Fred and Joyce, I had never raised the question of what he had done then—and to whom. Because my parents were Holocaust survivors and hated everything German, I had felt obligated to treat him decently, no matter what secrets might be in his family's past. How could he be blamed for any of it? My wife was Jewish, too, and Fred was always charming to us, so that seemed to end the discussion.

And I confess to finding him quite exotic. I'd never met any actual Germans growing up or in graduate school, and knew them only from my parents' sparse anecdotes, and from movies, whether about the war or in films by Werner Herzog. Germans had always seemed somewhat unreal to me, and given Fred's apparent wealth and his academic reputation, he in his own way fit that description, though he was very accessible.

Howells (and even James and Wharton) left Fred cold, but he loved talking literature with me (Joyce only read *Travel and Leisure*, *Vanity Fair*, and *Vogue*), and he could range widely, from the Greeks to Salman Rushdie. He read omnivorously, and given the fervidly narrow range of most academics, it was particularly surprising and commendable. A colleague in my English department had once confessed that he most preferred reading either Gerard Manley Hopkins or *about* Gerard Manley Hopkins: "Everything else seems so dull."

Fred was shorter than Joyce, a dynamic, beefy, muscular man with bushy eyebrows, large, thick-fingered hands and the kind of quiet swagger that I imagined probably made women of a certain age swoon, or at least take a second look. I ran into him often at the main gym on campus where he swam with a methodical, powerful butterfly stroke and though he might nod at people on the way to or from the pool, he had the air of a man absorbed by his own obsessions.

"It's his parents' fault," Joyce repeated with asperity, as if she knew my mind had wandered. "His parents never talked about the war. Never. Fred grew up here after his parents divorced and he always assumed the worst. Why not?"

I nodded. I knew that silence could cover many sins, but despite what had happened to my parents and most of their family, I was not personally given, as some Jews were, to demonizing all Germans no matter what their age. I wasn't squeamish about buying German products, the way many of my Jewish friends were, and I had in fact defiantly disavowed my parents' abhorrence of anything German. That wasn't a proclivity I ever shared with Fred, however, or even Nathalie. I just lived it out.

"So you wanted to talk to me about Fred and the war? Is that it?" I asked.

"I don't know anyone else in your position," she brought out anxiously.

That struck me as an odd, almost prim way to talk about my parents having survived concentration camps, but I let it go.

"Does Fred feel guilty about the Holocaust?" I asked.

"His whole fucking country feels guilty, so why shouldn't he? But he doesn't talk much about any of that to me. It's all work for him. I'm so bored!"

That, I guessed, was an occupational hazard when you were married to an academic and weren't one yourself, or even something close to it. My wife was a high school teacher (yoga was her hobby) and the chasm between us wasn't enormous: We both graded papers (she was doing so that afternoon, since she was stuck at home with a fever anyway); we both dealt with delusional student expectations; we both suffered through endless meetings.

Joyce wasn't actually anything. She shopped, she lunched, she drank. The rich woman's triathlon.

"And Fred keeps everything about money to himself," she went on like a guest on some pseudo-deep talk show unburdening herself to the nodding, smarmy host.

The best I could come up with was: "That's a guy thing."

"*Ach, so?*" she said, in a passable German accent that didn't sound too much like a caricature. Or like someone doing an Arnold Schwarzenegger imitation, though of course he was Austrian—not that most Americans could tell the difference. "Is it a guy thing to not talk about running up massive debts, about bringing yourself to financial ruin?"

"What do you mean?" I asked, starting to feel seriously out of my depth. We didn't know each other well enough for this level of confession—and wouldn't it have been more natural for her to talk to Nathalie, woman-to-woman, wife-to-wife?

Joyce shook her head like some diva annoyed by a reporter's too-personal question. And she glared at me, or in my general direction. "Do you and Nathalie discuss finances?"

"Sure." Too much so, but who didn't during this recession?

"Fred, never. Nothing. He pays the bills, says we either have more money or less money at certain times, but won't show me the bank accounts, the stocks, none of it. When we plan a vacation, I have the brochures, I choose the hotels, the restaurants, but he has the money. He has to control everything. Sometimes he's a little Na—" I knew she'd been about to call him a Nazi, and my face must have read surprise, because she blushed.

"He keeps me in the dark and God knows what he does or doesn't do with his money."

She sounded angry enough to hurl her glass at one of the beautiful shelves, but instead she set it down beside her chair and excused herself. Either she needed to go to the bathroom, or she was heading off for some Valium.

Though Fred had been raised in the U.S., I did wonder how much of his reticence about the money side of their lives might be Old World, or even specifically German. Her American love of liberty might be foundering on some idea he had of how husbands *should* behave.

Joyce came dashing back, red-faced. Had she been crying? She was no calmer now, though her voice was more controlled, the kind of control you see in parents choked by the desire to strike their badly behaving children in public. She crossed her legs sharply in her black pants suit and waggled her top foot in its sexy black pump.

"We've been married thirty-five years and he's *always* been feckless."

The mojitos were strong and I must have been a little drunk by that point, because I wondered if the opposite of feckless was feckful.

"Fred's brother and sister have amazing lives. Apartments in Paris, homes in Italy, boats. They cruise the Greek islands in their own *boats*!"

I'd never heard Joyce express an interest in sailing.

"His father was ruined in World War II, but he was smart enough to have a Swiss bank account and once the Allies rebuilt Germany, he was ready. When he died, the estate was split three ways, so they all started out with the same money. But Fred? He's squandered it all in stupid investments. If he buys gold, it goes down. If he invests in real estate, mortgage rates go up. The man has a *gift* for losing money. He's invested in oil wells that dried up, dot.coms that tanked, whatever's bound to turn to crap. You'd almost think he *wants* to get rid of his money, that he *wants* to go broke. And now he's after mine."

"Yours—?"

"My money, such as it is. I opened his mail by accident last week," she said

I thought, "*his* mail?" and also wondered where this was taking us.

"He's massively in debt and he never told me until I confronted him."

"Gambling?"

"No, no, no," she said. "Stupidity." She grimaced. "And now he wants me to help." Joyce evidently didn't like the expression on my face because she shot, "You think I should be helping him!"

"I don't know what you should do."

"He wants all my friggin' money is what he wants. Everything I earned when I was dancing and then teaching dance classes, the money I've never spent and kept in a separate account he can't touch because I was terrified he'd end up like this and we'd have nothing to live on when he left the university."

"But he has his retirement savings like all the rest of us faculty. Even with the economy down, it's got to be a pretty hefty sum." Fred held an endowed chair, so I guessed that he must have made easily twice my salary over the years.

Joyce grimly shook her head. "He's been raiding those funds, God knows why."

Maybe to pay for their biannual luxurious trips, I thought, but I didn't say it. Nathalie and I, we could only afford vacations in places we could drive to. We lived in a small ranch house. We owned second-hand cars. Our son's college tuition bills were killing us.

What if Fred had a mistress, I suddenly wondered, or was being blackmailed, couldn't that be as likely as his being so incompetent with money? Hell, it might be easier to imagine her husband was a lousy investor or a financial dolt than to imagine he was cheating on her, or had secrets worth paying to keep hidden.

As if guessing at my suppositions, Joyce launched into a litany of Fred's years of financial irresponsibility that were as detailed and depressing as the medieval chronicles of a prince ruined by war and plague and all the rest.

"He's not getting a dime out of me," she swore in conclusion. "Not a dime."

"If he wanted to get rid of his money, he could have given it to charity," I said.

"Oh, sure! He has no sympathy for anyone else's suffering, he's a friggin' German for God's sake."

Her face was bitter—a suburban Medea scorned.

I felt ambivalent. She was a friend, however recent, and I should support her with some version of "Stick to your guns!" but I felt almost sorry for Fred. That was easy, since I wasn't married to him and had no history. It wasn't much different from finding a friend's parents admirable and charming—they had never destroyed your morale or repeatedly embarrassed you in public, and you see them usually at their best. And there was actually something almost noble about him squandering wealth if he felt he didn't deserve it because of who his father was, because he felt ashamed to be rich at all after the war.

"I can't tell anyone about this, it's so mortifying. My girlfriends would laugh at me. All I've been doing is writing in my diary."

"How about seeing a shrink?" I asked.

"I need a hit man, *that's* what I need."

And then as if we were in some symphony where a giant pause preceded some momentous climax, the room fell silent, and eyes down, Joyce said, "I never tell people this, and you have to swear to keep it to yourself. I'm Jewish."

"You're *Jewish*?" I flinched. I had never guessed; she seemed Haute Wasp to me.

"That's not all. My parents were Holocaust survivors." And now her voice dropped as if she were afraid the room were bugged. "Not even Fred knows that."

I tried not to recoil, but all I could think was: "You married a *German? You* did?"

My face must have registered revulsion because she glanced at me and then averted her eyes, dropping her head as if ashamed.

"I thought *you* would understand," she said. "My parents came here with nothing and they had a terrible life. They met in a Displaced Persons camp, they were desperate to start a family and escape to America, but nothing my father did ever worked out. They argued over money every day of my life. My mother always called him a bum, and finally he killed himself."

I gulped at my drink, thinking of Primo Levi, of other survivors who had committed suicide. But as if an alarm bell were clanging in the background, I kept wondering how she could have married a German. I might drink Riesling now and then, and have a Krups coffee maker, but I could never have married a German. It would have seemed a perverse kind of betrayal, even though my parents had not struggled in America the way Joyce's parents had.

"Say something," Joyce begged.

"Uh . . . Did Fred meet either one of your parents?"

She shook her head. "Mom died a year after Dad. And we have no family anywhere—they were all murdered in Europe. But it didn't matter to me that Fred was German," she said, eyes wide as if seeing Fred the first day they met. "He was rich. I wanted to be safe. You get where I'm coming from, don't you? *Don't you?*"

Glancing around the overstuffed room, I saw it differently now. I knew enough about our peer group, children of Holocaust survivors, to see that she was living in a castle built against the darkness that had eddied around her as a child without connections, without history, without a reachable, tangible past. I'd briefly belonged to a children of survivors group with an on-line discussion board but the whirlwind of neediness, dysfunction, anxiety and rage sweeping across it all too often had made me quit. I found I had nothing to learn from these people except that somehow I hadn't dragged a Holocaust ball and chain through my entire adult life, as they had. Joyce, I thought, was clearly one of them.

"You know," she said. "I really figured that I could get over hating Germany, hating Germans. I haven't. I can't. It's worn me out over the years. When we travel anywhere even *near* Germany I want to *scream*. It was the stupidest mistake anyone could make."

"I don't know, Joyce, maybe it was brave?"

"What do you mean?"

"Maybe you thought you could change everything with one throw of the dice." I was trying to find something positive to say because her life seemed so murky. But even to me it sounded like an inane comment from a trashy TV movie.

"No. It was insane to marry him. I see that now. And don't even mention divorce. I'm too old for the trauma." Eyes down, "Everything would come out then. Everyone would know the truth about him, and me. I couldn't stand it. I'd look like a moron to have let it go on so long. A moron—or worse."

"Does his family know what he's been doing with his money?"

She laughed bitterly. "No, but his sister Renate warned me. She said he couldn't be trusted about anything, that he'd always had a screw loose. That's how she put it. She said he was dangerous."

"And they don't know about your past, either?"

"Well, they do know I'm Jewish, and they think that's great. Hell, they like klezmer music, too. Whenever we're over there in Berlin they want to schlep me to some godawful concert. It's a minstrel show, it's sick.

Jewish music without Jews. Jewish culture without Jews. I'm sure they were thrilled when he married me. I was their passport out of shame. Whatever their father did or didn't do, I saved them!"

I wondered then how therapists could take the endless stream of revelation from their clients because in just a few moments, I felt almost crushed by what Joyce had told me. Her life seemed so tortured and hopeless, and here my wife and I had been envying her and Fred their luxe existence, imagining staying in some of the fancy chateau hotels they seemed to take for granted as the only possible choice on vacation. From the sound of it, they were just high-priced prisons for Joyce.

"I've never met a child of survivors who married a German," I said. "I just can't get my head around it. It's so bizarre."

"Yup, bizarre. That's my life—in a nutshell." She didn't sound at all insulted, just mournful and depressed. I briefly thought of asking where her parents had been during the war, but the paradox of her marriage held me back. Somehow it seemed impossible to talk about them when all-too-German Fred stood in the way. And then I thought of Isabel Archer in *The Portrait of a Lady* marrying a man she hoped would open up a larger world to her, only to discover that she lived in "the house of dumbness, the house of deafness, the house of suffocation."

"You think I'm disgusting," Joyce spat.

"No. No way. *No*." But my denial was too fervent to be real. And I wondered how free I really was of my parents' past if I could have such a visceral reaction to her marrying a German.

"You know what the worst thing is?" Joyce asked, her voice hoarse. "I got exactly what I wanted in life. And it poisoned me."

I flashed on her father's suicide. Wasn't she at risk herself, given her family history?

I said, "Can't you ask Fred's family for help, or at least tell them what's been going on?"

"Never! It's too humiliating. I'd rather die first."

"But—"

"You want me to beg *Germans* for money?" She looked nauseated.

I deserved her contempt. My parents had never signed up for reparations from the German government for their years in concentration camps. They called it "blood money."

Joyce was gazing at me with wide, wounded eyes and I knew that a different man would have been tempted to take her to bed, hoping to conquer in the flesh the agony of her mind, however briefly.

After a painful silence, I skulked off, feeling stained by Joyce's confession, and ashamed of my own inability to say anything helpful because I was appalled by what she had unknowingly brought upon herself. Really, how could any child of survivors think marrying a German would be an escape from the past, from *anything?*

Driving home, I kept seeing Joel Grey and Liza Minnelli dancing lasciviously around each other in *Cabaret* and singing about money, money, money. I couldn't get the song out of my head; it had always given me the creeps, but now it struck me as something much worse, a dirge, a *Totentanz.* And when I pulled up to our house, I couldn't get out of the car. Here I was feeling superior to Joyce, the way I'd held myself separate from other children of survivors, thinking I had escaped their traumas, but I hadn't. I'd buried them, buried myself in William Dean Howells, for God's sake. I'd done a secondary bibliography of the man, as if it were a passport, a shield, something that could hide who I really was, where I'd come from. *I* should have been the one confessing to *Joyce*, but I knew I would never even tell all this to her, to anyone—even Nathalie. I was too afraid. I had always been afraid.

] Lonely, Lonely, Lonely Is the Lord of Hosts

Within the first year most of the grass had given itself over to mud, and by the third all the buildings were sagging inward or tilting sideways like three crooked rows of children. Now, in the fifth year, the gate to the dairy was hanging on by a tired nail, and the stables and the printing press were rotting side by side, adding a whiff of decay to the scent of manure that already clung to the colony newspaper. And though what had been completed of the schoolhouse had a guileless elegance, the project had been abandoned halfway through for lack of capital; Karl Tannenbaum, the Staatliches Bauhaus graduate who'd designed the structure, had gone off on a fundraising mission in January, but had written in May from St. Louis to say that he'd found a bride and a job with an architecture firm, and would not be returning.

Yet just now the New Marlborough colony was beautiful. The warm yellow of the Berkshire Mountain sunlight filtered, prism-like, through the red and orange blaze of the grand old elms the first wave of colonists hadn't had the heart to clear, and the last stubborn bits of green still clinging to the ground jumped out in jubilation; even the mud sparkled a rich, satisfied garnet between the hours of noon and two, which was when Anna usually walked the length of the farm, from her office to her bungalow and then to the dairy. She always took this circuit slowly, curbing her long strides so that instead of gamine she looked gangly, a change that wasn't lost on any of the other women who happened to notice her pass. She saw the smiles they exchanged but she didn't care. She invited envy and she knew it. You couldn't be Alfie's woman and not. There was nothing personal in it. If they rarely gossiped with her or poured out their troubles for her over weak tea, it was just as well; she didn't have time for their intimacies, her only leisure this slow, admiring walk each afternoon.

Back in Vienna, she used to stroll the parks of the Prater the same way. Alfie would tease her about her wide-eyed intensity, saying that her face lit by the sight of chestnut trees in bloom was insultingly indistinguishable from her face lit by love-making. One time she'd brought a hand-mirror to bed with them in the name of scientific investigation, but at the crucial moment she'd forgotten to make use of it.

Now at night in their bungalow, Alfie spoke. He spoke worlds into existence. He spoke himself out of the need for sleep and almost spoke her out of it as well. The rings under her eyes, which the other women smirked over, were not worth smirking over in that way. Sometimes they were, but usually no. Last night had been one of those sometimes. She had been turning down their sheets, inspecting for long-legged spiders, when she noticed the uncommon quiet. She'd looked up to find Alfie half in his clothes and half out, furiously pondering a spot on the floor. "Jack will come around," she'd told him. "He doesn't understand yet what we're trying to do in New Marlborough." "Yes, if only the others could see our purpose as clearly as you can," he'd agreed, and then he'd come for her, still silent, and pushed the hair back from her face with both his hands.

The door of their bungalow, which never fit smoothly in its frame, had swelled in the heat of the late afternoon. She had to give it a shove. The tangle of her blouse was over her head, her skirt kicked halfway across the room before she noticed the envelope lying on the rough-cut table. It had been nearly two years since she or Alfie had received mail from overseas. They rarely spoke about this, and when they did it was to reassure each other that no news was good news and that their families were safe. An Austrian who had passed through the colony last winter assured them that the wealthier families had abandoned Vienna for the Alps, waiting out the war in the resorts. Alfie had believed it absolutely, and Anna had tried to as well, but when she opened the envelope and saw her sister's handwriting she knew she never had. On her way to the dairy she thought how best to present it. The timing was not good.

[

] The trouble in New Marlborough had started the month before. Jack Friedlander had been with the colony only a few weeks by then, in the United States not much longer. No one knew how he'd gotten himself out of Lvov. He didn't volunteer the information and this was fine with her. He had impressed Anna as one of the precious few who would work their arms and legs more than their mouths. And so she'd been surprised, though not to say displeased, to see him duck into the meetinghouse that Friday night.

They were debating what to do with the inheritance Gittel Weiss had received from an uncle in Chicago. Everyone agreed that the money should be used to fix the hole in the roof of the meetinghouse—just now they were all huddled in the left half, to avoid the rain—but that was beside the point. They were ideologues, every one, and every decision brought them back to a war of fundamentals. Did the money belong to Gittel or to the community? If it belonged to the community, did Gittel have a bigger say in how it was used? If, on the other hand, it belonged to Gittel could she use it to buy more property than she could work herself? These were the questions they'd been shouting about— three, four voices at a time—for a quarter of an hour, when Alfie finally took the floor.

"Again with all the wrong questions," and the room had gone silent as it only did for Alfie. The man had a way of speaking. He spoke and you felt that you were speaking, speaking through Alfie's lips, saying words you hadn't known you'd wanted to say. He could announce, for instance, "Anna, we're going move to the United States of America in order to create a new basis for community that's going to be like God's own promised land," and even if you'd never before considered leaving your mother and father and sisters you'd say, "Of course we will," and feel as though he had read your mind. Alfie could read anyone's mind to them this way. It was why they were here, four dozen souls huddled in the left half of a ruined barn. "These questions," his voice was soft; the colonists had to strain to hear. "Why do you ask them? You know, my friends. You know that when one truly acts out of loving responsibility, the interests of the community and the interests of the individual become one. You know that labor and money are irrelevant. That class disappears. You! I say 'you' to you all, and the answer is plain. Are none of us Buberists anymore that I have to be so plain?"

"We say 'you' to the world!" had come the response, but it was bloodless. To be a Buberist was difficult, and the effort was telling on them all. Only Alfie seemed really to excel at it. Not even Martin Buber was such a

Buberist as Alfie. In fact, Buber was no Buberist at all. Buber was a Zionist, fled to Palestine. It took an Alfie, Buber's last student in Mainz, to come to America and make an ism of the man. That Alfie was a visionary no one doubted. But to be a Buberist was something harder than to be a visionary and that was the miracle of Alfie. It was one thing to dream up a community where the only laws were those that arose out of loving responsibility, where everyone was linked only by their natural desire to do right one by the other, where the only obligation was that each citizen see every other, at all times, in the wholeness of their humanity and behave accordingly. But what did it mean, in practice, to live that way? Only Alfie seemed really to know, but the rest of them had not stopped trying.

Nor did any seem inclined to doubt that it was *worth* the trying, this impossible, exhausting task, until that planning meeting when from behind the uninspired chorus Jack rose from his place in the back row, a small, narrow man, sickly-looking and pale, and asking, "But I wonder."

"But I wonder," he had said, "this money. Is it possible, perhaps, that we could send it elsewhere? I know a way, you see, to get this money into the hands of those who know how to help back home. We could use it to save lives."

But "New Marlborough first, the world later," Alfie had explained, so gently, so respectfully that who could doubt the wisdom of the plan, seeing where it could lead, to a man disagreeing just like this? The vote was taken then, the money slated for the roof, and there was every reason to think Jack's outburst had been a newcomer's misstep, like the time Moishe Nuiberg from Ukraine had suggested they build a synagogue and hold Sabbath services, a motion that was laughed down rather than voted on.

Jack, though, was not as easily put off as Moishe, who now went by the more modern "Mose." The following Friday, he was the first to raise his hand when the meeting was called to order.

"Forgive me. I am new, and still trying to understand," he'd begun, mild but not *so* mild. "But am I alone in my confusion? You speak endlessly of loving responsibility and of kindness here. But I hear no kindness at all in what you describe. Choosing to mend a roof over saving a human life? What sort of kindness is that?"

There was a whisper clotting through the small crowd, but it was silenced by Alfie's hand clapped affectionately on Jack's shoulder. "Ah, Jack, my friend, here's your mistake: the promises we make are only toward each other. That's how it has to be for now. One day we'll act with loving responsibility toward all mankind. One day we will, and I love you, my friend, for your impatience. But we are showing the way for all humanity. And how can we show the way out from thousands of years of human history, if we don't do right by our own small community? How can we show the way unless we focus all our resources on New Marlborough and make this the perfect model of what can be? This is why I say, 'New Marlborough now, the world later.' "

Outside the meeting hall afterward, people gathered in groups to discuss the exchange. It was the first time so much analysis had been devoted to words that weren't Alfie's.

[

] At the broken gate of the dairy, Anna stopped to watch the milkers lined up at cows' teets. The new recruits were pulling too hard, but Alfie walked between them whirring with praise and they smiled as they worked. Briefly she saw her family's dining room, Alfie ecstatically conversing on the imminent end of all allegiances separating man from man, the end of individuals dragged out from the vast warm pool of brotherhood and tossed in cold, barbed bands of friend and foe. Alfie had just started coming to see Anna then, and so, out of courtesy, they had let him talk uninterrupted, even her father holding his tongue while he kept his eyes trained on the flickering shadows cast by the Sabbath candles on the fine stitch of the tablecloth. Anna's mother and three middle sisters were throwing her desperate glances, but it was the youngest, Rachel, who interceded. "Are you real, sir, or from the radio?" It had grown so late while Alfie lectured that she had been sent up to bed, but now she stood, balancing on one foot, in the ornately sculpted arch of the dining room, dressed in her pale pink nightgown, scratching at a spot above her eye with a finger tangled in fine blonde hair. It was Alfie's delighted laugh, louder and more appreciative than the rest that Anna had thought about later that night, with a flush of warmth, after he'd left to the cool farewells of her parents.

She leaned against him lightly.

"I have a letter from Rachel."

Saying it out loud made it simple: France, alone, $1,000. $1,000 and her sister would be standing in this dairy, in the yellow stillness of this day. It seemed *too* simple, almost, to be important.

"I'm sure your family is still in the Alps," she added.

"Yes."

His eyes were on his happily bungling dairymaids, but she could tell that he was pondering, and this was good.

"The money from Gittel's uncle, maybe."

"No."

"We could start by selling one of the cows, in that case."

"No."

"What, then?"

He looked at her with some surprise. "What can we do? None of this is ours. It belongs to everyone. We'll earn the money some other way."

"But, Alfie, be reasonable. We don't have time."

He had taken her hand, and now he pressed it to his chest. There was nothing disapproving in his tone. "But I am being reasonable, Anna. You must be, too. Every person here has family. Every person in the world has family. Why yours and not theirs?"

"Because I have a letter."

"And what is a letter?"

And it was true, of course. What was a letter? What was a sister? A letter was a piece of paper. A sister was just another woman tied to her by accidents of birth. New Marlborough first, the world later.

[

] It was Alfie's idea that she approach Mrs. Van Orter, the town doctor's wife, for work. She went the next morning, foregoing her hours with the financial books. She left with a job: She would clean the Van Orter home once a week, on Thursdays, for a dollar.

That night she skipped the meeting to catch up on her bookkeeping. It was late when she returned to their bungalow, nearly dawn, but she found Alfie sitting at the table, his fist closed tight around a piece of paper. He held her eyes while he showed her the page and this made her feel less tired. The page was a newsletter. Not the newsletter Alfie wrote every week, but one filled with news from outside, news from Europe, about the war. So here was the reason Jack had taken on the printing press. For months after Abe Rabinowitz ran off to New York, the role had remained unfilled. Working the lever was tedious and difficult; the room itself stank of rotting wood and horses; and Alfie had considered it a peace offering when Jack stepped forward. The feint, the double-dealing of it, playing on Alfie's unfailing generosity of judgment—it caused a constriction in her that was pointedly un-Buberist. She could not think of Jack in the wholeness of his humanity that night, and it was his face, pale, feral, untrusting that she held in her mind as she lay in bed knowing: a dollar a week was not enough.

[

] On Monday morning, Anna woke early and went to the home of the town lawyer; his wife let her down kindly over tea. The grocer's wife wouldn't let her in the door. She tried several more houses—the banker, a schoolteacher, a man who came to the market wearing a fine pocket-watch—before giving up. When she cleaned for Mrs. Van Orter on Thursday she explained her predicament, but Mrs. Van Orter could not increase her pay. The rest of the country might be in a war-time boom, but surely Anna could see that only the weakest vibrations were hitting New Marlborough.

There was again a second newsletter at the meeting that week.

At home he said, "Why can't I make him see? He's protesting against paradise. How can it be?" and the sadness of his tone, the pure-hearted pity of it, pierced her through.

Outside, a low rustling groan swept through the unbuilt schoolhouse and a door nearby was protesting its poor construction against a wall. Beside them their stove sputtered sickly, giving very little heat. The newer stoves, the ones that worked, were reserved for families with children. All these years she'd brought small miracles out of columns of numbers, walked Alfie on roundabout routes to avoid the worst scenes of decay, while Alfie saw nothing but God's own promised land around them. She'd protected him from a discouragement of which he was not capable. Now, here, he needed her to shield him and all she could think to say was, "Give him time."

In the morning she found it hard to concentrate on her calcula-tions. She caught several mistakes in her arithmetic. She considered whether she should go through the long rows of sums a second time to be safe, but found herself rebelling against the idea. "It's not as if any-one would know," she said out loud, and though it was true that no one other than Anna looked at the books, the words distressed her.

Resting inside them—smuggled into the room and quickly taking over—was a shameful possibility.

[

] Anna knew what the colony could stand to lose, and she knew how best to lose it. What was a dollar or two fallen off the page every other week, another three or four pocketed directly when she went to sell their extra produce at the market on weekends? It was nothing, and it was a life, because by the end of the month she had gathered just over $70, including the money she had earned from the Van Orters. And she had ideas for how to make the pile grow more quickly.

Something from nothing, and yet she paid. She thought it might be better if only she had a friend. Just to say to someone: *This is what I have done, can you forgive me?* But she was alone. So alone she could not understand how she had ever *not* felt lonely here. But even here there was someone lonelier. In the few hours a night that Alfie fell still she sat in the almond light of a homemade candle, reading and rereading the pair of weekly newsletters, Alfie's and Jack's, each given over entirely to arguing with the other, and felt a loneliness so profound it was almost sacred: the loneliness of Alfie's immaculate goodness. In those hours, she burned with an excitation that directed itself at Jack. It was very far from loving kindness.

[

] There had been three more letters back and forth: two she had sent, and one she had received. Whenever she closed her eyes, even for a moment, just to blink, her sister was waiting. The last time she'd seen Rachel they had locked themselves in the attic, the youngest and oldest natural allies against the bland ones in the middle. "Can you keep a secret?" Anna had asked, and Rachel had narrowed those eyes set wide in the round ball of her head, making her look even more the wise old frog than usual. "But then you'll send for me," Rachel had insisted. "You have to send for me as soon as you arrive, or I'll put a curse on you and make all your hair fall out." That was Rachel at ten, a funny-looking, fierce little amphibian. What was she like at fifteen?

On Thursdays, on her way to the Van Orter's, Anna stopped at the post office. A man there had agreed to set aside her mail. The colonists seldom ventured into town, and so she didn't take precautions. Who would she meet? And even caught who would think to doubt her?

It was only luck that kept her from running headlong into Jack. She was walking fast, rounding the corner with arms swishing, when she saw him, bent, thin, chafing his hands and blowing into fists. She thought at first to get out of his sight, but why? If she had business to hide then so had he, and she had better know it. In fact, the longer she watched him—he had moved onto the green, onto a bench, and drew a hunk of bread from his pocket—the clearer it became that she *must* speak to him, to reason with the man as Alfie couldn't, perhaps even to plead.

If he was surprised to have his lunch interrupted, he wanted her not to know it. He slid along the bench to clear a spot for her.

"Rebbetzin, good afternoon." The white puff of his breath made her feel the wind worse than before. It was not respectful the way he called her Rebbetzin. It was because of "Rebbe," his name for Alfie. But Alfie it didn't bother.

"It's cold," she said. "So suddenly."

He broke his bread in half and offered her a piece, and since she couldn't think what to say next she took it. They ate in silence, watching a young man on a bicycle, then a mother rushing a child from the town's one store, then a round old man in an apron and a visor emptying a bucket on the ground. Each took his turn being the only thing to watch. The silence was restful, and after a while she felt herself bucked up by it, enough to ask, "Why do you stay?"

He chewed deliberately, his shoulders hunched against the chill. The muscles of his neck, inside his raised collar, looked taut and uncomortable.

"You'd like me to go?"

"I didn't say that. I'd just like to know why you stay. You don't believe in the community. Where's the sense in it?"

"You may be right. I myself don't know how much sense it makes."

"But really why stay and be that way? Or perhaps you do believe a small amount in what we're doing?"

"Well, when you put it like that, I'm not so sure. Surely there are some things I believe."

"In loving responsibility, perhaps."

"No, not in that. I'm too simple a man. I'm not so smart that I can wait each time for a theory to tell me how to be kind."

She stamped her foot, more from the cold than in anger, but realizing

at the same time that she had spent too long here, that she was expected elsewhere, and that this was his fault. "But, see, you aren't
fair."

"No?"

"No. That isn't fair at all to say. And it upsets him, you know, very
much, when you say things like that. When you're unfair like that.
You're making him unhappy." The words were thickening in her mouth
even as she spoke them. She was choking herself up and felt ridiculous.

"It isn't my intention, believe me, Rebbetzin." Now he was watching
the withered leaves chase each other around the base of a tree trunk,
and she watched them too because it was the only thing to watch. Her
eyes were wet; she was glad he didn't look at her. "You won't believe
me, I know, but it isn't my intention to upset him. I would rather it
weren't this way between us."

"So make it not that way. Or else—why not?—find somewhere else
to go."

"Maybe you're right. Maybe it's so, and I ought to leave. But—you
won't believe me—it's a great disappointment to think of leaving. I
hoped it might be right for me, this place."

It was very late, and she felt she ought to go and was foolish for
staying this long. How could she have thought that she would succeed
where Alfie had failed? How could she have thought that her words
would do better than Alfie's?

"No, maybe I'm too simple," he continued, "but for me the loving
responsibility, as you say, is just what isn't right. There's something not
right in what we're trying to do. It isn't for us."

"For you," she corrected. None of this had gone as she had hoped,
and now this "us." What was it? She suspected it wasn't nice.

"For all of us." His nose was running from the cold. Why didn't he do
something? "Human men and women. I don't know how to say it. We
can't try to see like God sees. We can't try to love like the Lord of Hosts.
To try is to become the opposite of kind. It's to become cruel. We love
who is beside us. We help who reaches out a hand. Maybe God's way is
smarter and more fair. Maybe. But for us it's not so good."

She was impatient with the glisten beneath his nose and wanted to
slide further down the bench, but something prevented her. It was his
hand in hers. Whether it was she who had done this or he hardly made a

difference. One of her hands was warm and moistly cradled, the other clutched cold against itself, and she preferred the cold and clutched. She stood.

"For you," she said, and left.

[

] That night she had no patience. The slow boil of the soup infuriated her, her mind shut down in the onslaught of Alfie's conversation, and then beneath him she lay stubbornly, and thought how strange it was: She felt his need, but she was not a part of where it led. He thrashed about ecstatic and complete, and what was she in this? Lonely, that's what she was, alone even in their lovemaking. The sorry oven belched and tried its best but she was cold beneath him, and lying there she thought she was aware of a chill desiccation throughout the colony, a withered groan all through the wood and stiffening mud, and it hurt her heart for Alfie, even knowing it could never make a difference. He was so lonely it could not make a difference what happened beyond the boundaries of his thoughts.

Later she drifted in and out of sleep as usual while he marched tirelessly through the tangle of his own ideas, waiting until she would again be needed. It happened close to dawn. Who should they send, he wanted to know. There would be snow before too long, and the meetinghouse must be repaired. Someone must drive to Pittsfield for supplies, and who could they spare just now?

"Send Jack, of course. A gesture of goodwill."

"Of course. There's no other answer. You understand so well." He pushed her hair back from her face, and stared at her delighted.

"I'm tired," she said, and turned away from him.

[

] "Why me?" Jack's back gleamed silver pale in the linty light, beaded and heaving as he worked the lever press to churn out Alfie's newsletter. The room's stink of manure and rot had been transformed by the addition of Jack's sweat, and for once was not so unpleasant.

"Because he's trusting you. It's a gesture of goodwill, a compliment. That's how you should take it."

"Pardon me for saying, but if he needs to trust that's no compliment." He lifted his shirt from the back of a chair, and wrapping it around his neck he smiled. "So, when? Today? You'll send me off with a king's ransom and hope that I return?"

She ran a finger through the condensation dripping down the dirty window, said, "What if you don't?" then looked to see.

Only the concave dip of his chest still moved; he watched her closely.

"Believe me, me you can trust."

"Yes, but what if you don't?"

He swabbed his forehead with the shirt, then put one arm in and the other. His voice was no longer friendly, but neither was it unfriendly. "Listen, do you want me or not? Truthfully, I'd rather not make the trip. You want me to go, I'll go. But maybe you should stop with so many compliments."

It was just like when she found her hand in his. She heard a voice saying, "Is it possible, perhaps, that we could send the money elsewhere?" and if it weren't the same one she'd always heard out of her mouth she would have believed it was someone else's.

He set his jaw; it didn't seem nice.

"I have a sister."

The nod was curt. He closed his eyes. It was a long time before he spoke. "You won't believe me," he finally said. "But I don't like to leave. I'll do what you ask, but I don't like to leave this place."

[

] She had no sentimental urge to gaze on Alfie in his sleep that night, but took one long look anyway, thinking that this was how she would remember him: contented and cut off, wrapped tight in his immaculate kindness.

Would he miss her, could he? She felt that he would not and could not, but this did not make her love him less. It only made her leave.

[

] And yet she never did entirely. At least my mother would have said so. If she knew what I know now, she'd blame those five years in New Marlborough for the chill remove she had always felt in her mother's way of loving. Not like the way her father loved, sweet, simple Jack, so easy and adoring; not like her fierce aunt Rachel, cursing your existence and then smothering you in kisses. No, her mother loved wrong, she'd always claimed, wept over little Vietnamese babies, marched for the children of Africa, but when you scraped your knee she might gaze down at your blubbering, snot-nosed self like you were anyone, just a child like any other. *Her* child, yes, but a child like any other all the same, and who were you to carry on like this? My mother said her mother had made her feel so lonely as a girl that no number of friends could warm her up. She'd piled on friends like sweaters, and it was never enough. I saw none of this in my grandmother.

But then one bloated afternoon in Palm Beach Gardens, while an August thunderstorm was steaming on the other side of the sliding doors, she pulled out an unfamiliar album. On the front page was an old photograph, a man I'd never seen among the besilked and befeathered Viennese she loved to bring to life in stories. "Alfie," she'd said, "like your uncle." A handsome face smiling out from the past, eyes cold with a righteous light. A very young man, so certain of the possibilities of human kindness, ready to share a burden with the Lord of Hosts.

I think she died still loving him.

] The Afterlife of Skeptics

Max Besserling awoke into a complicated thought. His meeting with Jakob Binder was imminent, and he had not managed to finish reading Binder's manuscript, *The Ontology of Doubt*. The only words that Max retained from his reading: *For E. M. Besserling.* Binder, for reasons unfathomable, had dedicated the work to him. This made it even more imperative that he greet the author with some insights, preferably trenchant. The unbound pages were heaped on his desk in a disquieting disorder. They must have spilled from his limp hands while he slept. Was there still time?

Apparently, he had dropped off just like that, sitting bolt upright as he read. The light from the floor lamp, its amber-glass globe just directly to the left of his head, cascaded down over his massive head of thick white hair. His author photos, always a headshot, were commanding. He was not a large man, but he had the head of someone large. He had worn his hair long enough to cover his cauliflower ears ever since Nina had made the suggestion. This had been in the earliest days of their courtship, and he had been elated. It had suggested genuine sentiment on her part.

His office used to get the morning light, but no more. The university, in its continuous eastward march, had floated the campus straight over Amsterdam Avenue. His office sat in the shadow of the overpass. Draped with an extra layer of dimness, the external world appeared today even more problematic. He had perhaps slept longer than he knew. His left arm was dead numb. He must have fallen asleep on it. His watch he could not locate on either wrist.

It was even possible that Binder had already come and gone. Though the door was closed, it was unlocked. It would be just like Binder to seat himself without ceremony, his arms serenely folded behind his head and his feet up on Max's desk, maybe moving the papers out of the way, maybe not. If not, then Max had real cause for vexation. A man must not put his feet upon another man's papers!

Even though he disapproved of Plato as an errant metaphysician who had much to answer for in the history of Western philosophy, Max shared Plato's indifference toward material objects. The particulars of the perceptual realm did not speak to him the way ideas did. He did not understand their language. He listened to how others described their properties, the evaluative terminology applied and the emotional colorations received, and he felt stark wonder. For an entire week, Nina had served him dinner on a new set of fine bone china until finally asking him whether he noticed anything at all that was different. A new hairstyle, he had guessed, since that had been the correct answer to a previous question along the same lines. And yet for some reason, he harbored a sentimental attachment toward the lamp at his side. To his mind it was beautiful, and he took a certain pride in his appreciation. Like one of the multitudes, he, too, could feel the influence exerted by things. Its glow was burnished and antique. Old it certainly was. It had been converted to electricity from the original oil. His sentimentality perhaps stemmed from all the reading and writing he had done by its light. The glass globe was etched with griffins and unicorns. Allegra, his daughter, used to copy them with her crayons. A princess with an abundance of brown curls and a tiara always dominated the picture discreetly from the corner. This was when she was small and her greatest pleasure was to accompany her Papa to his office, which happened to coincide with her Papa's pleasure, too. Though Allegra had been a child bursting with energy—never would she sit if she could walk and never would she walk if she could run—still here in his office she sat drawing. One could not say that she sat drawing quietly. She woke up talking and fell asleep still talking. In his office, too, she had spoken softly to herself the whole time, making up adventures for herself and the fantastical beings. Sometimes he would pause in his own reading or writing and ask her to tell him, and always he was amazed. He could never have invented such elaborate make-believe. He had an impulse now to reach out his arm and trace the creatures with his fingers. There were two pull chains descending beneath the lamp's globe, tiny strung brass beads dangling delicate as a woman's earrings. He should bestir himself and make the lamp go brighter. The scattered pages of Binder's manuscript awaited.

Nina had surprised him with the lamp. He had complained to her of how the university's lust for Lebensraum had cast his otherwise fine office into perpetual gloom. She had tsk-tsked in sympathy, a wifely sound, though how far down the sympathy extended he would forever remain in doubt. The next day she had shown up at his office, twirling the handsome lamp over the threshold on its embossed brass base, her dancing partner, she in her high heels. Always she had worn high heels, because of her height. It offended her that she was not taller, her elegance cut short by several inches.

It was not that she had been a frivolous person. Her book reviews, written with rare intelligence, appeared in *Commentary* and *The New Republic*. She had read Max's manuscripts with a red pencil. Quite often, there was not a sentence she had left as he had written it. Her style, certainly in English, was superior to his, and he had always acknowledged her efforts. *Last, but not least, I wish to thank my wife, who has read every draft of my manuscript and offered useful comments.* It must have been difficult for her to transport the heavy lamp across the campus. Perhaps if he got up and moved about a little then the numbness would dissipate. Like the lead cape they drape over you when they take your X-rays, so the lassitude lay over him. It was likely that someone had helped her with the lamp. Dormant gallantry had aroused itself around her. She had waltzed it into his office, and he had told her its illumination was more conducive to the natural light of reason, the *lumens naturalis*, than the natural light of Amsterdam Avenue had ever been. Quite often he had played the pedant for Nina. It was the least he could do for her. Her father, too, had been a professor, a philologist at Jagiellonian University in Cracow, and she had grown up basking in male scholarship.

The Ontology of Doubt. What did it even mean? Nothing at all was suggested to Max by the title. How could doubt, an activity of the mind that withstands the beguilement of answers, have its own ontology? Binder was still confoundedly, incurably obscure. His style was like a blind man's cane, tapping out the contours of a landscape that none but the blind could know. There had come a time in their relationship when the eloquent incoherence had made Max want to gnash his teeth in exasperation.

And to dedicate the work to him! Max had published nine much-cited works, not to speak of numerous scholarly articles. His typed curriculum vitae, which included eight honorary doctorates, framed and hung on the wall behind him, ran a full twelve pages. From Jagiellonian, too, he had received an honorary degree. He and Nina had returned together to the city of their births. Nina had not wanted to go. Not *honoris causa*, she had said. *Horribilis causa*. And not once had he thought of dedicating anything to Jakob Binder. The thought had never crossed his mind. It was not as if Binder had exhausted dedicatees. This was his first book. Yes, what had it all come to, the magniloquence of the metaphysician? To wait until one was nearly eighty to publish. It was true. Arithmetic does not lie. Binder would be an old man now. There is always solace to be taken in the sobriety of numbers. Who had said that? Possibly Max himself.

So Binder, through all these years of silence, had been thinking of him. Max could not deny that he, too, had thought often of Binder. Perhaps not so much these last few years, but certainly when Nina had still been alive. Binder had been then a frequent uninvited presence in their lives. They had all met as students at university. Binder was younger than Max by two years. Their philosophical orientations had diverged, both of them striding off like two duelers before turning and firing.

Had they been then such ardent friends that Binder should dedicate a manuscript to him? Yes, once upon a time, it was true, warm feelings had flowed between them. Binder, suffused with sentiment, had made declarations of eternal friendship. But to declarations, most especially those alluding to eternity, Binder had been predisposed. It was his religious past that was to blame. Unlike Max's and Nina's enlightened families, Binder's had been pious. He prided himself on having abandoned the old superstition, but it dragged behind him like a vestigial tail. The world to him was not an impersonal proposition. Ideas emerged from Binder like water that drips brown from rusting pipes. Of pure clear logic there was none. Instead he propounded upon the totality of existence, of whose infinite attributes, each of which expresses infinitude, we can grasp only the sublime and tragic sympathy in which the totality of existence beholds the totality of existence. That was how he spoke. In other words, he had a strong preference for meaningless assertions.

In Binder's enthusiasms Max had once seen a profligate generosity, and he had been initially charmed, though also, philosophically speaking, alarmed. A tendency toward meaninglessness is not to be encouraged. It is, philosophically speaking, a variety of vice. Unreason parading as reason can have deadly consequences. Who better than they to know? Was it so surprising that a philosopher of the likes of Martin Heidegger, capable of propounding such portentous nonsense as that *the Nothing nihilates,* had also proven capable of accommodating himself to the regulations of the new regime? Thought and deed: If you are less than fastidious in the one, then why should we expect you are any better in the other?

But untenable premises had occluded Binder's vision. He was unable to apprehend "the promised land of the new philosophy, the swamplands of speculation drained of cant and Kant." This was a line from Max's "The Eradication of Metaphysics through the Rigorous Application of Logic to Language." It was perhaps a bit too fanciful a phrase for such a paper, and yet it was his most-quoted. It had been Nina who had suggested it—for respite from the arid style, in her words. In a drawer not far from his knees were all the manuscripts chronologically filed, Nina's comments in their fading red. A red pencil, its eraser worn down to the metal clamp, a feeble artifact to flail against time, its markings had outlived her. Binder's excesses had helped Max to develop his own outlook in opposition. If not for Binder's rhapsodizing on the totality of existence, Max might never have clarified the empirical criteria for what can and cannot be meaningfully expressed. Max's ideas had proved influential, most especially in the bracing pragmaticism of his adopted country. He had at least been able to vouchsafe that much to Nina, who had grown up basking in male scholarship. At the least it could be said that her husband had received his fair share of academic recognition.

Binder would not have prospered in America as Max had. Max had felt compelled to remind Nina of this fact. Here they did not indulge those suffering from advanced cases of metaphysical dementia. With time, their relationship had taken on more the nature of a rivalry than friendship. There had come a point when Max could barely tolerate the sound of Binder's throaty voice, transparent with its throbbing emotion, or the sight of his face, towering half a head above Max's and flushed with the rapture of some pseudo-insight.

For Nina Orlofsky, too, they had been rivals. Their speeches to one another were obliquely directed at her, their eyes irresistibly drawn to hers as the only meaningful measure of the soundness of their reasoning. Binder's eyes were a child's blue. He and Nina were among the few in their crowd who did not wear spectacles. No doubt he had preserved his eyesight by possessing a mind sufficient unto itself for the deduction of the world. From first principles, of course! Nothing less than first principles would do for Jakob Binder. And yet it was Max who had done so much better for himself. Binder had loved with hope, vindicated by the totality of existence, as Max had loved without hope, convinced by the testimony of his senses. Binder was a handsome man, and even Max had once confused the grandiloquent web of his nonsense for the exuberance of a generous soul.

"Try to say it clearly, Binder," he had chided, a forefinger wagging in a way he intended to be playful, his eyes glancing quickly at Nina to take the measure. "Anything that can be said at all can be said clearly!"

"So you say."

"And I say it clearly!"

"As also clearly false."

It was incumbent on Max to laugh, and he did, and Nina, too, was smiling. Binder would no doubt have liked to let the matter rest right there, and why not? He had delivered a *touché,* and Nina looked as if she were lit from within. She seemed to Max not quite made of flesh, so slight a girl and blonde, with soft glows pooling in her eyes and in her smiles. In her very skin the photons danced.

"So you maintain that there are truths that, in their very nature, so to speak, cannot be expressed clearly?"

"All the most important things."

"Such as?"

"How can I say, when the whole point is that one can't?" Binder laughed easily. "We say by saying but also by not saying, by gesturing in the direction of the sublimities."

Max had turned to Nina, smiling. "Can you understand him? Do you know what he's going on about? How can silence speak of anything, much less of sublimities? Is there a perceived distinction between silences that express sublimities and silences that express, say, dumb stupidity? Really, you speak the most interesting nonsense, Binder. Doesn't he?"

But Nina Orlofsky had turned her miraculous eyes, mosaics of green and blue, on Binder. "I think it's like music, Jakob?" It was said more as a question than a pronouncement. Just hearing Binder's name in her mouth caused a sickening motion in Max, and Binder's eager look was repulsive. "Music, too, is something more than the notes. And the sublimity is not in the notes . . . " She paused, seeking encouragement in the foam of her beer, and her pale lashes touched down on the poetic line that was etched along the edge of her cheeks. "It's in the music."

"Yes!" Jakob had declared, simultaneously with Max's "Exactly so!"

"Exactly so, Max?" Binder's face had the blandness of handsomeness, but his eyebrows could be highly expressive, punctuating his statements with an irony otherwise missing.

"Don't you see, Binder? The game's up! Nina has just proved that you metaphysicians are simply musicians manqué. If you could compose like a Bach you wouldn't need to try to maintain that the totality of existence conforms to some mysterious harmony. If you could compose like a Beethoven, you wouldn't harangue us on the tragic sympathy echoing in inaudible chords throughout the infinite universe."

"Perhaps," Binder had murmured deep in his throat, also looking down into his foam, on his lips the enigmatic smile with which he often brought such arguments to a close. Was he conceding or simply seceding from further discussion? And what did it profit Max that his logic was unspotted, when Nina, too, was smiling enigmatically into her beer?

And what nonsense had Max been thinking to himself just a moment ago, weighing the possibility that Binder may have already come and gone? In youth it is one's self-image that is easily shattered, in old age it is one's sleep. The conclusion was undeniable: Binder had not yet arrived. It was childish of Max to keep picturing Binder as he had been when he had last seen him, two young men alone in a courtyard of the university, the ancient stones catching fire from the setting sun. Pillars and arches: Who would imagine the pain that lived on in such images, pressing down without mercy on his anguished chest? With great effort he tried to draw a breath and then another. Beloved archways and stairways and the end of summer, a ball of fire sinking below the medieval skyline. They had been walking with swift even strides and had stopped abruptly, at the same precise moment, as if their conversation had come with its own choreography. Binder had turned and gestured to the lit sky, sprayed with saffron and gold from the vanishing sun. Was it the totality of existence again? Could he still have been insisting, even at that late date, all the doors of escape clanging shut on them, on the sympathetic sublimity of the universe? Let the transporting spirit then spirit them out of Cracow. Let it transport all the doomed of Europe. The reddish curls that swept off of Binder's high-minded forehead had caught the last light. His right arm was extended straight out before him, pointing to something in the western skies. The emotion on his face had made Max turn away in shame. He could still remember the intense purity of his eyes.

Allegra's eyes had been just that shade of night-tinged blue, full of infinity. Sometime in the course of her first year of life, the color had changed. They're exactly your eyes, Nina had announced. My eyes are that color? His wonder had made him sound like a child even to his ears. Don't you know the color of your own eyes? she had laughed, ruffling his hair, playfully exposing the ears she had taught him how to hide. No, he hadn't known, but now he knew. Looking into his daughter's eyes, he learned his eyes were the color of caramel.

Allegra. They had both been so proud when they had come up with the name. Let us not give her any of the names of the dead. They had agreed on the point. None of the heaviness of the past. *Allegra.* Music floating on light-filled air, harmonies triumphant, the first syllable shared with the new homeland, the lilt ascendant, swift and sweet, as she had ascended swift and sweet, *allegra, allegra*. Allegra. The pink tutu and tiny dancing slippers: How old had she been when she had made the demand? Nina had searched up and down wide Broadway to find slippers to fit a ballerina so small. Allegra had wanted pink, but there were no pink in that size, only white, and she had pounced on them with no sign of disappointment. For weeks, months, until the weather turned too cold, that was all she would wear, pirouetting down Broadway to general acclaim. Max and she would make the rounds. Any sitters she considered her audience, congregated for the purpose of watching her. Quickly she had worn out the dancing slippers. Nina had to keep replacing them. A constant supply of tiny slippers. The old people sunning themselves on the benches that ran down the center of Broadway had dubbed her their own Anna Pavlova.

On certain afternoons, when the thick sun drizzled the world in a slowness like syrup, then Max, too, had partaken of the illusion. It was not that he and his daughter were chosen, but rather that everything in all the world had been chosen. Even Mrs. Projansky's anarchism had seemed a necessary part of the totality of existence. Her eyes, pressed into a Tartar tilt between the fatty pouches, had glittered with gratuitous well-wishing, and her overflowing bosom had heaved in time with the tumultuous Russian songs she sang to Allegra's dancing. The voice had been a rich contralto, sobbing with vibrato, and the songs were in a minor key, all the world's sorrow, but Mrs. Projansky would glance with a sly mischief before plucking the tax-payers' flowers and tossing them at Allegra's toes with a lusty *brava*. Did Allegra recall anything from the sweetness of those days?

Many times, he had tried to call her, but he was betrayed by his own emotions. He had her number programmed into the elaborate phone system the university had installed, the only such number, the fist at his heart now grabbing away all his breath. Socrates, dying from his quaff of hemlock, had described how the coldness was climbing up his body. When it reaches his heart, the jailer told the gathered grievers, he will die. The wife and little boy had been removed from the room, so that the philosophical conversation could proceed unimpeded by sentiment, but Appolodorus had broken down and sobbed like a woman, which had set all of them to weeping. It was unseemly, and Socrates had reprimanded them. But also it was right that the philosopher's death should cause those who loved him to behave as they did, and even it was right for the philosopher to know what his loss would mean to his many mourners, disapprove though he may. At some age beyond the tiny slippers, at nine or ten, she had switched allegiances. He had said something belittling to her mother, and an expression he had never seen before had come onto the child's face, the first sign that something irrevocable had transpired, that she had become Nina's rather than his, without Nina having said a thing to persuade her, of this he was certain. In Nina's character it would not have been to influence the child against him.

It seemed sometimes he could hear a chorus of accusations, but whose were the voices? Could they all belong to Allegra? Adolescents are known to be difficult, but Allegra had not shown difficulties toward anyone but Max. Had not Nina's mother, too, filled her husband's water glass when he raised it empty without his needing to utter a word? Was such a trifle sufficient cause to make a daughter rise up and hurl recriminations against a father and knock the glass from his hands, and when Nina had rushed to get the broom and shovel, Allegra had blocked her way, her voice terrible, "No him! Let him sweep up his fucking glass!"

Even for the accident she blamed him, Nina stumbling while she was crossing Broadway, a pothole the city hadn't gotten around to fixing after yet another harsh winter, her arms laden with grocery bags from Fairway. For weeks she lay unconscious and when she had awoken no words but two. *Pomóżcie nam.* Help us. Ah, Nina Orlofsky, to whom were you calling out for help, and for whom? This I would like to know, who was this *us*? Over and over, *Pomóżcie nam.* Max had spent the days in his office, unable to bear the sound of her plea, but Allegra had moved herself from her downtown loft into their apartment, giving notice at her work without a thought to her own future. Help us, help us, help us. Who could listen to those words, see the look in her eyes, and still keep hold of one's sanity? And yet: Was this, too, entirely his fault? Why not blame the pothole, the grocery bags? Why not blame the high heels?

Nina Orlofsky, combing her fingers distractedly through the ends of the lock of hair that nestled her shoulder as she concentrated on the questions swarming around them: Max had inferred a sensuous nature. He had loved without hope, but had he been a more experienced student of human nature he might have seen in the steadiness of her gaze her capacity for secrecy and suffering, and the late and dark afternoon in December, another snow storm just begun, an unforgiving winter, new flakes coming to rest on the snow already lying in soiled piles along either curb. The portentous skies having called him home early, he might have foreseen his stamping of boots on the front mat, calling out to Nina and hearing only a noise like someone being strangled. She was sitting on their bed, and he had gasped to see such grief, her face stripped bare. Allegra, Allegra, had something happened to their little girl? No, no, it was not Allegra, she made a motion as if to push away the air, the apartment, the totality of existence. To push away Max. Her eyelashes were white. He pictured her letting them catch the snowflakes, hanging her head out the window in unnamed despair. He leaned down over her and examined the crystals. They were not of snow but of salt. Her long lashes were encrusted in salt that had precipitated out of her tears. Seeing his wife's eyelashes sagging beneath the precipitate of her tears, he needed no further evidence. He left the room, pulling back on his snow boots to go and pick Allegra up from school, stopping for a treat of hot chocolate so as to postpone going back too soon, the child's chatter dropping unheard into his despair.

And still he could not let it go.

"Metaphysicians are musicians without musical talent. That was Binder. That was Binder down to the last sour note." He was determined to make her see. "He would never have found a place here. He would have known only failure."

He watched her face, remembering the smile as Binder had spoken, a flight of the luminous never seen again. Not even Allegra, with her tutu and her chirping, had brought forth that smile. To inspire it for himself, that he would not have dared to imagine. But still to see his wife's face arranged as it was now, a look that was something like terror rising up in her drowning eyes. That, too, he could not have imagined.

"Are you completely mad then? You pursue your rivalry beyond the grave?"

For himself, he had needed no further recourse to evidence. She had tsk-tsked in wifely sympathy and gone through the motions of a life of intimacy, and all the while she had been searching to find out how Jakob Binder had died. She had pursued the proper channels, made her inquiries in duplicate and triplicate. Binder had died, one way or another. There had been so many opportunities for death in those days. Nina had pursued the details, her passion far from the life they had seemed to share. He saw himself in her eyes, a man both small and foolish, his illusions looming larger than his life, thinking to himself that she basked in his insignificant accomplishments, and how can one defeat such a rival, how can one vanquish the remembered dead?

Allegra, I have had such a dream.

It was only a dream, Papa.

I cannot see how to go on after such a dream.

Don't be frightened, Papa.

It was a dream about a friend of your mother's and mine, a friend long dead. I dreamed he had dedicated a manuscript to me.

I'll tell you a story, Papa, and it will make the pain in your heart go away.

But the pain won't let him go, and the numbness in his arm and in his jaw and in his head is swallowed up in the pain that has his heart in its unforgiving fist, his suffering chest is collapsing into it, crushing all the air out of him, so that he fights to take in the breath that he doesn't want to breathe except for the necessity of forcing some air into the words so that she will be able to hear how it was that he had made a mistake, your stupid Papa, he did not know the place for what it was, had never called it by its name, though Jakob had gestured to me in the courtyard, turning away to show me the place so that I might find my way there, and I should have said the name aloud, and blessed the place where I had stood, but I looked away, forgive forgive, from that blessed place, my Allegra, my Nina, I turned my face, forgive forgive.

Like a miracle from the old religion, the page bearing the dedication has floated to the top of the scattered pages. *For E. M. Besserling.* It is an immensity that Max could never have imagined for himself. Against such largeness it is impossible to preserve oneself. He hears the fatal tear as he stretches himself out to reach for it, while Allegra, summoned by the voiceless call, runs out into the street to hail a cab.

] The True World

No doubt the world is entirely an imaginary world,
but it is only once removed from the true world.

I. B. SINGER, *Gimpel the Fool*

When the magazine *Omega* asked me to interview Saul Bellow, I jumped at the chance. Bellow had been dead for less than a year and this would be his first major conversation since departing. I'd interviewed plenty of writers before but there was no getting around the fact that they were alive. I was eager to reach a more mainstream audience. There were still a few old-fashioned periodicals that dismissed these pieces as "nobituaries," but now that literature was finished, more and more magazines were realizing they couldn't do without them. Clearly, the future was with the dead.

Omega was paying me three dollars a word, plus travel expenses. There are writers for whom one can earn more—Pound, Celine, Dostoyevski—but they're all in Hell and I hear the trip is very uncomfortable. Besides, I'd interviewed Bellow while he was still alive so I thought there might be some continuity.

It was with a light heart and a heavy suitcase (I always overpack) that I headed to Ellis Island. The departures terminal was on the far side of the island, out of sight of the museum and gift shop. It was in one of those buildings that had been ignored during the renovation. The outside of the building looked alarmingly shabby, with the word QUARANTINE still chiseled above the door, though above it a sign with the words "Mental Flight" had been painted in faded yellow lettering on a length of wood that looked almost as old as the building.

Inside, the vast building displayed the institutional grandeur of a bygone era. A high, coffered ceiling reminded me of the old Pennsylvania Station—which I had never seen in person, since it was torn down in 1963, the year I was born—but I felt not the bustling energy of a train station but the lingering chill of life suspended, a whiff of illness, deportation, and sorrow that no doubt remained from the building's original purpose. The day outside had been clear and bright, but, inside, the high windows scarcely admitted any sun.

There was a long marble counter against the wall with ticket windows framed elegantly in gilt, as if they had once held Old Master paintings. There was no line and I approached the first window. A tall, stooped man behind the counter in shirtsleeves peered down at me through Ben Franklin glasses.

"No baggage," he said.

"Not even carry-on?" I asked.

"No baggage."

He nodded toward a great heap of suitcases at the far end of the big room; some of the trunks seemed positively ancient. He slid some tags under the window.

"My bags are already labeled," I said. "I travel a lot."

He shrugged and withdrew the tags.

"You're allowed a pencil and a small notebook. That's all."

I took these out of my knapsack before placing it, along with my suitcase, on a cart that a short, slight man in a red cap had just wheeled over. The man seemed oddly familiar, like my uncle Eli, who used to run the Seders in Brooklyn before his death. He also looked a good deal like Bernard Malamud, with a small melancholy moustache and an expression of wry despondency. I wondered briefly if I was expected to tip him but when I reached for my wallet the man suddenly began to move away, pushing the creaking cart before him.

Turning back to the ticket window I cleared my throat and asked the question that had been on my mind since taking the assignment.

"I was wondering," I began. "My father . . ."

He was already shaking his head.

"I'm sorry. It's not allowed."

"I just thought, while I'm there . . ."

"Everybody asks," he said.

He was studying my ticket.

"Why is it just writers?" I asked.

He gave an odd shrug, a sort of nervous convulsion, but made no answer. He slammed a big old-fashioned rubber stamp down on my ticket and slid it back to me.

"You understand that this ticket is good only for a conversation with Saul Bellow?"

I told him I did.

"You are not to wander. You are not to talk to strangers. No photographic equipment is permitted and no sound recording devices. If for some reason you see a familiar you are not to address him or her. The consequences for such contact will be severe. You are traveling at your own risk. Mental Flight bears no responsibility for injury, death, madness, loss of faith, or any other form of spiritual, emotional, or bodily harm."

I said that I understood the rules.

"Sign here," he told me, shoving a ledger towards me. I was hoping to see the names of other journalists but he had opened to a blank page.

"Your boat's here," he said.

Somehow I had failed to notice a great open door, not ten feet from us. Beyond it you could see water and a wooden dock. A small, black boat, longer and slimmer than a rowboat, almost a gondola but with oars, was bumping gently against the dock. A hunched figure inside the boat was making it fast with a rope.

"Where is everybody?" I asked, realizing somehow for the first time that the entire place was empty. "Am I the only traveler?"

"Stop worrying."

"But surely others are going, too?"

I felt a chill in my heart.

"That boat is just for you," said the man. He shut the big ledger with finality.

It was cool outside and I wished I'd brought a warmer jacket. The boat did not look very sturdy and there was a filthy brown broth at the bottom.

"Do you have life jackets?" I asked, as I settled myself onto the narrow thwart.

The boatman did not answer but simply shoved off. His face was ghastly. He bore an uncanny resemblance to Marcel Proust, the orbits of his deep-set eyes were black, illuminating the pallor of his cheeks. He had a heavy overcoat and a thick, maroon scarf wrapped around his slender neck but he kept shivering with the cold.

"Are we going far?" I asked.

The boatman said nothing. He appeared unwell but he rowed with level, unhurried vigor, keeping his eyes on the receding shoreline. He never turned his head to see where we were going. We seemed to be headed straight for Liberty Island. I saw the great green lady rising up from the water, but as we approached, a sudden sweep of mist closed over us and I felt a sort of whirling in my soul. Though hardly a minute had passed since the mist descended, the little boat bumped against something solid.

"Is this it?" I asked the boatman.

"It ain't Jersey," said a voice above me.

"Mr. Bellow?" I asked, standing up and almost capsizing the boat.

There was a laugh.

"You'll meet him in a few minutes."

"Who are you?"

"I'm your escort."

He was a short, stocky man wearing a workshirt, with a faded blue bandana tied around his neck.

"I know you," I said, following him along the rocky path away from the water. "You're Henry Roth. You wrote *Call It Sleep*."

"Don't ask me about books," he said. "I don't give a shit about them."

"How is that possible? You spent your whole life . . ."

"Literature is for the living," he said, cutting me off.

"But surely . . ."

"I don't know why you'd want to come here at all," he muttered in a grumbling undertone. "This place is not what it seems."

"What are you saying?"

But he gave one of those shrugging shudders I'd noticed in the ticket seller and hurried me along the path.

"Watch your step."

The path suddenly widened and together we ascended a long flight of crumbling marble stairs. We paused before a great wooden door that he unlocked with a key hanging from a hoop attached to his belt. He paused for a minute with his hand on the knob.

"Stay close now," he said, "and keep your mouth shut."

With that, he opened the door and we stepped into an enormous room. As soon as we did a great wind began to blow and a deafening roar filled my ears. Roth grabbed my arm in a cold, hard grip and pushed me across the threshold.

I became aware of throngs of spirits that flitted in and out of view, transparent as sea monkeys. Dickens seemed to be having an argument with someone who looked like James Joyce, except he wasn't wearing glasses. I saw Virginia and Leonard Woolf talking quietly; I was glad they'd let Leonard in, even though he'd only written one novel. Hemingway and E. M. Forster whirled past, holding hands. I thought I recognized the Yiddish writer I. L. Peretz weeping in the corner.

Roth drove me forward at a fearsome pace. Despite the din, I heard him muttering under his breath: "I did not know that literature had undone so many." He chuckled grimly to himself. I felt somehow he was talking about me.

"Why is it just writers?" I shouted. "My father . . ."

But Roth put his fingers to his lips and gave me a furious look.

We had come to a stop in front of another door that Roth unlocked. We entered a corridor, much more quiet than the big room, though every now and then a shadowy figure fled before us. There were doors lining the corridor, with numbers on them like in a motel. We stopped in front of number 1915 and Roth rummaged for another key.

"Make good use of your time, " Roth said. "You won't have a lot of it."

Suddenly he was gone and I was sitting in a chair. Across from me, in an elegant velvet dressing gown, with gold, vaguely Turkish bedroom slippers, sat Saul Bellow. He seemed neither old nor young, the Bellow of *Henderson the Rain King* or perhaps *Herzog*. The room was unfurnished except for a small sink, Bellow's leather armchair, and my own cold folding chair. A shade was pulled down over the single window. It looked a lot like the examination room in Bernard Malamud's short story "Take Pity." I didn't read Malamud much these days and had always disliked the dyspeptic righteousness of "Take Pity," which takes place in the afterlife and features broken English, broken dreams, and a broken-down ex-coffee salesman named Rosen, but I was impressed that Malamud had been so prescient.

"Mr. Bellow," I began. "This is a very great honor. Perhaps you remember . . ."

"That was in another country," he cut me off. "And besides, the writer's dead." He laughed goodnaturedly at his own joke.

"I was planning to stay for a few days, but they didn't let me bring my bags."

I hadn't meant to complain. Bellow nodded sympathetically but looked, I thought, relieved.

"Our time is not our own here," he said.

"Do you think much about your time on earth?" I asked, flipping open my notebook.

"Bliss was it in that dawn to be alive, but to be Jewish was very heaven."

I scribbled down his words and added "jovial, jovian, Olympian, allusive." I like to work on a piece while I'm taking notes. I added: "Look up Wordsworth."

"He's here, you know," said Bellow.

"Wordsworth?"

"Of course, but we go to different shuls. He had a Reform conversion. He thought they'd let him sleep with his sister."

I nodded and kept on jotting notes.

"That's a joke," said Bellow.

"Of course," I said, crossing out what I'd written.

"Wordsworth's Orthodox. He sleeps with his sister anyway."

"Really?"

"No," said Bellow. "And if you print that I'm a dead man."

He gave another chuckle. "Don't tell Roth I was making incest jokes."

I crossed out everything I had written down except for "vaguely Turkish bedroom slippers." Somehow I'd been expecting more gravity from the dead.

"So how does it feel to be here?"

"It's comfortable," said Bellow. "Everyone's an immigrant so nobody has anything on anybody."

"Kind of like America," I said, hoping to start a conversation and show him how astute I was.

Bellow ignored my observation. I'd been warned that the most exasperating thing about interviewing the dead was the way they seemed to wink out all of a sudden and seem only partially present, leading some to wonder if they weren't in fact truly elsewhere and this was just a kind of conjurer's trick. There were darker rumors too about who was in control. Bellow had a frozen smile on his face, as if he were posing for a photograph, but then he snapped out of it and looked at me with large, alert eyes.

"You must have wonderful conversations about literature here," I said.

"Not really an interest anymore."

I found this hard to believe.

"Then what are you interested in?"

He gave one of those convulsive, shrugging shudders, like a jerked marionette. But he pulled himself together and leaned towards me.

"Politics," he whispered.

"Really?"

"The situation is very serious. Tolstoy talks of nothing but Israel. He's quite convinced . . ."

At that moment Bellow's eyes darted to the corner of the room and I felt, rather than saw, a kind of shadow lurking behind him. For the first time, I had a sense that we weren't alone.

"Has your thinking changed since *To Jerusalem and Back?*" I asked inanely.

"I should never have left," he murmured, half to himself.

It was unclear to me if he meant Jerusalem, Chicago, the earth itself, or wherever it was in the afterlife he spent his time before coming to this post-mortem motel room to meet me.

His face had grown very grave and again he darted anxious eyes at the shadowy figure in the room, which had moved closer and appeared to have grown larger. Bellow seemed afraid. I realized that he was holding out a tiny folded scrap of paper, inching it towards me. My hand reached out and he thrust the piece of paper into my palm; instinctively my hand closed over it.

At the same moment I heard sounds of struggle outside, the grunt of men grappling in the corridor. Someone cried out in Hebrew, though I couldn't make out the words. I recognized my father's voice, though it might have been Henry Roth or the wind, which had begun howling as it had in the room full of spirits.

"Father," I shouted, rising. "Is that you?"

As soon as I uttered these words there was a blinding flash and I felt a jolt, as if a powerful current of electricity had shaken the room, the floor, the building, my body.

When my vision cleared, Bellow, the shadowy figure, and the room itself were gone. I was staring into the pallid, impassive face of the boatman, who looked less like Proust than before. He was rowing us through the mist.

Ellis Island came into view. It was bustling with tourists. A wave of sadness came over me. There were so many questions I'd meant to ask. What was it Tolstoy was convinced of? And could that really have been my father's voice?

My notebook and pencil were gone. For a moment I wondered if the whole thing had been a dream, but then I realized that I was still clutching in my fist the note that Bellow had passed me. I hid the scrap of paper in the palm of one hand while I unfolded it with the fingers of the other, working stealthily though the boatman seemed not in the least interested.

Printed in neat, tiny letters, were two words: "Go home."

That was all it said. What could such a note, delivered at such obvious risk, mean? The oars, with their swift mechanical dipping, seemed to speak the words aloud. The last shreds of mist cleared and I found myself looking beyond Ellis Island, towards the bold, wounded skyline of lower Manhattan. Somewhere, hidden beyond it, was my wife, my family, my future.

It was time to get to work.

Acknowledgments

As editor of *Promised Lands: New Jewish American Fiction on Longing and Belonging*, I did not work on this collection alone. I am grateful to all those who collaborated with me on this book and offered support during the years of its preparation. First among them are the writers who contributed original, unpublished short stories for this collection. Simply put, without their overwhelming generosity and dedication to their art this book would not be here. My debt to them goes beyond this, however, for right from the start they believed in the literary value of this project and throughout the editorial process responded to my comments on their stories with an openness and with a professionalism that far surpassed anything I could have hoped for. I am eternally grateful to them for this, as it turned what, for me, could easily have become an agonizing editorial process into a joyous and fulfilling experience. Among them, in particular I would like to thank Thane Rosenbaum who, as we talked and talked and talked during wondrous strolls through MoMA, helped me to conceptualize the project and give it concrete form and often challenged me to rethink things in light of useful suggestions that he made. I am also particularly indebted to Binnie Kirshenbaum for generously bringing to my attention some very fine writers who, thanks to her, I was able to include in *Promised Lands*. Special thanks also to Melvin Jules Bukiet, who offered encouragement and inspiration, and didn't hesitate to share the contents of his voluminous address book when I wanted to contact writers he knew personally.

The people at Brandeis University Press and University Press of New England who worked on *Promised Lands* were terrific. Without exception, they were helpful, reliable, and efficient. I would especially like to thank acquisitions assistant Lori Miller for all her help and Phyllis Deutsch, editor-in-chief of University Press of New England, who when she received my proposal for *Promised Lands* instantly grasped the significance of the book and went on to work closely with me as my editor. I consider myself exceptionally fortunate to have been able to complete *Promised Lands* under Phyllis's guidance. Seldom does one come across someone who works so efficiently and rapidly, answering each and every e-mail with lightning speed and effortlessly removing obstacles that arise along the way. Her sensitive and astute readings of the stories in *Promised Lands* often prompted me to think hard about how they might be improved and challenged me to reexamine some of my basic assumptions about contemporary Jewish American fiction. I am greatly indebted to Phyllis, not just for making *Promised Lands* possible, but for helping me to improve it immeasurably and for placing her trust in me as editor of the book. I would also like to express my gratitude to the anonymous external reviewers for their expert, detailed comments that helped to make this a much better book.

I am grateful for the ways in which Utrecht University facilitated this project. The Research Institute for Culture and History of the Faculty of Humanities generously provided financial help that was crucial to making progress on *Promised Lands*. In particular, I would like to thank the academic director, Maarten Prak, and the managing director, Frans Ruiter, for their ongoing belief in this project. Special thanks go to my colleague in the American Studies program, Jaap Verheul, who supported my work on *Promised Lands* in various ways. Thanks also to my colleagues in the English Department, Wim Zonneveld, David Pascoe, and Roselinde Supheert for being supportive. Finally, two other colleagues, Hans Bertens and Rob Kroes, made useful suggestions that helped to move this project along.

Versions of the Preface and Introduction to *Promised Lands* served as the basis for papers that I presented at two international conferences: *Response, Remembrance, Representation: A Dialogue between Postwar Jewish Literatures*, Universities of Antwerp and Ghent, Belgium, November 6–7, 2006; and *Jewish Migration: Voices of the Diaspora*, Fourth International Conference on Jewish Italian Literature, Istanbul, June 23–27, 2010. My thanks to the organizers of these conferences for the opportunity to present my work and to the participants for their thought-provoking and encouraging responses.

There are others, friends and colleagues, who supported *Promised Lands* in important ways. I am deeply indebted to Stephen Hanselman and Julia Serebrinsky of Level Five Media for helping me to conceptualize and focus the book. Their generosity, sustained support, and unswerving belief in the value of what I was trying to do were crucial to laying the foundation for *Promised Lands*. I am also profoundly grateful to Gerald Sorin, director of the Louis and Mildred Resnick Institute for the Study of Modern Jewish Life at the State University of New York at New Paltz. Years ago, Gerry was the first person to put me in contact with some of the writers who have stories in *Promised Lands*. Moreover, in 2007, when this project was still in the early stages, he provided recognition and encouragement by devoting the Nineteenth Annual Louis and Mildred Resnick Distinguished Lecture Series to *Promised Lands*. Very special thanks also to Donald Weber for dropping everything when I asked him to read the final draft of my Introduction on very short notice; his astute comments and suggestions helped to greatly improve the text. Finally, I don't know what I would have done without Willem-Jan Goudsblom, who invariably answered my calls for help when things went amiss with my computer. Owing to his patience and expertise, work on the book could go on uninterrupted.

Last but most certainly not least, there is my family. I would like to express my deepest gratitude to my parents and my brothers, to each of whom I owe a debt far too great to be specified here. And then there is my wife, Marijke, to whom I owe everything. This book is dedicated to her.

D.R.

About the Editor & Contributors

] DEREK RUBIN was born in South Africa in 1954, grew up in Israel, and has lived in the Netherlands since 1976. He teaches in the English Department and the American Studies program at Utrecht University. He has taught American literature at various universities in the Netherlands and, as a Fulbright scholar, at the State University of New York at New Paltz. Rubin has lectured widely on Jewish American writing in both the Netherlands and the United States, at Princeton, UCLA, UC Riverside, and the University of New Hampshire, among other universities. He has published articles about Saul Bellow, Philip Roth, Paul Auster, and the younger generation of Jewish American fiction writers. He is coeditor of American Studies, a series published by Amsterdam University Press, and of the essay collections *Religion in America: European and American Perspectives* (2004) and *American Multiculturalism after 9/11: Transatlantic Perspectives* (2009). His anthology *Who We Are: On Being (and Not Being) a Jewish American Writer* (2005) won the National Jewish Book Award.

] ELISA ALBERT was born in Los Angeles in 1978. She is the author of the novel *The Book of Dahlia* (2008) and the short story collection *How This Night is Different* (2006), and the editor of the anthology *Freud's Blind Spot* (2010). Her nonfiction has been anthologized in *Body Outlaws* (2004), *The Modern Jewish Girl's Guide to Guilt* (2005), and *How To Spell Chanukkah* (2007). She lives in Brooklyn and Albany, New York.

] MELVIN JULES BUKIET was born in New York City in 1953. He is the author of four novels, among them *Strange Fire* (2001), and three story collections, including *A Faker's Dozen* (2003). He has edited three anthologies, most recently *Scribblers on the Roof: Contemporary American Jewish Fiction*, co-edited with David Roskies (2006). His work has been frequently anthologized and translated into nine languages. He lives in New York, where bad things never happen.

] JANICE EIDUS was born in New York City in 1959, and now lives in New York City and Mexico with her husband and daughter. Eidus has won numerous awards for her writing, including two O. Henry Prizes and the

Independent Publishers Award in Religion for her novel *The War of the Rosens* (2007). Her other books include *The Celibacy Club* (1997) and *Urban Bliss* (1994). Her writing appears in such anthologies as *The Oxford Book of Jewish Stories*, *Neurotica: Jewish Writers on Sex*, *Scribblers on the Roof: Contemporary American Jewish Fiction*, and *Desire: Women Write about Wanting*. She also publishes in leading newspapers and magazines, including the *New York Times*, *Jewish Currents*, *Lilith*, *Tikkun*, and the *Forward*. Her forthcoming novel is *The Last Jewish Virgin*.

] REBECCA NEWBERGER GOLDSTEIN was born in White Plains, New York, in 1950. She received a PhD in philosophy from Princeton University and has taught philosophy at Barnard College and Columbia University, as well as Trinity College. She is the author of nine books, seven of them fiction, including the bestselling *The Mind-Body Problem* (1983) and *Mazel* (1995), which won the 1995 National Jewish Book Award and the 1995 Edward Lewis Wallant Award, and *Properties of Light: A Novel of Love, Betrayal, and Quantum Physics* (2000). Two books of nonfiction followed: *Incompleteness: The Proof and Paradox of Kurt Gödel* (2005), which was chosen by *Discover Magazine*, among others, as one of the best books of 2005, and *Betraying Spinoza: The Renegade Jew Who Gave Us Modernity* (2006), which won the 2006 Koret International Award for Jewish Thought. The recipient of numerous awards for scholarship and fiction, including both Guggenheim and Radcliffe fellowships, in 1996 she received a MacArthur "genius" award in recognition of her unique talent for "dramatiz[ing] the concerns of philosophy without sacrificing the demands of imaginative storytelling." Her newest book is entitled *Thirty-Six Arguments for the Existence of God: A Work of Fiction*, published in 2010. She is a member of the American Academy of Arts and Sciences and was elected a Humanist Laureate.

] LAUREN GRODSTEIN was born in New York City in 1975. She is the author of *The Best of Animals* (2002), a collection of stories, and two novels, *Reproduction Is the Flaw of Love* (2004) and *A Friend of the Family* (2009). Her fiction and essays have been widely anthologized and translated into several languages. She is an assistant professor of English at Rutgers-Camden, where she helps run the MFA program in creative writing.

] AARON HAMBURGER was born in Detroit, Michigan, in 1973. He was awarded the Rome Prize by the American Academy of Arts and Letters for his short story collection *The View from Stalin's Head* (2004), which was also nominated for a Violet Quill Award. His next book, a novel titled *Faith for Beginners* (2005), was nominated for a Lambda Literary Award. His writing has appeared in *Poets & Writers*, *Tin House*, *Details*, *Out*, *Time Out New York*, and the *Forward*, and he has won a fellowship from the Edward F. Albee Foundation and a residency from Yaddo. Currently he teaches creative writing at Columbia University and the Stonecoast MFA Program.

] DARA HORN was born in New Jersey in 1977. She received her PhD in comparative literature from Harvard University in 2006, studying Hebrew and Yiddish. Her first novel, *In the Image* (2002), received a 2003 National Jewish Book Award, the 2002 Edward Lewis Wallant Award, and the 2003 Reform Judaism Prize for Fiction. Her second novel, *The World to Come* (2006), received the 2006 National Jewish Book Award for Fiction and the 2007 Harold U. Ribalow Prize, was selected as an Editor's Choice in the *New York Times Book Review* and as one of the Best Books of 2006 by the *San Francisco Chronicle*, and has been translated into eleven languages. In 2007, Dara Horn was chosen by *Granta* magazine as one of the "Best Young American Novelists," a selection made once a decade. Her third novel, *All Other Nights*, was published in 2009 and was selected as an Editor's Choice in the *New York Times Book Review*. In 2009, she was selected as one of the "*Forward* 50," the newspaper's annual list of the fifty most influential people in American Jewish life. She has taught courses in Jewish literature and Israeli history at Harvard and at Sarah Lawrence College, and has lectured at universities and cultural institutions throughout the United States and Canada. She lives with her husband, daughter, and two sons in New Jersey.

] RACHEL KADISH was born in the Bronx in 1969. She is the author of the novels *From a Sealed Room* (1998) and *Tolstoy Lied: A Love Story* (2006). Her short fiction has been read on National Public Radio and has appeared in *Zoetrope*, *Prairie Schooner*, *New England Review*, the *Gettysburg Review*, *Story*, *Wondertime*, and *Bomb*, in the *Pushcart Prize Anthology*, *Lost Tribe: Jewish Fiction from the Edge*, and in various other anthologies. Her essays have appeared in *Moment*, *Poets & Writers*, and *Tin House* magazines, as well as in anthologies such as *The Modern Jewish Girl's Guide to Guilt* and *Who We Are: On Being (And Not Being) a Jewish American Writer*. She is a graduate of Princeton University, and holds an MA in creative writing from

New York University. She has received a grant from the Whiting Foundation and has been a fiction fellow at Harvard/Radcliffe's Bunting Institute and a resident at the Yaddo and MacDowell colonies. She has been a fiction fellow of the National Endowment for the Arts and of the Massachusetts Cultural Council, has won the John Gardner Fiction Award as well as the Koret Foundation's Young Writer on Jewish Themes award, and was a writer-in-residence at Stanford University. She lives outside Boston, where she teaches fiction and creative nonfiction for Lesley University's MFA program, and is currently a Visiting Research Associate at the Brandeis Women's Studies Research Center.

] BINNIE KIRSHENBAUM was born in Yonkers, New York, in 1959. She is the author of one story collection, *History on a Personal Note* (2004), and six novels including *Hester among the Ruins* (2002), *An Almost Perfect Moment* (2004), and *The Scenic Route* (2009). Her short stories and essays have appeared in many magazines and anthologies and her work has been translated into seven languages. She is the chair of the Creative Writing program at Columbia University, where she is a Professor of Professional Practice.

] JOAN LEEGANT was born in New York City in 1950. Currently she lives in the Boston area, where she taught for eight years at Harvard University. For the last three years, she has been teaching half the year in the creative writing program at Bar-Ilan University outside Tel Aviv. Her published work includes the story collection *An Hour in Paradise* (2003), which won the Winship/PEN New England Book Award, the Edward Lewis Wallant Award, and was a finalist for the National Jewish Book Award as well as a selection for the Barnes & Noble Discover Great New Writers program. Her novel *Wherever You Go* is forthcoming in July 2010. Formerly a practicing attorney, Joan began writing fiction at the age of forty.

] YAEL GOLDSTEIN LOVE was born in Brunswick, New Jersey, in 1978. She is the author of the novels *The Passion of Tasha Darsky* (2008) and *Overture* (2007), which are actually the same novel. To make sense of that, you can visit her at www.yaelgoldsteinlove.com.

] RIVKA LOVETT was born in Wynnewood, Pennsylvania, in 1975. She received a Master of Fine Arts in Fiction from Columbia University in 2004, and is currently at work on a short story cycle. She lives in New York City with her husband and two children.

] TOVA MIRVIS was born in 1972 in Bethesda, Maryland, and grew up in Memphis, Tennessee. Her first novel, *The Ladies Auxiliary*, published in 1999, was a national bestseller and a selection of the Barnes and Noble Discover Great New Writers program. Her second novel, *The Outside World*, was published in 2004. Her essays and fiction have appeared in various anthologies, and most recently have been published in *Poets & Writers*, *Good Housekeeping*, the *New York Times Book Review*, and broadcast on National Public Radio. In 2009, she was named a Scholar-in-Residence at the Hadassah-Brandeis Institute at Brandeis University, and in 2010, was selected as a Visiting Research Associate at the Brandeis Women's Studies Research Center. She has a BA from Columbia College and an MFA in fiction writing from the Columbia School of the Arts. She lives in Newton, Massachusetts, with her husband and three children and is completing a third novel.

] LEV RAPHAEL was born in New York City in 1954. He is one of America's earliest second-generation writers and started publishing fiction about Holocaust survivors and their children in 1978. He has published nineteen books in a wide range of genres, including the recent memoir-travelogue *My Germany* (2009), and his work has been translated into a dozen languages. He has reviewed for National Public Radio and the *Detroit Free Press*, the *Washington Post*, the *Fort Worth Star-Telegram*, *Boston Review*, the *Forward*, and the *Jerusalem Report*. Raphael has published hundreds of stories, essays, articles, and reviews in a wide range of magazines and newspapers, and his fiction has appeared in several dozen American and British anthologies, most recently in *Who We Are: On Being (and Not Being) A Jewish American Writer*. Raphael has keynoted several international Holocaust conferences, appeared at the Skirball in Los Angeles in a reading series with Joan Didion, and spoken at the 92nd Street Y. He has done hundreds of talks and readings in North America, Europe, and Israel at Jewish Book Fairs, Jewish Community Centers, synagogues, Hillels, museums, libraries, colleges, and universities. Featured in two documentaries, he has been a panelist at London's Jewish Film festival. His stories and essays are on university syllabi around the U.S. and in Canada; his fiction has been analyzed in scholarly journals and books and at MLA. Raphael holds a PhD in American Studies from Michigan State University, where he taught creative writing before leaving academia in 1988 to write full-time. The Michigan State University Libraries recently purchased his literary papers and he currently reviews for Bibliobuffet.com and East Lansing Public Radio in Michigan. Raphael can be found on the web at http://www.levraphael.com.

] NESSA RAPOPORT was born in Toronto, Canada, in 1953; she moved to New York City in 1974. She is the author of a novel, *Preparing for Sabbath* (1981); a collection of prose poems, *A Woman's Book of Grieving* (1994); and a memoir of family and place, *House on the River: A Summer Journey* (2004). Her meditations are included in *Objects of the Spirit: Ritual and the Art of Tobi Kahn* and *Tobi Kahn: Sacred Spaces for the 21ˢᵗ Century.* Her essays and stories have appeared in the *New York Times*, the *Los Angeles Times*, the *Jewish Week* and the *Forward*, among other publications, and on faith.com. With Ted Solotaroff, she edited *The Schocken Book of Contemporary Jewish Fiction* (1992). She speaks frequently about Jewish culture and imagination.

] JONATHAN ROSEN was born in New York City in 1963. He is the author of the novels *Eve's Apple* (1997) and *Joy Comes in the Morning* (2004) and two works of nonfiction, *The Talmud and the Internet: A Journey Between Worlds* (2000) and *The Life of the Skies: Birding at the End of Nature* (2008). Rosen, who has received the Edward Lewis Wallant Award, the Chaim Potok Prize, and the Reform Judaism Prize for Fiction, is editorial director of Nextbook, where he edits the "Jewish Encounters" series, published by Nextbook/Schocken. He created the culture section of the *Forward* newspaper, which he oversaw for ten years. His essays have appeared in the *New York Times Magazine*, the *New York Times Book Review*, the *New Yorker* and several anthologies. Rosen lives in New York City with his wife and two daughters.

] THANE ROSENBAUM was born in New York City in 1960. He is a novelist, essayist, and law professor, the author of the novels *The Golems of Gotham* (2002), a *San Francisco Chronicle* Top 100 Book, *Second Hand Smoke* (1999), which was a finalist for the National Jewish Book Award, and the novel-in-stories, *Elijah Visible* (1996), which received the Edward Lewis Wallant Award for the best book of Jewish American fiction. His articles, reviews, and essays appear frequently in the *New York Times*, the *Wall Street Journal*, the *Los Angeles Times*, the *Washington Post*, and the *Huffington Post*, among other national publications. He appears frequently at the 92nd Street Y, where he moderates an annual series of discussions on Jewish culture and politics. He is the John Whelan Distinguished Lecturer in Law at Fordham Law School and directs the Forum on Law, Culture & Society.

He is the author of *The Myth of Moral Justice: Why Our Legal System Fails to Do What's Right* (2004), which was selected by the *San Francisco Chronicle* as one of the Best Books of 2004. His most recent book is an edited anthology entitled, *Law Lit, from Atticus Finch to* The Practice: *A Collection of Great Writing about the Law* (2007).

] JOEY RUBIN was born in New York in 1982 and raised in California. His essays and reviews appear in the *San Francisco Chronicle*, Nerve.com, the *Forward*, and *Paste* magazine. He recently left Buenos Aires for London, where he will complete a Masters of Research at the London Consortium in the fall of 2010.

] EDWARD SCHWARZSCHILD was born in Philadelphia in 1964. He is the author of *The Family Diamond* (2007), a collection of stories, and *Responsible Men* (2005), a novel, which was a finalist for the Rome Prize from the American Academy of Arts and Letters and the Samuel Goldberg and Sons Foundation Prize for Jewish Fiction. His stories and essays have appeared in such places as *Fence, Tin House, The Believer, StoryQuarterly, The Yale Journal of Criticism,* and *The Virginia Quarterly Review.* He has been a Fulbright Scholar at the University of Zaragoza in Spain and a Visiting Writer at the Netherlands Institute for Advanced Study. He lives with the writer Elisa Albert and their cool little boy in upstate New York, where he is an associate professor at the University at Albany, SUNY, and a fellow at the New York State Writers Institute.

] STEVE STERN was born in Memphis, Tennessee, in 1947. He is the author of eight works of fiction, including *Lazar Malkin Enters Heaven* (1986), which won the Edward Lewis Wallant Award, *The Wedding Jester* (1999), which received the National Jewish Book Award, and *The Angel of Forgetfulness* (2005). His most recent novel, *The Frozen Rabbi,* was published in 2010. He has been the recipient of grants from the Fulbright and Guggenheim Foundations. He lives in Saratoga Springs, New York, where he is a professor of literature and creative writing at Skidmore College.

] LARA VAPNYAR was born in Moscow in 1971. She immigrated to the United States in 1994. She is the author of two short story collections, *Broccoli* (2008) and *There Are Jews in My House* (2003), which received the National Foundation of Jewish Culture Award, and a novel, *Memoirs of a Muse* (2006). Her short stories have appeared in the *New Yorker,*

Harpers, and *Zoetrope*. She lives in Staten Island, New York, with her husband and two children.

] ADAM WILSON was born in Boston in 1982. He is a founding editor and the deputy editor of the online newspaper *The Faster Times*. In 2009, he received an MFA in Fiction Writing from Columbia University, where he was awarded a Merit Fellowship, and was Columbia's nominee for 2010 Best New American Voices. He has thrice been a finalist for Glimmer Train Story prizes, and was recently a finalist for the Canteen Prize for New Writers. His work appears in a number of publications including the *Forward, Gigantic, The Rumpus, Paste, BookForum*, and *Time Out New York*. He has an essay on "Golden Showers" in the anthology *Dirty Words: A Literary Encyclopedia of Sex*, and has read at such reputable venues as KGB Bar, The Museum of Sex, and the New York Public Library. He lives in Brooklyn.

] JONATHAN WILSON was born in London in 1950. He has lived in the United States since 1976, with a four-year interlude in Jerusalem. He is the author of two novels, *The Hiding Room* (1995) and *A Palestine Affair* (2003), two books of stories, *Schoom* (1993) and *An Ambulance Is on the Way: Stories of Men in Trouble* (2005), and two critical works on the fiction of Saul Bellow. His most recent book is a biography, *Marc Chagall* (2007). His short fiction, essays, and articles have appeared in the *New Yorker*, the *New York Times Magazine, Ploughshares, Tikkun*, the *Forward*, and numerous journals and anthologies, including *Best American Short Stories*. He was awarded a Guggenheim Foundation fellowship in fiction for 1994. He is Fletcher Professor of Rhetoric and Debate, Professor of English, and director of the Center for the Humanities at Tufts University.